IN THE SECOND YEAR

STORM JAMESON

IN THE SECOND YEAR

STORM JAMESON

Edited by Stan Smith

TRENT EDITIONS

Trent Editions
Department of English and Media Studies
The Nottingham Trent University
Clifton Lane
Nottingham NG11 8NS

The editor and Trent Editions would like to acknowledge the assistance provided by The Jameson Estate and Christopher Storm-Clark in bringing this edition to press.

Printed in Great Britain by Goaters Limited, Nottingham.

ISBN 1 84233 094 2

Contents

Introduction

I. Concerned with Change and Revolution

I have a good but not a great mind', wrote Storm Jameson (1891-1986) in her autobiography, *Journey from the North* (2 volumes, London: Collins and Harvill, 1969, 1970). That mind has received less critical attention than it deserves.[1] Jameson produced upward of 70 books between 1919 and 1979 – not only novels but short stories, essays, criticism and three volumes of autobiography, together with a vast range of uncollected literary and political journalism and social commentary. Virago Press republished several volumes in the 1980s, one collection under a title, *Women Without Men*, which seriously misrepresented her actual concerns. Jameson was an instinctive feminist, committed to social and economic equality. But her primary interests lay elsewhere, in the social and political analysis of British history advanced from the independent socialist stance common among 'progressive' middle-class intellectuals *entre deux guerres*.

Born in Whitby, Yorkshire in 1891, into a family of shipbuilders and merchant seafarers, Margaret Storm Jameson was in 1912 the first woman to take a First Class degree (in English) at Leeds University. Though first in her Honours class, she was, in the words of her autobiography, 'fobbed off' with a research studentship, while the man who came second was awarded a University lectureship (*Journey from the North*, vol. I, 58). A fellowship to read for a Masters degree at King's College, London University resulted in the publication, in 1922, of a critical study, *Modern Drama in Europe*. By this time she had already published the novels *The Pot Boils* (1919) and *The Happy Highways* (1920), set within the ambience of contemporary feminist struggles, with a strong socialist commitment to the emancipation of working-class women. Her first contribution to A. R. Orage's *The New Age* was published in 1913, and she was editor of the weekly *New Commonwealth* between 1919 and 1922. Jameson was President of the British branch of PEN ('Poets, Essayists, Novelists'), from 1938 to 1945, and a member of the governing body of PEN International, campaigning on behalf of refugee writers and intellectuals and helping to rescue many from the concentration camps and prisons of fascist Europe. Besides bringing out three volumes of autobiography (the first, *No Time Like the Present*, in 1933), she edited in

1975 the autobiography of her second husband, Guy Chapman, the socialist historian.

Jameson knew and worked with most of the significant writers and radical intellectuals of the interwar and postwar eras, many of whom became close friends. Several of them figure in disguised form in the pages of *In the Second Year*, her dystopian fiction published in London in 1936. One of these, Stephen Spender, is referred to by name, for, by the time the novel opens, in 1941, he has disappeared into a British concentration camp, become a 'non-person', dismissed with sadistic sarcasm by Richard Sacker as 'a solar myth'. Another, E. M. Forster, is reported to have gone into exile. The book is not, however, a *roman à clef*, though its translations into fictive form of contemporary personalities and events are an important part of its deeper political purpose. The novel imagines the second year of a British fascist regime only five years ahead of the time of writing. It explores the mixed feelings and double standards of those people who have connived at such a regime coming into being, or simply allowed the take-over to occur by their indifference or self-absorption. The book is thus both an admonitory vision of a future that might still be avoided, and a critical diagnosis of the mid 1930s present, exposing and analysing the impulses and attitudes which might allow such an eventuality to arise. The novel operates within a narrative double-take in which its disenchanted prevision of the near future aims to dispel those delusions and complacencies in the present which might make that future possible.

Despite Valentine Cunningham's inaccurate reference in *British Writers of the Thirties* (1988) to 'those sterner Marxists like Storm Jameson', Jameson maintained throughout her life the position of an independent socialist humanist. As is indicated by her hard-headed comments on Communist manipulativeness in her autobiography, she was never a fellow-traveller, but was nevertheless prepared to work with (and sometimes, in full knowledge, to be used by) the Communist Party in her campaigns on behalf of political prisoners in the 1930s – an activity she transferred, to the Party's chagrin, to the threatened intellectuals of eastern Europe after 1945, without ever becoming a Cold Warrior. Her admiration for the doggedness and dedication of Communist activists in *In the Second Year*, though tempered by distrust of their narrowness and dogmatism, is never deployed to justify the cynicism fashionable after the Hitler-Stalin Pact, and in this Jameson remains the stubborn representative of a principled third way of radical socialism largely ground out between the polarised allegiances of the 1930s and the Cold War.

Significantly, Cunningham discusses Jameson only with regard to her influential essay on 'Documents' in the left-wing little magazine *Fact* (4, 1937),[2] in which, as Samuel Hynes observes in *The Auden Generation* (1976), 'she produced the first theory of documentary as a literary form', distinguishing it from both the 'proletarian novel' and the bourgeois novel of private life. No more than Cunningham (who quotes exactly the same passages from Jameson's essay) did Hynes attempt a discussion of Jameson's own fiction during this period. But her account of what an authentically socialist literature requires can be seen almost as a manifesto for her 1930s novels, and in particular, for *In the Second Year*.

> Perhaps the nearest equivalent of what is wanted exists already in another form in the documentary film. As the photographer does, so must the writer keep himself out of the picture while working ceaselessly to present the fact from a striking (poignant, ironic, penetrating, significant) angle. The narrative must be sharp, compressed, concrete. Dialogue must be short, – a seizing of the significant, the revealing word. The emotion should spring directly from the fact. It must not be squeezed from it by the writer, running forward with a, 'When I saw this, I felt, I suffered, I rejoiced ....' His job is not to tell us what he felt, but to be coldly and industriously presenting, arranging, selecting, discarding from the mass of his material to get the significant detail, which leaves no more to be said, and implies everything.[3]

This is not to say that Jameson's novel dispenses with the interior view or with subjective self-expression. On the contrary, given that her British dictator is a Hitlerian windbag, surrounded by familiar representatives of the chattering classes, and opposed by intellectuals and militants for whom speechifying and preaching often take the place of decisive action, both elaborate monologue and extended dialogue figure largely in the novel. But both devices are articulated structurally within a narrative where the urgency of a politics which allows no time for talk finally disposes of all the brilliant talkers, bearing down on their self-centred personal obsessions with a brute force.

The novel's narrative point of view is predominantly that afforded by a taciturn, marginal observer who feels himself outside and uninvolved in the preoccupations of those around him, whether political animals or apolitical private citizens. But he finds that in the end he too is not a disinterested observer, a camera à la Christopher Isherwood, but an active participant in and potential victim of the forces he observes and analyses. A prime impulse of the novel is to demonstrate the ineffectuality of talk and subjectivity in a world rushing towards catastrophe. Unlike the inspiritingly optimistic novel envisaged by contemporary socialist realism, *In the Second Year* moves towards no happy ending and euphoric overthrow of capitalism, and it was not generally well-received by the cheer-leaders of orthodox Communism. Survival, the survival of a handful of right-thinking people, their understanding toughened by political exigency, and of the possibility of democratic and socialist renewal, is all that it can envisage.

'Literature concerned with change and the changing world is concerned with revolution, and all the stages of revolutionary action', Jameson wrote in 'Documents'.[4] This involves not the optimistic utopian celebration of inevitable revolution but a cold, hard look at all the processes by which such a revolution may be defeated and counter-revolution installed. This Jameson accomplished consummately in *In the Second Year*. But the novel is not a political tract. It is an eminently readable work of fiction, with vividly realised characters and an engaging plot. The novel has pace and a shrewdly diagnostic turn of phrase, the fine-tuning of which carries the reader into a series of discoveries which sustain the narrative momentum. Its ability to get under the skin and understand the motivation of its right-wing extremists makes it far superior to the leftist formula novels of the 1930s, while its dissection of the prevarications and evasions of well-meaning liberals and socialists offers no easy comfort to the godly. In this, as I discuss below, Jameson seems to be following a procedure similar to that described in Georg Lukács's contemporaneous study *The Historical Novel*, though it is unlikely that she will have encountered this work directly before the 1950s. It is more a question of ideas and critical debates that were in the air in the British and European left-wing intellectual circles in which Jameson moved at the time.

A book of this analytic and writerly calibre ought to figure in any serious reading of the 1930s. As a subtle exposition of dystopian writing, it can be set beside such works as Orwell's *Nineteen Eighty-Four,* Aldous Huxley's *Brave New World*, Rex Warner's *The Aerodrome*, and a host of similar fictions. But it is not just a document for scholars and socialists. It is a novel written for the general fiction-reading public, and, in its analysis of intelligent, well-meaning individuals caught out by a historical crisis beyond the scope of their imaginations or intellects, it remains, quite simply, a very good novel, a novel about the end of a world.

II. The End of the World

W riting in *Journey from the North* of why she abandoned the *Mirror in Darkness* sequence of novels, Jameson makes an important point about the fraught relation between the personal and the political in her writings. She felt, she said, 'a stifled instinct warning me that I was working against the grain of my talent':

> I refuse to regret the energy spent writing polemics against war and Fascism. Still less the energy given to helping a few, too few, men and women to escape the hell of German concentration camps, and then to keep them alive. Nothing in me is fiercer, more obsessive, more nearly involuntary, than my loathing of the cruelty that issued in Auschwitz, except the sense that exile is only the human condition pushed to its farthest limit ....
>
> I could not have held aloof. No regrets. A concern with politics, a conviction that political activity was obligatory at that time, was right. Wrong as wrong was the fallacy that political passions I could not ignore had somehow to be pressed directly into my novels. I confused an inescapable personal commitment with a totally mistaken and crude literary one.[5]

From this criticism *In the Second Year* is in her own assessment largely exempt. Written in the summer of 1935, just after Ramsay MacDonald's supposedly Labour-led 'National' government had mutated effortlessly into that of Stanley Baldwin's Conservative-led one, the novel is projected into the second year of the fascist regime that follows the collapse, in 1940, of another economically disastrous Labour government. Britain and Germany are not at war, though there is constant talk of it. Frank Hillier has become Prime Minister by largely democratic means, though on the back of the National Volunteer Guard, a private paramilitary army commanded by his friend from youth, Richard Sacker. Most of the story is narrated in the first person by Sacker's brother-in-law and Hillier's second cousin, Andrew Hillier (Andy), newly returned from his academic post in Norway, whom Sacker calls, with affectionate contempt, '"an unregenerate liberal"'. The timescale of the novel (late April to early July) suggests the accelerated pace at which events move once the constraints of institutional inertia are lifted, and politics is concentrated in a few hands. It also deliberately shadows, date for date, that period in the second year of Hitler's Chancellery in which he sought to neutralise not only opposition elements but also the very forces that had brought him to power, culminating in the massacres of the 'Night of the Long Knives' of June 30th 1934.

Jameson constructs some precise homologies between the events of the novel and those of Germany in 1934, but also significant divergences of detail. The old political parties have been dissolved or absorbed into the ruling National State Party. Two former Labour Cabinet Ministers, the suave career politician, Eugene Denham, and George Body, a trades union leader, have joined the presiding Council of Action, as they claim, 'in the national interest'. The trades unions have not been abolished, simply emasculated. Antisemitism is not a specific feature of the regime, but most Jews have lost their jobs, as the sacked minor civil servant Myers, himself a Jew, puts it sarcastically, 'for the sake of economy'. What are euphemistically called 'Labour' and 'Training' Camps have been set up for what is rumoured to be up to five million 'irreconcilables'. Hillier is now under pressure from the establishment, in the guise of the banker Thomas Chamberlayn, the most powerful member of the Council of Action and a past source of NSP funding, to bring the Volunteers under control, either by disbanding or substantially reducing their numbers, on the grounds that the country cannot afford to support them.

When the novel opens, Hillier and Sacker are on a collision course, but Sacker persists in believing that Hillier in his heart agrees with him, and is merely swayed for tactical reasons to listen to Chamberlayn. A half-hearted coup conspiracy, more talk than action, which he genuinely believes will save Hillier from his new false friends and preserve the Volunteers intact, involves Sacker with Body and with a disaffected senior Army officer, Major-General Smith. Denham goes along with the plotters, only to betray them to Hillier. On the night of June 30th they are seized and executed, the Volunteers crushed, five hundred 'journalists, writers, working men, suspected of seditious opinions' arrested, and new repressive measures introduced.

The purge of the Volunteers is organised by Sacker's main rival, the fat and loathsome head of Hillier's Special Guard, Colonel Frederick Hebden, clearly modelled on Hitler's second-in-command, Hermann Goering. The killing of General Smith 'while avoiding arrest' directly parallels the summary execution of General Kurt von Schleicher (1882-1934), the career officer who was Hitler's predecessor as Chancellor. Sacker himself is modelled on Ernst Röhm (1887-1934), the SA Chief of Staff, one of Hitler's earliest and most enthusiastic supporters, whose organisation of the 'Brownshirts' dated back to 1921, and also, possibly on Gregor Strasser (1892-1934). Sacker's anti-capitalist rhetoric and advocacy of a 'real English communism' echoes both men's 'national socialist' mélange of radical and reactionary ideas. He too wants a 'second revolution' against the capitalists and the old conservative political elite, and his end replays that of his German prototype. Hitler had ordered that a revolver should be left in Röhm's cell, but Röhm refused to commit suicide, remarking 'If I am to be killed, let Adolf do it himself'. Likewise, Sacker asserts defiantly that '"an officer does not shoot himself unless he is guilty. Send for Hillier. Let him do his own dirty work"'.

There are striking characterological parallels throughout the novel. Hillier, for example, exhibits many of his near-namesake's personality traits. In his 'frenzied speeches' he is 'like a man in a trance', 'working himself towards the state in which his acts and words became automatic', so that 'passions with which he had infected his hearers seemed to pour from himself, leaving him as dazed as a man at the end of a drinking bout'. Sacker's wife, Lotte, discerns in Hillier an emotional volatility playing across an 'inert and empty' centre: 'Wistful, kind, charming, gay, inspired, ecstatic, hating – he was a vessel to be filled with any of these emotions, emptied, filled, filled, emptied'. Her brother Andy watches the teetotal Hillier, 'sober as a judge', 'coolly watching' the drunken, intemperate Sacker, as if biding his time. Andy's assessment is revealingly duplex: 'detestable and supercilious I thought him', yet 'His voice when he answered me was full and kind'. Sacker, he thinks, 'knew less about his friend than I did. Richard trusted him. I never did'. Towards the end of the novel, Hillier reveals a deep and paranoid inferiority complex, telling of his recurrent dream of being a serf in another century, in an immense field, unknown to his remote master: 'I am unknown, lost, a speck crawling slowly along the furrows for ever, as long as I live'. He had forgotten none of his early humiliations, Lotte concludes, and 'hate makes him strong'. His charismatic appeal lies precisely in his power to speak to that same sense of lostness in the masses.

Jameson's narrative homology between the events of Hitler's second year of power and those of an imagined Britain in 1941 is not an arbitrary structural device, but central to her interpretation of contemporary history. *In the Second Year* subscribes to the orthodox 1930s Marxist interpretation of fascism, reading it, not as the momentary, opportunistic convergence of quite different national agendas brought on by global economic crisis, but as the generic mutation of 'monopoly-capitalism' in its imperialist phase. It is in such terms that the influential left-wing economist Harold Laski described it in his preface to Robert A. Brady's 1937 Left Book Club study, *The Spirit and Structure of German Fascism:*

[Fascism] has replaced capitalist democracy as a form of state because ... it proved impossible, under German conditions, to achieve that discipline of the working-class which is required to maintain profitability under monopoly-capitalism .... The lessons ... are of grave importance for ourselves. For wherever capitalism finds itself in the dilemma so ruthlessly solved by Herr Hitler, someone akin to him will arise to act, if he can, on its behalf. There is no reason ... to suppose that any nation is so inescapably wedded to democracy as to be free from the danger of Fascism ....

There is no logical reason I can see why Great Britain should have a different experience unless we are warned in time. The lesson of all foreign experience is that a governing class will not permit the use of democratic institutions to abrogate its economic privileges .... To the possibility of a British fascism, the weak reply only is made either that such an experience is wholly alien from our character, or that democratic institutions are here too firmly rooted to be overthrown.

But it was a favourite exercise of German observers before 1933 to explain that Germany was not Italy, and that the German national character would prove toughly resistant to Fascist ideas. In fact, German democracy... collapsed without a blow .... If in so brief a time so startling a transvaluation of all German values can take place, are we reasonably entitled to assume that, under a similar threat, we would act so very differently?[6]

This British fascism has different subjective inflexions, specific to its national culture. What Andy calls the 'half-mystical nonsense' of Sacker's reform programme, for example, echoes the currently fashionable prescriptions of D. H. Lawrence or W. H. Auden's semi-parodic *The Orators: An English Study* (1932, revised 1934) by urging the replacement of a world of 'Men selling their manhood and women losing their womanliness' with an English utopia, in Andy's words, 'like nothing more than a fearful sort of public school, with willing fags, a glorious hierarchy of heroes in the persons of himself and his Volunteers, and floggings for the unwilling or rebellious. For the rest, all stout and jolly together, and daring the other nations to come on and be licked'. Such differences of subjective content, however, hardly matter. Objective events unfold inexorably in the same direction as in Germany, driven by an historical momentum which dictates the grammar of events. The Professor of Economics, R. B. Tower (modelled in part on Laski, but primarily, as his name suggests, on the Christian socialist R. H. Tawney), a 'known socialist, making no concealment of his beliefs', has been allowed, as an internationally renowned Nobel Prize winner, to continue lecturing at London University, ostensibly because it would be 'un-English' to sack him. Tower compares the modern situation with the pattern of historical process at the end of the middle ages: "'Like maggots, they are devouring the world that engendered them. But the pattern was there before the carpet; it lasts, and what one generation sees lapsing and falling into disorder another restores, in another way'".

The generic pattern overrides the shifting subjective content of each specific historical moment. Reworking Marx's famous formula from 'The Eighteenth Brumaire of Louis Napoleon', that history repeats itself as farce, Andy scoffs at those 'Romantic publicisers of the National State Party after its triumph, men with pens to sell', who were 'apt to write of [Sacker] as a modern Sforza, or the new Göring, or of the re-emergence from the shadows of history of the great *condottieri*.' The 'truth of history' is that these soldiers of the Middle Ages were largely 'unpleasant brutes' and it was 'sentimental nonsense to speak of their re-emergence' in Sacker:

> History does not repeat herself like an idiot, but like an artist. The originals played their minor and bloody parts in the smelting of a European civilization. Richard Sacker was the opportunist and undertaker of its decay.

Sacker was 'out of his place in a country where civilisation and traditions are still secure. England when he was born was not ripe for him, but in due time this ripeness prepared itself'. Subjectively, he casts himself as the cure, when he is, objectively, a symptom of the disease. A deeper, impersonal historical logic moves the pieces about the chessboard. It is easy to see that the coldly fanatical Special Police officer, Eckhart, is a man 'out of himself', 'possessed' by fascism. But each of the lives in this story, for all their conviction of personal autonomy and volition, is possessed and finally broken by the forces of history. Even Hillier comes to seem, to Lotte, a mere instrument of impersonal forces, like, perhaps, the line of the prophets as she envisages them, mere 'hollow vessels, to be filled by voices from without and within the mind'. Lotte, who had sought to ignore her husband's politics as much as his affairs, is forced by his murder to confront both, when his former mistress, the opera singer Harriet English, visits her, offering to help in her escape. Lotte's final way out, however, lies in the complete abnegation of the personal, in suicide.

In this novel, each character, including the narrator, has to negotiate that disillusioning described in *Journey*, 'to eat away a double illusion: the face I show other people, and the illusion I have of myself – by which I live'. Lotte unwittingly adapts Adam Smith's idea of the 'invisible hand' in trying to explain to herself how apparently self-directing individuals are really the pawns of historical process:

> Perhaps there are times, in the history of a country, when naked forces take charge, needing only the covering of flesh as the hand needs the white glove. They rise from the ground, from the fields left unploughed by the farmer, from the spoiled orchard, from streams poisoned with oil, from dry wells. They fall from the air .... They find their hand and guide it, their brain and charge it with their electricity, their nerve and hold it stretched awaiting their time. The tongue moves but the words are given.

Her reaction is cast in physical terms, a kind of ontological *déjà vu*, as if 'she had lived in this moment before, and thought these thoughts .... It was as if her mind were living ahead of her body, or as if her body had a foreknowledge it could use, but only clumsily.' Later, she has a similar experience of being outside the narrative, 'the sense that this scene was taking place in the past ... as though she were looking back on it from some later moment, as though she were already an exile'. Among the students opposed to the regime, her brother Andy had likewise experienced 'the most curious feeling that I was not here in the flesh, I was a ghost living for a moment in the future'. Self and events seem somehow out of kilter. Their uncoupling is embodied in the physical sensation of being de-narrativised, exiled from the plot of one's own life. A similar process is figured in the aptly named Harriet English, who, though still in love with Sacker, has prudently transferred her (imputedly sexual) allegiance to Chamberlayn. Her operatic performance becomes for Andy a symbol of the national dislocation, singing superbly the words of a 'childishly poor' opera: 'whatever the quality of the music ... it really mattered very little to her what sounds she was called on to produce from her long throat.'

What Lotte's corporeal imagination experiences as vi   odied metaphor, Tower, Chamberlayn and Hillier alike see more abstractl   n Hillier's words, '"The heart of the State is an economic heart"', or, in Cl   layn's, that '"men are economics, are the raw stuff of economics'". From Tower's (as it transpires, illusory) intellectual detachment, human subjects are merely the site where economic forces realise themselves. He sees no prospect of revolution, but only "'praetorian revolt'", a "'change of dictators'", which, he says, is "'theoretically interesting, but not important'". At present, he says, in these awkward first steps toward dictatorship, "'the old forms'" are retained; but "'When things become worse economically, if disappointed or starving persons try to revolt before time, the repression will harden. It is the weakness of repressors, that their tenure of their slope depends on their claws and teeth'".

The day after the attempted putsch, Tower is proved right, butchered by Hebden's police, who burst into his room in the middle of a telephone conversation with Andy. *The Times* obituary records his death as 'suicide', and speaks with a dispassionate aloofness akin to Tower's own, admiring his intellect, but regretting his dabbling in subversive ideas. 'He believed as firmly as *The Times* in the essential decency of England. Perhaps he was right', Andy reflects, before turning to what he calls, sarcastically, the 'inspired musings' of the *Times* editorial, which dissembles its partisanship under a pose of disinterestedness. *The Times*, too, has an opportunist vision of history. Dictatorship, it suggests, can sometimes serve the long-term interests of democracy, by protecting it from 'the reckless ambitions of individuals', which would have plunged the country into 'untold misery, unpredictable in its consequences'. It congratulates the Prime Minister for his 'moral courage and energy', and pledges that 'The country is firmly behind MR. HILLIER and the State Council in any further measures they may decide to be necessary for the safety of our lives and traditions'.

The authoritative, trustworthy establishment voice is lying, as Andy knows for himself, having been, in Jameson's skilful manipulation of narratorial viewpoint, the unobserved sole witness, at a remove, over the telephone, to Tower's murder. His immediate response, then, had been a physical one, trembling in his whole body, and his conclusion at once personal and absolute:

> This was the end for me. My first separate thought was that it was the end of the world. There is nothing more to be hoped from a world which, deliberately, with deliberate cold violence, murders the best man living in it at the time .... None of us is clean any more, none of us is innocent – none deserves to live.

Even in this, however, he shares in a collective, transpersonal discourse. Tower had spoken of the world "'closing in on those of us who have sought truth'".

Early in the novel, the working-class woman compulsorily resettled with her husband in the Derbyshire Peak, as part of Hillier's work programme, says that "'It's like the end of the world'". A shy, starving student in a discussion group says that "'We're at the end of everything'"; and even the rich and trivial middle-aged woman at a dinner party thinks "'anything might happen, civil war, the end of the world, only God knows what'".

III. Not the Whole Story

Tower's last 'testy' words over the phone had been "'some men have come into the room. I must see what they want'", followed by the noise of shots. In *Journey from the North*, Jameson recalls that after Hitler came to power in 1933:

> I had the sensation, often, of listening to footsteps outside my room, drawing slowly nearer. If they stopped for a few minutes, it was only to make a bound and start up again closer. At moments the tension of listening became unbearable, as on the afternoon when I listened to Dorothy Thompson's account of the 30th June, 1934, one of the coldest of Hitler's bouts of murder, when he saw personally to the killing of a friend and followers he had no further use for. It was stiflingly hot in the room. I sat without moving a muscle, as cold as a stone, sweat running down my spine, my stomach contracted in nervous anguish. When I stood up I found that my whole body had become as rigid as a clenched fist, and I could scarcely move it. Something in the incident not, I think, the deaths, paralysed me with fear and curiosity. The curiosity of the writer. And perhaps fear of human nature itself.[7]

The echo of E. M. Forster's image in *Howards End* (1910), of goblin footsteps in the hall outside, called up by Beethoven's Fifth Symphony, presaging the coming war, makes Virginia Woolf's recent ambition for *A Room of One's Own* (1929) seem already parochially utopian and *dépassé*. Such personalist ambitions are shared by Lotte, who, 'For the wife of one of the saviours of the country... was shamefully uninterested in politics.' Her privileged resistance to politics is shared, for much of the novel, by her brother Andy. However, she is not that innocently apolitical. When he tells her "'I believe in liberty, and I don't like dictatorships even when they appear to be benevolent'", her response affirms the rhetoric of the new status quo identified with her husband: "'Liberty to drift and starve," Lotte cried'. His reaction is sharp and undeluded: "'Has the starving ended? Why are there so many beggars in London?'". Andy may be an unpolitical animal, but he is not a self-deluding fool. He may think he can detach his status of disinterested observer, with liberal but unacted principles, from his personal links to a family at the centre of current politics. His shared name and family connections may indeed afford him some discomfort. But they also give him privileged access to some of the darker corners of the regime, which, given his intellectual honesty, in the end makes his liberal fence-sitting impossible. In a moment of self-criticism, Andy acknowledges the moral limitations of his role as a supposedly disinterested witness: 'My mind noticed these details because it was not capable of dealing with what was going on'. Andy's crisis of engagement demonstrates the cumulative realisation that the personal and the political cannot be divorced.

Jameson recognised the same wishful apolitical tendency in herself. In September 1935, with a finished manuscript of the novel, she had 'felt an irrational gaiety and hope. The Abyssinian crisis was in spate, and I ought to have felt anxious. In fact I was convinced that there was no need to be anxious... from a purely irrational sense... that war was an insanity impossible in Europe'.[8] In her more mature assessment, such aspirations to a privileged seclusion cannot be sustained in a world rolling towards collective catastrophe. After the 7th March 1936, the day Hitler sent his soldiers into the Rhineland, she records, 'I seemed always to be listening to the sound of approaching footsteps and counting stairs'.[9] Jameson had started thinking about the story in Spain, in spring 1935, a year before Franco's rebellion, amidst a handful of German refugees. Until this year, she wrote, fear of another war had been balanced by a naive incredulity: 'It's not possible, after the hideous lesson of 1914-18, for even Hitler to risk war'. But in 1935, war 'began to flicker continuously, just below the horizon, a lightning flash, a sudden thinning of the clouds, another flash, another'. But her imagination was deadlocked until the glimpse of a 'personal', ostensibly 'private' exchange released it. 'During these weeks', she remembers,

> I thought constantly about a novel I had been meditating... ever since listening to Dorothy Thompson's account of Hitler's 30th of June murders. What I wanted to do was to expose why a dictator is forced, almost always, to kill the very men who fought for him when he was only a brutal adventurer. I thought I knew why, and I could imagine an English fascism, the brutality half-masked and devious, with streaks of a Methodist virtue. I saw scenes,

landscapes, figures, but did not yet see clearly the figures of the dictator and his friend.

One night, between dusk and dark, I glanced from my window into the courtyard. It was empty except for two men, Spaniards, sitting at one of the small iron tables, drinking. The light from a single weak lamp fell across their hands lying on the table, and over the face of the older of the two. I had an extraordinary sense of the tension between them, a tension which was part of a deep wordless attachment. It struck me that there is a homosexual relationship infinitely subtler and more powerful than the physical one, subtler than any mere sexual intimacy, or than intimacy between men and women. The two men I was watching knew each other at a deep level: there was attachment and hostility, both a little dangerous.

I had my English dictator and his friend, the man he would have murdered.

It was, however, Andy Hillier's role as internal narrator that provided the structural mediation of personal and political to give the novel its interpretative framework. Her intent, she says, did not conform to current left-wing orthodoxy:

Since my interest, as always if I please myself, was in the extraordinary way human beings behave when they imagine they are being simple, heroic, truthful, generous, it was a disappointment to my friends on the far left, who expected a direct attack on Fascism, with a Communist hero, and the rest of it.[10]

In fact, Andy corresponds almost exactly to the 'mediocre hero' described in Georg Lukács's *The Historical Novel* (1936) a product, like this novel, of the Popular Front period, though it is unlikely that Jameson would have encountered Lukács's ideas directly. Like the Lukácsian figure, Andy occupies a mediating position, morally uninvolved on the margins, and yet, because of his connections, accidentally close to the motive force of events. But for his family ties Andy would be a mere private citizen. An academic, in his own self-description 'not a brave man ... only conventional', with an edge of 'indifference' towards politics, he makes much of his liberalism. "'Is liberalism a luxury? It used to be a home-made article'", he says with unusual combativeness to Hillier, finding the latter's 'invariably charming' smile and 'supercilious look ... intolerable, or humiliating'.

He sees, without responding, Sacker's 'indifferent contempt' towards him, noting that 'I was scarcely worth despising'; as, too, he 'could feel Hillier's contempt for me, a cold reasonable contempt, not fanatical'. He notes how Lotte's housekeeper Annie ignores him, but can shrewdly generalise her parochial distrust of strangers to explain the reflex fascism of the politically innocent: 'I thought it only needed a few years of isolation of this part of England for them to begin burning witches again. Annie would have piled faggots with the cruel zest of a child to be helpful'.

Andy is an ideal narrator. Principled but undogmatic, he can remark with British understatement that, even without the Norwegian newspaper reports, it was clear that 'things were not going well' in Britain. A casual parenthesis is enough to suggest reservation, as when he alludes to Sacker's 'active soldiering – if that is what you call what he did during the troubles'. Likewise, when he says he never approved, but was never able to dislike Sacker, we recognise the kind of balanced assessment needed in a narrator seeking to understand this strange new world. Jameson has him reproduce her own Spanish illumination when he watches, unobserved, Sacker and Hillier in silent communion in the twilit garden outside his window. 'I don't know why this scene impressed me', he records, 'I wanted to understand it, and there seemed at first nothing to understand'. Unimportant in itself, it was the last of a line of earlier events, 'of which the first would emerge if I had patience to wait for it'. In seeking for the first, he is led, finally and ironically, to the last moment of this narrative line.

A teenager with a crippled arm, which left him both tolerated and patronised, Andy had learned early 'to keep quiet and to let my mind choose meanings for me.' As he says of one incident: 'I held my tongue. I knew it was not the whole story'. It is his liberal openness, that patient waiting for and persistence in seeking the whole story, which makes him such a reliable narrator. He keeps his counsel, does not make premature judgments or jump to conclusions – 'but I had not seen this for myself', he says of one report he is nevertheless minded to credit. In key chapters, however, the narrative is transferred from Andy's point of view to that of an impersonal and as it were subjectless narration, to depict events he could not possibly have witnessed, such as the graphic evocation, from within, of Sacker's death, the real end of the line, which alone could complete the whole story. This shift to an impersonal narration only serves to confirm, from an 'omniscient' narratorial standpoint, the revelation towards which Andy's confused, fumbling, but well-intentioned liberalism has struggled, in his negotiations with a fraught and opaque social reality.

Though Andy loathes Sacker's vision of the fascist utopia, he nevertheless 'felt the attraction of his vitality', and wonders whether even this violence and rankest sentimentality, in its energy, might not be better than the 'hardening and rigidifying going on'. In this, Andy honestly expresses the political ambivalence of his class, living through the contradictions of a historical crisis whose contours had not yet clearly emerged. Confronted by Denham's claim that the new regime, calling on national common sense and good humour, has saved the country from communism without violent repression, thereby ensuring that socialist planning can proceed, 'midwived', as so often in the past, by a Conservative Government, Andy is torn: 'I accepted the truth of all he said, [but] I detested him for it'. Andy wishes he had been born in the eighteenth century, when it was still possible to believe in progress, and a man could mind his own business with generosity. Now that there is 'no way out, but only barbarism in front of us, I am a lost soul. If I am to be dictated to, I prefer my own class to the communists'. But when this lost soul attends the funeral of the murdered Jewish communist Myers, whom he had tried to help, he is presented with a rather different historical perspective, in the young communist Lewis's assertion that the country has now '"returned to the brutal manners of the eighteenth century"'. Andy insists that he detests communism because it will not '"allow a man the free play of his mind"', invoking an exiled E. M. Forster as his ideal. He finds in this monolithic, intolerant 'religion', he says, '"no room … no air he can breathe, for a man whose cold passion is to balance all things fairly in his mind"'. But it is precisely in trying to follow through this cool judicious balancing that he discovers the insufficiency of a 'liberal' balancing act which is more self-interested than he had ever wanted to believe.

Andy's justification to Lewis is that he is '"opposed to all repression"'; but Lewis accuses him in characteristic communist terms of being a '"squeamish liberal"', ultimately the ally of Chamberlayn:

> 'You and your blood brothers in the Labour Party, who fought nobody but the communists … who worked for friendly relations with the owning classes and took their rewards, were decorated, knighted, wore silk breeches, who clothed themselves in righteousness of legality and held the door open for repression to come legally in.'

At this point all Andy registers is resentment at Lewis's unreflective arrogance, shared, he believes, with the likes of Sacker, who also 'divorces words from realities', forgetting 'that nations are made up of living human beings, with brains and heart'. If Andy rightly rejects Sacker's delight in war as 'part of his penny-dreadful imagination', his own generosity of response has to be seen as equally problematic. Such complete disinterestedness, like Tower's Olympian academicism, can easily become indifference. Andy's liberalism initially leads him to overestimate the personal at the expense of the political. He sees Chamberlayn at first and variously, for example, as 'the great financier ... kind and very simple': 'He struck me as a genuinely kind man', 'an astute, kindly, but dull elderly gentleman', his 'myopic kind eyes seeking mine now and then with a sly twinkle, as though we were old friends, with a secret understanding'. But he learns quickly: 'I was less certain than I had been of his simplicity'; now 'His smile was kind and sly', the second adjective complicating the first, so that 'the impression of kindly inquisitive dullness' fades before the revelation of a ruthless amorality in the pursuit of his class interests. Sacker, too, he says, 'could be kind and lovable when he chose' (that last phrase being crucial), but Andy has to learn to see beyond and through such personal amiability. In a 1933 poem, W. H. Auden contrasted the liberal-personalist satisfactions of 'our kindness to ten persons' with the stern demands of a genuinely collective vision. Such liberalist 'kindness' is deconstructed throughout this novel. Andy's trajectory follows that set out in Stephen Spender's 1938 Left Book Club tract, *Forward from Liberalism*. In this novel, however, Spender is named as one of the disappeared, probably murdered in Hillier's prison camps, '"a poet and a man of virtue"' personally known to Andy, jokingly dismissed by his brother-in-law as an invention of leftist propaganda, '"a solar myth"'.

Swept along by the role of intermediary others thrust upon him, Andy comes to play a crucial role in events. This in the end transforms his narratorial stance, taking him beyond liberal fence-sitting. 'There are times when I become an adept in listening to people's minds', he notes. When Harriet speaks in oblique warning to him of Sacker's danger, he acknowledges that 'My only genuine talent is for the receiving of unuttered messages'. 'At this time', he admits later, 'I was only interested in observing the effect on as many men and women as I could meet, of living in what is to all intents a dictatorship'. A self-styled neutral observer, he slowly comes to realise that there is no position above the fray, and ends a reluctant partisan. The narrative momentum thus carries us, as readers, from detachment to engagement. Andy is taken for granted by the big players, assumed to be a pliant intermediary and agent, with no will or ideas of his own. General Smith, for example, 'assumed that I was prepared to act as go-between. I suppose he thought I had political ambitions. Why didn't I tell him at once that his and Richard's interests were not mine? Their shabby and self-interested plots were not worth the trouble of an honest man. Partly, no doubt, out of vanity, out of curiosity'. Their presumption is such that, when he does express contempt for their plots, 'They turned to look at me as though a piece of furniture had spoken'. This Lukácsian mediocrity has its advantages. Because Hebden believes him 'only a tool' of the plotters he is released from interrogation, only a little roughed-up. There is, however, from the start, a certain cunning to Andy's indifference, enabling him, for example, to obtain from Sacker a permit to visit the nearby Winchell Labour Camp, where he sees for himself how the regime really treats its opponents, or to sound out Denham as simply 'an observer.... My sympathies ... neither here nor there ... only anxious to hear the truth.' But, he adds of this encounter, 'I had prepared an air of innocence. He did not put me to the trouble of using it', thereby suggesting the extent of Denham's cynicism. Andy's reactions in the end come abruptly, but they result from the slow accumulation of weeks of thinking, observing, and rethinking, crystallised finally by the movement of external events. With the plotters, for example, he 'was overwhelmed suddenly with a feeling of the worthlessness of all of them, and their plot'. Not one of them, he thinks, cares a tinker's curse about England, and on an impulse of disgust and excitement (very rarely, he says, does he feel strong enough to make such a rough gesture), he leaves the room.

The confusion of personal emotion and public motive figured in these exchanges is the key to Jameson's feminist reading of history. Though quietly informed by the Freudian insights systematised in Rex Warner's neo-Gothic allegory of a British fascist regime, *The Aerodrome* (1941), Jameson's novel is straightforwardly 'realist', deriving much of its analytic and narrative power from its observation of the way characters are constructed and used by the political discourses they think they control. There is a scatter of names that could be interpreted allegorically: 'Sacker', in particular recalls the barbarian energy of those who sacked Rome, a comparison drawn on several occasions. But the novel does not subordinate the particular lives it depicts to political allegory. They are unique and unrepeatable, and their tragedy resides in that fact. The experiential moment is absolute in its claim to narrative respect, not simply the replaceable carrier of some larger, 'historical' significance.

Everywhere in this text, individuals believe they are in control of events, when events are orchestrating them. Hillier, for example, engages in a long self-justifying rant near the end of the novel which leads Andy to reach the same conclusion as his author in *Journey from the North:*

> Even in my desperation I realised without shock that some of the
> men who help a leader to power are certain to be the actual men

he must murder or get rid of. He needs violent and unscrupulous men when he is struggling. Afterwards they embarrass him. They are a nuisance he can only ignore, and if they will not let him ignore them he has to find ways to silence them. It's the end of Richard, I thought.

Self-contradiction is at the centre of all these characters, and the narrator's own predicament differs only in the honesty with which he confronts the dilemma, as here, recognising, in crisply antithetical sentences, that 'I felt myself agreeing with him. It was abominable, to agree with him even for a moment'. Andy sees that the fascination Hillier here exerts over even his own 'cold passion to balance all things fairly' in part explains the hypnotic hold he has over the masses: 'People wanted to believe', he realises, 'Not reasons or facts. The narcotic of belief':

> Believe, and ye shall be saved. They had felt insecure for years and he promised them security.... He promised all of them what they wanted, and in their revulsion from despair and the cynicism of despair they never asked themselves if he were more able than others to give it to them. They believed.

Even when held by Hebden's Special Guard, Andy is a modest member of his class, with representative reactions, facing the 'cold enraged eyes' of a fanatic Hebden:

> I was at a loss. I was not frightened, in the sense that I did not believe I was in danger of death. As most men in my circumstances would, I believed in the reality of the world I was born into, a world kept in order by a known compromise between force and goodwill. Offenders were punished lawfully. A man was not shot in a room with an oilcloth-covered sofa, a coloured calendar on the wall, and a mahogany table bearing a trayful of broken cups. I was only afraid of making some mistake that would turn things to worse for Richard. Yet I am not a brave man, I am only conventional.

As readers, however, we know the limitations of this vision. In one of the moments of omniscient narration from which Andy is excluded, we have witnessed just how those cups got to be in that state, with Hebden hitting a tied-up Sacker whom he hurls at the table, breaking the tray of cups, to the distress about "'all my good cups'" of the working-class woman whose house it is. The narratorial shift here reminds that Andy is after all out of his depth in this gangster world. His reluctance to plumb the depths means we trust him all the more as a morally reliable witness. His very naivety turns out to have an edge of realism: he is indeed, as he believes, too unimportant to waste a bullet on. With a shock, too, he grasps the depths to which these villains have sunk when he realises that Hebden's interrogation, with its questions about Lotte's stillborn child, is only to find 'facts which he could use to mock at her'. What he should have understood before is that this regime practises not the cruelty of a savage ('almost decent on its level of instinct') but 'a corrupt civilised cruelty … hideous, nasty, and unbearable. It was a eunuch cruelty, which is never satisfied'. (Hebden is reputed to have been castrated by communists who took him prisoner during the fighting in Wales.)

At the same time, this slowness to credit is not just naivety. We have seen that he is a shrewd, self-effacing observer. We also see him learning, and learning radicalises, politicises him. At the end of this chapter he can for the first time acknowledge his own confused loyalties, his mind 'split and spilt over a number of shifting planes of dark and light'. When, at the start, he spoke to his sister of the country's decline, she responded that he had been away too long, didn't know "'what it was like before the new Government took things over'". He had no wish for an argument, and was ready to be persuaded. His private homecoming was more important to him than any argument about public policy. Somewhat belatedly, her husband dead, Lotte asks him, "'What have we done to deserve this sort of thing to happen in England?'". Now his reply is unequivocal: "'We did not prevent it. It is in any case too late to repent'". He has finally begun to grasp the whole story.

IV. Lost

Andy and his sister react physically to events: 'Our imaginations are wholly material. We see the physical image and strike ourselves on it again and again, trying to kill with the flesh what is rooted in the flesh.' This bodiliness, central to the novel, is focused in the symbolism of Andy's crippled right arm, which becomes as heavy as stone when he meets new people (he has to shake hands with his left). Explanation and sign of Andy's withdrawal from the world of action, the arm also reminds of the vulnerability and limitation of the human body. Under interrogation, he is humiliated by the demeaning, fastidious contempt of Eckhart (who had previously beaten Myers to death), who 'stepped delicately round behind me and lifted my "dead" arm. He held it away from my body, so that the hand hung down. He flicked at this useless hand with his thumb and finger. He looked into my face to see how I was taking it, and with the quietest curiosity'. This strangely chilling episode finds a coarser echo in the callow brutality of the country-boy soldier who 'took a pleasure in abusing and tormenting me … all his energy … found an outlet in treading on my hand when I lay on the floor of the lorry and telling me what had been done and would be done to Lotte'. The older soldier tells him to '"Give over now, Jim"' and is kind to Andy, reassuring him that he won't be killed. In cameo form, this contrast of generations reveals what the regime's 'eunuch cruelty' has already achieved in dehumanising the young. A lifelong campaigner against torture, Jameson reveals in these harrowingly understated incidents the irony that this most brutal violation of humanity is, in some senses, a defining feature of the human, containing a truth beyond ideology. 'Our imaginations are wholly material', rooted in a bodiliness which cannot be transcended. Pain is absolute. It is not constructed in and cannot be dissolved by discourse. And human beings are the only creatures who inflict it on others for its own sake, for amusement, spite, or sheer malignity.

Hearing his brother-in-law inveigh, early in the story, against 'the liberal-cum-bolshevik scum' he wants to extirpate, those fools, 'rotten with principles' he considers responsible for Britain's decline, Andy sees that, for all his vehemence, Richard Sacker is already lost:

> He was like an animal which knows it is threatened and cannot see the danger. His energy was drawn to a point in him, frantic to strike, but at a loss. I could see that his mind was at work, trying to foresee what was happening. He had an extraordinary imagination, sometimes acute, but oftener on the level of a penny dreadful. The trouble is that by some ghastly betrayal the violent and vicious sub-life depicted in these writings has been translated into actual life, and is worked out with real victims and real murderers, and given Spenglerian labels.

In an opposing camp, Andy nevertheless feels a corresponding loss, 'overcome by the strangeness and intolerable grief and pity of living in a Europe in decay. It has happened to Europe before but never to me'. At the Whitehall parade he grasps the full enormity of all this:

> With a shock I saw Eckhart's among the faces below the platform. He looked fresh, young, grave. I forced myself to look at him.

There, I thought, is the calm murderer of poor Myers. The young men on either side of him had much the same air. Would they, too – ? I looked at the people in the crowd below the stand. All these decent kindly anonymous faces, surely there was not an Eckhart among them? Then I thought that his calm, which had shocked me, was a sign that he was possessed.... Hillier was Eckhart's God. Everything he said Eckhart accepted. He was truly out of himself, both now and when he was beating Myers to death.

His spontaneous reaction is intemperate, illiberal: 'To hear them roar ... made me wonder why anyone has ever laboured to improve men. I think they are not apt to be improved. Let them be stupid. Let them be cheated and kept down. It is what they deserve'. Later still, released from Eckhart's attentions to be harangued by Hillier, he reflects inwardly, in a potent oxymoron, on Hillier's 'sublime trick', picking up that phrase 'truly out of himself' and relating it to the condition of the religious ecstatic – etymologically, one who stands outside himself. Hillier's charismatic sincerity resides in the fact that he himself believes whatever he is preaching, at least while he speaks: 'He caught people into his own ecstasy'.

Arrested a second time after Lotte's funeral, and then released with two days to leave the country, Andy visits the communist Lewis, only to be accused of '"running away"'. Lewis is disillusioned also, full of contempt for the workers prepared to betray their own kind to the new order; but a blind, persistent faith keeps him going. Andy still believes that revolution is not inevitable, because 'The English are different'. By evening he is at sea, bound for Norwegian exile, taking consolation that representatives of a younger generation, the former Volunteer, Ernest, Sacker's protégé and Lotte's godson, and his socialist girlfriend Steffy, are at least safe in flight – a tenuous promise for the future. Andy had earlier felt anguished at his 'powerlessness in the face of a society organised to keep misery within bounds and decently inarticulate'. But he lacks what he calls the 'rat courage' of Lewis to stay and fight, to make that struggle articulate. If all the dead of the past week were to meet together in one room, he reflects, 'still the truth of what each of them had hoped would be hard, no, impossible to tell'. The narrative, that is, cannot finally be comprehended by any single narrator, or even by several. As the novel's shift into omniscient impersonal narration at key points suggests, 'the whole story' transcends its individual actors. Andy's very self seems obsolete. He wanders the earth, as he had called himself earlier, a 'lost soul':

I felt myself empty, except for those who had died.... It seemed that my roots were too firmly and deeply curled round the past, round the old England, the old house and the old words and thoughts. In between these, the soil was dry and falling away, but my roots only clung the faster to what was left. I was not comfortable any longer in the past. Yet I could neither imagine myself living in a new way, nor wish it. I have lost both worlds, I thought.

The words 'loss' and 'lost' reverberate through the book, down to the empty resonance of its final words, which flicker only briefly and by negation, in the muted hope of that 'at first', with the possibility of a new start: 'at first I could only think of what I had lost.'

Stan Smith

Notes

Work on this edition has been assisted by Project ANGI-2002/2005 (Ayudas Nuevas a Grupos de Investigacion, Commune of La Rioja). The editor and Trent Editions would also like to thanks Christopher Storm-Clark for his assistance.

1. (p.vii) But see Jennifer Birkett, 'Doubly Determined: The Ambition of Storm Jameson', in Jennifer Birkett and Elizabeth Harvey (eds), *Determined Women: Studies in the Construction of the Female Subject 1900-1990* (London: Macmillan 1991); 'The Idea of France in the Writing of Storm Jameson', *Critical Survey*, December 1998 (French transl., *Annales de l'Université de Franche-Comté*, Besançon/Paris, 1999); Joanna Labon, 'Tracing Storm Jameson', *Women: A Cultural Review*, 8.1 (Spring 1997): 33-47; Phyllis Lassner, *British Women Writers of World War II* (London: Macmillan, 1998); Sylvia Vance, 'Lorca's Mantle: The Rise of Fascism and the Work of Storm Jameson', in Marolou Joannou, ed., *Women Writers of the 1930s: Gender, Politics and History* (Edinburgh: Edinburgh University Press, 1999).
2. (p.ix) Substantial extracts from this essay are available in Vassiliki Kolocotroni, Jane Goldman and Olga Taxidou (eds), *Modernism: An Anthology of Sources and Documents* (Edinburgh: Edinburgh University Press, 1998), 556-560.
3. (p.ix) Kolocotroni, op. cit., 558.
4. (p.x) *Ibid.*, 556.
5. (p.xi) Jameson, op. cit., vol. I, 344.
6. (p.xiv) Harold J. Laski, in *The Spirit and Structure of German Fascism* (London: Victor Gollancz, 1937), 11-13.
7. (p.xviii) Jameson, *op. cit.*, I, 320.
8. (p.xix) *Ibid.*, 337.
9. (p.xix) *Ibid.*, 39.
10. (p.xix) *Ibid.*, 333-6.

IN THE SECOND YEAR

The time of the book is in the future; from the end
of April to the two or three days following June 30.

To
AMABEL WILLIAMS-ELLIS
FOR MANY GOOD REASONS

PART I
APRIL

CHAPTER I

The house was built below the disused quarry on the edge of the heather. Last summer moor fires destroyed the trees on the slope of the quarry and burned the heather as far as the road. From the house the road was not visible; it lay at the back, across half a mile of moor, and in a dip of the land. The front of the house looked across the valley to the farther hill; the road from the south, from the town, descended this in a great curve, clearly visible from the windows. From the upper windows on this side, you saw the sea, a great way out. Very seldom, a ship passed, its smoke a brown smudge on the sky after it fell from sight. There were fewer ships all the time. Lotte had told me that the Tyne was a derelict place, with piles of rusted iron where the yards had been once, but I had not seen this for myself. It was hard to get into the derelict areas – that is, it was hard to get a pass for them with no excuse but that one wanted to stare.

It was two months since I left Norway and came home. So far I had seen nothing of England but the first sight of it from the aeroplane, then London, and then the journey up here by road. But it was clear enough, even without the little I knew from the Norwegian newspapers – but it was more than I found in papers at home – that things were not going well. There was hardship in Norway, with the closing of so many trade routes, but there people were never very rich. To be a little poorer than before meant less to them than it means to people here. London seemed normal except for the beggars. During the whole of the weeks I stayed there with Lotte and Richard I never became used to them. Lotte, who had been in Germany a few years after the war of 1914-18, when she was just married to Richard, said it was not much worse here now than then in Berlin with decent women offering themselves after dark, and a man who looked like a gentleman would suddenly ask you for a coin, anything, a sixpence, if you looked like a foreigner. I had not seen that, and what I saw in London horrified me. In Norway it would have been inconceivable. What struck me more than the beggars themselves was the attitude of the other people to them – indifference or impatience is the gentlest treatment they get.

I can tell you I was glad to come up here where there was plenty of grumbling, and the farmers burying part of their food and the fisherman keeping back a third of a catch and so on and afterwards selling it from house to house or exchanging it in the shops almost under the noses of the marketing officers, who are afraid to go too far with our quick-tempered fishwives and their men, and there was plenty of poverty too, but nothing like the feeling in London where it smelled to you from the pavements.

Last night, when we came here, Lotte said: 'Now you're home, Andy.'

'It feels more like home,' I said.

She sat at the table in my room, her elbows on it, her cheek on her hand. I thought she was tired, but her eyes, grey-green and bright, were inquisitive and merry, as always when she asked me what I thought of things. In growing old – she would be forty this year – Lotte had kept the face of a schoolgirl above her small stocky body. She had thin arms, small hands and feet, thin legs, but her body had thickened. Seated, this was scarcely noticeable. I noticed only her face, brown, with the pointed jaw like my own, the lines round her eyes, her schoolgirl's smile, mocking, seductive, half serious.

'Are you wishing you had stayed in Norway?'

'I didn't realise it was like this.'

'Like?' Lotte smiled.

'A country decaying,' I said. 'The sense that life is narrowing and closing in – like walking through the passage of a mine with the walls narrowing. I can't say that it's a pleasant feeling, Lotte.'

'You have been away too long. You don't know what it was like before the new Government took things over.'

'Perhaps you and Richard can persuade me,' I said. I didn't want to spoil the homecoming with argument. This house meant a great deal to my sister. I scarcely remembered it. Lotte stayed on here when our mother died and I was sent south, to live with a doctor, because of my arm. I never came back. I was in Norway during the troubles, and afterwards, after things quieted down, and Richard bought this place – it had been empty – Lotte wrote to me that it was like being young again. Young and happy, I thought she meant.

I thought of that this morning when I was watching the south road for Richard's car. As soon as I saw it, four miles away on the turn of the hill, I went downstairs to tell Lotte. On the stairs I met the servant – there was only one in this big house, a woman of close on fifty, from the village, bright eyed, with quick heavy movements, liking Lotte and as suspicious as an animal of everyone else. When I saw her, and heard her telling my sister what had happened in the village and at the port since she went to London, I thought it only needed a few years of isolation of this part of England for them to begin burning witches again. Annie would have piled faggots with the cruel zest of a child to be helpful. I told her that I had seen General Sacker's car. She turned and thudded downstairs again, crying out that if the master was coming he would want coffee, he would want this and the other. She called Lotte 'Mrs. Sacker,' and Richard was 'the master.' As for me she pretended not to know my name, although it is the same as the Prime Minister's – Frank Hillier is our second cousin.

Lotte was not in the house. She had walked down to the port to try to buy some fish before it went off by the market train or was hidden by the fishwomen. In London she lived as fitted the wife of General Sacker, one of the saviours of his country: up here she was Lotte Sacker, whom everyone had known well as a little girl. I heard a woman who came to the house selling fish call her 'Mrs. Captain, honey,' and the men usually addressed Richard as 'Cap'n.'

I met Richard for her below the house. He came round the sharp corner too quickly and drew up at the gates with a frightful noise of gears and brake. He was a bad driver. He had been allotted one of the best cars by the Government and in two years it was one of the worst. He was allotted a chauffeur at the same time, and got rid of him by frightening him until the man begged to be sent back to the army.

He jumped out and began to climb the path, walking slowly. He was only two years older than I and a year younger than Lotte, but he had grown heavy since he gave up active soldiering – if that is what you call what he did during the troubles. I never approved of his views or conduct, never from the beginning, and I have never been able to dislike him.

I watched him as he came up to me. He had the face of the Notre Dame devil,[1] except that it was a merry face, with deep downward-drawn laughter lines, out-thrust lower lip, eyes lively and quick, quick hands, ears pointed and set forward. He was smiling as he came towards me, the smile that drew out his long lower lip until it was the width of his cheekbones. He shouted to me when he was less than a dozen yards away, holding up a folded blue paper. I did not recognise it at once; we had no air-letter service yet in Norway. 'Hillier's coming to spend a night here on his way south. Where's Lotte?'

'Is he coming alone?' I said.

'There'll be his pilot. Now what is it, Annie?'

The woman had come running down the path from the house – she ran with flat feet, at great speed, like a bird. She was in a state because Lotte had the key of the coffee tin. It was the woman who insisted on its being kept locked. With coffee the price it was this year she would have thought it weak-minded to leave the tin open. She herself locked everything that would lock, pantry, meat-safe, coal house. She did it from pure peasant suspiciousness – a certain amount of house-to-house theft went on near the towns but here no one was actually hungry except, at times, in the winter. Richard laughed at her and set her scudding back to the house.

We reached it as Lotte opened the other door. She sent Richard a bright look when she heard that Frank Hillier was coming, but if it deceived him I guessed that she was disappointed. She went into the house and upstairs to get the rooms ready. I met her in the hall as she came down again. She had changed her woollen dress for a skirt and short jacket dragged over her tight round little stomach, and she had touched her mouth with red – it went well with her brown face and it was the only make-up she used.

I put my left arm in hers and we went out into the upper garden. The aeroplane had passed over the house twenty minutes since and we had not crossed the lawn before we heard the car. We turned back.

'Look,' Lotte said. 'Hebden is with him.'[2]

In uniform, with a belt round him, Hebden was enormously fatter. I loathed the man so much that he seemed to me more repellent, physically more repellent, than he was. In fact many people, and a great many women, found him attractive, for some boyish quality in his large face. In Norway they said that he had been castrated during the fighting in South Wales, and he had severe pain at times. He carried morphia pills. It may have been true. It would account for his increasing fatness and his quite pathological dislike of socialists and liberals.[3] He hated them as some men hate black-beetles. He was Hillier's other close friend.

He had dropped behind, allowing Richard to walk in front with Hillier. I watched them come. Hillier was a head shorter than Richard, slender, almost self-effacing until you were close enough to meet the gaze of his light eyes, calm, supercilious, not unpleasant. He rested his arm on Richard's shoulder and listened with a smile to something he was saying. You could think he depended entirely on Richard. There was an almost feminine curve of his body towards Richard's, yet he was not in any way feminine, in looks or manner. I found it hard to define in my mind the quality of the intimacy between them. It was very close. I guessed that at one time Lotte had suffered from it and that the time was over. At forty only a very few emotions are able to hurt deeply and these few are all to do with dying rather than living.

Hillier's manner with her was simple and affectionate, almost the affection of a friend who would like to be a lover. I did not feel that it was pretence. It was unreal, rather. Or perhaps it was only so sexless that its reality made no sense in me. By contrast, Colonel Hebden was flamboyant. He kissed her hand, leered at her, with the airs of a romantic amateur in women. He wore the uniform of Hillier's bodyguard, black tabs and a black stripe down the side of the trousers, honours of the Special corps of the National Volunteer Guard. He was its Colonel, and he was also Air Minister. They told in London of him that he possessed no less than a hundred and fifty uniforms, and made rather a joke of it.

During lunch – it consisted of the fish Lotte had brought and tinned pears – the talk became awkwardly political. There was a come-and-go argument between Richard and Hebden. Listening closely without seeming to, I thought there was a closer antagonism between them than showed in their manner. Hebden had said one word or other about the Volunteers. The situation was a little awkward. Richard, as commandant of the Volunteers, was Hebden's superior officer, but the head of the Prime Minister's Special Guard had almost an *ex-officio* equality with him. I gathered that Hebden thought there were a sight too many Volunteers on the pay roll at present.

'Half of them could be demobilised to-morrow with advantage,' he grumbled. 'What do they do? except cost money – three times what they'd cost in a Labour Camp.'

'They weren't recruited for Labour Camps,' Richard said.

'Perfectly. But they've done their work.'

'So you think you can get rid of them?' said Richard. He was at a disadvantage, because he was becoming angry and Hebden was his guest.

Hebden lifted his heavy shoulders and smiled. When he smiled two dimples appeared in his cheeks. I found this a detestable softness in so big a man.

'Not get rid of. Pension them – the older ones first.'

'That is, the ones who did the fighting.'

'Time they had a rest,' Hebden answered softly.

'In a Labour Camp?' Richard said. He turned to Hillier. 'You don't agree with this, Frank.' It was not a question.

Hillier had been listening to both of them with his slight smile. Now he smiled outright, with amazing sweetness. His lips, like his eyes, were pale. His face was noticeably sensitive, as though he listened with the whole of it. I had always the feeling that he understood very little through his ordinary senses.

'You may be sure we shall do nothing ungenerous,' he said.

Certainly Lotte noticed that he had not answered the question. I saw that by her swift sideways glance at his face. I doubted at the time whether Richard did. He seemed satisfied and dropped the argument. There was an echo of it again towards the end of the meal, when Hebden produced a newspaper from his pocket and showed Hillier an article headed: Ruinous Finance.

Richard looked at it with contempt. 'If I had my way I'd send the proprietor of that paper to a Training Camp,' he said.

'What are you talking about? Chamberlayn?' Hebden smiled.[4]

'Yes, I would. Thomas Chamberlayn himself. Close down his newspapers, take over all his financial and banking interests and run them for him – or rather, for ourselves.'

This time Hillier intervened. I had noticed how seldom he did it.

'Give me time, Richard.'

'Time for Tom Chamberlayn and the others of his way of thinking to undo all we've done,' Richard answered, but he laughed.

Hebden left after lunch. As soon as he had gone Richard and Hillier went upstairs to the library. It held more winter apples than books, and smelled of them. It was the only completely dry room in the house. In most of the others the sea air, or the rain, had found some way of blackening the wallpaper and warping window frames. There was no labour to spare to put it right. That seemed doubly absurd to me when I had heard the number of men in the Labour Camps given as high as five million. I thought this number was an exaggeration – part of them must have been in the other, what are called the Training Camps. The state of the house worried Lotte but she could not persuade Richard to take any interest in it. I found her near teatime in the dairy, skimming one of the flat bowls of milk. I spoke to her about Colonel Hebden, and she shut the door before answering.

'I don't like him,' she said. 'But you needn't believe all you hear about him in London.'

'I heard very little in London,' I said slowly. 'The worst I have heard has been printed in Norwegian newspapers.'

'He's not cruel. Not in that way. Look at him. He has no more cruelty than a baby pulling the legs off flies.'

'If the flies are human,' I said.

'No, I don't believe it.'

I had no reason to suppose she was not right. Norwegian newspaper correspondents have only the usual sources of information. Hebden was English and the English have no special ingenuity in cruelty.

'Why do we hear so much about Chamberlayn?' I asked. 'Bankers used to be anonymous – except Mr. Montague Norman.[5] And I think his notoriety was an accident, due to his having a beard. Beards are easy to draw.'

Lotte smiled. She sat on the only chair in the room and swung her legs.

'Chamberlayn used to be called the Enemy of the People.'

'Isn't he now?'

'I believe that most people in the Party, except poor Richard, regard him as our only Friend. He arranged the American loan when it had been practically refused.'

'But there were unpublished conditions to the loan?' I said.

'I don't know,' my sister said. 'I don't think so. Why should there be?' She yawned, tapping the back of her hand on her mouth. For the wife of one of the saviours of his country she was shamefully uninterested in politics.

Dinner was not a more elaborate meal than lunch. Lotte was really a poor housewife. Fortunately the Prime Minister was known to be indifferent what he ate or drank. He even sipped Annie's dandelion wine and sent her into chuckles of pride by complimenting her on it. It was nauseous stuff.

He made himself affable to me, too. He asked me what had been written in Norway during the fighting the year before.

'Very little,' I said untruthfully. 'It was difficult to get news.' The last at least was true. All the news was censored before it left the country. A Norwegian correspondent of a socialist paper resigned and came home with stories which were not wholly credited. I had met him in Oslo. He seemed to me hysterical and overwrought. During the evening he became drunk and spoke of Hillier and Richard as 'those cruel bastards.' It was he who spread the story about Hebden's wound.

'There was very little serious trouble,' Hillier said. 'What fighting there was Richard took care of easily.'

'The Volunteers were trained and well armed?' I asked.

'As well trained as the regular army. Almost as well armed. The officers of the first companies we enrolled – now five years ago – were all ex-army officers and N.C.O.'s[6] or from the Air Force.'

'Were you expecting trouble?' I said, as carelessly as I could.

'I ought to warn you that my wife's brother is an unregenerate liberal,' Richard said, with a laugh.

'He has been living in a country which can afford luxuries,' Hillier smiled. His smile was invariably charming. The supercilious look I found intolerable, or humiliating, was in his eyes and the persistent droop of the lids.

'Is liberalism a luxury? It used to be a home-made article.'

'At the beginning of last year,' Hillier said quietly, 'there were riots in almost every large industrial town. They were called food riots by the liberal and labour newspapers. Actually they were all deliberately organised. There was no starvation.'

'There were four-and-a-half million men out of work,' I said. 'Or so we heard.'

'They weren't starving.'

'The Labour government which went in in January had promised to double their allowances,' Richard said. He pulled down the corners of his mouth. Now he looks as malicious as the devil, I thought.

'The financial crisis broke as soon as they went in, as we all knew it must. Gold poured out abroad. The rioting became dangerous. Eight town halls were burned in one week.'

'Not such a loss,' I said.

'There were a great many people killed,' Lotte said.

I could feel Hillier's contempt for me, a cold reasonable contempt, nothing fanatical. And yet he must have been a fanatic. Those light eyes were not the eyes of a wholly sane man.

'Your labour and liberal friends did nothing at all,' he said calmly. 'They argued among themselves. A few of them were for what they called action. What action they could have taken heaven alone knows. Neither the Air Force nor the Army would have supported an adventure from their side. Nor the police. When the National Volunteers under your brother-in-law,' – I thought he spoke deliberately of Richard in this way – 'took charge, with the police and the Air Force looking on or at a pinch helping, they cleared the streets inside a week. If you ask me, I think most of the labour leaders were enormously relieved. At any rate they went quietly. The two of them who joined the National State government are both excellent men, at their own jobs.' He looked out of the window. I felt Lotte's foot hard against my ankle, and held my tongue. I knew it was not the whole story.

After dinner Hillier and Richard sauntered across the moor for a walk. It was a clear calm evening, warm for April. There was a full moon. The light seemed to come from behind the moors and to flow into the valley from its narrower end. The edge of the moor was black, without shadows, like a dead world. They came back about ten o'clock. I had gone up to my room. I looked down at them in the garden. Richard had fetched a jug and glasses for them from the house, and they were seated side by side at the broken down table, not talking, smoking. The curtains of the drawing-room must have been open and the light left on inside the room. It fell full on Hillier's face, and on the folds of the nearly white woollen overcoat he wore round his shoulders, the sleeves hanging. There was a mountain ash tree behind the table, the clusters of creamy flowers just visible between the leaves. The light came through it on to the table and on to their glasses. Richard was sitting sideways, his shoulders hunched to his ears. He wore his thick grey sweater and in this light it resembled a monk's garment. He was not looking at the other man. He had his head down and seemed to stare in absence of mind at the ground.

I don't know why this scene impressed me. I wanted to understand it, and there seemed at first nothing to understand. I did not move from the window. I watched until they stood up, still in their silence, and moved towards the house from my sight. I heard Richard come upstairs slowly.

I lay in bed and let my mind dwell on the image of the two men sitting in the darkened garden. I thought that if it were not important for itself it must be part of some earlier event, the latest moment in a line of which the first would emerge if I had patience to wait for it.

After a time I thought that the beginning had been a moment more than twenty years earlier, when I lay on the couch in my aunt's garden room and saw the two young men in the doorway. The room had been kept cool and dark with the sun blinds, and behind them the garden was brilliant with sunlight, colours wavering in the ripples of heat. They stood side by side, smiling at us with the half lovable condescension of boys of their age. They were both eighteen.

Lotte was with me. It was shortly after my father's death. My arm had been operated on for the third time. This was the summer of 1921 when the sun blazed day after day for weeks. In places the commons caught fire and smouldered all that time.

I was then sixteen. I hated the thought of going back to Eton with my crippled arm. The operation was a failure. By this time I had had all I needed of pain, and what with it and being alone often I had learned a number of tricks. One of them was to keep quiet and to let my mind choose meanings for me.

Frank Hillier, our cousin, was the shorter and slighter of the young men. In those days he was a little sullen with me. He resented the fact that his father had failed in every thing, last of all in the shop he opened in an out-of-the-way town. My father had paid for Frank to be educated at Thame Grammar School, and last thing before he died had put him into a solicitor's office. He failed his first examination and did not care to go on. Richard Sacker was the other boy. He had been Frank's friend at school. A year ago he had inherited money from a distant cousin – not a fortune, enough to allow him to do as he pleased. This was to fly. He had a second-hand aeroplane. He looked older than his age, thanks to the air wrinkles at the corners of his eyes and the deep lines down his cheeks. There was no mistaking the relation between them, or at least I could not mistake it. So far as I remember, I accepted it, with a certain satisfaction. It completed a circle in my own mind.

We had not expected them here. When Lotte saw them she got up slowly from my couch and went forward to shake hands. Richard explained that they were camping in the low field and had come to see how I was. He came over to me then and looked at my arm strapped to my side and sat down and began to talk.

He came every day after that. The fourth afternoon, when he was trying to distract me from the pain, Lotte came in and watched us. He asked her to fetch him a book. She went away and brought it in silence. He took it, looking at her with his wide smile.

'Do you remember slapping my face when you were Andy's age and I asked you to bring my mackintosh?'

'I was tired of fagging for you and Frank.'

'And now?' he laughed.

'I didn't bring the book for you, I brought it for Andy.'

'You wouldn't have brought it for me?'

'No, I would not.'

He seemed a little taken aback, but he laughed and began reading to me. The next day he came to say good-bye. Our cousin did not take so much trouble.

Richard came into another legacy at that time, almost three thousand pounds. He gave half of it to his friend. Frank Hillier invested his share while helping Richard to spend the rest. He bought another second-hand aeroplane, and one morning he set off unnoticed, with Frank as passenger, to fly to the Cape.[8] The enterprise came to nothing. They were forced to land somewhere in East Africa and the machine actually fell to pieces. Richard tried and failed to repair it. When they reached a trading station the newspapers had already forgotten them again. Hillier, I daresay, regretted this.

They came back to England early that year, and Richard settled down to study aeronautics. Frank decided late in the day to read for the Bar. In April Richard came to see us alone.

Lotte was about to be married. She was marrying an American called Lathan, a pleasant good man, older than any of us, kind, reliable, quick-witted. He was old enough to have been in the war, but he was not in it long enough to have become tired and nervously exhausted and restless as were the only Englishmen of his age whom we had known. There was none of that faint antagonism we felt – even I felt it, though I was not older than thirteen when the war ended – in the presence of old-young men with their fixed and incommunicable memories. Not that they tried to communicate them to young men of Richard's age. If we showed any curiosity about the war they made light of it, or told us would-be funny stories. In our turn we were hostile or jeering, to cover a sense of loss. Lotte's American, on the other hand, was almost too willing to talk. He had taken his war seriously, and had tried to understand it, and he was anxious when anyone asked him about it that they too should understand it. I became excited over what happened in this or that wood and on such and such a day. I could even imagine what it had looked like at certain times.

Richard saw him once at the house. Then the American went away and he stayed on. He was not living in the house, but he came in once or twice every day. He and Lotte laughed at each other, more kindly on Lotte's side than on his. There was a deliberate mockery in the way he smiled at her and in phrases he used. It was the clumsy mockery of a young man, but it was cruelly meant.

After a time she noticed it, and began to mock in her turn. She made fun of his adventures. She asked him what it felt like to be a rich and idle young man. (This was quite unfair. Richard Sacker was never idle and he was not well-to-do

– at this time he was living on thirty shillings a week: his experiments had swallowed up all the rest.) In a very short time the tension between them became unpleasant – more unpleasant to me, I believed, than to them. I was reading for an examination and I wished he would go and let us be quiet again. We had been quiet until he came.

He did not go away. He came to the house three times a day instead of once. One evening Lotte and I were sitting without the light, but the fire lit up the big untidy room. Richard came in from the garden and sat down in silence. He sat with his legs thrust out to the fire and his chin sunk. Even in those days he was broad, and his face heavy and severe. He was a forbidding young man unless he smiled.

'Have you nothing to do?' Lotte said.

He smiled and winked at me. 'No.'

'Is that why you come here?'

'Not especially.' He looked up quickly, and said: 'Are you going to marry this Lathan fellow, my dear?'

He spoke without affection and the word of endearment only made his question sound harsher and inexcusable. I felt that I ought to leave them and that it did not matter to either of them whether I went or stayed. They were as indifferent to me then as if I had been another chair in the room. I did not know how to go away without clumsiness.

'Certainly,' Lotte said, with an attempt at dignity. 'I shall be happy with him.'

'What nonsense,' he said. 'As if happiness is what you want.'

Her pretence of dignity broke down. 'What else should I want then? You tell me.'

He was not looking at her, but at the fire, his head dropped on his chest. He was wearing dirty shabby trousers and a thick sweater fitting up to his neck under his chin. It had the air of a uniform. 'Excitement,' he said in a quiet deep voice. 'Why on earth did you agree to marry him, Lotte?'

There was a short silence. Lotte said, deliberately – I saw her look at him – 'I can't spend the rest of my life waiting for you to care more for me than you do for Frank Hillier.'

They stood up at the same moment and stood facing one another. 'You're extraordinarily simple,' Richard said. Now he was laughing at her again and yet he was suffering, with the exaggerated abandon of the very young. I could not endure to be in the room with them any longer and with what there was between them, and I went out. Richard grinned at me over her shoulder. He was sufficiently detached from his desires to notice that I was there. I think that Lotte did not look at me.

They were married in the summer. Lotte was twenty and he nineteen, and neither of them had parents or any person to consider; between them they had an income of three hundred pounds. To speak of considering people, Lotte had promised me that when I was eighteen we should travel for a year, before I went to Oxford. She forgot even to tell me she was sorry this had blown away in a wind. I understood it, and I don't think I minded very deeply. My life had not accustomed me to expect the fulfilment of what were only pleasant notions, pleasant if they came to anything.

I supposed that Richard's marrying would at once alter or diminish his fanatical loyalty to Hillier. Only an event which took place much later surprised me. I learned then that a physical tie can be snapped without dying immediately. The two ends of the nerve go on living for a time. It may be a long time, perhaps differs with the minds and bodies involved – I don't know.

This is what happened. Five years ago, when she had been married and childless for fifteen years, Lotte had her child. The second (and last) General Strike began on the day she was to go into the nursing home. They were staying in a remote part of Dorset and their car having failed, there was no way of getting her to the home in time. She had a hard birth. Her child, a boy, was born dead and she was in despair. She was in such despair that it seemed she might die of it.

The Strike, as it turned out, was not to last more than five days, and then it was called off by its harassed leaders as hastily and with as bungling a diplomacy as it began. The five days were five too many for luck. There was tension and deep alarm in the country, because of the danger of war that month, but the Strike had been called for other reasons, the wage cuts and so on and the membership of the unions was falling very quickly with the unemployment in heavy industries. When the danger of war became acute the leaders themselves hurried to end the business without form, and to make speeches urging the nation to close its ranks and so on and so forth. They used every other smooth formula of our times.

On the second day of the Strike wireless news of communist outbreaks in Glasgow and Liverpool startled the country. On the evening of this day Hillier got permission to form a home defence corps, denied to him until now. The National State Party had had its fencing, flying, and rifle clubs. It had close on a hundred seats in the House, it was growing in the country. But until to-day authority had cut it dead in public, while recognising with polite bows such odd bodies as the National Service Women, who marched and drilled to their heart's content in uniforms of a singular horror. The leaders of a Conservative government, old and elderly men, with their own press shouting at them day in and day out to 'do something' – action, always action – had obeyed a sound instinct to do nothing, to take as little action as possible. Aware that any step they took must be a step nearer autarchy, not liking it yet not able to avert it, they held their hands. At last the old fingers moved, signing their own dismissal in the fourth year. And now at last, having brought authority openly to his side, Hillier hurried to turn every club into a company and company into a regiment. He sent a car for Richard to come to him in London at once. The moment must, he knew, be seized, lest the Government, becoming prudent again with the relief of fear, changed its mind.

I daresay Richard hesitated. I know he went in to see Lotte and even asked her what he ought to do. The local doctor had told him she was going to die. She was conscious and she told him to do what he pleased. He left her with uninterested strangers, and went off to Frank.

You could say it was Richard who made Hillier's victory possible. Without the National Volunteers there would have been no 'revolution' last year, no victorious National State Party and Council, no personal victory for Hillier. And if the first companies had not been formed then, in the emergency, would they have been formed at all? No one of the Party except Richard could have held them together and trained them for four years. No one.

The two of them could not want for thoughts as they sat in the garden. And it was perhaps thoughts and memories that kept them silent.

CHAPTER II

In the morning I helped Lotte to sort the apples stored in the library. Richard and Hillier had taken the car for some unspecified expedition. They went north, by the moor road. We worked on peacefully in the warm room, warm because it was over the kitchen with the peat fire kept going day and night. They had pulled the electric cooking stove out three years ago. The engine was falling to pieces and petrol was dear and rationed. Fortunately there was a broad chimney. It was easy to deepen the recess and make a bed for the peat with stone from the quarry. I liked it. I rejoiced that the stewed meat, although tough, tasted of peat smoke. So did the bread and tea and coffee and all that Annie cooked over it. She made admirable soup in an iron pan at the side, putting into it scraps of everything, even dandelions and fish heads. It tasted of peat like the rest.

'How long is our cousin staying?' I asked Lotte.

'Exactly long enough to persuade Richard to what he wants.'

'You mean to demobilise the Volunteers? Is that the whole trouble?'

'No, I don't think so,' Lotte said. 'It's only the immediate one.' She looked down at her hands, small and brown, moving over the apples. Her face was serious, with the triangular wrinkle between the eyebrows that meant she was not sure of herself. 'I think that Thomas Chamberlayn really is pressing Hillier to put down the Volunteers. But it's not a personal thing, as Richard thinks it is. The Volunteers are after all a sort of private army. You can't expect bankers, and business men, and civil servants, to approve of a private army. They might use it, but they wouldn't like it.'

'But Frank will go with Richard,' I said.

Lotte glanced up at me. She was smiling now, almost merry. 'Do you know what, Andy, you're very simple. You think because they loved each other they will always think alike.'

'Don't they?'

'Think alike? Love each other?'

I was so anxious, and inquisitive too, to know whether she had been happy during these twenty odd years that I was willing to risk hurting her. 'Did it work?' I asked her.

She smiled at me provokingly. We see through each other too well. 'Marrying

Richard? Yes, always. So far as I am concerned it does still. He wasn't faithful to me, if you mean that. There was always some woman. It surprised me, though I should have expected it. Yet in the end it didn't matter. He had been right: what I wanted was excitement. I'm not cut out for what you would call the life of the mind or the spirit. Married to a better man – better morally and spiritually, I mean – I might have been wretched.'

I thought of my own life. No, you could not say it had been anything but dull and pleasant. Lotte had half closed her eyes and folded her thin arms across her body.

'But when they were meditating the new Party you wrote to me in Oslo that you didn't care about it.'

'I know. I supposed it would mean that Frank took Richard away again.'

'Didn't it? Surely you've had very little of him these years?'

Lotte looked at me, steadily, and coolly. She knew how little warmth there was in my questioning and how much mean curiosity. 'You make a great many mistakes about Richard. Women have meant little to him in any sense, though he has gone through what he thought of as exciting and amusing adventures, when they were on the way. Always rather self-conscious adventures. I have been his good sensible friend and he has liked me. He likes very few people, and I think no other woman. He enjoys, really enjoys, an active life with a large spice of danger. He hasn't enough administrative intellect even to become a Minister. That is why all the important posts have gone to other men. But he can do anything with young men. The Volunteers are really his, his creation. He worked incessantly. I have known him sleep less than eight hours in a week – for six years until last February. It has meant more to him than his aeroplanes used to. More, infinitely more, than his wife would have meant. In any circumstances.'

'More than Hillier.'

'No, that's not true. It was to please, no, to serve Hillier that he kept at it. He admires Frank. I suppose he still loves him more than he loves anyone. Why, he even' – she smiled ironically – 'even tried to think for him. And you know that Richard has never been able to separate thinking and feeling.'

'So the country has nothing to thank our Richard for!' I said lightly. 'He was not even a patriot.' I knew now as much as I wanted to about her life apart from mine. Brother and sister born to old parents have the same dreams.

'You don't believe in the new Government, do you?'

'I don't think England has improved,' I said.

'When were you at home last?'

I counted years in which I had lectured on the same books and visited the same mountain valley. 'Not since 1935.'

'You didn't like it very much then.'

'No.' I remembered a supper party in a fashionable hotel and leaving it in the early morning with a quiet-voiced American who told me as we walked through the empty streets that he had visited five capital cities in the last few months, six, counting New York, and 'nowhere,' he said softly, 'nowhere are they spending money as you are here. I guess I felt a little ashamed being in there to-night. One of your countrymen said it was like 1913.' 'I can't recall 1913,' I said. I had felt deeply ashamed myself but it was no business of his. From all we heard his own country was not a colony of saints and idealists.

'It became very much worse later,' said Lotte. 'More vulgar and hopeless.'

'I believe in liberty, and I don't like dictatorships even when they appear to be benevolent.'

'Liberty to drift and starve,' Lotte cried.

'Has the starving ended? Why are there so many beggars in London?'

'Because,' she said swiftly, 'in spite of what your friends write about us, we don't imprison and flog unregenerate enemies. We leave them alone.'

'And Labour Camps? And what you call the Training Camps?'

'The first are for unemployed workers and the others for the men and women we consider worth disciplining to be able to live with us.'

She began to sort apples with sudden energy, to cover her irritation. She looked more than ever like a schoolgirl, quick, awkward, attractive. I felt very fond of her.

'Very well,' I said softly. 'Tell me something else. Will Richard sacrifice his Volunteers?'

'No.'

'And then what?'

'I don't know,' she said slowly. She jumped up from the floor, scattering the apples in her lap. They rolled under bookshelves and remained there. 'Why can't life be simpler and direct?' she cried. 'Why need there always be difficulties, and Mr. Thomas Chamberlayn making gloomy speeches and issuing grave warnings! As though he and his friends were in command. Why don't we begin to build houses, for instance? There's plenty of stone, and bricks, and men waiting about. Why ask civil servants and bankers, our servants, what we can and can't afford? Why don't we use what we've got?'

Before we left London I had sat next to the great financier at a dinner party. He was nearer sixty than fifty, a small dark man, kind and very simple. When he heard that I lived in Norway he described to me a walking tour he had made there years ago while he was at Oxford. I had been told, by a French banker, that he was 'a robber,' and by another man that he ran after women. I saw nothing of this in him. He struck me as a genuinely kind man, rather a saint, and dull as most mildly saintly men are. A saint needs a touch of savagery not to appear mawkish. The great saints have all been unpleasant, violent, or savages. His voice was so indistinct that it was hard to follow him when he wandered off into a sentence so long and meandering that any meaning it might have had at the start was soon lost.

'If Richard has all along been working for Hillier, whom did our heroic cousin work for? Did he work for England?'

'Do you remember that he disliked us when we were young, me as well as you, because ours was the rich half of the family?'

'What do you mean?'

'Don't you remember the awful clothes he came to dinner in?' Lotte said. Her nose wrinkled with laughter. 'At the time we were sorry for him. It is ridiculous and consoling now. Hanging round like a clown's. I am certain he has never forgiven life for humiliating him so many times in his youth. He had no decent clothes until Richard gave him the money.'

I was going to ask her what this had to do with Thomas Chamberlayn, or the Bank of England, or the expense of keeping up Richard's National Volunteers, when we heard the car below the house. I went downstairs. Hillier and Richard were in the hall. They had been driving in an open car and their faces were stung by the wind. Hillier was laughing and more animated than I had seen him, almost lively.

'If I let you drive me again I shall be as crazy as you are,' he was saying to Richard.

'There's nothing wrong with my driving,' Richard protested. 'I haven't killed anyone.'

'Why choose me?' Hillier retorted.

He went upstairs to his room. I followed Richard into the dining-room and watched him pour half a tumbler of whisky. He drank it as it was without water. Then he stood leaning on the table with one hand, the other spread on his hip, and smiled down at me.

'I've settled that business,' he said.

'They're going to leave you all your men?' I asked.

'They couldn't take them off me,' he laughed. 'Not a single lance-corporal.' He put his arm round my shoulder. 'You look thin, Andy,' he said, in a kind voice. He could be kind and lovable when he chose. 'As soon as Frank goes back I'll walk with you for a few days. We can't let you go to Norway looking pinched. They'll say next we're starving in England!'

It was not possible to feel indifferent to him. He had so much life, more of it than his share. I reflected that although Lotte had suffered, at the hands both of the other women and of Frank, she had not found her life dry. This even though for both of us Hilliers, for me and for her, jealousy is a physical torment. Our imaginations are wholly material. We see the physical image and strike ourselves on it again and again, trying to kill with the flesh what is rooted in the flesh.

'One of your foreign journalists, I'm not sure he wasn't a Norwegian, came to me about a man called Stephen Spender, a writer.[9] He said he knew certainly he was being done to death in prison. Do you know I had every camp and prison in the country combed for him? And never a trace. *What d'ye think of that, my cat?*' He put his head back and laughed. 'He was a solar myth.'[10]

'He was not,' I said. 'I knew him.'

'Then his body must have been hewn in pieces and sunk in the Thames.'

'It probably was – and by one of your more illiterate lance-corporals. He was a poet and a man of virtue.'

'Now listen to me, Andrew.' He brought both hands on to the table, leaning his weight on them and his face above mine. I felt weaker than new stubble under him. 'You think it's more important to keep individuals alive than to save the life of the country. But you couldn't even do that! What single thing did any liberal politician or liberal spirit do after 1918 to stop the country growing bewildered and more hopeless? They did nothing. They talked. They said it was disgraceful to stop communists preaching bloody revolution to workless men. And by God I believe some of you would let the communists put you against a wall and shoot you rather than take away their liberty to do it. Rotten with principles – and not a living principle among you.'

'Can I see over a Training Camp?'

'Yes of course. Why not?'

'Then you'll give me a pass?'

'You can remind me of it later.'

He took himself off, a little stiffly, vexed with me or with himself. I went upstairs to tell Lotte that the dispute was settled and in Richard's sense.

'If it's true, Hillier will go back to town before to-night,' she answered. 'He won't stay another night here; he doesn't like the north, and if his mind is made up he'll leave.'

I looked out of the window of her room and saw two young people coming towards the house across the moor. They could only be coming here, the path led nowhere beyond. I called Lotte to the window. She looked for a moment at the pair, both bare-legged, in grey shorts and sweaters, with rucksacks. Both were hatless and had short hair. Only the smaller bones, and the hollow in the narrow of the back when it was turned to us for a second, gave away the shorter figure as a girl.

'It's Ernest Sacker. That must be Stephanie,' Lotte said. She laughed for joy.

Ernest was Richard's nephew and her godson, and his parents both dead and she being childless she tried to think of him as her son. He might have been. He was born when she had been married a year. He was nineteen.

She ran downstairs and out into the upper field to meet them. I followed more slowly. When I am to meet strangers – I had not seen Ernest since he was a serious little boy and the girl might be anyone or no one – my crippled right arm feels as heavy as a stone. You see, I have to offer my left to shake hands.

Ernest Sacker was tall and very fair. He had a wide, loose frame, but there was no flesh on it to speak of, and what there was was as smooth as a child's. He was broad across the eyes, his face narrowing rather sharply to his chin. His eyes were remarkable, a deep bright blue, with large pupils, and set very low in his head. He shook hands with me with the frankest and gentlest of smiles. I thought him a delightful young man.

'This is Steffy,' he said, smiling.

His girl was as brown as he was fair, very thin, with grey eyes and a long brown throat. Her small hand grasped mine firmly, warm, and as smooth as a pebble lying in the sun.

Lotte took her away upstairs, leaving me with Ernest. He told me, but only in answer to questions, that he was a Volunteer. He had a fortnight's leave and he and Stephanie had walked from York, where he was stationed. They had been two nights on the way, sleeping in farms. He spoke easily and freely, as if he had known me all his life, yet as soon as my questions stopped so did his tongue. He was a very silent young man. It was less from shyness than from a fear of having nothing to say that his listener might wish to hear. I discovered much later that he was very intelligent, and a mathematician. I have the greatest respect for mathematicians. Mathematics is the only pure art. It is the skeleton of music and, I suppose, of the universe.

Seeking for something to entertain him I spoke of Richard. His face changed.

'Is he here in the house?'

'Yes. Do you admire him very much?'

He looked at me with an unusual steadiness, daring me not to take him seriously. 'I would do anything for him, as you might say.'

'Do your friends feel about him like that?'

'Yes, all of us do,' he said, in the same quiet firm voice. 'In a way, he is everything to us.'

'You like being in the Volunteers?'

'I don't particularly. The eternal parades, and keeping regular hours, are a bore. I don't get nearly enough time to myself. But I wouldn't give it up unless he himself told me to go. Others I know enjoy everything, even the parades and the marches.'

'Hillier is here,' I said. 'I think he'll be going before dinner.'

'If he doesn't, Steffy and I will eat in the kitchen with Annie. We're not dressed to eat with the Prime Minister,' he said calmly.

I went out, and met Lotte in the hall. 'I've seen Frank,' she whispered to me. 'He's not going until to-morrow.'

Before I could answer she touched my arm gently. I glanced round and saw Hillier coming down the stairs. He placed his feet on the edges of the stairs, making hardly any sound.

Dinner that night was a longer meal than usual. The chief dish was a whole salmon, served with a sauce of whipped cream as they serve it in Norway. That was one thing about Annie which was altogether unlike a peasant. She was willing to try new ways of cooking, even to make experiments herself. Before the salmon we had sorrel soup, and after it a curd tart with apples. Ernest and Steffy did eat their meal in the kitchen. I saw them before dinner seated side by side at the fireplace, sharing a plate; each had only an outer arm free. The inner pair was clasped loosely between them, finger between finger.

We burned wood in the dining-room, larch and pine, between dogs built of turves. Sparks from the logs set the peat smouldering. The smoke went up the wide chimney, but the faint acrid scent blended with the scent of burning larch. There were only candles in this room, set in pairs down the table. They gave less light than the wood. Richard had piled it up high enough to roast an ox. The windows were shut against the wind, which was strong up here, and the room grew unbearably hot. He was indifferent to heat and cold.

Lotte left us directly after the meal. I think she went to sit with the two young ones in the kitchen, and it was as well she did not come back. Richard had brought out four bottles of claret; since Hillier never drank anything at all and I only moderately he had almost the whole of it to his own cheek and the brandy as well. He began to say anything that came into his head and to walk up and down the room between the table and the fire, talking, singing lines from songs, stopping now and then to send a shower of sparks from the logs with the heel of his boot.

In a lull of the wind we heard an aeroplane pass over the house. 'Do you remember that morning in Africa?' he said to Hillier. 'Morning? It was a quarter past six and as clear as noon. There was a sharpness in the air you don't get in places like this country, where too many people breathe it. There was a cloud like a city, too.' He looked at me and went on talking to himself. 'The oil burst, and blinded me. I should not have put her down but for that. I was covered with it, black and oily to the hairs. Do you know what is the worst thing about being down, when you know you can't get away again? It's the being shut in. The edge of the earth turns over on you, like a ring pressing down. I thought, Well, I've done it this time. I don't remember ever feeling the air so cold on my face as I felt it then.' He stopped. 'That was at four in the morning. Soon it was burning us to the bone.'

'How long were you lost?' I asked Hillier. I hated the way he sat, as sober as a judge, the lids of his eyes half closed. He seemed coolly watching his friend drink too much and become tipsy. Detestable and supercilious I thought him. His voice when he answered me was full and kind.

'I don't remember.' He looked at Richard, and said with an absolute kindness: 'He carried me the last nine miles. But you don't know what that meant.'

Richard's mind had flown off on another curve. He stood beside me in his characteristic attitude, lounging forward, one hand spread out on his hip. He was laughing.

'Andrew. When you go back to Scythia tell the gentle barbarians from me not to put their trust in labour leaders.[11] I know you still have them there. Bloody Mary, you should have heard and seen ours when we invited them to confer. "In order to spare the country the pains of civil war we placed our resignations in the King's hands yesterday." "You can't resign what you've never had," I said, "the authority over the state. That belongs to us, to-day, yesterday, and to-morrow." Four of them were willing, God bless them, "to assist us in maintaining order." Can you beat it? Maintaining order! With the Air Force and the Volunteers keeping order all over the country and taking their instructions from me. I haven't laughed so much since. They were one sort of heroes. The rest, the men who folded their arms and walked out to tell their people how they fell, were the other.'

'The Scythians, as you call them, would rather know what you are going to do than what heroically you did.'

'We shall become a self-sufficing and self-contained people again,' said Hillier. He spoke in a monotonous voice, as though he were repeating a lesson, but with a kind of frenzied conviction in it somewhere. If it were only a lesson, he had learned it thoroughly. 'The world was going rotten with greed and looseness, everyone trying to become rich, and cheating and lying, as though money and trade were the be-all and end-all of life on earth. Men selling their manhood, and women losing their womanliness. It had to stop. We are stopping it. We have retreated into ourselves. We intend to have no debts to other nations and to rely only on ourselves. If it means that we are poor for a time, so much the better. We shall be all the sweeter for it. Some of the muck and rottenness will drop off. Sparta, not Athens, is going to be our model in the future.'[12]

Richard interrupted him rudely. 'Right,' he shouted. 'Tell the Scythians that, Andy.' He began to sing at the top of his voice, merrily and loudly: *'England was old England when Germany was a pup. And England will be England when Germany's jiggered up.* England for the English. No more foreigners allowed, except as envious visitors. No French, Boches, Eyetalians, or Scythians. The women shall spin English wool and the men wear it, and they shall eat English mutton and cabbage, and keep early hours.'

'Well, will you allow Englishmen to write and say what they please?' I said. 'It used to be an English custom.'

'Nonsense,' said Richard. 'Think of England in Elizabeth's reign. You were as free as air to get drunk, to sing in the streets, to break a neighbour's head. But if you offended the State you lost your own head or your ears or went to prison double quick and no nonsense about it. You can't say that wasn't a lively age.' He finished off the fourth bottle of claret to the great Queen. *'Sveiki!'*[13]

I rested my head on my hand. It was much too hot in the room. I looked at Hillier. Cool as a yellow cucumber. To please me Richard opened a window. The curtains blew in, floating straight out like flags. He had taken off his coat and stood there in his shirt, letting the wind blow on him.

'But the whole world was a scarcely opening market then,' I said to Hillier. I still thought he must have some doctrine other than this half-mystical nonsense. 'Now, three-quarters of the trade has stopped, in Asia and Central Europe they have gone back internally to barter – as they have almost up here. Every harbour in the world is filled with fine ships laid up and rusting. I've heard that you can walk dry-shod over the Tyne below Jarrow. Only coasting steamers put in to half the ports in England and the continent. Soon we shall scarcely know what the other side of the world looks like except from the tales of a few rare travellers. Was that worth taking away our freedom?'

At the window Richard sang softly: *'Stille Nacht, heilige Nacht.'*[14]

'There is no liberty except in obedience. In obeying as soldiers obey, in order not to lose their heads in a crisis', said Hillier. 'You were freer as a child than you are now, when your parents took the responsibility for you and you had only to live. When the State is your father and mother, you are free again.'

I believed, in utter amazement, that he felt what he said. Richard turned abruptly from the window, walked to the sideboard, and after struggling for a moment with his pencil and a notebook, came to me and handed me a folded piece of paper.

'There's your pass,' he said. 'It's for Winchell – that's the nearest Training Camp to here. You can walk there in a few hours.'

Hillier watched me fold it into my pocket. He said nothing.

'At Winchell,' Richard repeated slowly, leaning over me at the table, 'you will find only socialists and communists, the flowers of the field. Becoming fit for real English communism. I am drunk.'

'What is your kind of communism?' I asked wearily.

One Englishman, he said, was as good as another and worth three foreigners. All were equal in the sight of the State. None should be rich and none poor. Then suddenly he swept his arm round, knocking glasses, bottles, and candles on the floor with a shocking noise.

'Chamberlayn is the devil,' he said. 'You should keep him in order, Frank. Why haven't you put him under restraint?'

'He's a pleasant fellow, with a sense of culture,' Hillier said. 'He collects English painters of the seventeenth century – his place in Sussex is almost a gallery.'

'There, I've caught you,' cried Richard. 'You did go there that week. And after we'd agreed to keep him at arm's length.'

Hillier did not move from his careless attitude, arms lying along the table. His fine sensitive mouth alone smiled. 'I might have known you were not really drunk,' he said quietly.

'I think better when I'm drunk.'

'The fact is I was not there. An old friend of yours – Harriet English – told me about the pictures. She misses few of Thomas Chamberlayn's week-end house parties.'

'Do you deny Chamberlayn?'

'What do you mean, deny him?'

'Give me your hand,' Richard said, 'and swear to carry out our plans as we made them, regardless of Chamberlayn. Regardless of the devil.'

'I can swear that,' Hillier laughed.

Richard straightened himself and wandered over to the french window facing the garden. 'I must really see Harriet,' he said to himself. He sang softly: *'If I betray thee, thou nobl'st heart.'* Tugging the door open – it had not been opened this year – he walked away into the darkness. We waited a quarter of an hour and he had not come back.

'He's dropped asleep somewhere on the ground,' Hillier said.

'I'd better go after him and bring him in. It's too cold to sleep out.'

'Leave him alone,' he said, with a smile. 'He is tougher than either you or me.'

I rose. 'I shall go to bed.'

'Are you going to Winchell?' he asked, not moving.

'Oh I don't think so,' I answered carelessly. 'I mentioned it to Richard. It doesn't interest me.'

In the morning I looked out of my window and saw Richard returning across the fields, apparently from the village. I went downstairs. Lotte and Ernest were already at breakfast.

'Hebden is coming this morning to fly Frank back,' he said when he came in. He looked at Ernest. 'This time he's not flying the machine himself. Do you know a pilot called Eckhart?'

'Is that ass coming? Ernest said calmly. 'I shall go out with Steffy.'

'Report to me as soon as they go.'

'Yes, sir,' the boy said, in a quickened tone. He hurried through the rest of his breakfast and disappeared, with Steffy trotting beside him. I hoped he was not going to have much of this sort of thing. It was no good way to spend leave with your girl.

I was tempted to go out myself, but I wanted to see Richard with the others this morning. He was in a stiff ill-tempered mood. I saw my sister look at him anxiously. He could behave as he pleased with her, she had not criticised him for years, but she was afraid of the effect on a man like Hebden of one of his worst rages.

We heard the car, following the aeroplane. Richard went out with a polite smile to welcome Hebden and his pilot. Hebden this morning was in a fur coat to his ankles, in which he looked like a fat yellow seal. To my surprise, Eckhart was a boy as young as Ernest Sacker, good-looking, with dark smooth hair, and rosy cheeks. He was not an Air Force pilot; he wore the tabs, stripes and wings of a flying member of the Special Guard. He spoke in a gentle polite voice and effaced himself at the side of the room. I saw from the way his face brightened when Hillier came into the room that he was a humble worshipper of 'the chief.' He was almost as devoted to Colonel Hebden, running up like a puppy when that mountain lifted its finger, blushing with pleasure in being asked to do something for it. At the same time I did not think he was an ass. I thought he might be one of those simple but not always stupid young men who become fanatics for a cause they gulp whole. They did not stay more than half an hour. Hebden took a drink of whisky, Eckhart refused everything. Nothing of importance was said until Hebden was being helped again into his furs. Then he said jovially: 'Are you giving up half or only a third of your Volunteers, Sacker?'

'Not a drummer boy.'

Hebden had no tact, or saw no occasion for it. 'Well, what the devil,' he began.

'In any case I shouldn't be discussing it with you,' Richard said.

The other's eyes narrowed, and the flesh of his face seemed to darken. He glanced aside at Hillier. But the great man was seemingly lost in thought, or in the view from the windows. It was a fine one. The mists were lifting from the moor, and below them trees, grass, even the loose stone wall dividing the moor from the shabby orchard, caught the sun and gleamed. Hillier gazed at it all like a man in a trance. When at last he roused himself it was to put an arm on Richard's shoulder and draw him gently towards the door. As they passed me he said:

'This place, and you in it, do me good, Richard. I'll come again soon, if Lotte will have me.'

I followed them at a proper distance, catching up with them at the car. I heard Richard say: 'I can count on that?'

'You can count with absolute certainty on me,' said the other, quietly.

Hebden and Eckhart were on my heels. They climbed into the car, Eckhart at the wheel, and drove off.

I followed Richard into the dining-room. Lotte was still there. She had been looking at the marks made on the table by the broken glass. Had he been angry or drunk? she asked, mocking him. Both, he said. He put his arm round her. There were no marks of a hard night on his face. The colour across his flat cheekbones was high, and the lines less deep than usual. He was like an animal which knows it is threatened and cannot see the danger. His energy was drawn to a point in him, frantic to strike, but at a loss. I could see that his mind was at work, trying to foresee what was happening. He had an extraordinary imagination, sometimes acute, but oftener on the level of a penny dreadful.[15] The trouble is that by some ghastly betrayal the violent and vicious sub-life depicted in these writings has been translated into actual life, and is worked out with real victims and real murderers, and given Spenglerian labels.[16] The hero-gangster of a certain kind of American novel and film steps off the page or the screen and plays his horrid part in what is called the regeneration of his country. A disgusting cinematograph psychology becomes actual, as in a nightmare.

I saw Lotte look at him and avert her glance. My sister had no control over him. She could only watch him as one reads a book, turning the page to see what happens next. She was nervous and looked her age, haggard. She asked me to give her a cigarette, and sat smoking and listening, with bent head.

'When Smith told me this was in the wind I didn't believe him,' Richard said.

I glanced at Lotte. 'Major-General Smith,' she said, without lifting her head. 'I suppose you want to go back to London.'

'I'd better see Smith at once,' he said.

'I seem to remember,' I said vexingly, 'a great many speeches about the financial revolution that was going to follow the political one. You were going to repudiate the war loan. Disestablish the church. Quite a new society.'

Richard looked at me with an indifferent contempt. I was scarcely worth despising. 'I know all about that,' he said. 'They can have their new society if it's what they want. And I can talk about it with the best. I have, too. It makes no difference to me what sort of society I live in. I know where *I* am and what I can do. I was only concerned to tread out the liberal-cum-bolshevik scum. But they can't do without the Volunteers.'

'But Hillier knows – ' I began.

'Frank knows what he's told,' Richard said. He pulled at his long lower lip. 'I've left him too much with Hebden. I've had a load of trouble policing the country since last February. And Hebden is always in debt, and running to his bank to pull him out.'

'The whole of the State Council isn't in debt,' I said. 'Hillier – '

'I'll tell you something about Frank. Our Frank has a weakness for statesmanship. He wants to seem as solid as a Gladstone and as clever as a Baldwin. [17] Anyone who can persuade him that it is more statesmanlike to do things this way rather than that can move him – not the whole way but far enough. I suppose the City, or the Bank of England, or the Treasury, whatever hole these rats live in, has talked to him. Tom Chamberlayn has shown him columns of figures he can't understand – but he pretends he can. Appeals to his mature judgment and all of it. I know that smooth-haired ape, Chamberlayn. He'd persuade a virgin to seduce herself for him. Frank is a sort of virgin, you know,' he finished, with a sharp smile.

'But if it's a question of expense. The Volunteers must cost a fair sum.'

'Not more than they're worth. They keep the men out of mischief. And what's more, they're half trained. Better than half. Three weeks after the war begins they'll be a trained force, fit to use anywhere. It's all nonsense to say that wars can be fought now without men. If you don't want them in the air you want them at home, on the ground. To keep up supplies, to keep order, to man the submarine food-ships. And to shoot down strikers and so-called pacifists. Why, man, they're a perfect instrument. And I created it. And now a skinflint banker and a fat soft-bellied *spoiled* soldier – that's what Hebden is – want to break it up. But I can make Frank see reason. He always listens to me in the end. Always did.'

'All this war talk isn't taken seriously by the Government, is it?' I asked. It seemed to me that I had heard little else since I came back. At every dinner-table, wherever two or three men and women were gathered together, they began to talk about war. It was like an infection, or a sore spot that must be scratched.

'Is it not! How much longer do you imagine the tension in Europe can last, without a break somewhere? With Germany grinning from her empty pantry. Now, maybe you could have bought her off for a few years, letting her eat up Central Europe, country by country, beginning with Austria. But you can't sate a man-eating tiger. And you can't go out hunting with it, not to feel brotherly. And Russia a rogue elephant in the herd, chock full of mischief. But you'll be safe in Norway,' he grinned.

He went on talking in this horrible way, which divorces words from realities, so that it is possible to forget that nations are made up of living human beings, with brains and hearts. Many people, who have been educated out of their senses, talk about war in the same way. Richard was not educated, but delight in war was part of his penny-dreadful imagination. I soon gave up listening to him. Suppose I were to stay here? I thought. It is my country. Norway, for all I am comfortable and happy in it, is nothing to me. I ought to see the thing out here, if there must be war.

Then it occurred to me that on the other hand perhaps I ought to see about getting as many valuable and important books and documents as possible over to Norway. If there is war, and London is bombed, and Paris and Berlin, not to speak of Vienna, which would be a greater loss than all the others put together, a great part of the civilisation of six centuries will be engulfed, burned or scattered. No doubt the war will not last a long time, but when it is over the first care of whatever authority remains will be to feed the survivors and prevent them from turning into thieves and *routiers*.[18] There will be no money or energy to save the records and precious things of the past. I had a vision of the stones of the National Gallery being dragged away to rebuild Charing Cross station and the canvases burned to warm the sweating or freezing workmen's tea. Some of them were worth little else, but others would be a heavy irrecoverable loss.

And after all not so great a loss as this house, I thought. It would be deserted and fall to ruin. And with its rafters and stone walls and the orchard and the terraces, even as they are overgrown with peonies and southernwood, it is more English than the National Gallery. In any case I can't take away the paintings. Or the contents of the Bodleian. Or the Henry VII Chapel.[19] Or the close of Salisbury Cathedral and the magnolia tree. Or the lawns of Trinity with the crocuses out by the river. I was overcome by the strangeness and intolerable grief and pity of living in a Europe in decay. It has happened to Europe before but never to me.

PART II
MAY

CHAPTER I

On the first of May I walked across the south moor with Ernest and Stephanie. We walked in the direction of Winchell because I intended to go on there when they turned back. I had not told even Lotte that I was going. I had some fear of the permission being withdrawn by a sober Richard, if I reminded him of it.

Spring was early this year. In the valley, as we crossed it to reach the other moor, the may was full out. I never saw it fuller than that year. The branches fell down under their weight of blossom, white against the blue of the sky and the green of the grass. Never were such colours, except in my memory. The bees were already out as busy as in summer, and in the lilac in cottage gardens. It was very warm in the valley.

By noon on the moor we were glad to rest. We found a grey rock under a pine and Ernest and I sat leaning our backs against it. The girl stretched herself on the rock with her feet over the edge. I watched her as she lay there. Her small breasts, soft frail flesh, as melting as a child's, made no curve under her dress. Her legs were naked from half-way down the thigh. They were thinner than any boy's and below the knee there was scarcely a moulding of flesh and at the ankle none, only brown skin over the small bone. Each shoulder would have fitted into the palm of the hand like a warm brown egg or like the knee-caps. I was almost moved to lay my hand over these, for pure pleasure in holding what is alive, complete, and small. She had closed her eyes against the sun coming through the young leaves and I was afraid to disturb her.

Ernest had no such fears. He found a long grass and gently stroked her face. Without opening her eyes she brushed her hand over it thinking that a fly touched her. He did it three times and then she caught him at it. At once she slipped off the rock and hurled herself on him, overturning him by surprise. They wrestled for an instant, laughing and gasping. Ernest's face fixed in a smile. Then he picked her up, struggling, and laid her back on the rock. He was very careful with her in spite of his show of force, and she with him.

'Now lie still, dog.'

It was their most endearing term. They avoided the least caress before others. They were always cool, off-hand, even rude. I did not understand such manners and thought them badly brought-up. I was surprised when Lotte had told me that the girl was the younger daughter of the Master of Balliol. In my day Masters of colleges either had no daughters of eighteen or did not allow them to stravaige[20] about the country with young Volunteer soldiers. Probably she had told her respectable parent some lie or other. That Mrs. Sacker had invited her. That she was studying botany with a head mistress. What did girls offer nowadays?

'Then don't disturb me. Dog yourself.'

I seemed not to be looking at them. Thinking themselves safe they exchanged glances so exquisitely gentle that I could have cried. My own youth gave me no such glances when I called it before me.

Of course they were lovers. I was sure of it now. I thought that Lotte possibly did not know and might not care for it if she found out. But she would be kind and clever. The Master of Balliol would hardly be either. He would no doubt say that Ernest had seduced his girl. It was quite as likely to have been the other way about. I imagined myself trying to explain to him that with the very young seduction is easy and charming. That nothing need be ugly, hurried or rough in it when seducer and seduced are eighteen and nineteen and are neither afraid nor reckless.

Ernest opened his rucksack and brought out the milk, apples, and bread Annie had given him. He shared it with scrupulous fairness. Steffy sat up, crossed her legs under her, and bit into an apple.

I was anxious to know what boys and girls of their age thought about the 'revolution,' but hesitated to begin. I knew that Ernest thought the whole world of Richard. Did that mean he approved of everything Richard had done in changing the shape of life in England?

The girl herself gave me my chance. 'We are eight miles from Winchell Training Camp,' she said.

'I thought of going on there.'

She opened her eyes widely. 'They won't let us in.'

'They'll let me in. I have a pass. I'll go on alone. You might tell them at home that I shall stay the night.'

Looking away from me, Steffy said: 'I don't believe they ill-treat the prisoners.'

'Certainly not if they behave themselves,' said Ernest.

'But after all why are they there?' I said calmly. 'For holding views about property which were held by Jesus Christ and, strange as it seems, are held partly by General Sacker. I have heard him say that there ought to be neither rich nor poor. And if that isn't socialism.'

'I am a socialist,' Steffy said.

'Then why aren't you in Winchell?' I said, smiling at her.

'Because she is only a silly little goat,' Ernest said softly. 'And by socialism she means something else. The poor devils in Winchell – think of being a prisoner behind barbed wire to-day – wanted to take away private property. That's pure bolshevism and anarchy.'

'Property,' I said, like a don (I am only a don), 'is a natural human right.'

'We ought to have brought out a blackboard,' Ernest said. His smile took any offence from the words.

'Andy is perfectly right,' said the girl. 'Every little child, as soon as it can crawl, before it speaks, will take some little thing and hide it. Perhaps a little empty box. They love little boxes.'

A flame of passion and mischief came into Ernest's eyes. He picked up a slice of bread and butter and held it out to her, in order to give her something. She took it and broke off a small piece, which she held out on the end of her fingers.

'Animals and birds run into Steffy's hands,' Ernest said to me. 'Watch now.'

We sat still. In less than a minute a small field mouse ran out between the roots of the heather, crossed the rock, and leaped into the girl's hand. It sat there nibbling the bread and looking round it with bright calm eyes. My heart came into my mouth. It was like watching a miracle. At last she closed her fingers over it and put it down gently in the heather and it ran away.

'Clever dog,' Ernest said, in his slow quiet voice.

CHAPTER II

I reached Winchell at four o'clock. It was on the moor itself, on ground levelled from the heather, three miles from the village of Winchell, and that was no beauty spot for artists or holiday-makers, but a starved tumbledown street on the edge of poor fields and the wells never full enough even in a wet year.

I came over the slope and saw a quadrangle of barbed wire, I reckoned it not more than five hundred feet across and twice it in length. The wire was ten or twelve feet high. When I came nearer to it I saw that there were actually four fences, with a passage between them for the sentries. There were wooden watch-towers at the corners, like those erected for point policemen at certain busy crossings. Here shared by a brace of Volunteers and a machine-gun. I showed my pass at the gates and one sentry eyed me while the other carried it across to a hut outside the wire, one of six set down there on the moor without benefit of wire. One of these I guessed to be the Camp-commandant's hut by the attempt at a garden behind whitewashed railings. There were ragged wallflowers and a thorn hedge, mocked by the gorse which alone flourished up here. I wondered what sort of a man Steadman was, who was in charge of this place and had no more humour than to plant wallflowers on the full top of a moor.

The sentry came back without my pass and invited me civilly to go to the Commandant's hut to be inspected. I went. I found myself facing a man between fifty and sixty, in the uniform of Hillier's Special Guard. He was a big man, full stomached, but not fleshy or repulsive with it, as Hebden was. He was clean-shaven, with a pursed mouth and cold light eyes. He looked like an admiral; he had the very air of conscious authority and assurance that absolute mastery over an isolated community gives men.

He looked me over without a smile before asking me to sit down. I saw that he had my pass in his hand.

'General Sacker gave you this pass for some special reason?'

'No,' I said. 'I live in Norway. I am a professor, and I am eager to have a sight of your methods of dealing with anti-social elements. It may at any time be necessary even in Norway. Who can tell?' I felt that I was talking far too much.

'But you are not a Norwegian.'

'I live and work in Norway. General Sacker is my brother-in-law.'

'You are not a journalist.'

'Certainly not.'

He eyed me with the same unconscious insolence, second nature with him, as I felt, for another minute. I hesitated about telling him that I was the Prime Minister's cousin. I was not anxious to trade on the relationship or to have it known in the camp. He made his mind up first. Calling in an officer, he sent me with him to the camp, with an instruction to let me look where I liked and talk to any of the inmates, alone.

'You see I am trusting you,' he said, with a polite smile. 'Lies have been told about us in other countries. You can perhaps do a little to kill them.'

I thanked him. We went back to the gates.

I tried to look unconcerned as we walked through them into the camp, past the sentries. If I close my eyes now I see it as distinctly as though I had lived there. There was a path down the centre, and the huts, fifteen of them, stood end on to it. One of them was marked 'Stores.' A man came out of it carrying a plank. My escort beckoned him. He put the plank down and came up at the double and saluted. 'Show this gentleman over the camp and answer his questions,' said my officer. He left us.

'What do you want to see?'

'The camp,' I said, like a fool.

He took me, this man, whom I judged to be sixty years of age and a Yorkshireman, from hut to hut in silence, merely indicating in a word the use of each place as we entered it. Eleven of the huts were the sleeping and living quarters. One, separated from the rest by a slightly wider space and barbed wire fences, was for women. The windows facing the wire were boarded up. I made one or two attempts to start conversation with my guide, and failed. He could not have snubbed me more coldly if I had been the prisoner and he free. I became numbed by the discomfort and naked misery of the huts, each alike with its rows of sleeping bunks and the bench and table between. There was no washing arrangements in any of the huts and the latrine near the gates served for everyone but the women. Suddenly, as I was following him from the kitchen, which had impressed me with nothing except the unsavoury smell of the soup cooking for the evening, it smelled like rotting vegetables, I knew him. He was not sixty. He was not much more than forty, and he was a well-known journalist. I had met him only once, years ago, but I could not mistake him any longer. I completely lost my head.

'You're Holman,' I said.

He stopped for an instant, then walked on. 'Is there anything else you must see? I don't suppose you want to stare at the women. Their hut is exactly like ours.'

'For God's sake, trust me,' I said. 'I want to know the truth.'

'What truth?'

'What goes on here, what Steadman is like, what the rules are, anything. I don't know anything yet.'

'Is there any reason why you should?'

I could have implored or struck him, a prisoner. 'Every reason, if anything is wrong here, that people should know.'

'Five months ago,' Holman said slowly, 'we had an American journalist visiting us. Someone talked to him. He went away, printed the whole thing in his damned paper, and we paid for it.'

'Well, I can't convince you,' I said hopelessly. 'But I swear – I am an historian, you don't remember me but I met you at Philip Jordan's eight years ago, I swear I'll only record it for the future. And I might be able to do something. I can try.'

I could not bring myself to tell him who I was.

'Jordan isn't here, I don't know where he is,' said Holman. He stood looking at the ground. It was black, the peat earth trodden in. He looked up. 'All right. And if you're tempted to make capital out of us, remember that we're dead and can't reproach you.'

'Must we stand here?' I said.

'We can look at all the huts again. We have almost an hour before the working parties come back. What do you want to know?'

We set off, very slowly. I looked at everything with intense care. I summoned all my wits to remember what I heard and to judge if it were true or the natural extravagance of a man who knew himself imprisoned unjustly. Holman had not wanted to overturn the State, only to change it slowly and peacefully. As I listened to him I realised that he could not help telling the truth. His training and his Yorkshire shrewdness would not allow him to exaggerate. He even used the phrase – 'I don't want to say too much,' when he showed me the state of his own body.

That was later. 'Who is here?' I asked.

'Communists – Pennock, Straker, are both here.[21] Together with known socialists from the Labour Party, myself and Mellor. Eight of the irreconcilables, you know that's what they call Labour members who refused to join the National State Party last February, some Trades Union officials. My wife is among the women and so is Mellor's young wife. They are supposed to be going to have a separate camp, three miles off, but it's not built yet.'

'Then what do the working parties do?'

'Build roads from nowhere to nowhere, work at digging ditches on the moor, then filling them in. Not so bad at this time. Hell in winter.'

We were standing side by side looking into the Medical hut. 'Is the discipline strict?'

He looked up and smiled at me. 'You mean, is it true that we are flogged regularly? It is true.'

He spoke in a quiet soothing voice. I felt the wooden frame of the door under my hand. Why are you flogged? When?'

'When we break a rule,' Holman said. 'There are a great many rules, more, many more than there were in the army. I was in the army as a boy, did you know? I enlisted in the last year of the last war, when I was sixteen, I gave my age as eighteen, of course.'

'What rules? Don't be so correct,' I mumbled. I felt unfitted to play his game with him.

'Disobedience. That is, not running quickly enough when called, forgetting to salute, slackness in drill, persistent untidiness, that is folding blankets the wrong way. And of course any serious offence, answering back, trying to send unauthorised letters out of the camp, deliberate refusal of duty. Don't get a wrong impression. It is all done legally and according to form, with a doctor in attendance, the number of strokes counted, and iodine for the wounds. And my God, how that burns.'

'But here?' I said. I believed him and yet I did not believe. 'In every Training Camp?'

'I haven't been in every one. Mellor was at first in one run by the men themselves, under the benevolent nose of the young Commandant. There'll be other like democracies – behind barbed wire and by the O.C.'s leave! A place near Glasgow is much worse than this. Don't look sick. Why are you so surprised? It's not, after all, such a long time since they gave up flogging as a regular punishment in the Navy. And some living judges have certainly enjoyed being able to order the cat. And there was a man in my company in France, a sergeant, who shot a German prisoner for the sake of his wrist watch. Other ex-soldiers have seen such things, done in cold or hot blood. Steadman is a bully and a hard-souled brute, and there have always been such men and they have often been in positions of authority. The chance to put the fear of God into communists and such riff-raff must be a god-send to the Steadmans. Do you want to know any more?'

'You'll have to forgive me,' I said.

He smiled again. I thought, I shan't forget his smile.

'What for?'

'For being able to walk out of the gate,' I answered. It sounded like clap-trap.

I could not say anything else.

'We'll all do that some day,' said he cheerfully. He looked at me kindly. 'The first time I was flogged I raged all night wanting to do murder. The next time I cried. I thought at first that Steadman might be shot in the back by one of his own men, as it happened once or twice during the war. The men don't much like it, you know, except two or three of them, natural brutes and corner-boys, from some slum I shouldn't be surprised. Something much worse than the floggings happened, the men grew indifferent to them. They don't enjoy them but they don't mind very much. Some of them try to be helpful afterwards. But it's part of the routine. The lash is not the only punishment used here. A week's "solitary," in an underground room as narrow, dark, damp, as the grave, and smells worse – I'd near as soon be flogged.'

We had come to the end of the track again. I stood looking toward the women's hut. All at once a thin voice, I thought it was a child's and my heart turned only to think of a child in there, began to sing inside the hut. When it began I could not hear the words. And when I heard them I laughed.

Me farver was the skin of a Spanish onion
And so was Ma
So there you are.

'You have heard Sophie Burtt's song,'[22] Holman said, smiling. 'It is the only one she knows, and some of us think she remembers it a little wrong. You don't recall the whole song, by any chance?'

'I never heard it until now,' I said. I laughed again, foolishly, to save myself the shock I felt coming. 'You don't mean the writer Sophie Burtt, of course.'

'Who else am I likely to mean?'

'I supposed, I read it in *The Times*, she had gone abroad to live. Are you sure?' So far as I recall, I did my best not to believe him.

'Oh, that's what they put out, is it? Very ingenious. She used to travel a great deal, alone. Well, she has been here as long as I have. I knew her outside. She and my wife are friends, they're both Yorkshirewomen. They help each other by thinking in the same idiom. I'm glad for Win's sake. The National Service Women who warder them are breastless by day and bowelless by night, says my wife. If you believe me, they volunteer for this job.'

I think I asked him why she was here, but I have forgotten what he told me next. There had been no reason given. She had no family or near relatives, to make trouble. She had a bitter pen, and she was honest, incorruptible. It crossed my mind that in Germany they would have boasted of destroying her, but the

English are more expert in suppression.

'She is the only woman who has been flogged,' Holman said. 'Stop me if you have heard this one; or don't want to hear it. She has a sharp tongue, always had, and one day when Steadman was poking among the women's poor few things, God knows what looking for, she up and asked him why his mother hadn't smacked him out of prying when he was a boy. He ordered her ten lashes, and in consideration she was a woman they were not given outside, but in the hut, with the other women looking on. It was known in the camp five minutes after he gave the order. We sent in a protest, as a first move, and were answered that any failure of duty anywhere in the camp would double the number of lashes ordered for the woman Burtt. Have you ever felt absolutely without-God helpless?' He paused. 'There's no communication between the men and the women, but of course it goes on. Breastless and bowelless the National Service Women may be, but they are not pocketless. I heard from my wife that Sophie told them she was afraid of pain. She looked at them in such a way when she was laid out, with her clothes up. It seemed a century between each lash, my Win said. She was brave for five centuries but lost her nerve in the end. Out here we heard that, and believe me or not it wasn't twelve hours until we heard her singing.'

I was sunk. 'It must be stopped.'

'Oh, yes?'

'Could I see her, speak to her?'

'You could go in there alone, but they won't want to see you. They're such sights, and d'you know, they feel it. For the matter of that – look. She's there.'

Sophie Burtt had splendid red hair and large rounded white arms. I saw a woman with grey hair and a fleshless body cross from the hut to the latrine, but it was the same woman, my soul on it. There was no mistaking the face, eyes, the aquiline nose, the mouth.

'I'll raise heaven and earth to get her out.' Holman looked at me in a way I did not understand. 'You'd better leave her with her friends.'

'She has friends outside,' I said.

'No one here has any other friends he can trust.'

He turned to walk back and I walked beside him. 'We have some relief at the week-ends,' he said lightly. 'Steadman spends his in London. He has social ambitions, wants a title, they say. He was an unpleasant lecher in his youth, and since that sort of thing is frowned on in the most influential circles, I mean Hillier, he has to show himself in another light and at the best dinner-tables as often as possible. God ennoble him, he has the tastes of a Labour leader.'

'Can I rest?' I said.

I forget a little what happened next. I may have gone out for a few minutes.

I remember that I was in one of the huts when the working parties came in. I had a meal with them, but could not drink that soup, or chew that bread, as bitter mouthful as I ever tried. I thought Steadman had forgotten I was here. Holman made plans to keep me the night. The camp had, of course, its concert party, an orchestra of jazz players, able, so Holman said, to knock a professional rhythm from two tins and a wooden board. A thin boy, as thin as a nerve, face and accents of a Liverpool slum, ran about with a crazy gaiety preparing a show for the evening, for my benefit. I sat talking, no, listening, to men Holman presented me to as his old friend Andrew Hill. Secure that he had forgotten me, I gave him that name. I was ashamed of my own.

I thought I should remember all that was said. But I don't. There was a middle-aged writer, another novelist, and he was the only man without any hope. I should have been like that man. He saw nothing for him outside this place where he was not allowed to write. He was done for. His world had narrowed to a few yards between barbed wire, and he could conceive no new one rising out of the old after bloody sweat. His world had been good enough for him, a library, some book-shops, talk in quiet hours, striving to think clearly, a few weeks enjoyed in other countries, the cafes in Paris, the Ring in Vienna,[23] a Norwegian island. Useless to talk to him about the possibilities of a new world. It wouldn't be his, not look the same, smell, sound, as good. He had lost all. He was nearly helpless here, too. His daily life was an agony, the lack of privacy, the dirt, the digging. He could not use himself to these things, nor soften them by any of the tricks practised normally by men used to working lives. I was so sorry for him I sat as far from him as possible. When I knew who he was I had asked him if I could send him in some books.

'We have very little time to read,' he answered.

'All the same I should like to send you something,' I persisted.

'Send me a history of Europe in the Dark Ages,' he said quietly.

To my surprise – but why should I have been surprised? – the quarrels these men had had outside were still bitter here.

'The leaders of the Labour Party put us here,' Pollock said quietly to me. 'For ten years, after they lost office during a crisis, they threatened socialism. They promised the earth. When they went in again last January, what happened? What could happen? A financial crisis, partly real, the fears of people innocent enough to believe that this time they meant it, partly induced by persons whom the Government of the country does not control at any time. Did our leaders of revolution try to behave as socialists? They did not. Some of them were for staving off the crisis once more by cuts to the bone. These were said to have a high sense of duty to the nation. The others held up holy hands against cuts in wages. There'd been a plenty, they said. They had a duty to their class. Unfortunately they had no plan for driving their socialist cart and plough in an emergency. And weren't some of them relieved to be let off! I could repeat sayings dropped in committee, about the time not ripe, folly of swimming against the current, and the rest of the bladder noises that pass with them for wisdom. And so they went, some here, some there. The National State was dressed up and pushed on in front. Wage cuts are forced on now instead of being eased on, and protests choked back by decree instead of with butter. The wily Denham and the efficient Body saved their skins and their bums in office by joining the National State. More in sorrow with their late colleagues than in anger.'

'Yes,' Holman said. 'You'd have had us rush on into civil war.'

'Why didn't you call out every worker? They couldn't kill the whole of the working class. Why wait to be divided and driven off into pens like this?'

'It won't happen next time,' said Holman, with a strange twist of his face.

At my side there was a little man called (I never heard another name) George. He was childishly gentle. He now looked up and said mildly:

'Democrats can't appeal to violence. We can't throw away all our principles because the rest of the nation has gone temporarily mad. They'll come back to us. You'll see. They'll come back.'

Even Holman laughed at him. In my ear he said: 'This fellow, when he was on the Executive of the Labour Party, used to exasperate us all beyond decency. We forbear him now. He came here from the camp near Glasgow I told you about, where the Volunteers had a down on him, and put him through the most filthy and obscene torments. He was out of his mind, out of what mind he has, when he first came.'

The others were teasing George. 'What would you say to Hillier if he called you up to-morrow, and said "Now, George, I'm going to get you to help me"?'

He looked round at their faces and smiled with the cunning of a fifty-year-old child. 'I should begin by giving him a piece of my mind,' he said slowly.

'Good God,' Mellor said. 'It would be like splitting the atom.'

I joined in the laugh. George was not put out. 'You all like to laugh at me,' he said. 'And it doesn't hurt me at all.'

I nudged Holman. 'You,' I said, 'you who were not a communist, have you given up belief in democracy?'

'Does it matter what we believe in any longer? The haves won't surrender the least of what they have – we've learned that at last. It leaves the others with a choice of giving in like fools or dying in the civil war that they force on us.'

'It would have to be forced on you,' said Pollock, in his soft voice.

'I should have thought,' I said, not caring to argue with these men without a future – so I saw them – 'that democracy was the only thing worth believing in now.'

'Yes, and we must educate them,' George murmured.

'Merciful God,' said Pollock. 'If you are going to wait to educate people when you have the chance given, you'll end up here again, and serve you right. Make no mistake. That road is up. You can't go round, you'll have to go directly under or over.' He turned to Holman. 'If you like to join us you can. If not, why the devil didn't you follow the example of Body and Denham while you had time?'

I am a liberal, a mule, as Pollock would say, an animal without hope of posterity. But I had a qualm here. If they had not, both of them, made more mistakes and sent out more blundering orders than the leaders of a party, any earthly or heavenly party, can afford to do, they would not have been here. Is that the opinion of a defeatist? Very well, then, it is defeatist. But I could not for the life of me see that men who could not survive in an emergency could in any circumstances master the country. And here they were still quarrelling.

Holman looked at me. The thin merry nervous boy had come in looking for a spare coat for a charade, and gone out again. 'I'm going to tell you,' he said quietly to me, 'a story. The others all know it but it won't do them any harm to hear it again, and remind some of them that even Labour leaders can fight a revolution. And I want you now to hear it. It should be called "The Life and Death of Tom Lloyd" except that it doesn't concern his life but the end of it. Did you know Tom? No? He was the leader of the Welsh miners. Some of us didn't approve him willingly. We said he was too young for his place, or too fond of eating and drinking and sleeping. But Tom, when the trouble came, was in Wales. He hurried up to London and begged them there to call the General Strike. They were afraid of that, not without reason, so Tom tried next to bring the miners out. But by this time the lines were down and he had no answer to his appeals. What was he to do? He had a letter from George Body in his pocket inviting him to join the State Party. He went back to Wales and asked the Welsh miners if they wanted to give in without a fight. They came out everyone of them, to one man. He went from place to place, one night in a village in the hills, by morning in Newport, speaking, begging them to stand quietly, waiting for the others to join them. The Yorkshiremen at worst would have joined in if they had known in time what was happening. It's known now. In Wales there was the police and the Volunteers stirring up trouble, and hunger, and the first shooting was in Newport of all places.'

'I read in Norwegian papers about the fighting in Wales,' I said.

'Yes?'

'Lloyd was censured by them for persuading the men to a hopeless resistance.'

'Then all leaders of all forlorn hopes should be censured,' said Holman. He spoke as quietly as before. 'They didn't say that if Tom had not put himself at the head of the men they would have stood there without a leader? Well, then, you know what happened, how he and five hundred men were forced back into one of those valleys of dead bones over the mines, and how the Government offered all except Tom a free pardon if they came in before noon the next day, and how five only went down and were received in silence by the Volunteers and one of the five drowned himself afterwards when even his wife would have nothing to do with him. And how the others were bombed out of their place, and Tom, seriously wounded, was taken to Newport jail, and the others, except the dead, were sent to prison. He, under martial law – declared, mark you, after the attack from the air – was patched up, and hanged, not shot. They let his wife in to see him the evening before he was hanged, for one hour, and they took her back through the yard where the men were preparing the platform for next morning. He saw a friend for ten minutes, David Morgan, and Davy asked him for a message to pass on. Know that Tom spoke English like a Welshman all his life, with the stress falling on unlikely words and his voice rising at the ends of words and of the sentence. So you must hear it as he said it, his message and the last of his sharp speeches and his last laugh. "Tell Denham I always knéw he was a bráve mán but I did not know he was as bráve as denýing himself the easy lífe I have léd and the easy deáth I am dýing, and condémning himself to the Spartan lífe of socíety, and the company of austere mén such as bánkers and Márquises."'

What I would have said, if Mellor had not spoken, is unimportant, 'better tell the truth once in a while,' he said. 'We shall none of us get out of here while we're alive. Our last breath will be our next as free men. In fact we're dead here in good company. We've got ours.'

The young leader of the orchestra broke in again, nervous with excitement. 'We're ready,' he began. He turned his head at the noise of the door opening behind him, and stiffened as if he were on a wire. The other men jerked to their feet and stood at attention. I remained sitting, too surprised, and unused to this serious lunacy, to stir.

Steadman came a few steps inside the doorway and bawled at me from there. I saw that two Volunteers with rifles were standing immediately behind him. I gaped at the scene.

'You'll leave the camp at once, Mr. Hillier.'

I was close enough to the man next me to feel the jerk of his arm at the name.

'What is the matter?' I asked. 'You have my pass.' I had the fear that I had brought trouble on these men.

'I'll keep it.'

I thought I felt a trace of perplexity in his rudeness. 'Why am I being turned out?'

'I have had an order to-night from the Government not to admit any visitors. Even with passes.'

'My pass is signed by General Sacker himself.'

This seemed to decide him. 'An order from the Prime Minister overrules anything else,' he snapped. 'At once, please, Mr. Hillier.'

I turned to look at Holman. 'Good-bye,' I said, trying to be civil, yet not as civil as to bring any suspicion on him. He did not move his eyes to look at me. I glanced at George. His eyes met mine, with a steady distrust and shrewd quiet bitterness. I knew what he was thinking.

I had only to walk to the door to be out of their sight, but it was a mile. The cold on the moor when I walked and stumbled down to the village revived me, but to feel the more. I felt despair and anger. All the fears of my childhood rushed through me in a dark flood. I fell on the moor and passed the night there, with my face on the ground.

CHAPTER III

Richard and I drove to London. Lotte went by train, with Steffy, who had to return to her home and the Master of Balliol, and Ernest, who had still four days' leave and wished to spend as many of them as possible near Steffy.

We made a long detour, through east Lancashire. At six o'clock in the evening we were passing through what had been a centre of industry. The doors to the buildings were barred, windows boarded over, chimneys cold and smokeless, empty sidings. Men stood about at street corners and a few listless children quarrelled in the gutter. I have seen deserts, but I have never seen anything to equal in desolation this region of derelict mills. A cold shabby Purgatory. New grass will cover even battlefields, but here it had died under a million tons of brick, metal, concrete. It would take an age for these valleys to return to life, and in the meantime what became of their human scrap-iron? Scrap-bone and flesh.

'You don't seem to have had much effect here,' I said.

'We're not responsible for the state of things,' Richard answered. 'We shall cure them in time. Believe me.'

Time will cure them, I thought, by smelting bone and iron together. It was useless to talk to Richard. Smiling, he hung over the wheel, and sung lines of songs in a low voice. To be on the move made him as lively as a young man with a girl to meet. Towards dark, when we were climbing a hill, the car stopped suddenly. We got out and Richard poked this and the other part of the brute's body with no effect. It was ten or more miles since we had passed the last roadside garage. There were only fields here, with not even a house. We walked to the top of the hill and saw a small cottage in the trees at the side. It was now dusk. Richard brushed aside my suggestion that we should walk on until we found a garage, and knocked at the door of this house. There was no sound from inside, and no light in any window. He knocked again.

'The place is empty,' I said.

Richard pointed to a rubbish heap at the side of the door. On the top of it were fresh peelings of potatoes and a knife dropped on the ground. I should have stood beside them for an hour and noticed nothing.

He raised his voice. 'Answer the door.'

At this there was a noise as though something heavy were being dragged away at the other side of the door. It opened on a chain, and a man holding a candle looked at us. Seeing Richard's uniform he sighed heavily, and unfastened the chain, and let us in.

'What's the matter with you?' asked Richard. He stepped past the man into the room of the house. A young woman stood leaning against a chair, with a white startled face. The man had followed him with the candle.

'Can we do anything for you, sir?'

The young woman had said nothing, only looked at us. Now she spoke, with what might have been a laugh if she had not been out of breath.

'It's all right, Tim, can't you see?' She took a step nearer to us. 'Excuse us, sir, but we've had several frights lately. Monday last week four men came in here when I was alone and took every morsel of food we had in the house. We had no money, of course, but they weren't looking for that. And last night one stopped my husband in the road and said he'd cut our throats if we went to the police again, whatever happened. So you see we were anxious when you knocked.'

She spoke quickly, as if she were reassuring herself. She and her husband were both young, thin, and strained looking.

While she was speaking she had moved round to him. She stood with her hand on his arm. He put the candle down on a table and smiled at us awkwardly.

'It's like that,' he said.

Richard sat down, thrust his legs forward, and rested his hands on his knees. 'What is this place?'

It was, explained the young man, one of the settlements. I forget how many of these had been parcelled out this year among workless men. They were supposed to feed themselves and their families, but not to sell to market. They grew vegetables, kept a few hens or a pig, and for what they wanted in the way of clothes or soap, or tobacco, exchanged their eggs or their cabbages at the nearest shop – if they had to spare. Since none of them were farm labourers before they were set down on their acre or two, and the soil was in no case of the best, most of them had been put to it to live at all. I had a feeling that I was in the room with two young creatures who were already desperate.

'Where is the next village?'

'Five miles.'

'Are there any other settlements near here?'

'No.'

'There's not a soul near us,' his wife said. She might be nineteen or twenty. Her dress was pulled round her, she was perhaps undressing when we knocked.

'What men are they who come about here?'

The young man looked at us. 'How do I know?' he said slowly. 'From the town, I suppose. I don't blame them. I've been hungry.'

His wife moved to pull a curtain closer. 'Better not show the light.' She stopped beside me and I saw the grey colour of her skin. She would have been pretty but for that and her half-starved look. She had blue eyes. The young man was short, dark and stolid. He looked no surer of living than she did. They both looked as I could imagine people cut off by the tide to look, on their last edge of dry ground.

'Shall we ever get back to work, I mean to something safer than this?' he said.

'What is it like here?'

'Like nothing. The place was never touched before, and we're not country people.'

'It's like the end of the world,' his wife murmured 'And when those men come.' She stopped, and looked with a ghost of a smile at her husband. 'Maybe we'll get through one year and the next will be better,' she said softly to him.

'Why, if you can't work the place, don't you apply to go to a Labour Camp?' said Richard. He was frowning. He was angry and at a loss before a dilemma he was not able to shoot down.

'Ah, she couldn't come with me. Could she. We were married only this year.'

Richard could borrow nothing he wanted in the cottage, and we set out to walk to the village. He soon outdistanced me, as anxious as I was to abandon the young man and his wife to the darkness.

CHAPTER IV

At thirty-nine years there were two fixed points in Richard Sacker's life, only two, his love and loyalty to Hillier and his constant liking for his wife. All other persons, the women he had had and the men he had worked, bargained, and quarrelled with, were as little and as much in his mind as cities in which he had walked, quays where he had stepped ashore, cafés where he had eaten and drunk. He was at home in a great many foreign cities. There were the four years, from 1929 to 1933, when he left England and Lotte and went first to China and then to South America. He might have stayed abroad, if Hillier, feeling his way to the beginnings of the National State Party, had not asked him to come back. He came at once, although it meant the loss of a large sum of money to him to leave Bolivia at that moment.

The republics of South America, and China in disintegration, were his proper field. He was out of his place in a country where civilisation and traditions are still secure. England when he was born was not ripe for him, but in due time this ripeness prepared itself.

As soon as he began to look round him he was in conscious revolt against the social traditions of his own country, in which the manor house still played nearly as large a part as the bank. Romantic publicisers of the National State Party after its triumph, men with pens to sell, and especially a silly young woman who began to write key novels of the *haut monde*,[24] were apt to write of him as a modern Sforza, or the new Göring, or of the re-emergence from the shadows of history of the great *condottieri*.[25] Quite apart from the truth of history, which is that these soldiers of the Middle Ages were for the most part unpleasant brutes, whose followers burned the huts of defenceless peasants and raped their women, it was sentimental nonsense to speak of their re-emergence in Sacker. History does not repeat herself like an idiot, but like an artist. The originals played their minor and bloody parts in the smelting of a European civilisation. Richard Sacker was the opportunist and undertaker of its decay.

He was a violent man, with strong physical passions which he could still control. To live well he needed perpetual excitement. For that he would run into danger as other men take trains. He was physically reckless and he had the vanity of his nerves. All his early adventures were imagined before he undertook them.

As he grew older, imagination played less and physical need a greater part in his acts. He had escaped having scruples. He would cheat any man out of his money and any woman out of her honesty and think them fools when he succeeded. In short, he was an energy which a civilised state, if it could not put him to work making roads or testing engines, would do better to kill. This is the dilemma of all past civilisations. To be resolved in the next?

All this being said, note that Richard Sacker attracted women, and more especially intelligent women, very young men, and men who had the worser part of women in them. He was quick with physical energy, like a handsome and unbroken animal. He suggested danger and excitement. When his emotions were involved he was delicately kind and thoughtful, and this lasted so long as they were involved.

There were violent contradictions in him, living side by side, and never coming into conflict. He could think and plan like a politician, but the only things he ever did were kill, cheat, lie, raise an army – act, in short, like a soldier of fortune plundering a country. He was inconceivably insensitive to the suffering of persons whom he disliked. When he was in love he was as quick as a woman. He never fell in love with stupid women.

One of his mistresses, the only one who had come near being important to him, and given Lotte sleepless nights, was Harriet English. She was still fond of him.

On the afternoon of the day he reached London he went to see her in her hotel. She lived rent-free in a hotel near Berkeley Street, for the reputation she conferred on it. She was now thirty-two. She had sung only in England and America and in England and America she was considered a great singer. However, she was not one of the great singers. Her voice was a pure and light mezzo,[26] very beautiful in its way, but it was not the way taken by the legendary ones. Her legend was fulfilled during her life and would scarcely outlive it.

She had played her part in creating it. She was fat and sentimental when she was seventeen, with fine eyes. A year later, after she had been seduced by an ageing and internationally famous conductor, she began to reform herself. She became notorious for her witty and unkind speeches, she grew thinner, and waved her hair. As for the conductor, she made use of him to achieve a position as a singer far sooner than she would have managed it on her merits, on the merits of her voice. He was generous to her and settled a fair sum of money on her. Nevertheless, she was very bitter when he left her, and always felt that she had been cruelly treated by life.

With success she became very shrewd and saving. She invested her money on the advice of Thomas Chamberlayn, and as a reward treated him so distantly that he became obsessed with the idea of marrying her. Now that she had turned thirty she was beginning to consider it.

Her sharp tongue had made her more admirers than enemies. She had the sense not to attack people who could be useful to her. Like many brutal-minded and malicious persons she was exceedingly sensitive to slights on herself. Her friends had constantly to comfort her and to write letters of protest to critics who had ventured to be critical. Aside from this common weakness, she was honest and intelligent, but badly educated. To her friends she was a good friend.

Her fine dark eyes welcomed Richard. She liked to see him sprawling in her room. The physical attraction he had for her was almost as strong as during the two years he was her lover, but it had become a pleasure in watching him. In order to keep him her friend she talked to him of political events, and made much of the political gossip she picked up at dinner-parties. She was jealous of his wife, and supposed, quite wrongly, that Lotte influenced him. She had taken care not to know her.

'My dear Richard ! Why are you in London?'

'To hear you sing at Covent Garden next week.'

She accepted this, but laughed. 'Have you seen that it is an entirely English season? To seal the national uprising. Even Handel is banned from it, and apart from Purcell it is a riot of Wallace and Balfe. The Prime Minister's taste.'[27]

Richard saw nothing unfortunate in it. 'Do people care what you sing, so long as they hear your voice?' he said soothingly.

'*Scenes that are brightest,*' sang Harriet. 'I suppose it is good enough for you. Anyone who prefers music can go to Austria in the summer.'

Richard looked at her with his charming smile. He wanted very seriously to know what was being said in London about Hillier but not as it concerned his taste in opera. He did not know how to question Harriet without arousing her avid curiosity. At last he said:

'You were anxious about your money. Are you satisfied now that we're not going to take it all from you?'

'Perfectly, thank you,' said Harriet. 'The talk of a financial revolution alarmed me, and not only me. But office has sobered your friend Hillier, as we thought it would. He is a sensible man, after all, and if his musical taste was not execrable I should admire him more than I do.'

'There will have to be a financial revolution,' Richard said, watching her. 'But your money is quite safe. It is all in armaments and chemical industries, isn't it?' He had discovered early on that Harriet was extremely nervous in anything to do with her money. She was afraid of dying in poverty. To ask her for ten pounds was like asking her for a pint of her blood.

'You are out of date and out of touch, my poor Richard,' Harriet said with spite. 'Why don't you stay in London? If your wife hates London let her live alone in the country. You can't afford to know nothing of what goes on.'

'And I suppose you know everything,' Richard smiled.

'I know,' cried Harriet, 'that when Hillier wants advice on finance he asks Thomas Chamberlayn for it, not you. They have met in this very room to discuss it, and more than once. Now do you believe me that you are a fool to waste your time in the country, drinking too much, and holding reviews of your precious troops!'

'We shall see,' Richard said calmly. 'In the meantime you are too pretty to understand politics.'

Clever though Harriet was, she had never realised that he despised women and was sentimental about them from the same impulse. He knew what they were made for and what all of them, even the clever ones, wanted. He had been very fortunate in not knowing a woman who would continue to despise him even if he had her flogged. His impenetrable assurance made Harriet very angry.

'I'll tell you something, Richard. A word of advice. You don't understand your friend Hillier if you don't know that he is eaten up with vanity. Vanity has been the moving spring of his life. When you gave him a private army you fed it, and he loved you for doing it. Now he no longer needs your army and he resents having to board and feed it, and make unnecessary ridiculous speeches to it about the social revolution. He has other food for his vanity now. He grows quietly fat on power, and who feeds him with it? Why, who but Tom Chamberlayn? At Chamberlayn's house, Hillier meets international financiers who talk to him as if he were one of them. They even ask his advice. I have heard it done, and seen your Hillier licking his lips like a cat for pure pleasure!'

Richard stood up. He walked across the room, and looked down at her. She had no idea whether or not he was angry, but his body near hers awoke an old excitement. Stung by it, she went on:

'After all, we all know that Thomas Chamberlayn gave the Party three-quarters of a million pounds four years ago. Did you imagine he did it for love? Or for you?'

Richard stroked her hair gently. She jerked her head aside. Still smiling he left her. She heard him speak to her secretary in the next room, and the woman's amused answer.

CHAPTER V

It was thought unwise for Richard and General Smith to meet openly. I was sent to call for Smith at his club, at the corner of Pall Mall, facing the Athenæum,[28] and to bring him to an unlikely café in the Euston Road. I was very willing. I did not at this time believe in the seriousness of Richard's 'conspiracy.' Richard as a conspirator made me smile. I had not then made the acquaintance of the American armaments manufacturer who employed Richard to sell arms to both sides during the war between Paraguay and Bolivia, and had I done so I should not have felt that plotting in South America was a test of discretion. But I should not have smiled. Nor did I later, when I began to realise what was involved, and the persons involved. At this time I was only interested in observing the effect on as many men and women as I could meet, of living in what is to all intents a dictatorship. And I was not able to forget the image of Winchell, always in my mind, and I tormented myself with doubts and anxieties, afraid to take a step that would bring punishment on the men there without saving them.

In Smith's club I was kept waiting in the hall. After a time I caught the name 'Sacker,' and listened. Two middle-aged members of the club had paused to talk close to me. One had a newspaper in his hand and he was pointing to a paragraph. The other laughed in a mild barking way, and said:

'I don't see why these chaps, Sacker and Hebden, shouldn't have their titles. After all, there is the Salvation Army with its Generals and Colonels.'

Both barked together for a moment. They moved off. A phrase floated back to me. 'Hebden comes of a decent family, I believe, but the other bounder – '

Hearing this gave me a mild shock. I had never realised before that Richard was outside the ruling caste in England. Hillier was outside it too. But he had perhaps been adopted into it, for reasons of policy? Policy might dictate a very different attitude to my brother-in-law. I began to wonder what this meant for his future. For the first time I felt uncertainly that there might be danger in his conspiracy, nebulous as it was.

Smith was smiling his pleasant, rather meaningless, smile as he came toward me. I knew him a little already, and Lotte had sketched his career for me. He had taken a commission in the army when the war of 1914-18 broke out. He earned a D.S.O.[29] as early as 1915 and was taken on to the staff of the brigade.

He decided to make the army his career, worked hard, made useful friends, and at the end of the war he was given regular rank as a Major. He went to the War Office. He did well for himself by his marriage, and between luck and genuine cleverness he rose very high before an unfortunate deviation ruined him. He became interested in the finance of armaments manufacture. He discovered that a proportion of the money spent could be saved if certain changes were made. In his enthusiasm he did not notice, or did not properly realise what it involved, that these changes meant a loss in money to certain people who were in a position to suppress him before he had done them too much damage. They did it with the greatest smoothness, and without the luckless officer being able to explain to the country at large that he had been ruined for trying to save its money. His fall was an awful warning to other intelligent officers never to allow enthusiasm to cloud their judgment. This had happened three years since. He was now an active man of fifty-two, intelligent, discontented, adroit, with too much sense to make a fuss, and end for good any chance of recovering. He still had useful and faithful friends in the Service and in the former Conservative Party (now laid up in the bosom of the National State Party like the sinner in Abraham's). He had his wife's money and his ambitions were sharper and more biting than before. Could he believe that the part of saviour of his country was out of his reach?

We took a cab in the Haymarket and drove to the restaurant Richard had discovered, a small place run by an Italian. It was out of the way for the people who could have appreciated it, and was nearly empty. The proprietor, made morose by his misfortunes, never left his dark room behind the café, and neither of his foreign waiters was likely to recognise Richard or Major-General Smith.

They sat down, ordered coffee and vermouth, and began at once to talk like men who knew each other's minds. I am certain that Smith had as poor an opinion of Richard's subtlety as I had, but he had a respect for his practical intelligence, and he knew that the Volunteers would obey him in any adventure. What I did not know, and never shall know, was how much sincerity there was in his dislike of reaction. He said a great deal about it, more than necessary if he were not talking only for the sake of talking or to try Richard's mind. On his side Richard was uninterested in any theory. What he knew was that the turn of events was going against him and his Volunteers, and if the influences at work were reactionary then he was opposed to reaction, and ready to begin another revolution next week. His idea of revolution was a simple one. The men, the money, and the guns, and the will to use them to impress, alarm, and at proper times shoot down resistants. He was grateful to the handful of communists who rose up against him in the crisis, and gave him the chance to use his willing young men in something more serious than a street fight.

Sincere or not, Smith did at this meeting – it was not, I learned, the first or the second – talk at tedious length about the need to bring back liberal elements into the Government.

'Liberal!' said Richard. 'You've got Denham and Body on the Council. How much more liberal do you want to be?'

'Precisely. We've got them, but what do they represent? Only themselves and their anxieties. The men and women in the country who used to vote Labour at election after election, the men who used to be members of a Trades Union, millions of them still, everywhere, although they've lost their way and don't know what to hope – do you suppose they have any love for their two ex-leaders? Or any faith in them? And do you suppose that Body and Denham themselves are comfortable in being leaders without followers? On sufferance in the National State Party? Hated by their old friends and at best tolerated by new ones?'

'What are you thinking?'

'Nothing very definite yet,' Smith said. 'But as a start I suggest that it will be worth our while to take the minds of three men. I'll make a list of them.'

He tore a leaf from his pocket-book and wrote on it, one below the other, his three names. I looked at them.

George Body, Minister of Labour.
Eugene Denham, Minister of Social Service.
Professor R. B. Tower.[30]

'I suggest,' he said, with a smile toward me, 'that your brother-in-law is a very suitable person to make the approach. There may be good reasons for leaving them outside. I may be mistaken in them, they may be perfectly happy as they are. But I don't think that.'

'Yes,' I said, 'but I don't follow how men whose own class no longer trusts them can be of use to you.'

'Because they are, after all, socialists. Or were. They know the ropes and the language. If they saw any chance of reviving the Trades Unions, and with them, their own real influence, they could – well, what could they do? – arrange a general demonstration of workers in the country? create an agitation? And if it happened at the same time as the manoeuvres of the Volunteers in Richmond Park? Isn't it at least worth discussing?'

He assumed that I was prepared to act as go-between. I suppose he thought I had political ambitions. Why didn't I tell him at once that his and Richard's interests were not mine? Their shabby and self-interested plots were not worth the trouble of an honest man. Partly, no doubt, out of vanity. Out of curiosity.

Partly because I suddenly saw in all this a glimmering of hope for the men in the Training Camps.

'Who is Tower?' I said. 'Do you mean *the* R. B. Tower, the economist?' I thought I should be very glad to interview this man.

'Of course. He is a remarkably sensible and very wide-awake man,' Smith said. 'His advice is worth having.'

Richard had all this time been watching the other man. If Smith were aware of his gaze he sustained it more coolly than I could have done. Now he said gently:

'You'd like to take Hebden's place as Air Minister?'

'I should prefer to go back to the War Office,' Smith answered. He smiled slightly again.

'As the head of the State, Hillier mustn't be involved in any way, at any stage before the final one. You realise that?'

'Oh, quite. Shall we dine here? It seems a very decent place.'

Two men came in and took the table next ours. Smith tore up the paper with the names and began talking of books. He was an admirer of the sedate poet T. S. Eliot and of a new writer whose work I had not read. Smith quoted a verse or two in a light melancholy voice, suited to the words. I complimented him on his memory.

CHAPTER VI

Abroad, the National State Party had made discreet signs to draw all eyes to their toleration of R. B. Tower. Here was this man, it was whispered, a known socialist, making no concealment of his beliefs, allowed to retain his post in the London University. Even his letters to *The Times* arguing against the economic policy of the Council were printed. Even his previous books not banned, and his public lectures allowed.

It would have been hard even for Hillier to behave in any other way. Tower was a Nobel Prize holder, he was known in every country, the Socrates of our time, and a time and a nation which prefers to starve or smother rather than openly to murder its Socrates. For the Council to injure him in any public way would have been more than tactless – un-English. I was overjoyed to have an excuse to see him. The visit was arranged for me by his close friend who was also a friend of Smith's friend.

I was shown into a large room of heavenly disorder, books on the floor, on the mantelpiece, on the table with the coffee cups, on the bed, on all the chairs. In the middle of it, Tower, broad, shabby, shaggy, smiling. He cleared a chair for me by adding the books on it to the tottering pile on his desk, which fell down at once, breaking a glass and raising clouds of dust. 'Don't trouble yourself,' he said. He smoothed out a book which had fallen open on its face and let the others lie as they fell.

Not even Smith, who intrigued as naturally as he breathed, had any thought of conspiring with R. B. Tower. But Smith had perhaps a false idea of his influence. The width and depth of this man's influence on men's minds is not measured. Not yet.

Smith needed advice on the politics of the young men, and I was to ask for it, but in Tower's real presence I felt like a schoolboy.

Tower made things easier for me by asking:

'Let me see, now, you live in Norway. What do they think there of our changes?'

He was astonishingly shabby. There was a large burnt hole in his jacket. He had a pipe which must have been choked, it would not keep alight longer than a minute, he lit it again and again, and knocked it out, until all his chair and the floor round him were covered thick with matches and tobacco. I wanted to remember his face, and stared at it. I was to see it many times, but what I remember best are his eyes. They were bright and serene, the eyes of Socrates in the head of a professor of economics. What age was Socrates when they killed him? Tower this year was fifty. I had heard him spoken of as 'a saint,' but if he was a saint he was certainly no mild one. He could be very testy, very arbitrary. There was even a line of cruelty in his mouth. He was merciless with fakes and self-seekers.

'Mostly as I do,' I answered. 'That it is a pity England has thrown away her freedom.'

'Well, well,' said he, 'I think you take it too seriously. We never had more than the freedom to talk. And that most of us still have. Any number of my pupils call themselves socialists and communists, though in fact they will have to recant to get jobs. A few of them I can find posts abroad but the rest will have a poor time. They'll starve or dig. Some of them will give in, the others will be the yeast of a reformation.'

'When?'

'Not yet. I shan't see it happen. You must have noticed that we have only taken the first awkward steps towards dictatorship – call it what you like. The Absolute State. Autarchy. Fascism. I prefer to talk of the Disintegration. We are some way from the final stage. We still keep the old forms, but the Cabinet has become a Council of Action and governs by decree. Comparatively few persons were arrested for sedition last year, very few were shot and those were almost all communists. What we prefer is to starve out our tiresome persons. It is the blockade method, an old and tried method of ours. My most brilliant assistant, Lewis, was dismissed a year ago, he wouldn't get a job in England now as an usher. And we don't go to the trouble of abolishing the Trades Unions, we pull their teeth by forbidding them to take any part in politics, to levy political dues, or to maintain district or national units – they can mumble in their parishes as they like. When things become worse economically, if disappointed or starving persons try to revolt before time, the repression will harden. It is the weakness of repressors, that their tenure of their slope depends on their claws and teeth.'

'Surely it could have been avoided?' I cried, forgetting to keep up my calm in front of him.

'What are you?' He glanced at me shrewdly.

'Still a liberal,' I said.

'Well, well, you are partly responsible,' he said, spilling a pipeful of ash on his knee. 'If you had accepted the truth that there is no half-way house, but only brief rests between a caste society and one in which there are no classes except of individuals, of like mind – we should perhaps have saved ourselves this interregnum. The days when liberals could avoid looking at very unpleasant facts by dealing with others that were unpleasant but manageable are over. I think you should have noticed it.'

'An honest liberal,' I said, 'could not swallow your denial of liberty. You're killing the enterprise of private men. A man should have his own business to mind, as he had once. Not so long since.'

'Well you have had to swallow much worse,' he said cheerfully. 'And I doubt very much whether the bottom of the cup is even in sight.'

'If the liberal state of mind,' I said humbly, 'had prevailed against the fascist –' I would have added 'in your own party,' but I was afraid of rousing his anger. I felt it in his mind, a hot core of impatience and anger, hidden over by patience.

'That's what you think, is it? Well, do you know, I was mistaken myself. I had always supposed that the time for revolution would come when the rich could no longer be squeezed. And I imagined that that time was a great way farther off. I was wrong. Instead of continuing to surrender step by step, to their last ditch, the Chamberlayns stood last year. And beat us. In the first trial, that is. Don't think it's over yet, or predict an end. We used to talk a great deal about the irrational forces in society. Certainly they exist – the brute in us that was afraid of any further civilising of the world – say, the formation of a united Europe. The thoughts of civilised men were feeling slowly toward that – hence the need to deny thought. Chamberlayn is not an irrational brute, but a rational and very wide-awake man, with his private ends to serve. Violent men are his instruments. He was able to count on the brute, and on the spiritually immature, and on the despair of men without a future. Men whose livelihood was failing through causes they did not relate to Chamberlayn, whose sons had been trained for positions they were not asked to fill. It was partly your fault, but more ours, the fault of us socialists, that we did not give these people a hope and a faith, and that Hillier did. The worst of all is that the common men and women we failed are suffering and will suffer.'

This was my chance. I began to tell him about Winchell. He seemed to sink into himself and to become older and grimmer. He scattered a great many more matches, one of them alight. It burned a hole in his tablecloth before he smelt it and put it out absently with his thumb.

'If there were some safe way of getting Sophie Burtt out of the place,' I said. 'I think of the waste of a mind like hers.'

'She wouldn't thank us for making her a special case. I can't see my way yet. We must think of something, some way that won't bring her into danger. I don't know what danger – yet how can they let her out to talk abroad about what she's been through? It wasn't very clever to shut her up there. In fact it was very stupid, as stupid as the Germans or the Italians. It was not in the least like our much subtler and cleverer methods. You would probably find, if you could find out anything at all, that her arrest was due to the mistake of an important but ignorant official – ignorant of her reputation as a writer, I mean – a mistake that every other official is now bound to keep covered up as long as possible, forever if possible. I suppose you are too young to have heard anything about a Miss Douglas-Pennant, a lady who had the misfortune during the last war to be strangely treated by certain prominent officials. Her only blunder was that she was honest and upright, and had the innocence to believe that official justice existed, but it was enough to ruin her.'[31]

'But how on earth or in hell is a man like Steadman able to keep in his place?' I cried. 'There must be decent authorities who know what goes on at Winchell.'

'It is the chain of responsibility, my dear fellow. Steadman's conduct, if it were published, reflects on his superior and so *ad infinitum*, the big fleas protecting the lesser ones. You may find, if things quieten down for a time, that someone exaltedly important will discover Steadman and quietly get rid of him. He might even fall a victim to the new illness, and be shot resisting arrest.'

'I should like to have the shooting of him.'

'I think, yes, I should hang him,' Tower said mildly. 'Shooting is rather a decent death, you know. I shouldn't mind being shot.'

There was a wood fire in the grate. It had been growing lower, and was now nearly out. Tower got up to lay fresh wood on it, but forgot what he was doing. He put the wood down on the hearth and wandered toward the table. There was a clock lying face down among the books.

'It won't go any other way,' he said, turning it over to look at it. 'I'm afraid I have a lecture. Don't lose your mind over this business. The Steadmans are fewer among us than you think now. Do you know the history of the naval mutinies in the eighteenth century? There were worse than Steadman among the officers, and they were Englishmen, but not the English. Repression is the opportunity of bullies and ill men. It is not set going by them.'

I stood up to go. I had forgotten my mission until it was too late. I said hastily: 'You spoke of socialists among your pupils. Do you mean by it that there would be support for a revolt?'

He gave me a queer sharp glance, and I felt small and empty.

'There will be no socialist revolt for a time yet,' he said quietly. 'A change of dictators is always possible, of course. If the army and the Air Force were inclined to back another candidate for empire. A praetorian revolt. It's theoretically interesting, but not important.' He sighed. 'Not in the least important.'

His coat had ridden up round him but he did not notice it. Holding out his hand, he spoke to me in the tones of a kindly sergeant-major addressing a recruit.

'We must talk again later. Come to see me. One thing that interests me is the effect of violence and violent events on decent people. I believe that many of them were only thankful to read of communists being shot and sent to jail. Now of course there is no news in this sense, only rumours and the foreign newspapers. And what decent person would believe a foreign newspaper? The end of it, I think, is that most people don't believe the rumour of unpleasant things going on behind locked doors, and don't want to. If you try to tell them, you will only come up against the national dislike of unpleasant truths. Repression is evil not only for its floggings and torturings, but because it makes people lie to themselves in the privacy of their hearts. It makes lies the common food and poisons the wells. That is what I feel. It is what I hate. The world is closing in on those of us who have sought truth, shutting us off from other human beings. And this is the worst thing of all. The awful isolation.'

CHAPTER VII

Winchell Camp, Holman, and Sophie Burtt, haunted my dreams. To forget the nightmare when I was awake, I sought persistently for ways to help them. For this reason, I was more than anxious to see George Body, late an official of the Labour Party. Now Minister of Labour in the National Council. Calling at his office I was told that he was on holiday in Scotland. I resigned myself to see Eugene Denham first.

I knew the reputation of this man. He was the son of a Treasury official, educated to the same sort of career, who had joined the Labour Party, and by hard work, devotion, and the fortunate friendship of the leaders of two of the largest Trades Unions, had reached the Executive at a fairly early age. He had sharked for[32] himself in two Labour Governments, the one which fell ignominiously in 1931, and the last, which did not so much fall as scatter like chaff in a gale. It was not all chaff, however. An ear or two fell into good ground and bore fruit of a sort. The translation of Eugene Denham from the Labour Party to being Minister of Social Service in the National State surprised only his friends, and not all of these. He was not the man to go into exile at forty-eight.

I had no liking for the defunct Labour Party, which had always seemed to me to be engaged in selling the liberal pass. But I feel a slight qualm when I see a turncoat. Denham repelled me in other ways, too. He was physically displeasing, with a large smooth face, light eyes without eyebrows, and a wide and too well-turned mouth. He had a habit of turning his eyes up to the ceiling when he was on view, which gave him the air of a Chinese executioner. Not that I have seen one of these gentlemen. But I am prepared to accept Eugene Denham as their fleshly counterpart.

He received me very affably, told me that he had half an hour to spare, and asked what he could do for me. I had come to him as the brother-in-law of General Sacker, and a lecturer in Oslo University, visiting my country on behalf of Norwegian academic circles. He was always very anxious to be respected by scholars. He had pretensions that way.

He had an extreme elegance of manner. As he faced me, pressing together the tips of his long fingers, I was very conscious of my crippled right arm. I try to sit with my left side toward strangers, but he had placed me so that my right hand, which is half the size of a normal hand, was in full view.

'You have been seeing a number of people here?' he began.

'I had the good fortune yesterday to see Professor Tower.'

That mobile mouth stretched into a venomous smile. If ever I saw hate I saw it wearing the finest grey broadcloth, hand-made shoes, and a linen shirt.

'You admire him?'

'I think he is one of the greatest living men, the greatest mind.'

'He is eloquent,' Denham agreed. 'But, I think dangerous. I am anxious to see that every opinion has its chance of expression in the proper places, but I admit to being a little doubtful whether a University seminar is the proper place for Tower's views and doctrines.'

'He has a great reputation abroad,' I said.

'I am aware of it. And now, Mr. Hillier – by the way, are you related to the Prime Minister?'

'We are second cousins.'

'Indeed! Then you are a sympathetic observer, not a critic!'

'I am an observer,' I said. 'My sympathies are neither here nor there. I am only anxious to hear the truth. You, who have written on both sides of the slate, as it were, can tell me more than anyone.'

His face became a mask, with the eyes out of sight. I had prepared an air of innocence. He did not put me to the trouble of using it. Instead he said quietly:

'Yes. We can congratulate ourselves in this country on our national common sense and our good humour. We Englishmen are realists. Every country in the world has faced, or will face, the crisis which we faced last year, of falling exports, unemployment, loss of credit, in a degree which practically forced a revolution on us. It was necessary before anything to restore credit and to keep the peace. Anything in the nature of a civil breakdown, strikes, disorders, would have sent our credit to the bottom of the sea and ruined us. With the most terrible results. I daresay that in Norway you scarcely realised the acuteness of our crisis. I think we kept up appearances. And what happens? In any other country, violent repression would have been needed. Here all parties are of one mind. The rising party, and the rising man – Hillier, your cousin – seek the help of their political enemies, to the effect that all classes, from high to low, collaborate in saving the state.' He parted his fingers and joined them again, delicately. 'I think I can say with humility that without George Body, and myself, the National State could never have brought the workers calmly and loyally into line – as it happened. Our reward is that socialist planning will now go forward on a national basis, and socialist measures will be midwived, as so often in the past, by a Conservative Government.'

'A great achievement,' I said.

He looked at me now. Impossible to tell, from his face, whether he were going to turn me out or encourage me. The strange thing was, although I accepted the truth of all he said, I detested him for it. I suppose the truth about myself is that I should like to have been born in some other age, say the eighteenth century, when it was still possible to believe in progress. And a man could mind his own business, with generosity. Now that progress has brought us to confusion, with Thomas Chamberlayn on the one hand and Winchell on the other, and I see no way out, but only barbarism in front of us, I am a lost soul. If I am to be dictated to, I prefer my own class to the communists. But why, why, was it necessary? And why did the aspirations and the pennies of decent men and women have to be spent on raising Eugene Denham to office, in order that he could rob them of both?

'The credit belongs to the nation,' he said pleasantly. 'Except for the negligible few communists, there has been none of the harshness that would have been needed in another country, in Germany, or America.'

'What was the intention of your Training Camps?' Trust me, I said to Holman, I'll do something for you, trust me.

'To train men and women in citizenship,' he said mildly. 'We recognise that circumstances have been against some actually decent men.'

'Do you inspect them? There have been reports – in Norwegian papers – not pleasant reading.'

He stood up suddenly. 'If I had reports of that sort, from a respectable source, I should look into it instantly,' he said. He thrust his mouth out.

I should have spoken, I think. But then we were interrupted. The door opened, and an old man came in with some papers. He looked at me as he laid them on the desk. He seemed very tired or ill, and sagging feebly at the knees.

'My secretary, Sir John Megan,' said Denham. 'Mr. Andrew Hillier.'

Sir John bowed, and smiled, with overdone dignity. I wondered where I had seen his face of a Nonconformist Don Quixote before. I remembered as he was going away. It was at the head of a deputation of the English Labour Party to Norway in 1935. He was made much of by our, I mean, the Norwegian Government, and he impressed us all with his charm and tact. That was some years ago, but not, after all, long enough for him to have become a senile old man. I was at a loss.

'He is really useless to me,' murmured Denham. 'I have another man, two men, to do the work, but it makes the old fellow happy to feel he is still in harness.' He looked at his wrist watch.

'You have been very patient,' I said. 'I have only one further question.'

I made six of it before I came to my point, which was to find out, if I could, whether he was aware of the close relations between Hillier and Thomas Chamberlayn and whether he were easy about them. I remembered that in the old days, before his translation, the banker had been an object of his bitterest attacks. He had written a book largely to prove that any progressive Government would have to draw the claws of Chamberlayn and his friends in order to live, let alone act. This book was written in a sarcastic sharp way, with a liberal use of epithet to describe the banker and his habits. Parts of it must have gone home to the victim. I wondered how the two met now that they were bedfellows. Did they embrace with joy or lie apart?

Denham was cautious, he had the most adroit and slipperiest of minds, but he grasped that I was not inquisitive. He began to hint that he thought Chamberlayn distorted the Party.

'The aims of an international banker are not in all senses ours,' he said. 'We can make use of him. But national economy and international finance are oil and vinegar.'

'Powder and a match,' I suggested. He smiled politely.

I broke off to question him about the Trades Unions. About the wisdom of strengthening them, to increase his own strength in the Council. If he had an organised working class behind him again, I hinted, in place of one deliberately disorganised?

I was in no doubt that he understood me very well. I spoke of the 'liberal element in the country.' Of the 'emergence of youth' – in the uniform of a National Volunteer. I smelled Winchell here suddenly, in this room faintly scented with leather and carnations. I lost my head for a moment, and spoke too frankly.

We parted very smooth friends. I asked him to dinner with me in Richard's house. He thought it pleasant, very pleasant, and he looked forward to it, all in an exceedingly amiable voice.

On the way out I met Sir John Megan again. He was standing in the hall and I had the absurd idea that he had been waiting about for me. In fact all he said was to draw to my attention to the Cuyp on the wall, and to tell me that it was he who had bought it at Christies.[33] He seemed very anxious that I should admire it.

CHAPTER VIII

Ernest's Steffy was a student at London University. Her father, the Master of Balliol, must be criminally careless, I thought. But when, invited by her and Ernest, I went to see her in her room I learned that he was only displeased. He wished her to come home and to look after him, he was a widower, and a year ago he had cut off her allowance. But Steffy had a little money of her own, almost a hundred and twenty a year, left to her by her mother. On this she lived in a room in Endsleigh Street and paid her fees and studied, I believe, anthropology. I can't imagine why. What did she want to know about it?

She had one large room, with a bed that became a couch by day. There was a gas ring in one corner, and she kept her clothes in a box under the bed. She was wearing her navy shorts, she explained, because it was the evening. Ernest was in uniform. He had been ordered to London by Richard, who kept him running errands of a vaguely confidential sort all day and not seldom at night. There was nothing unusual, to start questions, in the sight of a Volunteer carrying messages from one company to another between their officers. I thought it a little unfair to involve him in the business, but Lotte, when I spoke to her about it, seemed unconcerned. In the meantime he was overjoyed to be in town and able to run to Steffy's room whenever he had an hour, or a night, I daresay, free.

Steffy was boiling water in a pan on the gas ring. She had a huge jug beside her, large enough for a school treat. On the table were a tin of biscuits and a bowlful of apples. The couch was covered with an extraordinary array of garments, underclothes, trousers, jackets, all laid out as if it were a second-hand clothes stall. The two of them watched me solemnly while I gaped at these things, nudging each other like school-children. Suddenly Steffy burst out laughing. She had the softest laugh in the world, like a very small cloud.

'Do you need anything?' she asked. 'A jacket? Is your shirt worn out? Have you one to put on while it is being washed? I can manage your size, I think.'

'It is what Steffy calls being a socialist,' Ernest said gravely. He smiled at her. 'If you want to do anything for her or me,' he said to me, 'you can take her out to lunch or dinner when I am away. She spends her money on other people and lives on air.'

'I live very well, thank you,' said Steffy.

'Now I must go,' Ernest said. 'My uniform would spoil the evening for Steffy's other friends.'

'You needn't wear it, dog.'

'I'm on duty.'

He smiled at me from his young height and blitheness, and went away. Steffy went with him to the landing outside her room. Leaning forward a little, I saw them lay their arms on each other's shoulders and silently kiss. Ernest took her hands, kissing each palm, and closed her fingers over them. He went off, running quickly down the stairs, and she came back smiling to herself. She became serious when she remembered I was there, and told me about the clothes.

I had had no notion how serious things were for the young at the universities. So many parents of boys and girls who had expected to complete their education by taking a degree, or studying for one of the professions, were ruined or nearly so. The depression that began in 1937 was worse than any other if only because it started from a lower level. Old respectable firms went bankrupt, others halved their staffs and salaries, towns and cities cut down their municipal services, dividends vanished, doctors, architects, even lawyers, carrion crows who can usually pick up a living when finer birds are dying of hunger, found themselves without money. Oh, the middle classes were caught in an ill wind this time. Their sons and daughters leaving school had nowhere to turn to find shelter. In Norway, reading in an English newspaper that the numbers of students at the universities were higher than ever, I had taken it for a sign of stability. Nothing of the sort. Their parents scraped up the fees, often with incredible pains, and the children went short of clothes, short of food. It was better than hanging about idle. And the parents at least had not given up their sad belief that somehow, somewhere, a degree must bring its owner in a living. Those who were not able to live at home were the worst off.

Steffy was now a rich young woman in comparison. Her room had become a kind of meeting place for her poorer friends. The clothes on the bed had been begged from her relatives and her father's friends in Oxford. She went home every few months on what she called a raiding party.

The first person to come in was not a student. He was a thin Jew, I guessed about thirty, his name Myers, remarkably haggard, pale, and affected. He was a poet, said Steffy. At once, like a poet in a farce, he pulled a paper from his pocket and read me out his newest poem. It was very bad, and he talked utter nonsense. Yet I did not dislike him. He had a curious tart spirit. He assured Steffy he did not need any clothes, and I am certain he had nothing at all under the scarf and jacket he wore.

Before long there were not less than fourteen young men and girls in the room, none older than Steffy. They were all shabby, all, unless I am much mistaken, underfed. The large jug had in it cubes of meat extract. Steffy poured on the boiling water and the young men handed it round in cups, glasses, even vases. I never ate at a gayer feast. Everyone laughed. A boy sitting on the floor strummed very lightly on a stringed instrument of some kind, heaven knows what, but he was happy, his round young head thrown back and a dreaming smile on his face. The clothes were shared out with complete frankness. A girl, half crying, half laughing, ran about holding against herself a cherry-coloured silk sweater. 'Am I pretty? does it suit me?'

I had the most curious feeling that I was not here in the flesh, I was a ghost living for a moment in the future. I saw faces, heard young excited voices, but their owners were living in another moment as children, and I, only I, knew what they were living toward.

Four, I found, were R. B. Tower's students. I asked one of them how Tower spoke to them.

'Oh, he's splendid. He makes the whole thing as clear as day, so that you know what's wrong and how it could be put right. When you're listening to him you can even believe it will come right one day, and that you listening are going to make it come.'

'If Tower would do it, he could lead the movement,' a boy said, seriously. 'All of us would follow him.'

'What movement?'

'Why, to the new age. There must be a new age, you know. We can't go on starving and hoping for ever.'

'Then we shall have to find the way to it ourselves,' another said, slow and laconic.

'Why won't Tower lead?'

'He doesn't want disciples.'

'He has too sharp a sense of humour.'

'He's too subtle.'

'Too honest, you mean.'

'Too saintly or too lazy.'

'No, he's a teacher and what we need are strategists and workers.'

I found Myers at my elbow. 'Are there many socialists at the universities?' I said to him. Why should I imagine he knew, except that he was nearer my own age and I felt, with what justice, that he was less of a poser than he seemed?

'No, very few. But I think there are still five millions of them in the country. But they've had the heart knocked out of them. Starved out during the years

between 1931, when the last Labour Government collapsed, and last year when
it went in again and immediately fell with a crash into Ly-cester Square – ' he
broke into song –

> *While the rich man drives by in his kerridge an' pair.*
> *What does he care?*
> *What does he care?'*

'But what's become of them?' I persisted.

'Some are in the Training Camps,' he said lightly. 'Some of them are crazy
with nerves, some have given up. Some are carrying on with their teaching and
speaking, waiting to be arrested one evening, as they sit at home.' He was not,
I felt, taking me seriously.

'Denham, the slimy beast, came to the school to speak to us last Monday,'
said a tall, pale girl. 'He told us to have faith in the future and to think of those
who would come after us.'

A silence came over the room, and a young man broke it to say: 'But who
will come after us? *We* shall never be able to marry.'

> *'Goldilocks, Goldilocks, will you be mine?'* sang Myers.
> *'My dole's been adjusted*
> *From twelve bob to nine.'*

There was a rush of laughter, as if they were all glad to have escaped. A fair
boy jumped on to a chair. He was the thinnest creature I ever saw out of an
hospital. He had lines under his blue eyes, and his mouth was pinched as if in
sarcasm or pain. He began, at first shyly, then with excitement, to make a speech
to his friends.

'Myers laughs at everything,' he said, 'and he's wrong, it's wrong to laugh. We
ought to be thinking of the men in the Camps, and of the others. What about
that peasant in 1516 who led the rebellion of the starving peasants and they
captured him and put a crown of nails on him and burned him slowly alive? And
what about the Austrians fighting in Vienna in 1934? And Rosa when they
murdered her and Liebnecht in a Berlin garden.[34] We should not laugh. We have
to choose. Those who sneer and those who want to seem better than they are
– and to talk as though they had been at Oxford – well, we're not like that. We're
at the end of everything. Yes, we're at the end – with works closing down, and
no jobs for us, and the only factories that are always busy are making shells and
poison gas for our deaths. And our mothers tired out, worn, harassed to death,

our mothers. And the streets full of other lads drawing their dole, and no life for them, no life for us. Why are they destroying looms and spindles in the North, and breaking up ships? Tell me that. Don't we need jackets, and wouldn't we like a drink of coffee sometimes?'

'I can answer that,' drawled a lad. He was eating an apple. He bit into it, held it in his cheek, laughed, and said: 'It's because we're so clever we make a million yards or so of cloth with one spindle. And only a boy minding it.'

His friend had listened with impatience. He did not like having his eloquence spoiled by an interruption. 'Please listen,' he said. 'But do we make them? Look at Phil there! He wears that sweater of his every day because his jacket has gone at all the seams. He's grown out of it anyway, the fat boy. There's no profit in making cloth from one spindle, so our Phil goes without his coat. But if *they* can't use the spindles, we naked ones could.'

He hesitated, blushed, and jumped quickly from the chair. 'I'm not running you down,' he said anxiously to Myers.

'When you're over thirty, like me, you'll be glad to laugh,' Myers said, in his slow, self-conscious voice.

'Where I live when I go home,' a boy said softly, 'we have a green hill behind the farm, and in front only fields and a stream. At the other side of the stream an old house is still standing, with a lawn and terraces, and a man and his wife living in one wing of the house. One side of his face is scarred, I suppose he has been a soldier. He spends all his time cutting and rolling the grass. She peels potatoes into a china bowl for their dinner. It is the most peaceful place in the world. I should like to live there until I die.'

'Don't worry about lawns and old houses.'

'We'll go back to them some day.'

'Why not?'

'Why?'

'My mother is angry with me, and disappointed. She hoped I'd go into the church. You can be sure there of an income, and her own family would like to have a parson for a nephew. She has done everything to help me.'

'If only they left us alone!'

'My father is a little like that. He has kept his end up all these years, and held on to the house and the land, while we have grown poorer and poorer. He goes up to stand at the Cenotaph once a year on the day,[35] and at supper in the evening he tells us that there are worse things than a good, clean war. I'm sorry for him, and yet I can't stand him. At his age, he joined the Volunteers. He thought it absolutely right to bomb the Welsh miners who went on strike – they were *enemies*.'

'Poor people *are* enemies when they try to change their lives by violence.'

'They should be patient and wait another century.'

'The birth rate is going down.'

'It doesn't fall half fast enough!'

The girl holding her cherry-coloured silk garment whispered to Steffy, I overheard her:

'Do you know, a friend of my father's wants to marry me! He's fifty-one, and he believes everything he reads in the newspaper. *We shall have to have a war,* he says, *to bring people to their senses. Ah, if only I were young enough to fight!* What must I do? I do want to have children, Steffy. Sometimes I think about them.'

'But to bring them up like that?' Steffy whispered. She was leaning against the wall, because her guests occupied all the floor as well as all the chairs. One thin brown leg was crossed over the other, and her hands were folded. A young man seated on the floor at her feet took her ankle between his finger and thumb.

'They are all crazy here, and you are as crazy as the rest,' he said, smiling at her. 'Of course I don't believe in Hillier's promises. I know they're what Tower calls delusive! But I'm not going to say so and go to jail. I shall keep strictly to science.'

'And they'll have you in a war in a year,' Myers retorted. 'And you and your science will go to heaven together.'

A boy with a soft, very young voice, spoke. 'Friends, eaters of Steffy's apples, and wearers of the cast-off duds of Steffy's cousins,' he cried softly. 'We are not going to be killed in any war. Are we? We'll dig our way underground like moles and work there.'[36] He laughed at his own joke. 'And we'll hang old Denham on a sour apple tree!'

'You will all be killed,' Myers laughed.

'No, not I.'

'Nor I. The greedy old men with their bank balances are making their last throw. They've lost, lost, lost. Bank balances are not immortal, and we are. We may be poor, and Phil has no jacket to his backside, and he coughs when it's cold, but we are the future and the future is us.'

'We are the future and the future is us.'

Who said that? I wondered. I looked across the room. But there were so many of them, four more had crowded in lately. They were talking all at once, and laughing at once, no one could be sure who said what and who laughed.

Steffy was tired. She had been standing there for hours. Myers noticed it as soon as I did, and he began to push the others out of the door. He and I stayed to help her to wash the cups and bowls. Then he asked me if I were walking his way. I agreed. We had just left the house when I saw Ernest hurrying towards it as fast as his long legs would stretch. He looked tired and rather anxious. I thought with pleasure that they would lie asleep, side by side, wake together, and eat breakfast cooked on the gas ring. Less like lovers than like children married in a game.

CHAPTER IX

'So the darkness closes down on them,' said Myers.

I was vexed by his drawling voice now that I had it to myself. I wished I were walking alone through a part of London I know better than most. How often, when I was younger than Steffy, I had prowled these sad streets about the University and wished I had company.

'Poor young devils!' he added.

'What do you do?' I said, meaning to bring him to earth. 'You are a Jew. Is it true that your race is worse treated here now?'

'No laws have been made against us. And hungry East-enders smashing up little shops in Whitechapel[37] are usually sternly reproved by the magistrates, who realise very well that property ought to be respected by the propertyless, even if it is a Jew's. But see what happens to me. I am − I was − a minor civil servant. I was not dismissed last year because I am a Jew, but for the sake of economy. The same grounds served for all the Jews in my department and in others. Some of us have been absorbed in the Jewish business houses, but it is not always convenient to have no Christians on your staff. And I, alas, have no head for business. Many Jews, you may be surprised to know, have not.'

Why don't you speak naturally? thought I, irritated by him. 'Then what do you do?'

'Live on my wife,' he answered airily.

We were passing a street lamp. I glanced at him, and saw so much anger and misery on his face that I was glad to look away again. It made me uncomfortable to feel it beside me, and I found an excuse to leave him at the end of Gower Street. Before he said good-bye, he had asked me to come and see him one evening and I had promised, out of curiosity and pity. I thought him indiscreet as well as affected. Yet I liked him.

The next evening was the first of the Covent Garden Season. Lotte had taken a box, as she was forced to do. And she would be forced to appear in it on the opening night. It was unfortunate that the season opened, not with Purcell, but with the opera which Hillier was known to prefer over all others, *Maritana*.[38] My sister plays, or used to play, the viola better than an amateur. She loves and understands music. It was, to say the mildest, a disappointment to her.

Richard and I dined alone, while she rested and dressed. He was silent. He asked me suddenly what I saw at Winchell.

I was unable to avoid a start of fear. Richard's voice, when it is not friendly, finds me at home in the pit of the stomach. My body expects involuntarily a blow. I had not known that he knew of my visit.

'From what I saw, not from anything I heard,' I said hurriedly, 'I was not impressed. I don't care for men of the type of Steadman.'

'He's stiff, eh? Well, you can't deal with communists and rattlesnakes with a lace handkerchief. A flogging is all they understand. I don't follow why the hell you care about the treatment of communists. If they got loose they would destroy everything you say you care about. They're the murderers of society, yet you'd keep them alive. Upon my soul, you liberals are the murderees of our day – you were born to be kicked.'

'I don't like brutality,' I said. 'I don't like a society founded on it.'

He pushed his coffee cup and glass out of the way and sprawled forward on his arms on the table. 'Sometimes I think you're worth talking to,' he said. 'At other times you make me yawn. Listen. In February last year we had a bloodless revolution in this country – apart from the drops of blood shed by your Red friends. We partly cleaned up the Constitution – instead of Parliament gabbling and evading, the State rules and is going to rule. We're freeing industry; we're cleaning out nests of bolsheviks. When the *second* revolution is under way, you'll see that the Chamberlayns toe the line along with the rest. Or else we'll hand them over to Steadman.' His bad humour went off with a laugh. I could never resist him when he laughed, it was mischief let loose. He had drunk too much already, enough to make it wise for us to-night to avoid Colonel Hebden.

He began describing the England he would create when he and his friends were in charge. It made me wince. It was like nothing more than a fearful sort of public school, with willing fags, a glorious hierarchy of heroes in the persons of himself and his Volunteers, and floggings for the unwilling or rebellious. For the rest, all stout and jolly together, and daring the other nations to come on and be licked.

Even now, when he was spreading out this frightful and detestable vision, I felt the attraction of his vitality. In spite of my will and against my nature, I felt it. Some fraction of my mind or my nerves responded to it. I wondered whether his violence, joined though it was to the rankest sentimentality, was not better in the end than the hardening and rigidifying that was going on in England now. His utter indifference to the processes of culture, his disdain of intellect, were rooted as much in energy as in ignorance. I compared him in my mind with the barbarian coming down on a Roman villa, sacking, defacing, stabling horses in the library, lighting a fire over the mosaics. Yet the Roman culture was not in its owner's dead brain. It soaked into the ground and was resurrected through other minds.

I believed him when he said, with tipsy energy, that he was Hillier's man. He was Hillier's when he was sober. When he was in drink, as now, he imagined himself and his Volunteers rescuing 'the chief' from the ogre's den. Chamberlayn, of course, was the ogre. It was a ridiculous picture. I sat on the floor of my mind and giggled at it. But it was I who was the fool. Richard had his own reasons for running into danger, he had to save his position and his Volunteers, but he was not a coward. And his love for Frank Hillier was a constant in his unbalanced life. Nothing in my life is constant except my avoidance of it.

To-night I saw that his loyalty to his friend was rooted in the same level of his life as his vision of England. It was part and bone with it. All his violent desires were fixed on the stages of his life he should have passed when he was a schoolboy. He was that tragic and detestable figure, a man with adult desires, energies, courage, wits, wrapped about the images of his youth.

I suppose that in my cold way I loved him as well as Lotte did, but not kindly. I came to know him too well to keep even a rag of respect for him. Except that the words are too good for such as he I could have said over him: *'Raging waves of the sea, foaming out their own shame; wandering stars to whom is reserved the blackness of darkness for ever.'*

Lotte came downstairs late and we drove to Covent Garden. Thank God, Richard did not drive. I had no wish to be killed hurrying to a performance of *Maritana*.

We were scarcely in time, and I had only a glimpse of the audience before the first act. I had noticed that the Royal box was occupied, but not by royalty, and that the box facing it, decorated with laurel, was empty. Then the lights went out, and the performance began.

Lotte had arranged her face into lines of civil attention. I sat well back in the box. As for Richard, he closed his eyes at once, and slept. It was not a criticism of the music, he had never been able to tell one note of an opera from another, and to him any instrumental music was a noise. He liked songs and choruses and the marching song of the Volunteers, a bastard version of a tune which was in fact not bad enough to deserve its fate.

I was a little excited. It was not to me torture to sit through an elaborate performance of a childishly poor opera. I could even listen, and watch the absurd plot unfold itself. Harriet English sang superbly that evening, whatever the quality of the music. Perhaps it really mattered very little to her what sounds she was called on to produce from her long throat. She looked beautiful, too. To avert any taint of foreignness the Spanish setting had been abandoned, scenes and dresses were late Victorian, copied from Du Maurier drawings:[39] Don Caesar wore a frock coat and a rake's superb top hat. In the palace scene there were no less than six magnificent cases of wax flowers on the stage, and a tablecloth with fringed tassels.

Hillier had seated himself in the back of his box with the laurels ten minutes late. Next day the newspapers suggested that this was his tactful way of avoiding a demonstration. If it were his object, he could have chosen a better means. At the end of the act, when he moved to the front of his box, the audience rose to him. He bowed slightly, smiled and modestly waved his hand towards the stage and the great conductor, in an effort to draw their eyes from himself. The great conductor knew his duty, and the strumped-up version of *Land of Hope and Glory* poured through the theatre. Richard started awake with a loud snort of surprise at finding himself at the opera. The stalls rose. After the least pause, so did Lotte, and I followed her. I kept my eyes on Hillier's pale, smiling face. With every other Volunteer in the house, Richard had risen, and they stood at the salute, elbow away from the body, the palm of the hand open and straight. No foreign salutes for Englishmen.

The strange thing was that the stalls obviously liked the song. They even forgot for whom it was being sung, and with glazed eyes gave themselves up unashamedly to an emotion, the hopeful nostalgia it roused in them. To me, born too late to remember what security feels like, it was an ironic thought that this music, the voice itself of imperial magnificence, should have been composed at the moment when all that solid splendour, the fruit of greeds and disciplines of heroic size, all that treasure of blood and wealth, was being scattered. 'Land of *t-um* ti *tum* ti' – old Park Lane, the wall of Devonshire House,[40] the unhurried days, dividends coming in, safe investments, safe seats in the House, safe, safe, safe, or at least they had felt that they were safe.

Lotte nudged me with her sharp elbow. 'Frank is fairly in heaven,' she whispered.

We sat down. Richard muttered half to me, half to himself:

'It was I put him there. He'll never forget that. He has more brains than I have – he is a genius, you know. And he knows fast enough that it was the Volunteers who lifted him into his place. He needs us, you know. You'll see *he* knows it. Wait and see what you'll see.'

I began to look round me with curiosity. The gallery and the amphitheatre were practically empty, there were scarcely more than a dozen of those solemn or smiling young men, old men frowning at innovations, young men with their girls in voile frocks and beads, who fill the cheaper seats to overflowing. Below me in the stalls I saw the only musical critic I knew. He was staring in front of him with an air of boredom so intense that he seemed to be bald from the back of the neck to the chin.

Hillier was receiving visitors in his box. Thomas Chamberlayn first. I renewed my memory of him as an astute, kindly, but dull elderly gentleman. He stooped his grey head so nicely to Hillier's fair one, and seemed so grateful for the Prime Minister's smile. Then Colonel Frederick Hebden, enormous in the uniform of the Special Guard, carrying his stomach as though it were a basket between clasped arms. He was all smiles. It was no use, I loathed the man. I have never been able to stand that combination of cruelty and amiability. I saw him speak to someone unseen at the back of the box, then present Steadman to Hillier. Seeing Hillier seated between these two, I wondered what he had in him that made him master over them. Surely more than cunning and oratory? He could not move a Council with the tricks he used in the Albert Hall.

In the second interval we left our box. Richard went to see Hillier, and Lotte and I walked about. I saw my musical critic leaning against a pillar.

'What are you going to say about this?' I asked him.

'I think I shall write about A Day in the Country,' he said thoughtfully. 'I'm too old for politics.'

Strangely enough, perhaps not strangely, his was the only doubtful voice I heard. It is true that few of these people had come to hear the opera. They had come, in all the glory of their diamonds and pearls and cloth-of-silver and lamé, to a social duty. Lotte stopped to speak to a brace of elderly dowagers. One of them had tears in her eyes. She dabbed them away before they had done any mischief.

'How it takes me back,' she said, simply and gaily. 'I thought I saw my dear Father again, dressing to go to the Queen's Jubilee. He was such a handsome man, and his sword was heavy, he let me hold it in my little hands. I can feel it now, and his moustache tickling my face when he lifted me up to kiss me.'

'Such pretty wholesome tunes,' her friend sighed.

Behind me a group of very young men and two somewhat older young women were in ecstasies. 'My dear! Enchanting is the right word, and the right period. Too dear and lovely altogether. And did you notice the table cloth?'

'How can one find out where they bought it? I *must* have one.'

'But, darling, the music. I almost cried with happiness.'

'Darling, so did I. Why haven't we heard it before?'

'The usual mustiness of critics, darling. They only like what they know. Wagner and all that.'

'Please let's go back,' Lotte whispered.

We went back. I watched the stalls and the boxes filling up, and meditated on time's revenge. But my heart was less light than it had been. The evening had ceased to be amusing. After all, I thought, there is something disturbing, even painful, in the sight of all this pomp and circumstance enshrining a triviality, a pinch of bitter dust. As it turned out at the end, there was at least one other person in the house who felt as Lotte did. When Harriet came before the curtain alone, to take the last applause of the stalls, a voice from the all but empty gallery called down:

'Oh, Harry, Harry, that you should come to this.'

Come now, that's better, I thought. I pinched Lotte's arm, but she had only a thin sour smile to spare. Richard had just told her that he and I were invited to supper with Harriet. It was the first I had heard of it. I said I had no wish to go. Lotte whispered: ' Go, go. I'd like you to go, Andy.' She was so jealous of Harriet even now, that she would feel happier if I were with her husband. I saw her into the car. I wish now that I might never forget her thin arms in their long gloves, her round little body, and her face, too young for her experiences, too gay for tragedy.

Hillier himself was going to Harriet's supper party. He had offered to take us there in his car. Richard was in a boisterous mood, he swayed from side to side, hummed the opening line of one of Harriet's songs – it was all he remembered of the opera and he thought it a very pretty catchy tune – and tapped his friend's knee.

'You looked the part to-night, Frank,' he said, swaying and smiling.

'Well, that was a good thing!' Hillier laughed.

'And now we're going to drink Chamberlayn's best burgundy, supplied for the party. What a pity you don't drink! Why have you and I always got on, we're as alike as blood and water?'

'For that reason,' Hillier said gently.

Harriet arrived scarcely in front of us, in Chamberlayn's car. She sprang out, still in her dress of the last act, and ran across the wide entrance hall to the lift. We followed her. Her apartment had been decorated by the hotel with flowers, orchids, her chosen flower, in the most extravagant way. She was shaking with excitement and the strain. Ignoring even Hillier, she took the arms of two guests who were already in the sitting-room, and swept them with her to the piano in the next room.

'Play, play,' she said to one of them, pushing him into the chair. 'I sang badly at the start, I know I did. This line was wrong. Listen.'

She sang a phrase, then others, while the man at the piano followed her as best he could.

'It should have gone like this. Oh, how bad I was!'

'You were perfect as always,' Chamberlayn soothed her. 'And now don't you think you had better eat something. She never eats before singing,' he told us, with a fatuous air of pride, as if he had created her. He was acting as host, greeting her guests when they came in, and giving orders to the servants who were waiting about to serve the supper laid in the dining-room. Since he had provided the wines, and, if rumour were true, he paid the greater part of all Harriet's expenses, it was no more than his right.

Harriet apologised to us in her quick way, looking from one to the other with a restless smile. She brought up those of her guests who did not know him to be presented to Hillier. The man at the piano was a middle-aged critic of music, Maurice Gardner. His wife, a slender woman, pale, very plainly dressed, had come with him. She was insignificant, and yet sure of herself. The second man was Charles Dalton, the novelist. I need not have been surprised to see him there. He moved in most circles of any social importance. Always a professor of tradition, in art and in life, he was the first well-known writer to attach himself to the National State Party. It was a sound instinct rather than any political acumen. From youth he had showed an exquisite skill in making his career. He never made an awkward friend, or lost a useful one. Of decent middle class birth, he enjoyed and knew how to praise just that mellow and polite England of which country houses and the Eton and Harrow match are comfortable symbols. Moreover he had a charming literary style, and a feeling for the half-mystical half-idealist sentiment which Englishmen treasure in their literature. It is the absence of it in French writers that chills us. But that is another story. I gazed at Charles Dalton, whose novels I have never been able to read beyond the opening chapter, and liked his looks than otherwise. He looked well-bred and delicate, almost sickly.

I turned round and saw Sir John Megan coming in. He looked about him, lost and somehow avid, until his eyes focused on Harriet. He came over to her and kissed her hand, and made her a little speech about her singing. He had clearly rehearsed it, to the gestures. She was kind to him.

A woman of forty, dressed below the waist and scarcely at all above, except for her jewels, came in and rushed to Harriet and embraced her, with what seemed uncontrollable enthusiasm. 'Like an angel,' she cried hoarsely. 'You sang like an angel, dearest. Looked like one.'

She had been followed into the sitting-room by Colonel Hebden. I began to suspect that he was actually in the habit, or felt the need of drugging himself. His very short light eyelashes scarcely veiled his eyes. I did not think they were the eyes of a man in his whole mind. Or else his mind was not such as I should care to have about me. He was smiling widely. He kissed Harriet, kissed the other woman, and would have kissed Mrs. Gardner if she had not backed gently out of reach. He had changed his uniform for the mess uniform of a colonel in the Air Force. I saw Hillier look at him with an indulgent eye.

At supper I sat between Thomas Chamberlayn and the enthusiastic woman. She was a Mrs. Amy Dale, a very rich woman and patroness of music. She had, I suspect, more taste for patronage than music, but she was one of Harriet's earliest and most devoted friends. She had the largest hands I have ever seen, and she used them and her eyes to caress every man she came near. For the moment, I was thankful, she talked to Sir John Megan on her other side.

The meal was elaborate, beginning with sole cooked in a sauce of Moselle and white grapes; *suprême de volaille*, with lobster and mushrooms in the cream, new peas, asparagus; a *Venus Tort*; and a savoury I had never eaten before. It was as stimulating as the wines we had been drinking, and had a flavour which pricked the back of the throat very delicately. Harriet had the Prime Minister on her right, of course, and Chamberlayn had to content himself with talking to me. He spoke in so low a voice that I had the greatest difficulty in following him and I had to lean almost over his plate.

'You must forgive me for not knowing who you were when we met the first time. I have such admiration for your sister. It is a great pleasure to me to meet her brother and to tell you that I have a profound admiration for her. For your sister. She is a good intelligent woman, very attractive, I suspect that is why she is not here to-night. My Harriet does not like rivals.'

What a simple old gentleman you are, I thought. I made up a remark signifying that his dearest need not fear rivals. He beamed at me and went softly on. His voice flowed under the noise and the laughter, his myopic kind eyes seeking mine now and then with a sly twinkle, as though we were old friends, with a secret understanding.

'You know I also admire your brother-in-law, General Sacker. I have so little recklessness myself I can admire it in others with a whole heart. I think I know what his nature is. I think the State should be able to use such men and to employ them so that their wonderful energy is not entirely destructive. Do you agree? I am so glad we agree. It is such a pleasure to me to meet you and to tell you again that I admire your sister. I fear I don't know her so well as I should like to know her. Perhaps you will tell her how profoundly and with deep respect I admire her. I have no doubt that Harriet admires her in her heart. One should not judge Harriet by ordinary standards. She has a remarkable mind. I find that I can discuss problems with her and she understands me when I say to her that this should be and that should not be. And I tell her that the State is this and it is not that. I give a great deal of thought to the State, my dear fellow. I think of it – somehow conceive it – as springing from my own head. Isn't there an old story to that effect?[41] And I think of it with love and pity, as though it were an infant and I ought to care for it. You know I have never had a son. If I had I think I should like him to be a soldier, not a banker, not a dull worldly man like myself. But all this is only in my head, and I often hold it and wonder how to end this tangle we are in, and which is the least wasteful way. I need armies and Air Forces, to help me and enforce my poor will and needs, and when I tell Harriet this she smiles. She smiles with wisdom and gentleness, and there is nothing I would not do for her. For your sister, too. You can count on me, my dear fellow, to do nothing, say nothing, that could conceivably wound that delicate nature. I want to say this to you – ' He broke off suddenly, turning from me. 'Yes, my dearest,' he said in the same even voice, answering Harriet's question. 'Only listen to me a moment, and I'll tell you everything.'

I was sure he was sober when he was making this fantastic speech. It had rambled on through two courses. He picked at his food and drank nothing. It was an extraordinary experience, to sit in that over-decorated, over-warm room, straining one's ears to catch words of which the sense was buried in complete nonsense. I was left with a slight feeling of uneasiness. I was less certain than I had been of his simplicity.

I had no time to reflect before Mrs. Dale hooked me. She and Sir John Megan were talking about artists. He was trying to tell her about the pictures he had bought, not for himself, for some great lady. He told us what the great lady had said to him, correcting and repeating himself, anxious that we should not miss a word of conversations which clearly were sacred to him. Amy Dale was bored with him and his gossip and his great ladies. She put her hand on my arm, squeezed it, and said in her deep voice:

'Do y'know what I think, I think anything might happen, civil war, the end of the world, only God knows what. But what's the good of harping on it? Do y' know, I was in New York the April night America declared war in nineteen seventeen. I think they were right to say let's make whoopee while we can. What's the use of crying over what can't be helped. We did, and others did, too. You never saw so many people ravin' tearin' mad, whether it was liquor or excitement, I was excited myself, I can tell you, though war was no joke to us then and God help you, I said, you don't know what you're in for. What was I saying?'

'You were saying, Eat, drink, and be merry, for tomorrow we shall have headaches,' Sir John encouraged her. He smiled. I looked away from him, not liking the sight.

I looked at Hillier. He had a bottle of Vichy water beside him. He was very sober. He leaned back a little in his chair, with an air of quiet assurance that he was a centre of attraction. He was charming to Harriet and not more than polite with Chamberlayn. Harriet now took us into the other room. She sent the servants away and asked her guests to pour their own drinks from the bottles and decanters on the sideboard. She seated herself on the couch, between Richard and Chamberlayn. They paid her extravagant compliments, trying with an air of good humour to outdo each other. Richard in this stage of drunkenness was flushed and attractive, and Harriet certainly did not dislike it when he began to stroke her arm and bare shoulder. I was caught by Sir John Megan. Now I began to realise what was wrong with him and why he had become a foolish old man within a few years of impressing us all in Norway.

He looked round the room and said softly:

'When I was a boy I used to wonder if I would ever see the inside of rooms like this one. And now I know them better than I knew my own mother's kitchen. And they mean nothing to me in comparison with the great work of reconstruction which is going on in the country and I am privileged to take part in it. And I mourn, yes, my dear fellow, I mourn over those of my old friends and colleagues who shirked their duty and in the day of trial and testing were found to come short of greatness, and put their personal vanity before their country. It's hard for me to condemn them. Hard. And life is hard, very hard, and which of us ends it as we hoped? We can only do our hard duty.'

The spectacle of a man who, having first lost his honesty, has lost his soul with it, is an unpleasant one. I escaped from him as quickly as I could, and looked round me for Charles Dalton. An idea had come to me during supper. He was standing a little apart, talking to Blanche Gardner. She was smiling into his face with an air of cool intimacy which conveyed the sense that she despised all the other people in the room.

I began by speaking of Hillier. I was afraid to say what was in my mind until I had felt theirs.

'A very subtle and a great man,' said Dalton.

'He saved us,' Blanche Gardner said gravely.

'He has saved the country,' Dalton said, 'including the people who would have ruined us. I was always willing to admit a strain of idealism in socialists, I am not a bigot. And yet. Well, let us say that I am England's bigot, or no man's.'

'Think of having to share one's house with three awful families,' Mrs. Gardner said lightly. She shrugged her thin shoulders. 'But, you know, my small dividends have not gone up yet as I hoped.'

'Blanche, I can recommend two aeroplane firms to you,' Dalton said kindly.

'Both of them a sound buy, even at the present price.'

'I wonder,' said I, in as level a voice as I have, 'whether you know anything about Sophie Burtt.'

'But I used to know her,' said Mrs. Gardner. 'I liked her once. She didn't improve with time. She was misguided and unbalanced.' She looked sharply at me with her serene cold eyes.

'I knew her moderately,' said Dalton. 'She could write, but she took too serious a view of life. I told her so. It ruined her as a writer. And after all, as I told her, there *are* a great many pleasant, good, innocent, quiet things in the world, and so much beauty and joy – why not write about them?'

'In some foreign newspapers there were rumours that she is in prison,' I said.

'Oh, nonsense,' Dalton exclaimed. 'She's abroad. She was in Biarritz last month. I saw her and talked to her.'

This remark so shocked me that for a moment I had nothing to say. Our eyes met. I was convinced in that moment that he knew where she was.

He turned his back on me. I think I felt only bewilderment, then horror. Did he only suspect? Was he reassuring himself? Did he know? I felt alone in the room. It had become very close, and the noise was overpowering. In one corner Hillier was talking with an air of quiet friendliness to Colonel Hebden. I saw Harriet shake off her two admirers and walk toward them. Hebden stooped over her hand in his flamboyant way. Amy Dale, with a half-smoked cigar in her mouth, had followed her friend. She rested one of her vast hands on Hebden's shoulder. At once he put his arm round her waist, sat down, and drew her on to his knee. She lay across his stomach.

A voice in my ear said: 'Not very amusing.'

I turned and found myself looking into Maurice Gardner's sallow discontented face. He was nearly sober.

'That incredible performance to-night,' he said, glancing over his shoulder. 'You didn't like it, did you?'

'I thought it trivial.'

'Trivial? My God, when I think what is happening, what is going to happen, to art in this country, squeezed between the police and the Government. Do you go to the theatre? There is not a play worth watching. Only little personal problems – the linen basket emptied out on the stage, and carried away in the last act.'

'Is it important?'

'Only if you believe that civilisation is important. I used to think it would last my time. I'm not so sure now. I'm not a socialist, mark you, and I do feel that they must take a share of the blame for having provoked the repression. But the world has gone mad. War, they say, is only a matter of time – short of a miracle. I don't understand the world any longer. Tell me about Norway. Could one retire there, and begin to build a monastery of some kind?'

'Do many people think as you do?' I asked.

He dropped his social manner and said quietly: 'Of course not. If you could take a cross-section of the ordinary decent families, you'd find that nine out of ten of them have no idea that anything is wrong. They have their own worries and pleasures on their minds, they are busy with marriages, births, and deaths. They don't think about anything.'

'Could we open a window, do you suppose?' I said.

He looked at me with a smile. 'In here?'

'Where did you think?'

'Sacker is very drunk,' he said suddenly.

I turned to look at Richard. He was sitting on the couch alone, with Harriet facing him in an arm-chair. Every second minute he stood up, walked slowly to her chair, bent over her, resting his hands on the arms of her chair, and kissed her deliberately, on the mouth. Then he went back to the couch and sat looking at her, with a slight smile.

'I adore you,' he said seriously. 'And you love me, don't you. And that's ideal. And I don't believe in ideals, so what's to be done?'

He stood up, kissed her again, and went back to his place.

'The only thing I want to say to you is that I adore you, Harriet.'

He went through this by-play several times. Thomas Chamberlayn watched it from his chair, and at last, in his mild voice, said: 'Sacker, I don't think I can stand this. If you go on I shall kick you.'

'I want to say that I understand your feelings,' said Richard solemnly. 'Harriet, I adore you.'

'Not still,' she said, laughing.

He walked over to her again. But this time she stood up, smiling.

'Will you do something for me?' he said, and putting both arms round her, kissed her again, pressing her head back. She made the least convincing protest. Now everyone was watching the absurd scene. Before anything more could happen, Hillier rose, walked over to Harriet and took her hand in both his hands. He thanked her for an enchanting supper party and an enchanting, memorable evening.

'I shall never forget your singing of *Scenes that are brightest*,' he said simply.

He turned to Richard, and said smiling: 'Are you coming with me, or are you too comfortable here?'

'I'll come with you,' Richard said promptly.

He did not kiss Harriet when he assured her for the last time that he adored her. I thought she regretted it.

I went away with them. When we left the hotel I noticed a young member of the Special Guard standing in the entrance hall. He stood rigidly still, his head held back. He had clearly been standing in that place and that posture for hours. It was young Eckhart. As soon as we passed through the doors he followed us. Three more of them had waited beside Hillier's car. The four stood at attention. Hillier took no notice of them beyond a kindly glance. He told the chauffeur to drive to the end of the street and wait for him, and with his arm in Richard's he walked on very slowly. I followed. The four young men kept a few paces behind me.

The silence, after Harriet's room, and the dark empty street, soothed me. I walked close behind the other two, hearing their voices, but scarcely at all what they said. I didn't know what had gone when I heard Hillier say: 'I realised to-night, Richard, that not a soul in that room, none of those men or women, had an inkling of what I am after, nor could ever imagine what you and I have lived through and thought.'

'Good Lord, no,' Richard answered. His voice sounded sober.

'I never knew anything but poverty and insecurity from the time I was able to look round me and compare my life with other children. It is what has formed me. It gave me a key to the minds of common men. I knew what they feared, and how to comfort them.'

'You know more than that,' Richard said tenderly.

'My only luck as a boy was that I was born and brought up in the country. And in that part of the country especially.'

'I liked it, always did,' Richard said. 'Have you forgotten the woman who was supposed to be out of her mind, and the stream that went with her cottage?' He laughed. A clanking lorry drove past, carrying away the rest. '... reached it through the field, and lie there between the trees on our stomachs trying to catch a young trout in our hands.'[42]

In the circle of light spreading out from the street-lamps I heard less well than in the darkness, or they lowered their voices. I missed a sentence or two. Then Hillier said:

'Well, England made me. Kind for a time, then half starved me in London. Well, I have saved her in return for it. We're only middle-aged. Thirty-nine is hardly middle-age.' He coughed and added: 'It wouldn't have happened as it has without you, you know.'

'Drilling men is my line,' Richard laughed. 'As saving countries is yours.'

I don't think he had any aptitude for talk of this kind. He must have listened to it very often. I doubt whether Hillier would have opened that curious receptacle, his heart, to anyone else. Its turgid flood went in at one of Richard's ears and out at the other, and he took it all in good faith, as a part of his friend's nature which was beyond him. I believe he was very bored.

Hillier must have realised suddenly that I was following them. He glanced round, and halted long enough for me to come up with them. He spoke in a persuasive voice, lightly.

'Did Richard ever tell you how nearly all was lost before it was even thought of? He might have bled to death. It was when we were fourteen! We had a scare, I can tell you.'

'What happened?' I asked.

'It was Frank's fault,' Richard laughed. 'He had been reading in some tale about Germany about two men swearing *blut-brüderschaft*.[43] Nothing would satisfy him but our going through the same thing. Well, we made a careful cut in his wrist and that was all right, but the pen knife slipped when I came to cut mine and I jabbed the artery!'

'I thought nothing could stop the bleeding,' Hillier said, smiling.

'We were a couple of innocents.'

We had reached the end of the street. The car was drawn up at the side of the pavement. The bodyguard stood still, three of them together, and one, a short distance away, in front. The one in front was Eckhart, and even in the darkness his face looked set and solemn. You could see that he regarded his duty as a sacred trust, and I think he would have died now without noticing it. Hillier took the trouble to speak to him before stepping into the car. The boy's already stiff body jerked into a further degree of rigidity and his chin lifted.

CHAPTER X

The next evening – I can fix it by what happened later – Lotte, Richard, and I were at dinner. Ernest came in a little late, and handed Richard a note. 'Sit down,' Lotte said.

He smiled at her quickly, and stood waiting. Richard read through the note. He frowned. 'I shall want you to take an answer,' he said. 'Have your dinner first, boy.'

With a sigh Ernest slipped into his place, unfastening the belt of his jacket. He glanced at me as though he had something to tell me, but when I began a question he pressed his mouth close and gave me a warning look. Richard was reading the note through a second time. He sat sunk in himself, his eyes restless, for some minutes. I should not care to be the man in his way, I thought. Yet a doubt did attack me, whether he was as adroit as he was unscrupulous.

When the coffee was served and the servant left the room he said:

'There's no doubt Hillier is being pressed to get rid of the Volunteers. Pressed hard. A fifty per cent cut as a start. Denham's very careful, he wouldn't make so precise a statement without being sure.'

'Is that note from Denham?' I asked, in surprise.

Ernest shook his head slightly. 'Lord, no,' said Richard. 'He'll not write anything. Much too cautious. But the figures are his, all the same.'

I wondered how much Ernest knew of the business he was engaged in. The boy looked numb and rather tired. He kept his head down and ate as though he were heavily preoccupied. Since he came in he had not said one word. I saw Lotte look at him.

'Is it certain?' she asked. I tried to guess whether she were anxious, but her voice was as level as always, and her face only grave.

'Nothing is certain. Except that it would suit more than one person and group to weaken the Volunteers. And to save money on them.'

'A nice reason for sacking us,' Ernest said softly. He looked down at his hands as he spoke. He never liked to show that he was moved, or nervous. I have never known so reserved a young man. I suppose he talked to Steffy, but even with Lotte he was silent about himself and his thoughts.

'You're not sacked yet,' Richard said dryly. He got up and went out of the room. A moment later he shouted impatiently from the next – 'Lotte,' and my sister hurried to go to him.

Ernest went on stirring his coffee. He had dropped six lumps of sugar into the cup. It must have been syrup. I waited.

'You can't help wondering sometimes what's going to happen,' he said, in his quiet young voice. 'I've always been expecting there would be a war. We've been hearing about it ever since I was at school. I remember one Armistice Day when a boy was sacked for giving out a lot of anti-war leaflets among the chaps. I don't think he'd have been sacked, but one of the chap's fathers wrote in and protested against his son being contaminated in that way.'

'When *I* was at school,' I said, 'the last war was just over and everyone was saying Never again. I can't remember exactly when the tone changed and they began to discuss rearmament, and say This year, next year, some time – Some of them are still saying Never, but it's become a prayer with them.'

'It must have been different in the old days,' he said. 'With no thought of war. I can't sort of imagine it.'

I tried, and failed, to imagine *his* mind, the mind of a boy always hearing echoes of the fear or the expectation of war in the adult voices about him. Strange is hardly the word for it. It must have been familiar with him from the first.

'I always meant to join up in the Air Force as soon as the war started,' Ernest said lightly. 'No mud and rats for me. I read a story about it, and I know I couldn't stand that. A quick death for me.'

'You'd better come to Norway.'

He gave me one of those secret looks in which boys express their hopes and diffidence, both bottomless. His eyes were bright and very clear, between long thick lashes.

'I'm looking forward to flying,' he said. He smiled.

'It's a damned shame if they put down the Volunteers,' he went on, after a moment's silence. 'It'll break a lot of fellows' hearts. His, too. And after they'd promised us the earth, to give us a Labour Camp in exchange, or the dole. It shows you what to expect in politics,' he said, in a flat bitter voice. He dropped his head. 'Do you know what's going on?'

'You mean the plans for a – for a demonstration,' I said.

He stood up, pulling his belt round his thin waist. 'Call it what you like,' he said. 'I call it waste of time. If I could I'd shoot that swine Hebden, and tie a few others up to lamp-posts. He is worth a hundred of them – ' he nodded at the door of the other room. 'But they'll do him in. He's not – necessary to them.'

I was so astonished at hearing this piece of political cynicism from him that I had no answer ready, and lost my chance of coming further at his mind. He began whistling, stopped in mid-breath, and said: 'Oh look here, I've something to tell you. There's some trouble, I don't know what, but Steffy wants you to look into it. She's only had a message. It's about one of her *intellectual* friends. A man by the name of Myers, a poet. He wrote a parable in verse, doggerel I called it, making fun of Hebden and Hillier – perhaps it was really funny – it made me laugh. It was printed in a leaflet and it got about everywhere. Steffy had a copy in her room. Well, at any rate, now something has happened to him. *I* can't go to enquire, can I, and I'd rather she didn't. Will you go? She'll go herself if you don't.'

I saw that he was really anxious for Steffy to keep out of trouble. I agreed to go to Myers's house. I felt reluctant, tired, and I wanted to sleep. I changed my clothes before I went.

I had imagined him living in a room or two above a shop, but when I found the street, near Gray's Inn Road, I saw a haggard reddish building, a block of workmen's flats put up in the worst period of liberal benevolence. I crossed a flagged yard, found his entrance, and began to climb stone stairs, narrow and very cold between dirty plastered walls. It was already dark. There were no windows on the landings, only a gas jet giving a little light. I began to be oppressed by the silence. Surely there should be a child playing, even at this hour, or a woman's voice, or women gathered round the sink placed on each landing. At last, when I had passed two floors a door opened and a man in shirt sleeves stepped out.

'Shall I find Mr. Myers's flat higher up?' I asked.

The man looked at me for a second. He whipped back into his room and slammed the door.

Taken aback, I stood a minute. I went on. On the fifth floor I found his number. I knocked, and had no answer. Knocked again. Again, louder.

The door opened suddenly. The man standing there, with the light behind him, looked at me with suspicion and anger. He had a dark face, yellow, out of drawing. When he spoke I saw that his teeth were bad.

'What do you want here?'

'I'm a friend of Myers,' I said. 'He asked me to come.'

'And when was that?'

I lost my temper, and my voice rose. 'For pity's sake, don't shout here,' the man said earnestly. 'Come in.'

I stepped inside and he scrutinised me in silence. At last he half smiled at me, with an unexpected shyness, and said: 'Well, forgive me. We're pretty much on edge. My name is Lewis.'

'Mine is Andrew Hillier,' I said.

I had expected a movement of repulsion, but he nodded: 'I've heard of you. Come in, then. His wife's out and I'm waiting. Don't stay long, will you?'

Puzzled, and afraid to seem ignorant of something I ought to know, I followed him into the room. I had a feeling of stuffiness and shabby disorder. There was a bed between me and the closed window, and a figure in the bed. Myers. I saw this in the first second, then that he was wrong in some way. I went close, and saw his ghastly face between the bandages. He winked at me slowly. I bent down, holding my breath because of the unpleasant smell.

He spoke, moving only his lips.

'Good chap to come. You see I was wrong. I said the Dark Ages, but it's the eighteenth century.'

'I don't know,' I began.

'You hired bullies then to beat up your enemies. We're going back in time. Reverse movement. Eighteenth, sixteenth, Dark Ages. I'm sliding quicker than the rest of you. I shall reach my Dark Ages before night.'

'Can't you stop showing off?' Lewis sighed. 'Don't talk.'

'But I still have a whole tongue,' Myers whispered. 'A pity not to use it.'

The lids came down slowly over his eyes, not the whole way, a line of white persisted under the lashes. His mouth smiled and the tip of his tongue came out between his teeth. 'That for you,' he said.

I drew back, with the smell in my nostrils. I looked at Lewis.

'We're going into the other room,' he said to Myers. 'To talk where you can't interrupt. I'll leave the door open.'

The other room was a kitchen. I was glad to sit down. I could feel my dinner in my throat. 'For God's sake, what happened?' I said under my breath.

'Don't you know what happened to him? Well it was early this morning. About two, I think. Someone knocked, they thought it was a friend needing a bed or a hiding-place, and Mrs. Myers opened the door. There were five young men, two of the Special Guards and three others. They came in and one held Mrs. Myers while the others got him out of bed. The one holding her told her calmly that if she kept quiet and waited nothing would be done to her husband. "Just a little correction," he said. He told her that one of them would come back to see whether she had kept quiet, and if she had they would bring her husband back intact; if not, she might be very sorry when she saw him. Then they tied her in her chair and left her, taking Myers with them. She waited two hours, until four o'clock. Then the same young Special Guard returned, asked her whether she had screamed, whether she had been uncomfortable, unloosed her, and went outside and beckoned over the stairs. The others came in carrying Myers. He was in – I don't think any part of him was whole. He was unconscious. She thought at first he was finished. They laid him on the floor and went away, telling her to hold her tongue, or next time they came it would be worse for him. Do you want to hear the rest of this? She tried rousing her neighbours. The man came, looked, said he'd get help and went back. She heard him arguing with his wife, wanting to keep out of it, but the woman came in and helped her to wash him a little. There was so much dirt mixed with the rest. He did come round and he told them what happened. The five men took him in a car to some room, put a blanket over him and battered him with spanners and a leaded stick. The leader, the young man who did all the talking, was called Eckhart. He was very young, almost a boy, and perfectly calm all the time. Two of the others – it came out in the talk between them that they were students of University College – were very nervous and anxious to get it over – and one of them was sick. Eckhart reproved them in the coldest way. They put a rope round Myers's neck and dragged him up and down a passage after the beating. He said he thought they had lost their heads, except Eckhart. Without Eckhart they would either have let him off with an ordinary thrashing or killed him out of nervousness. Eckhart looked him over and said: "No, don't quite do for him."'

I relaxed.

'You've been to the police,' I said.

'Don't be a fool,' he said curtly. 'Do we want to give them an excuse to take all Myers's friends into custody as suspects?'

'Well, have you got everything you want for him?'

I would have given my sound arm to go away again. But I was ashamed.

'Yes, thanks. At any rate – you can ask Mrs. Myers when she comes back. She had to go to work. She cleans offices at night. It's what they have to live on.'

He slumped in his chair and half closed his eyes. I looked at him. He was a little older than I am, muscular, looking underfed and not well. He was not a Jew. He spoke like a north-countryman.

When he opened his eyes I began to question him. In spite of myself I felt sleepy and my lids kept dropping. Since his dismissal, he had been living on the research he did for Tower, but he was not Tower's only pensioner and the living was not fat. At the end of my questions he asked me very sharply where I stood.

'I'm a liberal,' I said. 'I'm opposed to all repression.'

'Yes, you would be,' he sneered. 'You instituted the dole system. Well, that's one thing the last few years has done. It has logged the depths of the abyss that exists between the squeamish liberal who wants to be kind to the honest worker and those of us who have never wanted anything short of a classless society.'

'At least we liberals would not have behaved like this, if we had remained in charge,' I said, resenting him, and his arrogance.

'No,' he answered. 'You worked your betrayal by refusing to face facts. You kissed us, slipping sixpence into our hands, and exposed our naked backs to the stab.'

'Well, what are the facts?'

'Do you want a lecture on economics?' he asked ironically. 'I'm out of practice.'

'I'm not an economist,' I said.

'No. Do you know what you are, my friend? By chattering of peace where there is no peace you have become the ally, the cover for Thomas Chamberlayn. You're joined to him, and beyond him to Hebden the bully. You murdered Myers. You keep up the Training Camps. You and your blood brothers in the Labour Party, who fought nobody but the communists, who held back here, and retreated there, who opposed reaction with their tongues and turned their bottoms to it to be kicked, who worked for friendly relations with the owning classes and took their rewards, were decorated, knighted, wore silk breeches, who clothed themselves in righteousness of legality and held the door open for repression to come legally in. Damn them, damn them, damn them.'

Because of Myers in the next room he had never raised his voice, though it nearly choked him. His face worked. A little slaver came in the corners of his mouth.

'Some of them are in the Training Camps,' I muttered.

'Thank God for a small mercy.'

'How could they or you have fought against bombs and modern artillery?'

'That's what they always said,' Lewis whispered. *If we go in for force we shall be beaten.* That is, *Do what you like with us, we shan't resist.* As if any force could massacre the whole working class of a country. If it did no more than line the streets! But why talk of it.'

'You'd have had civil war,' I whispered back.

He looked at me. 'Oh yes? What have you now? I suppose it's not civil war when one class in a nation does the work for the rest, starves on a dole, and goes to jail or a Training Camp if it kicks.'

'This is a phase,' I said. 'It will work itself out. There'll be a return to democracy. You'll see.'

He looked at me with the grimmest contempt. 'I'll see the sun set in the east, a Chamberlayn resigning his power, a rich woman attending Ascot in sackcloth, a Tory peer sharing his house with ten families from the slums. I'll see the heavens open and a dove descending. I'll see miracles.'

I said nothing for a time. He went to the door and looked in at Myers. He came back softly.

'What are the communists doing now?' I asked.

'Minding their own business.'

I ought to have expected that. More to cover myself than anything, I said clumsily:

'I spoke of a phase just now. I don't mean a brief phase. For my part, I can't see anything in front of us but a long period of reaction.'

To my surprise Lewis smiled, his shy, rather kind and plaintive smile. It changed his whole face, one could forget his bad teeth.

'Yes, you people have always felt that,' he said softly. 'But I'll tell you something. Put it in your pocket, my liberal friend. The hangmen and jailers, Metternichs, Thiers, Goerings, Hebdens, Hilliers, come, use their whips, and go.[44] We remain. Kill us and we rise again from the dead. We come again. It couldn't be any other way. Starvation feeds us. Jails set us free. The ground you fasten us to breeds us. The womb you starve gives us birth. When you choke us, our breath goes into other throats. In the end, in the end – '

We heard Myers groan, then a very curious sound. I had never heard the sound in my life, it might be no more than a sigh, but my knees gave way. Lewis had run in. I followed him slowly. I saw him lift Myers up, then lay him back in the bed. The bed-clothes had fallen off him. He was naked but for the bandages, and blood and dirt were still pouring out between his legs. My stomach gave way. I stood; I could not go near him. Lewis was handling him with the quietest care, very gently. He placed cloths, and laid a rag soaked in water and brandy between his lips. After a few minutes he came over to me and looked in my face.

'You'd better go,' he said, without any contempt, almost kindly.

CHAPTER XI

Eugene Denham talked of books to Lotte throughout dinner. Richard, who by some accident had read, after he left school, a volume of Swift, and later a modern English novel he found lying about a hotel in Monte Video[45] was very silent. The conversation gave him no opening to speak of either of these events. Lotte left us at the end of the meal. We drank our coffee, and I stood up to go.

'You had better stay,' said Richard. He turned to Denham. 'My brother-in-law prefers Norway to this country and has no axe to grind. I like to have his opinion.'

'I hope that none of us is carrying an axe in his pocket,' Eugene Denham murmured.

'I don't know about you, man, but if I were satisfied with the way things are going in this country I should be sitting quietly, not chasing my tail in politics. It's a mug's game at the best,' Richard said curtly.

'I have a very small axe,' I said, smiling. 'A reward for running errands.'

'Indeed?' Denham smiled.

'Very small. Only the release of one person, not politically important, from a Camp, and the dismissal of one Camp Commandant.'

'And who are they, your axes?' asked Denham.

'I'll tell you later,' I said.

Richard looked at me drily. He knew the name of the Commandant at least. Turning from me, he said: 'Well, those were your figures I had? The Council is to be asked to recommend to the Prime Minister the dismissal of half the National Volunteers at once, and a half of those left next year.'

'I thought you would be interested in the figures,' said Denham. 'That is why I passed them on to you. Changes in the status of the Volunteer force don't affect me in any way, of course.' He leaned back in his chair, with crossed legs, one foot moving rhythmically, and the tips of his fingers pressed close, his pose during any discussion. I believe he meant to wear an austere calm.

'No?' Richard said swiftly. 'But what does affect you is the proof it offers that the man who is giving orders to the Council is not Hillier, not you, not me, but Tom Chamberlayn. Mr. Thomas Chamberlayn. This month it is my Volunteers who are to be sacrificed to his economies. Next month or the one after, it will be your precious schemes, for socialising industry. I think it's what you call them? And the month after that, perhaps you yourself will be found superfluous on the Council. After all, what is Social Service? What are your schemes worth to you on paper? Where is the importance of a Minister with nothing to do because he can't get the funds to carry out his plans?'

I was constantly surprised by Richard's quickness in grasping the significance of events of which he had no direct understanding. It explained his success in South America. He would arrive in a capital city, live in the hotel, and in a week or an evening learn the lie of the political land, the names of the important persons, and the right doors to approach them. His weakness was that he had only one method of dealing with men. No doubt it was the correct one for South American presidents and would-be presidents, who are for the most part simple-minded realists. It was the wrong method for a cultivated English politician, who is also a realist, but not simple-minded. Centuries of diplomatic practice have gone to the making of a Eugene Denham. He could, on occasion, speak the simple truth, but it was always the right occasion.

I saw that he winced inwardly at the crudeness of Richard's speech. I saw a great deal more that evening. There are times when I become an adept in listening to people's minds. I heard Denham acknowledge to himself the truth of Richard's diagnosis, and I saw him squirm and twist to find another way off the hook on which he was caught than by jumping into Richard's basket. He was prepared to jump if he must. He asked about General Smith, anxious to learn how far that astute soldier had committed himself. And about Body, ex-Trades Union leader, on whom I was calling the next day.

The conversation lasted until midnight. At the end of it only a child could have remained ignorant of the truth about Denham. Denham felt sincerely that a cause was just if it was successful. He would sincerely have persecuted the Christians in one century, and sincerely joined them in another. His head was his fortune.

In the morning I went to call on George Body, Minister for Labour.

I had prepared myself for another Denham. It was a mistake. The man I had to talk with this morning was a simpler man, less adroit, less intelligent, less sure of himself. I suppose that Body had been a very efficient officer and director of the Labour Party. He looked like the efficient head of a department. Come to that, he looked like an honest clerk. You would never suspect him of stealing the stamps. I think that it must have been very easy for him to convince himself, during the crisis, that his right place was in the National State Party. He had been allowed to retain, that is to save, everything that mattered to him, the comfortable offices of the Labour Party, his own room and desk, such of his old staff as were willing to stay and work side by side with energetic young men of the National State Party. When he came in of a morning, and placed his gold-topped umbrella in the corner where he had placed it on the morning he inherited this room from its former occupant, it must have seemed to him that nothing had changed. He had saved the Party. He still had his beautiful umbrella.

And when he dictated letters, they were in the same style as the letters he had been dictating for sixteen years, and concerned with much the same things. Nothing had changed. Nothing was lost.

He regretted sometimes that the man who had been his chief assistant for many years had acted foolishly and wildly and was now in Winchell Training Camp. He missed that man. No one else remembered that he liked clean blotting-paper every morning, a new thick pad, and a new pen. Fountain pens bothered him. He never used them.[46]

I found him very pleasant, though a little stiff. He was not, like Denham, all things to all men. He liked to understand his visitor's position before unbending with him. When he knew that I was Hillier's second cousin his manner noticeably softened. This was not snobbery, it was the habit of an official. A man was precisely his place.

He spoke readily about the collapse of the Labour Party. 'If my advice had been taken,' he said, 'we should never have accepted office last year. We had a majority, it's true, and that was the primal error. We had got it by promising to do what every sensible man knew we could not do. We could not restore cuts. We could not begin vast socialist schemes. The situation was far too delicate. Financially and economically, the country was in a bad away.[47] Millions had been spent on armaments. In our election talk we promised to reduce that. How could we? It was madness. I advised and begged that we should take every proper means to avoid having to take office at such a time. In the end I was overruled, and you know what happened.'

'You don't think,' I said, deferring to him, 'that a show of firmness, say, a General Strike, would have altered events?'

'Altered them in the most desperate way,' he exclaimed.

A few drops of rain spattered on the glass. He looked round him. His umbrella was there, in its place. He sighed. 'At that moment there were such fears in the country, such ridiculous resentments – and the financial crisis worsening every day – almost every hour – do you know I believe that civil war would have broken out in a week if the Labour Party had attempted anything? What could we do – a peaceful law-abiding party, pledged to use democratic weapons? There was only one thing to do. And the Party, alas, was not equal to it. A few of us did stand firm, I'm very thankful to be able to say.'

'Yourself,' I said.

'Myself. Others. Well, we have our reward. In two ways. We can say with truth that the *real* enemy has been defeated. We have heard the last of communism. And certain revolutionary Trades Unions have had a salutary lesson. Second, the fort has been held for democratic socialism. It is all very much in our English tradition, Mr. Hillier. The direct assault fails, but the reforms are brought in next day by the back door. We are a strange, but a great people. H'm.'

His very simplicity made it hard to talk to him. Was he genuinely satisfied? Did he believe that all was for the best, for an ex-Labour leader, in the best of repressive Governments? Almost by accident I found the way to an organ in him less dry than his mind, as shrunken and withered perhaps, but sweeter. His heart. I mentioned the name of a man I had known slightly many years ago, who was afterwards a Labour leader. He had died in 1937, before he had to choose between Winchell and a room blessed by the National State Party. Body's face and voice changed, grew gentle, trembled a little.

'Did you know Alec? Well, think of that. I remember Alec when we were both boys, not nineteen, and we were working in Portsmouth in those days. I remember one evening after a supper and Alec and I were helping to wash up and Alec was drying cups and jigging about, he was always one to dance, loved dancing, and he dropped a cup, crash, bash. And old Mother Ransome, she was treasurer of the branch, clattered his ears for him. You never saw a boy so taken aback, then he laughed, he – ' His voice died away. He blushed. 'What am I talking about? You don't want to hear old gossip. Where was I? Yes, h'm, h'm.'

He became the efficient head of department again, but his tongue was loosed. He rambled a little about the old days for a time. I thought that he had had a qualm of conscience thinking of his friend, or perhaps only of old Mother Ransome, who was certainly dead now, too. Or perhaps nothing so clear and inconvenient as a qualm. Only an uneasy wish to feel an old warmth about him, the feeling you would have coming on a coat in the attic and remembering the day you walked in it in the rain, a hunk of cheese in your pocket, and the smell of grass or peat. No fear in your young bones of catching cold. Well, those were days.

It was natural that he should go on to speak of his lingering doubt. Had it been politic to flatten out the Unions? Ultimately, he mused, they must be re-built. A change would slowly and certainly come about, he said. Democratic habits would assert themselves. There must be no premature act, no repetition of the mistake of last year, no bid for power before power was safe to handle. But perhaps the least little show of spirit. Only a ripple. A murmur. Perhaps remind the Council that the workers had, after all, leaders, and those leaders the right to be taken account of. He thought he might have a word with his old friend Eugene Denham. In my mind's eye I saw him dictating a letter. It began:

In re Suggested Rally of Democratic Elements, or would it be, *Tendencies?*

Our talk, he said, had been very valuable to him. And, yes, he would like to meet General Sacker. He had not the pleasure of knowing him personally, and he had a great respect for him. He started round suddenly.

'Is that more rain on the window?'

It was, a very heavy spring shower.

'But you have your umbrella,' I said soothingly.

'In fact, I don't need to go out,' he answered. 'Do you know, we can serve a very good lunch here? Yes. In the basement. It is a part of our staff organisation of which I am proud. You must lunch here with me one day. It can be delightful. Cool, with the fans going, and dark green matting on the floor.'

CHAPTER XII

Myers died, and was buried on the day of national rejoicing decreed by the Council, popularised by the newspapers, and carried out with every mark of gladness by poor and rich. If there were any dissenters they held their tongues.

He was buried in the early morning in the Jewish cemetery. It was at the earliest hour possible because the Jewish officials were afraid of inviting the displeasure of the authorities if there should be disorders. There were none, since all who might have thought his grave a proper place to air their ideals were busy. Only a few Jews, his relatives, and two students, went with him.

There were a great many trees in the place, which made it dark and shady, and as already the day was hot that caused this place to seem pleasant. One policeman and two National Volunteers had stationed themselves near the grave, but they looked politely away while the business was carried through.

I had followed a long way off, thinking that I had no right, of friendship or any other, to show myself among mourners. There was no woman with them. A man in a raincoat came in late and stood apart. I thought he was Lewis. I could not get a full sight of his face until the time came for handfuls of earth to be thrown into the grave. Then he stepped forward and I saw that it was Lewis. He had earth in his hand. When he raised it to throw, moving his lips, he raised it in the forbidden communist salute. My heart came into my mouth. It was enough, if it had been noticed, to have him taken off for one of the dreaded examinations by the newly-formed special police, and that would certainly end badly for him. But the Volunteers were still looking studiously away.

I joined him afterwards in the street and we walked under the flags and the ropes of coloured paper and flowers withering in the first heat. He said that he was ashamed of giving way to a sudden emotion. 'It was inexcusable,' he said.

'It impressed me.'

'Oh, it would,' he said. 'Undisciplined fool, ass, I should have known better.'

I had asked him if there was anything I could do for Myers's wife, and he said he was on his way to her. I went with him, not eagerly. When the door was opened by a young boy I heard a woman crying, but it was not Mrs. Myers. It was his mother and two other old Jewish women. His wife was as quiet as wood.

She was not Jewish. She was a countrywoman from somewhere in the west, I thought by her accent. She had a small stubborn face, a great deal of coarse hair, and rough hands.

No, there was nothing she needed. She was going back to her own people. 'And I shall show you what I am taking back,' she said quietly, and held up to me a shirt and a jacket, both cheap shabby garments, now torn and covered with dark stains. 'They were his. It is to show what was done to him, if someone says, "I do not believe it." Then I shall say, "Look for yourself."'

Since there was nothing to do we left, and left the four women, three sunk and one buoyed up by dear knows what pride or hard bitter anger. It was now close on noon, and the bells ringing everywhere. We heard the salvoes in Hyde Park even at this distance.

I invited Lewis to eat with me. We entered a small cafe in which the dish of the day was potatoes roasted in their jackets and served with a dab of butter substitute that had a very sour taste. An old man waited on us; his son, the proprietor of the cafe, son's wife, and all theirs had gone out to watch the Review.

'I was thinking of what Myers said to you,' said Lewis. 'That we had returned to the brutal manners of the eighteenth century. But apart from the fact that there is no return and if we are on the same level of brutality as that age it is at a point on the descending slope – apart from that, I say, he had no need to go so far back. I have collected a very pretty list of common cruelties from the last century, employment of infants, flogging in jails, and so forth. You might be surprised to know how few years we had to retrace to come to this moment.'

'I should be more surprised,' I retorted, 'if you had the fairness to add that it was liberal ideas which made us ashamed of brutality. As the liberal faith has declined, so violence and cruelty have returned.'

'I don't deny it,' Lewis said mildly. 'I only ask you why your faith has declined, and why we have become less not more liberal.'

'I detest all religions in their first stages,' I said. 'I detest communism because it will not – cannot, if you prefer it, but it is no better – allow a man the free play of his mind. He must accept *your* truth, hate your enemies, look for the dictatorship of the proletariat, the Second Coming, throw himself into the struggle – all the rest of the litany, I haven't patience for it all. I don't say that a thinker or artist could not live by your faith, if he accepted it with his heart, and had passion. But there is no room in it, and no air he can breathe, for a man whose cold passion is to balance all things fairly in his mind. To relate them, to be tolerant. You have no use for so exquisite a mind as E. M. Forster's – whom you may never have heard of, since unfortunately he ceased to write long before he was an exile – '[48]

Here I was interrupted by the old man's turning on the wireless in the back room of the café, so that we could not hear ourselves speak for the noise of eight military bands playing the marching version of *Land of Hope and Glory*. The noise deafened us. There was nothing for it but to pay our bill and go. We stood a minute in the street, but every open window blared on both sides, for the enjoyment of the old or bedridden.

'I am too bitter and heartsick for this,' said Lewis suddenly, and left me.

I knew that Lotte was keeping a place for me beside her in Whitehall, to watch the march past of the Volunteers. I made my way there. The sun was now like a molten ceiling over the city. I had my official pass, and that procured me a way through the crowds, the cordons of police and soldiers, and so into the yard of the House of Commons. I was barely in time. As I clambered to my seat, Hillier and Richard came out of the House together. Their passage to the gate was lined by the Special Guard, and Hebden stood at the foot of the steps of the platform, which was set up outside the gate. When Hillier and Richard had mounted the platform, Hebden placed a number of his men round it. But the two of them were alone on the narrow canopied platform. The march past of the Volunteers began at two o'clock. They came down Whitehall, between cheering crowds, past the platform, and turned along Victoria Street. They marched in double column for four hours. Whenever I looked at Hillier he was smiling slightly, as though he were inwardly excited. Richard had an impassive face throughout. I thought he would have dwarfed Hillier on the platform, but curiously, although they stood side by side, Hillier's was the figure that obstructed the light.

Wherever I looked there were crowds, wave on dun wave, along Victoria Street and the Embankment, the length of Whitehall to Trafalgar Square, and heads in all the windows. I felt brittle and unsafe between the weight of the heat and the pressure of these waves of flesh and bone.

With a shock I saw Eckhart's among the faces below the platform. He looked fresh, young, grave. I forced myself to look at him. There, I thought, is the *calm* murderer of poor Myers. The young men on either side of him had much the same air. Would they, too – ? I looked at people in the crowd below the stand. All these decent kindly anonymous faces, surely there was not an Eckhart among them? Then I thought that his calm, which had shocked me, was a sign that he was possessed. I had been right. He was one of those young men, of no special intellect, to whom an idea becomes a religion. They serve it blindly, without thought. Hillier was Eckhart's God. Everything he said Eckhart accepted. He was truly out of himself, both now and when he was beating Myers to death. If Hillier had ordered him to turn his rifle on himself he would do it that instant. Suddenly the brassy heat made the boy standing next him collapse and fall forward. Eckhart did not so much as glance at him.

When it was over Hillier made his speech. It was a superb piece of declamation, in which he quoted that passage from the *Aeropagitica*[49] which is quoted by every politician seeking gold to gild his cracked pots. There was not one solid piece of reasoning in the whole speech, not one fact to support all he said of revival and prosperity. I am sure the crowds did not observe it. To hear them roar and split their throats at him made me wonder why anyone has ever laboured to improve men. I think they are not apt to be improved. Let them be stupid. Let them be cheated and kept down. It is what they deserve.

Towards the end of the speech Lotte and I slipped away and ran behind the ranks of the Special Guard into the House. At one of the swing doors a policeman and a man who looked like a clerk were betting solemnly on the number of minutes Hillier would speak. We went along the corridor and into a room where there were tea-cups beside a decanter and some glasses. Lotte sat down, swung her legs, and hummed. I looked out of the window at a tree shining in the sun. We heard Richard's voice in the corridor. Lotte looked down with a light mischievous smile. Richard opened the door and held it with his arm for Hillier, then came in quickly and closed it.

'Lord, the heat,' he said.

Hillier was more moved than I had ever seen him. He put his hands on Richard's shoulders, smiling into his face, and said:

'It was your day, Richard.'

'Mine?' said Richard. 'Nonsense. Every man of the Volunteers is your man, and the crowd out there felt it. Listen, they're still cheering. You'll have to go out again.'

'In a minute,' Hillier said. 'Let me stay here quietly a minute. And when I go you must go with me. They must see you to-day.'

He went alone in the end, and after a time we heard the volume of cheering swell to a deafening broadside, then a silence when he must have said something, then another broadside. 'And in this heat,' Lotte murmured.

Fortunately Richard did not hear her. He held his glass up and said: 'To the day!' Then he turned to me and gripped my arm. 'You see, Andy,' he said. 'That's the real Hillier. That's the man I'm counting on. And by God, can't I? It's now or never, the break, and Hillier with us!'

PART III
JUNE

CHAPTER I

On the third of June we went back for a few days to the house in Yorkshire. Annie greeted us with the story she had been repeating for years, there were some queer people about, she wouldn't put a name on them, but she had her suspicions and she was not blind yet, and wood didn't get up and walk off the wood pile nor legs of mutton unlock the door of the larder and vanish overnight. What was more, only the evening before this, coming home late from the village, she had found a piece of tarred string in the yard. It was not there when she went out, no person had a right in the yard, no person lawfully dropped string in another's yard. 'There's something in it,' she said energetically, 'mark my words, it doesn't mean nothing.'

Lotte tried to soothe her. She listened with a bright sly smile. It was plain that she thought Lotte, although a kind woman, neither more nor less than a fool.

'Is it right what we were reading in th' paper?' she asked. 'The master was two hours, was he, standing in London on a platform on Tuesday?'

'Quite true,' Lotte said.

'Well, I saw a photograph of him doing it. But you can't be sure of anything, can you? Still, of course if you say he did.' Smiling, she padded off to her kitchen, and we heard her singing at top voice, *Shall we linger at the fountain?* until Richard shouted at her to hold her tongue. She did – for as long as ten minutes.

That evening the fishermen and some others came up from the port, with a band and flags, as the crown of their national rejoicing, to welcome Richard. They gathered on the upper lawn and played the inevitable air at funeral pace, then followed it with *Now the labourer's task is o'er,* singing mournfully a bar or so behind the music. Richard came out and roared at them as if he were in a temper, while the great fools stood grinning and nudging each other in delight. He spread his arms out and invited them into the kitchens to drink beer.

He drank it with them. There were two fishwives had come up with their men, harridans who would have the skin off you if you vexed them, as strong as men and more merciless and sharper-tongued. Calling Richard 'bairn' and 'honey,' they hung on his arms. He paraded them the length of the kitchen, one on either arm, and at the end kissed a brown wrinkled cheek of each. They screeched with joy. Annie, in the meantime, was in a frenzy of locking cupboards and hiding tins and jars, and keys. Some of our keys were lost for days.

These men and women liked and understood Richard. They admired his violence and hot temper. Grinning, they recalled the day when he had kicked one of them from top to bottom of a flight of steps for a single impudent speech. The man broke his leg and owned afterwards he had deserved it. Yon's the sort of man he is, they said openly. He's a rare one to fight, is Sacker.

That was the way it went with them. Scarcely one would think of giving Richard his title, or taking a cap off to him. They stood in front of him with thumbs in the band of their sea trousers, and grinned in his face. But they knew he was superior to them. The boldest did not deny it for a moment, nor feel that it was aught but right he should be. They had the differences of class in their bones, and yet their bones would not bend before any man's, not if he was King. Nor, which came nearer home, if he was the lord of the manor and owned the salmon fishing from the source to the harbour mouth. Last year Richard had jailed a dozen of these men for taking salmon in the harbour. It did no good. The others went on with it, taking their boats out under the noses of Richard's watchman and the police. One rough night they threw the watchman in the water and fished him out when he was as near drowned as makes no matter. They would have done the same by Richard himself if he had come on them at the time. He was in London and could only write furious letters to the magistrates. They were of his way of thinking from the first, but were helpless to put a stop to it. They could not jail every fisherman in the town, and if they had, the women would have gone on with it.

The men had no ill feeling for Richard. He was only looking after his own, as any one of them would have to do in his place. But come the proper time they would take his salmon in the harbour again and let him burst his bowels with rage.

It struck me that up here Lewis was irrelevant. These men had all the independence they wanted or could use. All they really wanted was a better market for their fish and to be let alone. Why must Lewis try to force on them a destiny they had not asked for? Well, I thought, they would throw him in the harbour as fast as the other, if he tried talking to them in the way he talked to me. A man who began by taking Richard's property from him would as like as not take theirs. Into t' watter wi' him!

I watched Richard for a time. He was thick in a knot of three men, arguing on the right way to net a lobster pot. He could sink himself in any talk that had to do with the way men work or act. You would suppose he had been setting lobster pots half his life, and the other half yarning about it. He is a simple man, I thought. Compared with Hillier he is simplicity itself. I wondered whether

Hillier's complexity were more in his mind or in his nerves. Patient, crafty, wallowing in delays. Moving with violence when he was forced by events to move at all. I felt at this moment that Richard knew less about his friend than I did, and God knows that was little enough – except that Richard trusted him. I never did.

CHAPTER II

In the morning I took bread and cheese in my pocket and walked across the moors northward. This side of the moor was bleaker and less pleasant than the south, but I disliked that now, because Winchell lay on the other edge of it. I preferred to walk over these bleaker miles, with the sea on my right hand and a few wild valleys on the left, where were now and then poor farms or a struggling village. In the afternoon, when I was thinking of turning back, I came to a deep disused quarry. I thought there might be a spring on the slope below it, or a few wild strawberries. I found a path by which I could scramble down, holding by my one hand to jutting stones and the tough stems of the mountain ash.

The path was steeper at the last than I had expected and I fell a short way on to a bed of ling and brambles. I lay on my back for a few minutes, getting my breath. A few feet from me, at the back of the quarry, was an overhanging ledge. It was deep enough underneath as almost to form a cave screened by brambles. I became certain that there was something, some large animal, there behind the bramble bushes. There was no movement, or none I could detect. But I felt in my nerves the nearness of something alive. I knew that I was being watched.

I got up, turned my back on the ledge, and walked a few steps in a parallel direction. Turning suddenly I walked directly to the back of the quarry. There was a man crouching on the earth under the ledge, a small man with an unshaven dirty face. We stared at each other in silence. It was the mild little man from Winchell Camp. George. I knew him almost at once. He did not move, only looked at me from unblinking dark eyes, like a child or an animal.

'Well?' I said.

'I'm running away,' he said softly.

He was even smaller than I remembered, and his face was wizened and puckered. His hands were like claws.

I sat down on the ground, with a vague idea that I must hide too, to keep him hidden.

'Where are you making for? Can I help?' I said.

'I don't know,' he answered. He looked slyly at me. 'Are you really a relation of Hillier's? We discussed it very often at Winchell after that evening.'

'Yes,' I said.

He was silent. I waited. After a minute I said as well as I could that we can't choose our relatives.

He sighed. 'It doesn't matter,' he said softly. 'You're not going to give me away, are you?'

'Good God, no,' I cried. 'Can't I help? I'll do any thing.' I pulled the remains of the cheese out of my pocket and offered it to him.

'I'm not hungry,' he said. 'I stole almost the whole of a leg of mutton from a large house over that way, two nights ago.' He unfolded a piece of sacking and showed it to me, chuckling. 'I was downright clever.'

'Where are you for?'

'I'm going home to Corpeth in Northumberland. It's my village, where I was born.'

'You'd better let me try to get you to Norway,' I said. 'You'd be safe there.'

'It's kind of you, but I'd rather stay here,' he answered. 'I've lived in England all my life and I'd rather go on living here even if I had to eat roots. I shouldn't take well abroad, you see.'

'But if you're caught.'

'Perhaps I'll be sent to another, better camp. There are some better ones. It's a bad place, is Winchell. Do you know what, I used to think that Steadman was mad. Sometimes, if he happens not to go away for the week-end, he gives us a sermon on Sunday. Never about religion but always shouting against immorality and indecency. He talks about street girls and Jews and indecent books and pictures and so on, you'd think he had a very close acquaintance with all of them. But he's not mad. That's the awful unbearable thing I discovered. He's as sane as anyone else – but he's evil. Perhaps he's the Evil One himself. You know we're told he is to be loosed for a time. Well, when I knew that evil exists – really exists – not just goodness gone wrong – and I saw it living in Steadman I couldn't stay there any longer. I escaped from a working party one day, and I've been a fortnight on the way already. Safe and sure is my motto.'

He said all this in his soft voice with its northern accent as quietly as if we were sitting over lunch somewhere and he were talking to a friend. I felt very anxious about him.

'You're not likely to be sent to a decent camp if you're caught,' I said roughly. 'Suppose they sent you back to that place near Glasgow?'

'Then I should kill myself,' he said as simply as a child.

We sat in silence for a minute, while I tried to think of some help or advice I could give him. He was a feeble little man. And I felt that I was more helpless now than he was.

'There are people who help such as me,' he said brightly at last. 'I haven't bothered anyone, because I know where I'm going. Holman had the name of one of them, and one of our chaps ran away from Winchell this March and he was out a fortnight before they caught him and fetched him back. When he was getting better from – from what they did to him, he told us how he managed. He used to lie up all day, then go to the front door of a house in the evening and ask to see the master, and when he came, or it might be a woman, if they looked safe decent sort of people he'd ask them to let him sleep for a few hours in the kitchen – it was as cold as death that month. He says when he'd decided a man was safe he was never wrong. They guessed where he'd come from all right, and one would give him a little money and another a change of clothes or food. Well he got to the fellow's house he had the name of, and it was a great place. The man himself was a big arbitrary man, he was a Yorkshireman, a writer. He told our chap to stick around for a day or two and he'd get him out of the country. "I've helped others to get away," he says, "and I'll help you." Our chap was very curious why he was doing it, he with all that money and that house, and he says, "Aren't you afraid of the law?" But this fellow only laughed. "I've as much respect for the law as anyone," he says, "but I'll not be bullied, nor if I can help it I won't see other chaps bullied. Where do you want to get?" Our man wouldn't wait, though, he was set on seeing his girl again, so he only took a little money and went on home, and there the police were waiting for him. They said they'd been expecting him for a week. Escaping prisoners always make for home.'

'But you're going home,' I said.

His face clouded for a moment, only for a moment. He was soon smiling. 'It's different for me. There's no one I want to see. I shan't go into the village. But there's caves in the hills where I hid as a boy. I can live there all summer, and maybe by winter comes they'll have given up looking for me and I can come in of nights.'

He looked round him. 'It's not bad here. But you should see the hills above Corpeth.'

'They'll get you in the end, George,' I burst out. 'You'd better come away.'

He looked at me, as it were from the far back of his eyes, from the place where he was alone. So much had happened to him during the past year and a half. His not very quick brain had not grown used to it. He had not changed in himself. If I had known him when he was a member of the Executive of the Labour Party I should have thought him a very limited stupid sort of little man, not fit to hold a position of authority. But now I felt humble and uneasy with him. It was because he had accepted his life, which I have never had the strength to do.

'No, leave me be,' he answered, half impatient.

I asked him whether he would now act very differently if he could put the clock back two or three years.

'Ee, how could we act differently?' he said quietly. 'Our enemies are violent men. They believe, y'know, that they're justified in using any illegal, violent means to get their ends. And we others have always stood for peaceful methods. For democracy. If we had tried to use any others we should have betrayed ourselves, and our ideas. All we stand for would have been declared false – false – because we abandoned it in the crisis, in time of trouble. Surely *you* don't think we ought to have done that?' He looked at me with reproach.

'I don't know what I think now,' I muttered. 'My head, my mind – I find everything confused.'

He made a little clucking noise with his tongue. 'Dear, dear,' he said sympathetically. 'It *is* hard, I know. The only thing one can do is to cling fast to principles.' He put his head on one side, and considered me. 'Perhaps I shouldn't tell you this. But when I used to read a lot as a boy – I was fond of reading, that's how I came to do so well, in spite of our being poor. There were eight of us children, and my mother and father, living in two rooms – as I was saying, I used to read about people being racked for their faith, or tortured, in the old times, and think no I could never stand that. I should have to give up. Now I know you *don't* give up. It's so easy to go on from day to day, standing anything. Only I couldn't stand that place in Scotland again. I s'd have to kill myself.'

I gave him what money I had with me. I told him I was going back to Norway in August and made him repeat my address in Oslo until he had it by heart. Rødhusgaten 91. When he was tired of his cave, I said, he should write to me, or get in touch with the Yorkshireman who would have helped him, and we'd find a way to get him safely out. I did not believe in any of this myself. I thought he would be caught before long.

He thanked me in a rather casual way, much as you thank a man for an invitation neither of you takes seriously. Heaven knows I was serious about wanting to help him. In his dogmatic unintelligent way he was as incorruptible and alert as R. B. Tower, and as much and as little of a saint. He had the brain of a rabbit. Towards evening, after I had left him, I found tears pouring out of my eyes because of him. This was at the moment when I remembered he had said my name didn't matter. It seemed to me that only a good man could have said that in such a way, in such circumstances.

CHAPTER III

Sacker was more at ease with Smith than with the other persons he had drawn into the loose conspiracy. So far it was only a conspiracy of talk and talkers. Smith had talked to the sympathetic ones among his friends in the Service, and to Eugene Denham. Denham and Body went cautiously to work to sound the minds of various ex-Trades Union leaders – not, you understand, the foolish ones in the Training Camps, but those who had fitted themselves, insecurely for the most part, into the new frame of industry. Richard had no desire to meet any of these awkwardly placed men. He was not at home with such allies. If he had not wanted to save his Volunteers he would not have troubled himself with what Smith called indifferently the 'demonstration,' or the 'financial readjustment.' He himself spoke of it as the 'second revolution,' and the 'clean-up.' He could not let himself be pushed aside without a struggle. He had to struggle, to resist.

He knew where he was with the regular officer. Disliking and despising the way in which things are done in the army, he understood them. He knew how much Smith's ability had counted for in his rise and how much was due to his friends. With only the least trouble he could talk Smith's language. It was not more difficult than talking Spanish to a Paraguayan general.

They dined once or twice a week in the little restaurant in the Euston Road. The melancholy dirty Italian, when he had spied on them from his back room for a time, one evening emerged from it and suggested with a truckling smile that the gentlemen would like to sit by themselves in the room upstairs. He had a nose for a plot, that one. He could not recognise Smith, but he had soon discovered Richard. And he hoped that something would come of his politeness to General Sacker.

From now on they sat upstairs, in a smaller room with four tables. The other three were never occupied. The food was not intolerable, though it was dirty and oily, and the waiter effaced himself as much as possible.

Their talk on this eighth evening was of Eugene Denham. The soldier distrusted him, instinctively, and because he had suffered once already at the hands of the politicians.

'He'll crawl along the top of the fence and come down only at the very end.'
'Then it's our business to see that he prefers to come down on our side of it,'
Richard answered. 'He's double faced, but he's no fool. He's on the wrong side
of Thomas Chamberlayn, and he knows that.'

'We shouldn't count on him.'

'We can count on Denham,' said Richard, 'to join the successful side at the
earliest possible moment. That's why he'll hold his tongue about what he hears.
He'll wait to see what happens to us and what action Hillier takes. Then you'll
find that he's been with us from the beginning. I know Denham.'

He knew Smith too. In a few minutes Smith would come round to his own
share in the spoils. He would be very mannerly, unassuming, quiet. A slight smile,
half a sneer, would move his fine nostrils. He had conceived the notion that
there was no one who could be trusted to take Hebden's place at the Air Ministry,
and since he wanted the War Office himself, he wanted the two posts to be
combined, at any rate for the time. And he wanted the suggestion to come from
Sacker.

Richard was by no means sure that he cared to see so much power and glory
in one adroit pair of hands. It had occurred to him, too, that he would feel safer
and less exposed if he were at the War Office. There he would control both
armies, the regular and the irregular. An unshakable seat. But he was prepared
to give it up, recognising Smith's prior right, and to take Hebden's place as Air
Minister. That would be almost if not quite satisfactory. It was easier for him,
too. He had friends in the Air Force and none in the Army. He knew very well
the contempt with which regular soldiers looked at his Volunteers.

'My own belief about Hebden is that he is mad,' Smith said quietly. 'A temper
so little under control as his – and then his wounds – I should imagine there
would be no trouble in finding a doctor to certify him as insane.'

'Shut him up in an asylum, you mean.' Sacker roared with laughter. 'I like that.
But why not shoot him? He'll give us the chance, you can be sure of that.'

'Do you know, I don't like shooting people. Not in that way. In war, where
you never see what you're doing – and even that's bad enough when you see the
wounded men. You've never been in a field hospital, have you?'

'I'd rather be shot than shut up for the rest of my life in Broadmoor.'[50]

'Leave it to the event,' Smith counselled. 'It's more important to find a man
to step into Hebden's shoes at the Air Ministry, at once. I don't know what you
feel about it. For my part I am inclined to lay some stress on the advantages of
a unified control of all the forces. At least during the critical weeks or months.'

'All of them?' said Richard. He looked up sharply and shrewdly. 'Come, come,
my dear chap. A single control is all very well, but I can't add War Office and

Air Force to the Volunteers. It's a little too much. One of them, perhaps, but not both.'

His slight smile flickered on the soldier's face. He knew when he had been put down. He could appreciate the quickness of the answer too. He was up again at once, with no ill-temper. Indeed he felt none. He was too old a campaigner to lose his temper when he missed. And too sure of himself. He had more staying power than the other man, although he was older, with a lower physical energy. In his smooth way, too, he liked Sacker. Occasionally, as at this moment, he felt a clear respect for him.

Their talk lasted almost until ten o'clock. Each knew what the other wanted, in the event of success, and was prepared in the due time to come to terms. The Prime Minister would have two chief men to help him in pulling the country round, not one. For the time both of them were ignoring the ambitious Denham. Richard because he disliked, and Smith because he distrusted him. They parted in good spirits, on the best of terms.

Richard walked home to his house in Regent's Park. From the road he saw a light in his wife's room. He went in to talk to her. He had a respect for her judgment. He rarely obeyed it, because she was cautious, and all his success had come from disregarding caution and common sense. But he liked to talk to her and to have her mind.

She was sitting up in bed, reading under the lamp. He sat down on the bed and rested his legs in knee boots on the chintz-covered chair at the side. Lotte made no complaint. She liked to see him there, and he could rest his boots on her sheets for all she cared. Her heart beat faster for his nearness, even though she reminded herself that she was less to him, as a woman, than the no doubt worthless creature he had taken up with for a few nights. A young woman of the under-bred and over-photographed class. Lotte knew all about her. She smiled at Richard through her straight eyelashes, without allowing a trace of her jealous discontent and anguish to appear. She had the sense to know that she would get nothing from him in that way. She was disciplined. Richard, she thought, had broken and disciplined her. She meant that she had broken herself, in order not to lose him and her own mind and health. And it had become easy – it was easier now every year.

'I have been dining with Smith.'

'Yes?'

'We discussed whether Eugene Denham is to be trusted.'

'I should have thought – not for a minute,' Lotte said. 'He is a man who can persuade himself of anything.' She waited, and took her courage in her hand. 'Like Frank Hillier. He is like Hillier in that one quality.'

Richard gave her a slow, thoughtful look. 'Have you ever liked Frank?'

'No, never.' She glanced at him with a sharp taunting smile. 'You remember the accident in Switzerland, all those years ago. When he saved you. At the time I almost wished he hadn't.'

'Kind of you, my dear! To be sure, you would have been spared something if he had let go of me. I shouldn't have come back to England, and married you.'

'I thought of you very often at that time. You were the person in my day-dreams. The deliberate day-dreams of a girl of eighteen are not always innocent or gentle, let me tell you. I was jealous of your friendship. When I read the account of the accident, and of Hillier's coolness and his courage, I was furious because he had been given the chance to pose as a hero.'

'He was heroic enough,' Richard said curtly. 'When my foot slipped, and my head struck the ice, I was unconscious. I was a dead weight on the rope. If he had chosen to cut it – what was left of it – he hadn't even to think that I should know what was happening. No one would have known.'

'I believe now,' his wife said, 'that Frank Hillier is capable of any deed, even one involving danger to himself, danger of death, perhaps, if he has been pushed, or has pushed himself, into being obsessed with it. If he can *see* himself doing such things. He will be like a man in a trance.'

'He was certainly not in a trance that day. The Swiss guides congratulated him afterwards on his presence of mind. To this moment, I can't imagine how he managed to bring it off without killing himself too.' He was displeased with her, and spoke with a little scorn.

But *I* can, thought Lotte. He was obsessed with the desire to appear heroic in the eyes of those people, us for instance, who had blamed him for taking so much money and help from Richard. He saw himself a hero and all of us compelled to eat our words and praise and admire him. She could imagine the gleam in his light eyes at the time.

'Well, forgive me,' she said lightly. 'I was jealous. It's a very long time ago.'

'More than twenty years. Half a lifetime,' Richard laughed.

'I hope we shan't die at forty,' said Lotte. She looked at him keenly. 'You can tell me – since it's so many years. I have never, at any time, been to you, in any sense, as much as Frank. Have I?'

'You had no right to ask. It was foolish. I shall not tell you.'

'Are you angry?'

'Not at all.' He smiled at her. He leaned forward, and stroked her arms. She sat very still, defending herself from him, from being moved by him. 'You have pretty arms. They're too thin for you, but I like them.'

'I thought you preferred large white arms. Like Harriet English's lumps of white flesh,' she retorted.

'I like you very much,' Richard laughed. 'Better than anyone in the world. Tongue and all. I wouldn't change you for a fortune.' He swung his legs from the chair and bent across her, half roused, affectionate, smiling into her face.

CHAPTER IV

The newspapers were controlled as in time of war. Two of them had been proscribed. The rest toed the line, to receive their iron ration of news. When a short paragraph, the same in each paper, stated that certain changes were contemplated in the National Volunteer Guard, every reader assumed that he was reading an official announcement. Three days later another paragraph contradicted the first. Between the two there had been unreported meetings of local Volunteer bodies. Resolutions were passed in the old way. There was even some talk of a national petition. News flew about the country, by word of mouth, carried in the motor cars of Volunteer officers, and tucked into the inner pockets of pilots. It was said that the Volunteers were to be disbanded at a week's notice and the men who could not find work sent to the Labour Camps, whether they were married or unmarried. It was said that the Special Guards, the so-called bodyguard, was to be strengthened, its pay raised, and its duties stretched to become a more powerful secret police. In three cities a gale of trouble blew up between the Volunteers and the Special Guards, two men were killed and several wounded. Neither the wireless news nor the papers spoke of any of these things. Nevertheless a great many people knew about them.

It was in this atmosphere of unrest and doubt, scarcely allayed by the second official paragraph, that Sacker went down to Chequers.[51] He was to stay the night, two nights if one were not enough to clear up all that must be cleared up. That at least was Sacker's reading of the invitation.

But when he arrived he found his friend in what was for him an hilarious mood. He would have no serious discussion. With his arm in Sacker's he sauntered about the garden, and talked of the season at Covent Garden, of making Harriet English a Dame of the British Empire, of the past, of Colonel Hebden's new green uniform as a Royal Forester,[52] of any and everything not tainted with politics.

They were alone at lunch. After lunch Hillier excused himself for two or three hours. Richard sat in his room and reflected drily that there had been a time when he would have gripped Hillier's arm and said: 'Now, listen to me.' Why could he not do that now? The change was not in their friendship nor in himself, it was in the other man. Without ceasing to be his friend, to talk to him with an intimacy that was like the past, Hillier managed to erect round himself a curious sense of discomfort when Sacker wished to talk on an awkward subject. The barrier could be knocked down. But what had put it there? Success? The virtue of power?

Sacker fumed for an hour, then went downstairs and sat drinking and weaving plans and conversations until Hillier showed himself. By this time his temper was simmering. He brushed aside an innocent remark, and began:

'Look here, Frank. I want to talk to you about the future of the Volunteers.'

'You always do,' Hillier smiled. 'I never knew a man with so few purposes.'

'The Volunteers were a useful purpose of yours not so long since,' Sacker retorted. He swallowed his anger. He must keep calm now. To lose his temper meant only that he would talk too much, while Hillier listened, soothed him, and said nothing of importance. He had learned that.

'They're useful to me now,' said Hillier gently.

'Then why treat them or allow others to treat them in a way that will end in making them useless, if not a source of danger?'

Hillier looked at him, a slow reflective look. Damn it, I've said too much, thought Richard. I've given him an opening for a speech. He waited. Hillier said nothing.

Richard felt vaguely uncomfortable. 'Is it or is it not true that the Council will propose disbanding half of the Volunteers at once?' he said.

'What the Council may propose is one thing and what is done is not necessarily the same thing.'

'To my knowledge the Council is not in the habit of making unwanted suggestions,' Sacker said.

Hillier bent his head. A rather melancholy look crossed his face. 'You know, Richard,' he said softly, 'you have never given yourself the trouble to wonder whether a Party seeking office and power is in the same position as a Government. You assume, I think for your own convenience, that because you and I could take decisions and enforce them on the Party – because we *were* the Party – that I can behave in exactly the same fashion now, when I am the head of a Council with at least two opinions. There must be some give and take, some form of co-operation.'

'Between Hebden and me? Or between you and Tom Chamberlayn?'

'Between all honest men.'

'God Almighty, if honesty is a matter of opinion, why don't we invite delegates from the Training Camps to give theirs!'

'You're being perverse now,' Hillier smiled.

Sacker felt anger and an impulse of despair. This whole business had become too complex for him, he wanted violent action of some kind, to cut loose, turn the Volunteers loose, smash, destroy. He put his hands on his knees and pressed down, fingers gripping the flesh, to calm himself.

'I must know where I stand,' he said. 'If you're going to turn my men off – ' He stopped, not knowing what to say.

Hillier was looking at him with kindness. 'I'm going to do nothing at any time without your will and approval,' he said.

'You don't expect me to approve your cutting the ground from under your own feet. Where would you have been without the constant backing of the Volunteers? Who would have believed you that you could restore order, stop the riots, if you had not had the men to do it?'

'There are no riots now.'

'There may be.'

'Where? Who will make them?'

Richard said nothing. After a minute, Hillier said gently:

'Before last year – when every kind of subversive element was allowed to work openly in the country – there was need of a body of men, a citizen army, ready first of all to defend the whole nation against the wreckers. Now the need has changed. The army is not needed, but the citizens are. The actual fighting is done. Finished. We've won, we're in charge, you and I. *Now* we need to stabilise. We need peace, security, economy, the co-operation of all honest men. I'm sorry to offend you with that word again!' he said, smiling.

'And the price of co-operation with Chamberlayn is – '

'Don't run away with the idea that your advice has less weight than his.'

Sacker felt the tension in his body relax. He was not deceived. Far from it, he told himself. But now the thought that had been in his mind all along, a thorn, pierced deeper, to the bone. He was certain now that Hillier was morally afraid of the financier, afraid of his influence in the country, of the feeling he could mobilise. But two can play at that game he thought. If *I* mobilise opinion first – what then? He felt a sudden lightness and merriment lifting in him at the prospect of surprising his enemy. He looked directly at Hillier.

'Only ten days ago,' he blurted, 'when you were speaking at the Review, you promised that every man who had fought for the Party should be retained in his position until he reached pension age. It was not a new promise. It is the one you have made for years, again and again.'

'I shall keep it.'

'How?'

Hillier was standing up now. He came round the table, and rested his arm on

Richard's. It was a caress.

'We can decide it together.' He paused. His voice rose a tone from its deep note. 'And now, my dear. Fred Hebden is driving over for dinner. Try not to argue with him. He's been – unwell.'

How I should grieve if he became so unwell that he died of it, Richard thought. He shook his head. 'I'll behave myself.'

In fact the argument that broke out towards the end of the long meal was less his fault than that of the other man. He drank himself into a good temper, and kept it up for a time. But Hebden was either unable or unwilling to keep his distaste for Sacker's company within bounds. He was deliberately rude and abrupt. He looked ill. His skin was a dark greyish yellow, his lips pinched, his eyes fixed and staring. At moments he clattered his fork against his plate as though his hands were not in his control. He spoke in a low voice to Hillier, raising it, with a subtle suggestion of command, as though the other man were a servant, when he had to speak to Sacker. For the time Richard ignored it.

As for Hillier, he sat between the two men, his closest friends and supporters, like Alice between the Red Queen and the White. Or a woman between two admirers. He gave a soft, almost an ingratiating turn to his voice and manner. He was easy, smiling with a slow self-satisfaction, affectionate.

He told them the story of his visit to the headquarters of the National Service Women. Their commandant, an elderly woman with the face of a sly horse – curious how so many old families develop the facial characteristics of animals, as if by a devolutionary process of some sort, or it may be Nature having her little joke – booted to her knees and above that breeched and belted round her ample stomach, led him up and down the lines of women standing rigidly at attention. As he approached them he was struck by the extraordinary appearance of a line of women in uniform, their female hips swelling out behind and their breasts pouting in front. The slender women were the least laughable, naturally, but even they presented, as it were from the shadow cast by the others, the comical effect of a parade of penguins in clothes.

'Something will have to be done about it,' he laughed. 'I can't answer for my dignity if I have to attend any more of these shows.'

Richard roared with laughter. The comment he made was a natural one. Hebden cut it short by rapping on the table.

'Too much mummery altogether,' he said curtly. 'Women, and amateur soldiers – I'd wipe up the whole mess if I had my way.'

Sacker felt his anger rising in him again. It was like a rod thrust into him, he felt it in his stomach and his throat. He saw Hillier look earnestly at him, and took no notice.

'I suppose you don't include the Special Guards in that definition,' he said.

'No. I do not,' said Hebden. But as if his words had given him some relief, his voice became nearly conciliatory. 'I don't think you've considered one thing, Sacker. That is the imminence of war. There is certainly going to be war in Europe, whether Germany moves south into the Danube countries, or east against the Soviet. And we are not going to keep out of it. How can we? And why should we?'

'I don't see that this allows you to insult the Volunteers.'

'Why talk of insults?' Hillier said softly.

'I'm not insulting anyone,' said Hebden. 'But wars are fought by regular troops and with new, that is, costly arms, aeroplanes, poison gas, incendiary shells. It all costs enormous sums of money. Then how on earth can one justify the spending another million on an army which is useless for war?' He spoke calmly. 'That's all.'

'It's enough,' Hillier said, rising. 'I've had a hard week. I didn't expect to spend my weekend in argument.' The other two had risen with him. He spoke coldly to Hebden. 'You kept your car? Or shall I have one brought up? It doesn't matter.'

Whatever Hebden's feelings were, he swallowed them. He nodded to Sacker when he left, and Hillier walked with him to the door and bade him a smiling good-night. He came back to the windows.

'A lovely night,' he said, half sadly. 'I should like a walk.'

'Shall I come with you?'

'Do, Richard.'

The night was warm and cloudy, with the feeling of rain in the tepid air. The leaves of the trees were turned for rain. At a short distance searchlights from an aerodrome built up a curious scaffolding of light on the clouds, a modern Jacob's ladder. Richard pointed to it.

'They say we've destroyed a great deal, pulling down old houses, and turning lanes into motor roads. But so long as we can do that sort of thing I don't see why anyone should complain.'

'I have a dream in which I am a serf of some sort, in another century,' Hillier said. 'I seem to be working in an immense field, far out of sight of the lord's house or castle, or whatever it is. He has never heard of me. I am unknown, lost, a speck crawling slowly along the furrows for ever, as long as I live.'

'Damned silly dream,' Richard said.

He repressed a boisterous longing to shout, or clap his friend on the back. But he could not help humming, and he walked with a slight swagger that let out a little of his energy and sense of triumph.

'I thought it might be a way in which my mind relieves itself of a burden.'

'What burden? What's worrying you?'

'The burden of being a leader,' Hillier said, in a simple voice. 'The awful responsibility. To know that everything depends on me. On me alone. If I died to-night what would happen? The country would be plunged back into doubt and confusion. No one would feel safe. None would *be* safe. It would be like it was two years ago, hopelessness, unemployment and fear of unemployment on one side, and wild promises and fears on the other. It would be worse than that, because men have grown used to thinking that now someone is in charge. Me. They rely on me. To think for them. To find the way out. And there is no one to follow me.'

'You should marry, and bring up a son,' Richard said, smiling in the darkness. No song in his head seemed appropriate to the conversation, and his humming became soundless, the monotonous repetition of a single line – *Roll along, sister Susy, roll along.*

'I have a feeling against marriage. It's scarcely intellectual – only an instinct – that for me to marry would be an anti-climax of some sort. Besides – one can't ensure sons,' he laughed. 'You have never had one.'

'Mine died that night.'

'Yes, you came that night. I shan't forget it.'

Roll along, sister Susy, roll along. 'It was the only thing I could do. I couldn't have left you in the cart at that moment,' said Richard. He remembered his excitement when he was hurrying to join Hillier, but he had forgotten what Lotte had said and what he had felt in leaving her. *Roll along.*

They turned to go back, and Hillier put his arm in Sacker's. He leaned on him and yawned. It seemed that he had nothing further to say, but he walked more and more slowly and dragged on the other man's arm, almost as though he were an old man. He seemed to need the assurance of personal touch, and when the path made walking side by side difficult he still held on, putting all his weight on Sacker. He has grown heavier during the last years, thought Sacker: heavier or older. He shortened his steps to suit his friend's slow ones, and to distract his mind and keep from humming aloud he watched the searchlights turning over and down, like the spokes of a wheel entering the earth.

CHAPTER V

When we returned to London in the second week of June, I went directly to see Tower. I had had no excuse to go earlier, since Smith and Richard had concluded that he was useless to them at this, perhaps at any stage of their schemes. But now he had invited me to come and see him. I went eagerly.

He was wearing the same jacket with the hole in the pocket. He saw me glance at it, and said ruefully: 'You wouldn't think how I did that. I put my pipe in my pocket one day when I got onto a bus, and after a few minutes my jacket burst into flames. The tobacco had been alight.'

Some attempt had been made to clear up the room since I was there, but books were already stealing back into all sorts of unlawful places, and an old boot had found its way on to the desk, where it was on duty keeping down the leaves of a folio. I looked round for its fellow but did not see it. Perhaps he had lost it.

'I've been thinking about Miss Burtt,' he began at once. 'What we can do about her. Merely to say that she's in Winchell won't do any good. They'd move her and invite us to come and look. Far the best thing would be for you to go back to Norway and form a committee, it doesn't matter what you call it, the Happy Folklorists if you like, to award an international prize. Your first award is to Miss Sophie Burtt, and then the hue and cry begins. Where is Sophie Burtt? We're betting on the chance that the proper authority would like to *discover* her, and set her free with apologies for the regrettable mistake, even at the cost of having her publish what she's seen. She can only do it abroad. And you remember what little lasting effect tales of German concentration camps had in other countries. People tire so soon of stories of suffering. Don't you think it's a very good idea?'

He looked at me with sly pleasure, waiting to be praised for his ingenuity.

'It's as good as anything else,' I said. 'We'll try it.'

'Oh. Can you think of anything better?'

I hurried to assure him without a lie that I could not. We talked for a moment of the other well-known writers; the three including Charles Dalton who were found to prefer the new régime, one because he had principles and the other two because they had none; the few in exile; the rest living uneasily at home.

'We don't persecute writers,' Tower said. 'In the first place because we have no respect for them, and in the second because it is much easier to starve them out by a censorship. Poor Sophie Burtt is the exception.'

I wondered whether he knew about the grumbling among the Volunteers. I asked him. Yes, he knew as much as I did.

'Do you notice something else?' he said. 'More significant. People in London are growing very bad-tempered. They scowl at you and snarl in the buses if you stumble against them. They're impatient and rude. There's a nervous tension. As though they were expecting a blow, or a danger of some sort.'

'I hadn't noticed it,' I said.

'Ah, I do,' he said, rather sadly. 'London is different. It used to be a friendly place.'

'Well, what is in the air?'

'It could be anything. The beginning of disillusion – sure to begin in the cities among restless and sophisticated men. One helping cause of Hillier's success has been men's need for an absolute faith. Something in which they can believe, in the breakdown of churches and all the airy fairy notions of progress and innate goodness and the rest. Men are innately nothing except weak.'

'You think that only disillusion is in the air?'

'Only disillusion! You're much younger than I am.' He knocked his pipe testily against the leg of the table, so that the ash flew everywhere. 'It could be something definite, of course. If anyone or any group of men were plotting a change, the premonition of it would be enough to disturb the highly charged air of a city.'

He looked at me kindly. It was on the end of my tongue to tell him that Smith, Denham, and Richard were – plotting was much too definite a word for their business. But I had no authority to open it to him. Would it have made any difference, for him, if I had spoken then? I shall never know. It is one of the doubts that will plague me to my last day.

'What is going to happen to this country?' I said.

I felt that if any man knew, he did. Oh, he was the greatest man in England. His mind carried a light into the tomb of knowledge. I shall never know such another.

'How can I tell you? I could draw a convincing parallel with the decline of Rome. There are many likenesses – the vast area of the old empire, the different nationalities it covered, and the standardised Roman culture taken everywhere with the conquerors. A Roman in Gaul did not go native any more than an Englishman in India or Africa may. There was world trade, too – Greek wine, British oysters, corn from Egypt and Spain: trade with India and China, trade routes through Mespot[53] and Turkestan, and a permanent fleet running between the Red Sea and Malabar. The decline begins in the third century, a hundred and fifty years before the barbarian invasions. We have to guess a little at the causes. But these were among them. A bad fiscal system, heavy taxation to cover the immense expenditure on armaments, that is, to guard the frontiers, and to provide doles and jubilees for the city populations. The small farmer was ruined by the taxes. The rigidification of classes. You have it here in the strata landlord-tenant-labourer, of which the lowest stratum can never rise. And in the new class of unskilled town worker which is smothering the old skilled artisan class, and can never move into the new hierarchy of technician. Race suicide. The Roman middle class, like the English and the American, was unwilling to breed, under the pressure of the taxes. Under the other worse pressure of fearing and not knowing, the uncertainty of the future; the sense of the abyss. The increase of disease, malaria with them, with us cancer and nervous illness, true maladies of anxiety and artificial living. The ruin of farming. The break-up of the empire into separate units, with interests which could become inimical to each other. Autarchies as now, and then the trade decline. The widening of the gulf between the few rich and the many poor. People were losing heart. They became hopeless of finding any solution. You have cautious elder statesmen waiting for a miracle, and impatient careerists. It took a long time for Rome to break up, and even then you had something left. Dreaming on. Cologne was destroyed twice, and still it shows the Roman street plan. And that's very interesting, and very delusive. To my mind it is delusive.'

He was prowling about the room, poking books out of shelves and dropping them.

'Have you lost something, sir?' I asked.

'No, no.' He sat down, but it was only for a minute. He was up again, rolling up and down the long room, scattering matches and ash. His coat was rumpled up about him. His face wore an air of shrewd, serene interest, bright-eyed and yet absent. His mind was more present than he was.

'Shan't we decline?'

'I have never known what is meant by decline,' he said, smiling at me slyly. 'You and I will decline. I have declined by several years more than you have.'

'But England. Europe.'

'Faiths decline, you know, and men live by faith. They live by putting boots on their books, too. I wonder where the devil the left one is. The decline of the faith that held Europe together began with the Renaissance. There was then a spiritual government, which all men acknowledged, though they did not all obey – nor at all times. You know what became of that, and what has become of the forces that rose against it and undermined it. Like maggots, they are devouring the world that engendered them. But the pattern was there before the carpet; it lasts, and what one generation sees lapsing and falling into disorder another restores, in another way. You can't have the mediaeval church back, but you can have something else. In my not too humble view, the successor to the old spiritual empire is the new one of international socialism. The new Messiah, like the old, is a common man. If I call myself a Christian it is something more to me than going on my knees in a church. I have been to church sometimes, you know. Chiefly to please an old friend, but partly for the assurance of – of continuity.'

His eyes twinkled. 'Have you heard me called a subverter of authority?'

'Yes,' I answered truthfully. 'And more than once.'

'Well, the truth in it is that I advise young men not to put their trust in earthly leaders, but to cling to the one true faith. That is, the eternal infallible debt of man to man. Not one man is greater than others, but only as all are reflected in him. A new idea, a new invention, has its roots in common minds. Beside this, I keep up a correspondence with men in other countries, with as many as possible. We do not know very much of the future. But we must keep a few of the channels cleared. I hope in time, when I lose my job at the university – and that won't be long, you know – to make something a little more definite out of it. Perhaps no more than a skeleton frame stretched across the world. Web joining one man of good will to the next. You think that's only dry bones? Well, there can be a wind to breathe life even into dry bones. The skeleton can cover itself with flesh, and sluice itself in the fountain of blood. What do you think?'

'I think,' I stammered. 'I think – do you believe in that?'

'Oh, I believe, I believe,' he said.

'You ought not to stay in London,' I blurted. 'You'd be safer abroad. Couldn't you come to Norway, sir? The university at Oslo would gladly have you. I know it's small, and nothing like the scope you have here, but you could be sure of continuing your work, in peace.' In safety, was definitely what I meant then. I had a dreadful sense of urgency. It was like, a little like, the sense of danger in sleep.

'Dear me, that's very kind,' he said carelessly. 'But what on earth should I do there?'

'Teach,' I said. I had a distinct vision of him – small, as if I were looking at it from a height – walking across the mosaic of coloured stones in front of the university. He came from between the trees, crossing Karl Johansgaten in sunshine. 'You could be safe there.'

'I'm not in danger,' he said, slowly. 'Or if I am, it's nothing to make a fuss about. What is coming, comes. One has only to keep quiet.'

He laughed to himself, in his chuckling way. '*I* can't run about from place to place. Do you know, I hate travelling. I forget which train I'm going on and I leave things behind and have to write for them. An awful nuisance.'

CHAPTER VI

My sister was unwell these days, sleepless, irritable. Her face looked sallow, and pinched at the nostrils. Only when she laughed she was herself, awkward and quick-witted, as ignorantly reckless as a schoolgirl beneath her years of experience of life. The experiences gave her a look of authority, which fitted her small thickened body better than the clothes she dragged round it.

She disliked London. She had no feeling for the softnesses of living, and was happier in the discomfort of the Yorkshire house, working with Annie, than she could ever be in London, with a staff of servants, her own bathroom, and a woman to brush her hair and lay out her clothes.

I found her this afternoon, reading Charles Dalton's new novel, her cheek on her hand. When I came in, she closed the book with a sigh. 'So nicely written, about an old house in nice country, and a family which has lived in it for centuries – and so dull, dull, empty, *worthless*. How can he go on doing it?'

'Because he takes care not to enquire into anything,' I laughed. 'He knows that curiosity killed the cat, and he enjoys his saucer of cream and his cushion.'

'Where is Richard?'

'I think with Smith. Perhaps Denham.'

Her forehead wrinkled with the old discontent and doubt. 'Nothing but a disappointment will come of it,' she said; 'He will give Hillier an excuse to dismiss him, and that will be the end. Have you ever thought what would happen to us if Richard loses his job? He'll be forty next year, and the only thing he is fit for is soldiering. *I* could grow old happily in the country, digging a potato patch.' She looked at me with a sharp smile. 'But I wouldn't change him. I don't idealise him at all, Andy. He's as useless to the world as that wretched book – a pure waste of energy. But to have lived with his energy all one's married life, to have been angry, hurt, tired, but never bored. If I were a good woman I ought to hate him. Instead of hating, I let him do as he likes. I'm not a Jael.'[54]

She broke off as Ernest came into the room. He was vaguely embarrassed and in a hurry. He hung over her, and smiled, with his young half-ironic self-confidence. He had come to tell her that he had no money and he wanted to take Steffy out to dinner. She gave him a pound note. He kissed her, and went away at once, without even the polite pretence that he had come to see her.

'Is he going to marry that girl?' I asked.

'I suppose so. I hope so. Steffy's kind and unexacting. She won't mind very much when he forgets her for days at a time. She's complete in herself.'

'Now I come to think of it, they're both remarkably self-assured young persons,' I exclaimed. 'No respect for their elders, and no sense of duty to them. Steffy neglects her father and Ernest only asks you for money.'

'Thank God for it,' my sister said. 'I'd cut every single emotional attachment between the generations, if I had my way. Let them be separate, let them think only of themselves. It's the proper way. Let us have done with all the clinging of the old to the young and the young being reluctantly sorry and responsible for the old. If Ernest wants money, or if he's in trouble, he turns to me, and when he's happy he forgets me. That's as it should be.'

'Is he ambitious?' I asked.

'Yes. In an impersonal way. If we lived in a decent society, he'd be working in a testing shop on his designs for a new aeroplane engine. No one would blame him if they were a failure, and if they were a success he'd hand them in and go on to something else. Steffy, too, has no ambitions for herself. I can see her in charge of a nursery of a hundred children, thinking as much of the ninety-nine others as of her own lamb. I'm sure there are more like them. I daresay they've been born too soon, before society is fit for them.'

'A society made by Hillier, Hebden, and Richard is fit for nobody but adventurers and opportunists,' I said. I felt an extraordinary bitterness. The beauty of trees and grass outside the windows was darkened by it. As I watched, it was darkened by a tangible shadow, flitting across the grass. I looked out and saw a small aeroplane gliding towards the landing roof above St. Dunstan's. The afternoon sun caught its wings, turning them to a glory of silver. It seemed as transparent as glass. In my mind it was part of a flight of seagulls over water and a rock in Norway, the wings flashing silver against the sky and the shadow following below, dark on the water and the rock.

Lotte had said nothing. 'I am sorry if I hurt you,' I said.

'You don't hurt me. I agree with you about them.'

'They'll bring us all down. England. Europe.'

'Sometimes I think we tried for too much,' Lotte said. 'We set up ideals, of sexual purity and social sympathy. Even when they were being ignored, by men who only wanted money or power, and by stupid, greedy, complacent women, even then we kept them held up, as marvellous shining ideals. And people did sacrifice to them. I used to know a man whose life and mind were consumed by his passion for international peace. And do you know, Andy, such purity is somehow repellent. I used to look at him – he was good-looking, but so thin, and as dry as a bone – and feel repelled. Yet I approved of every word he said. And now it is as if the others, the Hilliers and Hebdens, and yes, Richard, had got loose, to rage and destroy us. After we had tried to preach them down.'

'You can't preach to wild beasts. You can only exterminate them.'

'And what then?'

'And if they do the exterminating? Don't let's talk about it,' I said. 'Let me take you out to dinner. To balance your accounts.'

My sister smiled at me sweetly.

'Dear Andy. I'm very fond of you. I wish I hadn't deserted you when you were a schoolboy. I always felt guilty about that.'

'You needn't,' I said.

'Do something for me now. I'm too tired to go out. But I want *you* to make an excuse to call on Richard's flame, Harriet English. You can do it.'

'Why on earth?' I began, astonished.

Lotte began to talk volubly, persuading herself. Harriet was Chamberlayn's mistress or his future wife, or both. She knew what was intended for Richard, if he were to be given other work in exchange for his Volunteers, if Hillier would protect him. His schemes, and Smith's, were futile, and we must prepare ourselves. In short, she fairly pushed me out of the house on this ridiculous mission, which I had no hope of carrying out. To please her, I rang up Harriet. I asked her to let me see her 'before I returned to Oslo.' It was six o'clock. She invited me to come round to her hotel at once, to drink a glass of sherry.

I found her alone. She was charming to me. I suppose she was used, as a famous person, to visits like mine. We talked of art, and books. Her opinion of Dalton's novels was as low as Lotte's. 'Emotional diarrhoea,' was her compact phrase for them.

'But what can you expect,' I said cautiously, 'under a censorship? Writers must have perfect freedom.'

She gave me a very sharp glance, as direct as a man's. Brown eyes are not supposed to show intelligence, but hers had a searching and intimidating depth.

'I detest communism,' she said. 'To avoid that, I'm prepared to put up with a great many disagreeable things. Even to read Charles Dalton.'

'You don't think there's a middle course?'

'Of course not. Not at this stage.' She looked directly into my face again. 'If anyone were to disturb, or undermine, the present security, he would be a social danger. He would have to be stopped, ruthlessly.'

My only genuine talent is for the receiving of unuttered messages. I felt perfectly certain now that she was expecting Richard to give trouble. She could not know anything. She was going by her knowledge of his nature and instincts. I wanted to ask her whether she had discussed him with Chamberlayn, but no form of words covered the impudence of the question. Just as I had opened my mouth, to make a neutral retort, the door opened and Chamberlayn himself walked in.

He came forward with his kind smile. He kissed Harriet's hand, and said to me:

'This is an unexpected pleasure, Mr. Hillier.' He laughed gently. 'I think I shall call you Mr. Andrew, to avoid confusion.'

'Call me anything you like,' I said. 'I was just going.' I rose.

'Now that is a pity,' he said. 'We have never had a quiet talk yet. We must meet some day when you have time to spare.'

'That will be very pleasant.'

I looked at Harriet to take my leave. She held out her hand, but instead of releasing mine at once she kept hold of it, dragging slightly on my arm, so that I was forced to bend over her in a strained, awkward attitude.

'I want you to take a message for me,' she said rapidly. 'I don't know your sister, and I should like to. Will you tell her that? Tell her I am sorry we have never been friends and that if she will come to see me or let me come to her, it would give me – much happiness.'

'Me, too,' Thomas Chamberlayn said. 'I like your sister. My dear Harriet, you always say the right thing.' He smiled at her, seated looking like a gnome in a frock coat on the very edge of the wide couch. His smile was kind and sly. It was difficult to feel about him that he was a financial or any other power. And yet – the impression of kindly inquisitive dullness I had formed of him at our first meeting had faded completely. I had begun already to find him very curious, and difficult. The epithet 'robber' applied to him by the French banker seemed less inapt. If he robs, I thought, he will do it neatly, high-mindedly, and without the least roughness.

In the entrance hall downstairs I brushed against Maurice Gardner, the critic. He remembered me, and came forward with a very friendly smile. His friendliness warmed me. He was on his way to call on Harriet, but when he heard that Chamberlayn was with her, he turned away. We walked out of the hotel together. Somehow, I don't recall how, we found ourselves drinking coffee together, and growing confidential.

'I wanted to see you again,' he said.

'Yes?'

He seemed embarrassed. Stirring his coffee with energy, and with his face averted, he said:

'I felt the other night that you and I hold the same views about what is going on.'

'What is going on?' I asked.

His rather sallow face lengthened. 'Nothing pleasant. It was not too comfortable a few years ago, with – do you remember the petition sent formally from one of the derelict areas? – *Shoot us and pension our women.* But now, when such a thing couldn't happen – and yet one knows that the men *are* hopeless and the children *are* hungry still. And the feeling of worse things than that going on. That we don't hear about. Do you suppose there's any truth in these tales one hears of floggings in the Training Camps?'

'I know it's true about some of them,' I said. I told him about Winchell, and described the marks on Holman's body. He turned pale.

'Oh my God,' he said to himself. 'It must be stopped.'

'How do you propose to stop it? Complain to the police? They have no authority over the Camps, even if you assume they want to interfere. And why should they? The men in those Camps are nearly all men who wanted to overturn society, one way or another.'

'The Prime Minister doesn't know that such things are done.'

'He could know if he chose,' I said. 'He doesn't choose. Let not your right hand know what your left hand is murdering. He wouldn't thank you for putting trouble on to him.'

'But you're not reconciled to cruelties?' he exclaimed.

'No more than you are.'

It was myself I was tormenting, not him. My own powerlessness in the face of a society organised to keep misery within bounds and decently inarticulate.

'Are you prepared to risk making trouble about it?' I said. 'They'll call you unbalanced or destructive, or a socialist. You'll lose your job, if that's the worst that happens to you.'

'I'm not a socialist.'

'No. Nor I.'

We finished our coffee, and parted. Our sudden intimacy had withered, and it seemed that we had no longer anything to say to each other. Neither of us felt easy in the presence of the other uneasy and defeated creature. If we meet again, I thought, we shall take care to discuss Dalton's novels, or Elizabethan music. We shall turn over some lovely perfect thing in our hands, and feel thankful for it. We shall cover our eyes and stop our ears with its perfection. There is much in life that we can be thankful for – if we are not workless, or half hungry, or young men without a future, or women worn with early toil, or child forlornly asleep in a slum bedroom.

CHAPTER VII

For the first time all three men, Smith, Eugene Denham, and George Body, met together in Sacker's house. They had dined together, with Lotte at the head of the table, and afterwards withdrawn to the small room in an angle of the first floor, which Richard called his office. Its one window looked over Regent's Park and the water. It contained a day bed, a table, Richard's desk, and half a dozen chairs. In one corner was a cupboard with a tiny window, a sink and a tap. The room and the cupboard had been snipped off a large drawing-room for some purpose of the original owner of the old house. Sacker had a curious fondness for it, and resisted all his wife's efforts to move him to a more convenient place.

The day had been the hottest of the year. There was no breath of wind, the trees were as still as if they were painted on the colourless sky. People lay relaxed on the grass. Even the dirty infants who make their way to the park from the stews of Paddington and Marylebone were too listless to give trouble to the shrewish little girls responsible for their safe conduct between slum and canal.

No air came into the room. After a few minutes Sacker took off his coat and sat in his shirt sleeves. The others, except Body, did the same. Though he was so hot that he was melting, Body could not bring himself to such a disregard of convention. He had spent too many of his early years in shirt sleeves, you may say.

A tray, with decanters, glasses, and syphons, was placed on the table, but only Richard touched the whisky. The other three kept on helping themselves to soda water. There was an air of undress even about their conversation. The heat made coherence very difficult.

Denham was in a mood to lecture the others, as though he were in a seminar. Tilting his chair back, he composed his hands, rolled his eyes almost out of sight, and gave them his views on events past, present and to come. Smith sat with bent head, his fine sensitive face almost vacant. The fixed smile lifting his nostrils could equally well be politeness or boredom. Richard yawned and fidgeted. Only George Body listened with rigid interest. He had the habit of it from his youth in a political party which loves to hear itself speak.

'As I see it,' Denham said, dictatorially, 'we have gone to a great deal of trouble only to place certain financial interests more firmly in the saddle. Where at one time they had to persuade or outwit a number of persons to do their will, now they need only convince one, or at most two. We have really saved them a great deal of trouble by muffling the House of Commons and the press and leaving them only the Council to manage.'

He took out a large white silk handkerchief and wiped his forehead. Richard watched him, with the concentration a certain amount of drink invariably gave him. He was used to allowing men to talk their guts out, to quote his own words, in the expectation that they would afterwards act as he wished. But Denham's capacity for talk seemed bottomless. He'll go on talking while we act, Richard decided. Then he'll come to us and say, Didn't I always tell you, you were right?

Without moving his head, he glanced round at Smith. The soldier's vague meaningless smile no longer irritated him as it would have done once. He recognised that it was Smith's cover for his thoughts. He smiles and I drink, Sacker said to himself. But the whisky had become a necessity to him. He could not work or think without it.

Body had lifted up his voice during one of Denham's pauses for breath. He had only one thing to say, but he was determined to say it.

'The Trades Unions must be revived,' he said. 'They have had their lesson.' He repeated it. 'They have had their lesson.'

His mind yearned over the obscure hard-working officials, secretaries of branches and the like, whose life was bound up with their work. How loyal they were, and persistent, one in faith, one in hope, and one in charity with the men whose cause they tried to serve. Some of these had written him bitter ill-judged letters when he joined the National State Party. They were not one in charity with him any longer. Dear me, no. But they would be. Once they understood, once he had spoken to them and put plainly to them the terrible dilemma of the man who must put his country above his class, above all that narrow futile bitterness, they would listen to him again. They would believe in him. And in return he would give them back their power and pride. With a vague wide gesture, as if he were opening his umbrella over the whole dejected multitude of them, he invited them to come in out of the rain and be warm and snug again inside.

'We must put the machine on the road again,' he murmured. 'We've gone too far in one direction. We must get back. The old ways are best.'

Smith looked at him quickly with an absent kindliness. His smile wavered, and spread to his bright quick eyes. He arched his fine eyebrows.

'But of course,' he said, gently. 'I am all for a more liberal attitude. I don't like this dictatorial atmosphere and methods. It doesn't suit us. We're used to compromise and argument, and the next best thing. In government as in other things, *Le meilleur c'est l'ennemi du bon.*[55] Eh, Body? Don't you agree?'

'Certainly, certainly,' said Body. He thought the General was giving him a Latin quotation and wished for the thousandth time that he had had a better education. He had sent his own son to Harrow and Cambridge, and it was not his fault if the boy could not bandy quotations with the best. He felt a little melancholy.

'Then you think that the time may be ripe for some, let us say, gesture?' said Denham. He had brought his pale eyes from the back to the front of his head again. He fixed them on Smith's face, as though he were seeking to disconcert him.

Smith smiled again, with a little sadness. 'You mustn't go too fast,' he said politely. 'Any very sudden step might have the worst effects. Before making any move – however discreet – it is as well to be sure that you have the sympathy of the services, the Army and the Air Force. I'm sure you – '

'But you are not suggesting anything violent?' George Body said hurriedly.

'Good heavens, no, my dear fellow. But suppose, let us just suppose, for the sake of a hypothesis, that the annual general manoeuvres of the Volunteers near London were taking place at the same time that something in the nature, I only say in the nature, of a general strike, broke on us. And then if the Volunteers announced their sympathy with the objects of the strike – it would be, would it not, let us say infinitely preferable that the soldiers and the Air Force should feel a friendly neutrality towards both? Don't you think so?'

Body nodded in a bewildered way. He was so hot that he thought he would have to go. He saw Denham rise suddenly and leave the room, and with an automatic longing for relief he followed him.

Left alone, Richard and Smith looked at each other. Smith lifted his fine nose slightly as though he were sniffing something. Perhaps he smelled a politician. Richard went to the tap in the cupboard and ran off a glass of water, and swallowed it. He came back into the room and stood, swaying gently, with his thumbs in his belt.

'Friendly neutrality,' he echoed. 'Friendly — is all we shall get from those two. We shall have to move alone, when we do move. Don't you think so?' He mimicked Smith's voice.

'Oh, I don't know,' Smith said vaguely, smiling. 'You and I can't direct strikes, you know!'

He went away a few minutes later. At parting, he squeezed George Body's hand and said in a light gentle voice:

'We must meet again, my dear Body. We have much in common.'

He left. Body and Denham went soon after him, and Sacker was left alone.

But not for many minutes. The telephone on the desk rang, and when he took it up he heard Hillier's voice, inviting, no, entreating him to come as soon as he could and talk to him for an hour. Richard looked at the clock on the desk. Half-past eleven.

'I'll come now. What's the matter with you?'

'Nothing at all,' Hillier's voice answered softly. 'Only this awful infernal heat. I can't sleep, and I have to travel and make a speech to-morrow.'

'I'll come.'

'Good chap.'

Richard stood with bent head for a moment, thinking rapidly. He decided that there was nothing at all in the incident. But he felt a queer repressed triumph. It was still to him that Hillier turned when he needed relaxation and rest. Not to Hebden, or any other. No, he'll never let me down, he thought. Never.

He had the big open car brought round, the car he used in the country, and drove it himself. The slight breeze of the motion cooled his face and hands, and exhilarated him. He drove recklessly along Oxford Street and stopped with a screech of his brakes at the Circus. A policeman came up to the car to deal with him, but stepped back when he saw who it was, and saluted. 'Have a heart at the crossings, sir,' he said, smiling.

'God bless you, I will,' Richard answered.

If I could drive straight on, he thought, down the Duke of York's steps – I'll try it one night. When he drew up at the house the door was opened before he had left the car. 'Where is the Prime Minister?' he asked. He noticed, as he noticed every such detail, that the usual four of the bodyguard standing about in the hall had been increased to ten. The young man Eckhart was with them, as usual.

Hillier was in his bedroom, and writing at the desk in the middle of the room. He put his pen down and smiled eagerly when his friend came in. His hand moved heavily to his head in a gesture of fatigue.

'Come in, my dear, sit down. I hope I didn't interrupt a party.'

'No, I was alone,' Richard answered. He drew his chair under the lamp and sat down with knees wide apart and his hands resting on them. 'Are you ill?'

'Not in the least. Only tired out. And I've been sleeping badly. That's new for me. I suppose I could take something, but I have a horror of drugs.'

'Well. I'll sit here all night if you like,' said Richard. He was wide awake and watchful. His eyes took in the room – books, books, a photograph of himself, a bronze head of the great Duke of Wellington. Hillier made the most of a slight resemblance between himself and the Iron Duke, but his features, for all their slenderness, were coarser and blunter, and his head narrower.

'Would you like a drink?'

'Have you anything here? All right. I don't want anything.'

Hillier moved to an arm-chair and let himself loll forward in it. His arms hung down over the sides.

'We were better off in the past, you know, Richard,' he said, in a warm, quiet voice. 'Our trouble then was to get time to sleep, not to sleep when we lay down. Upon my soul, there are times when I wish we were still running about the country, talking our heads off. And marches. And holding endless conferences about the funds. As I look back, life was much simpler then.'

'You shouldn't look back,' Richard said. 'No sensible man looks back.'

'Yet I've heard you telling stories,' said Hillier. He smiled a little sharply, his face lifted, and bloodless in the yellow light from the lamp.

'That's another matter. But when it comes to regretting anything, why, I never do. When a woman says to me, But you promised you would never leave me, I say, That was yesterday.' He laughed gently.

'Happy man,' his friend smiled. 'But you haven't a whole country on your mind. One trusting woman is easier disposed of.'

'What's on your mind?'

'Nothing but the eternal difficulty. How to keep things straight now we've started them going straight, how to prevent idealists without facts and factual men without ideals from running their heads together and splintering me between them. In short, how to make men obedient without destroying them for our purposes.'

'*Our* purposes?' said Richard, looking at him without lifting his eyelids.

'Yours and mine are the same in the end,' Hillier said. 'We both wanted to save the country from being destroyed by the socialists – I don't between ourselves say they're all scoundrels, but I do say they're fools. And if I find ways to do it, I can count on your supporting me. Can't I?'

'I've never let you down yet, have I?' Richard said quickly.

'No, that's true.'

'Then why should I – ?' He debated a moment with himself, then thought, Better let him have it. 'If you're going to ask me again to disband the Volunteers, I can't do it. You'll have to do it over my head. And if you want to do that – ' He made the gesture of turning down his thumbs, his face almost blank.

'Now what does that mean?' Hillier smiled.

Richard felt an anger rising in him, which he could scarcely control. He was afraid – afraid to quarrel with the other man. He no longer knew where he stood with him. Hillier watched him. A nearly indulgent smile came on his face.

'Listen to me,' he said, softly and persuasively. 'You know I want nothing for myself.' (That's not true, Richard thought; you've always wanted to be liked.) 'If

I ask other people to obey it's because I'm obeying something myself. The idea of England – England becoming great again. It's because of *that* that I have the right to ask men to obey blindly, like good soldiers.'

'I don't see how you make England great by turning my men off into the streets and the Labour Camps,' Richard growled. He was utterly uninterested in this theory of the omnipotent State. If he had ever pretended to be interested it was because he saw it as the excuse for his Volunteers. But now they had created it he expected it to support them. Tit for tat, like a game.

'We have neither time nor money for idealist ways if England is to be made strong. Just as we have no money to pull down every slum in the country – as we said we would – until we have made ourselves secure in the world. Security first, and idealism afterwards.'

Richard looked at him with a wide smile, sharp and malicious. 'And the voice was the voice of Chamberlayn,' he said.

A glint came into Hillier's pale eyes, it could be a rising flame of anger, or only pleasure in hearing his own voice. He went on speaking gently.

'You will persist in talking as though Thomas Chamberlayn dictated to me. Let me tell you that he has never tried it, and if he did I should know how to put him down. *He* is not the master of this country. The National State Council is that, and I am the elected head of the Council.' His voice changed, becoming as coaxing as a woman's. 'I shan't give either of us the trouble of going over this again. But one last word, my dear. Will you trust me?'

'How am I to trust you?' Richard said slowly.

'Not to do, or say, anything that spoils your position in the country. Your dignity is quite safe with me. Do trust me, Richard.'

Richard sat and looked at him with a tense alert quietness.

'What the devil do you think I care about my dignity?' he said, quietly. 'I'm not a dowager. Or Hebden. Or yourself. I only care about the men who've trusted me – and you because I taught them to trust you. It's not a month since you repeated your promises to them. Not a month.'

Hillier looked steadily into his eyes, as though he were hurt, hurt and grieved. 'I'm not going to disband the Volunteers,' he said. 'Only to weed out the least efficient. With your help. Do you imagine I want to break a promise, or disappoint a single man? But if sacrifices, for the country, are necessary, then everyone must be willing to make his. Beginning at the top with you and me.'

'You'd like to keep the men on? If it weren't for the money?'

'Yes,' Hillier said, as if reluctantly. He added: 'And the certainty in responsible circles that the money could be better spent. I'd like to pull down the slums, too.'

Richard had been sitting with his hands between his thighs. Suddenly he slapped both hands on his knees. He laughed. 'Trust *me*,' he said. 'Trust me, I'll get you out of this.' He jumped up and rested a hand on his friend's shoulder. 'What did I say? Never look back, eh?'

Hillier looked up at him with his faint smile.

CHAPTER VIII

On June the eighteenth Sacker left London, meaning to be away six days. He was making a round tour of inspection of the Volunteers. Their force in the country (1,600,000 men) was divided into sections, companies, districts, areas, and commands. Counting the London one, there were six commands – Southern, Western, Midlands, North-East, Northern. He meant to visit them in that order. The idea was already in his mind that he would have to act alone, without Smith. He was becoming impatient with that careful soldier's insistence that nothing could be done, not a man moved nor a voice raised, until the Army and the Air Force gave the word – or, at least, signified their readiness to hear someone else give it.

Before he went he had another talk with Lotte.

She sought it. By himself, Richard Sacker would have gone off as casually as if this were an ordinary journey and not, as she guessed it to be, a reconnaissance. She had gathered this not from anything he said – he said little these days – but from his repressed gaiety. In twenty years she had become clever at reading him. It was necessary, if she wanted to know anything. He never told her.

It had taken her some time to realise that she had *no* control over him. As a lively, attractive young woman she had assumed that there are always ways of handling a man. If he pulls against the reins you may try coaxing him. By one method or another, by force of will or by friendliness, he will become malleable and manageable. Richard was never the one nor the other. He was accommodating in small things, watchful, kind, a marvellous travelling companion. But in what concerned his manner of living – when he had decided to take some step of which Lotte disapproved or she dreaded it – he was not to be moved. Lotte was strong-willed and very obstinate. She did not give in without a fight. And in time what defeated her was not so much Richard as a failure of her own will. She could provoke him, at first, to anger, violent anger. She expected him to strike her. He never did. In the final moment he simply turned away, and left her alone – for days or weeks, coming back as calmly and assuredly as if nothing had happened. She had either to accept him or to go away herself.

Many times during the first years she was on the point of going and then drew back from the point. She realised that it was her heart that would be pierced. Richard would dislike it if she went – he would even be deeply grieved – but he would recover and his life would go on much as if she had never been part of it. Hers would not do that. Without him her days would have neither joy nor purpose, she might as well put her eyes out as leave him.

When she realised this her strength to fight against him left her. She accepted what he did and what he was, not without railing and scolding, not without some tears, as if he were the rain and the sun. In her life he was. She was satisfied. She was not always happy. When he was away, and she knew that he was taking some other woman to please himself, even for the time in love with her, she suffered. Her sharp, bitter tongue struck at him when he came back. He minded it very little. He would perhaps have been disappointed if she had lost her spirit. That her will was no longer in the field against his he knew without thinking about it.

He began to rely on her. After he ceased to feel toward her as a lover he found in himself a spring of liking and warm kindness for her. Not respect. He respected nothing but a greater cunning or strength.

She remained very young in the face, and her eyes were always those of the schoolgirl, by turns eager, mocking, seductive, grave. She allowed her body to become perfectly round. Why take any great trouble to remain shapely, she felt, since she had no lover and no wish for one? There remained, between her and Richard, a physical sympathy which enabled her to know his mind. Beside that, she knew so well now how he would act, with an adroitness that was never patient enough, and a reckless physical courage that courted danger from an adolescent sort of vanity.

She asked him bluntly about his tour of inspection, did he mean to take any of the higher officers into his confidence? Not more than four or five of them, he answered.

Was it not a little early? she said. Richard looked at her with a familiar quickness. Early for what?

'For the safety of your plans,' she answered.

'There's no *safe* way of carrying out a revolution,' he laughed.

'There are wise ways and unwise ones,' she retorted.

He looked down at her with a derisive smile, yet warm with kindness. 'You're worrying, aren't you? You've no need to, I know what I'm doing and how to go about it.'

'You have not got Hillier with you.'

'Listen, my dear girl. I've got Frank just where I want him. Do you want to know that two nights ago he admitted to me that he would like to retain every

Volunteer?'

'*Would like to* means less than nothing.'

'It means this. Don't you remember four years ago this very month, when we had planned an assembly of the Volunteers, and almost at the last minute we were asked, not ordered but urgently asked to call it off. And Frank was for obeying and wrote out an order to cancel, which I tore up, and went on with it on my own authority, and told him when it was too late to withdraw. Afterwards he thanked me for forcing his hand. Remember it?'

Lotte did not answer. She was trying to recall whether what Hillier had said at that time was – if the assembly had been the cause of riot – that he would have repudiated Richard, or he ought to have repudiated him. She supposed it made a difference. But it was one that Richard would ignore, if to ignore it saved his vanity. Her civilised mind recognised and despised this obtuse self-assertive vanity of his, but her mind had no influence with him and none with herself touching him.

'Does it ever occur to you,' she said, 'that there are other ways of bringing about a change than by violence? The kind of violence you may be starting.'

'Certainly there are! If you leave a pear on the tree long enough it will rot and drop into your hand. I prefer to pull mine and eat it.'

'You may find it is still sour,' she mocked him.

'I may.'

'Then what?'

'Oh, then, we'll run away and begin another life in another country. What d'you think of that? Will you come?'

She rested her head on her hand and did not speak. To her surprise, she found that the mere thought of going away injured her. It tore the skin of her mind and left her exposed and quivering as if she were to step out naked into cold air. I am too old to live in another country, she thought wearily and sadly. Yet if it came to going away with Richard she knew that she would go, and she felt already the grief and reluctance and heaviness she would feel when the time came to go. It seemed to her that she would have to move herself like an old woman across the room to the door and from the door into the car and the car into the train or the aeroplane and so on to the end of her days in a foreign city, where she would never, until that moment, feel at peace. She looked up at Richard and nodded.

'Good,' he said, smiling. He had not expected anything else.

Lotte watched him move across the room, with the slight swaying of his heavy body she knew so well. No, I can't bear it, she thought. The weight of her life on her at this moment became intolerable. If she could only slip off the years like a garment, and stand up free, as free as a girl. She felt that she must speak to someone of this burden. Her mind was humming with words but when she opened her mouth to say them all that flew out was:

'I love you.'

Richard stood still, arrested in the middle of the room, as he was going out. He turned to look at her, half frowning. I have never until now seen him look surprised, Lotte thought. And she felt a small triumph in it.

'But I have not even been, as they would say, faithful,' he said. He said this from a feeling that he ought to be candid with her, as if it were the last time.

'I know, I know,' Lotte said impatiently.

'I can't say that I've respected you very much. I think I haven't any natural respect for women.'

'I have always known that,' she said in a dry voice. 'You're sometimes sentimental over us, like a schoolboy. But you never grew out of that. You're not, when it comes to speaking frankly, civilised or mature. I know that.'

He smiled, quickly and subtly. It looked subtle, and, though she knew that it was not, her heart moved to it. 'Well, then?' he asked.

'Nothing. It makes no difference.' She came towards him and put her thin arms closely round his body. Her eyes looked into his face, cajoling and merry. 'But do something for me, will you?'

'What?'

'Give me something to do while you're away. It doesn't matter what, but let it be something which is useful.'

'Very well. I meant to do it when I came back next week. Go through the papers in my desk and where you find a list of names on a sheet of paper, or only one, or two names, destroy it. Destroy everything, in fact, that is not obviously a routine document. There is very little which is not, you'll find, but better now get rid of that. Now I must go.'

As soon as he had left the house she went up to his room with his keys, and went through every drawer and pigeon hole. As he had said, there was little that was not official forms and records. But she found some slips of paper with the names of officers in the several Commands, and these she took away and burned. She was sorry he had given her a task that took so short a time.

That was in the early afternoon. Towards nine o'clock that evening she was sitting over a book in her own room when a servant came in and with a flutter of excitement told her that the Prime Minister was downstairs, asking to see her.

'Where have you put him?' she said.

He was in the sitting-room on the ground floor. She decided to go down to him rather than ask him into her room. But when she crossed the landing to the head of the stairs she saw his head below her at the turn of the staircase. He carried it poked forward when he walked, so that for a second it was all of him that was visible. He emerged into the full light from a window, and at the small sound she made glanced up at her.

'Just what I was trying to prevent,' he said smiling.

'What?'

'Forcing you to come downstairs.' He continued to come up, and stood beside her on the landing. His light eyes, with their look of almost supercilious calm, rested on her face for a moment, with affection. Putting his hand on her shoulder he led her into her room.

'This is a great pleasure,' she murmured, hardly noticing what she said. 'But you know that Richard is away, don't you?'

He had seated himself opposite her.

'Yes. I am not sure where he has gone.'

'Oh but surely you knew!' she cried. 'He is inspecting, as he always does at this time of the year. He has gone first to Winchester.'

'He didn't give me any information. Except, last week, that he would be away this.'

Lotte wrinkled her forehead, gazing at him. 'I don't understand it,' she said, bewildered. 'I am certain he sent you an official letter, enclosing a personal one. I was in his room when he wrote the second. He tried four times yesterday to see or speak to you, but you were always busy.'

'I was idle all day yesterday,' Hillier said, smiling again.

Lotte spread out her hands. It was beyond her. She had nothing to say.

Neither, it seemed, had he. He leaned in his chair, and looked abstractedly about the room as if his thoughts were far far from her. She began to feel irritated, and obscurely anxious.

At last, rousing himself, he said: 'You know, it's not of the least importance, but for the fact that Richard had some papers to give me. And they *are* rather important, it is important that the Council should consider them to-morrow.'

'Oh,' Lotte said, with relief. 'You want me to find them for you.' She rose.

Hillier rose, too. He accompanied her across the room, held open the door, and walked through it after her. He is coming with me, she thought. She was suspended for an instant in pure fear. Her body went forward mechanically, and she was able to recover her senses. She reached the door of Richard's room first, and opened it, turning on the light.

'Come in,' she said quietly. 'I'll open the desk. The keys are here.'

He seated himself at the desk, and let her unlock everything. He began to take out papers, spreading them open, one after the other. She watched him for a minute. He looked up with his abstracted smile.

'Don't wait, Lotte. I can do this better alone.'

She went away, back to her own room – and waited. He came in after three-quarters of an hour. She looked up at him without speaking.

'It's all right,' he said, kindly. 'I found it.'

Did I leave anything? she wondered. She knew she had not, and yet she could not help being afraid. He sat down and began to talk to her in the kindest way, like the very old friend he was. She asked him if she could give him anything. Would he smoke? She put her hand out to the bell behind an angular steel figure in a recess of the grey wall.

'Do you know,' he said, with a bright archness in his look, his head turned on one side, 'I should like some tea more than anything. Could I, do you think? At this hour?'

'But why not?' Lotte said.

She ordered tea. He sat sipping it, and looking about him, with the same slight, supercilious smile. He was not supercilious. His talk was of the simplest things, a painting he had bought, the work of an unknown young artist, his early morning walk in St. James's Park, his only relative, an old man, who was staying with him. Lotte listened, and nodded. She was wondering whether the smooth, almost vacant, look on his face, opposite hers, was actually its proper expression. It is like a blank sheet, she thought, waiting for the image. His eyes were without a centre, rather, the centre was inert and empty. At once, with sharp clarity, she realised that he was in a sense faceless. Any one of a multitude of images could take possession of that vacant surface, with the least trouble. Wistful, kind, charming, gay, inspired, ecstatic, hating – he was a vessel to be filled with any of these emotions, emptied, filled, filled, emptied. Ah, but who fills the vessel? she wondered. Perhaps the succession of prophets, she thought, was a line of such hollow vessels, to be filled by voices from without and within the mind.

Talking of the old man, his relative, he said:

'It's hardly a pleasure to have him in the house, I can tell you. His mind has begun to go, he forgets where he is, and lives nearly the whole time in the past. This morning when I went in to see him he told me that I had dirty ears and had better wash them before I carried out the parcels to the customers.'

He said this in an indulgent tone, gently, as though it were pitiable for the old man to imagine that the Prime Minister, the almost dictator of his country, had been his errand boy. But he was errand boy in his father's little shop, Lotte thought quickly. She glanced furtively at his face. It was fixed in a glare of hate, the lines drawn downwards, the eyes staring. Ah, Lotte thought, startled. She felt the fear again in her body. Then she had to hide her smile. He has forgotten none of those early humiliations, she thought: he is afraid to admit them; he is a vain man with a gift of words, who has taught himself to hate, and the hate makes him strong. She was not satisfied with this image; it was too simple, like a formula describing the flow of water, which describes neither the flow nor the water. She looked into his face and spoke recklessly.

'Do you know you gave Richard the impression that you would be sorry to disband the Volunteers?'

'Oh, nonsense,' he said, roused. 'He asked me whether I'd like to keep the men on, if it weren't for the expense, and I told him No, absolutely not – it was a matter of policy, not money.'

'Did he understand?'

'Perfectly.'

But Richard's memory was remarkably accurate. He would never remember a no as a yes. Hillier was looking at her with delicate sarcasm, his hands holding cup and spoon in an almost womanish gesture. She tried with all her power to penetrate his thoughts. *Is* he treacherous? she wondered. Is he deceiving himself? For a moment she thought that she had grasped something in him, before it slid away under her hand like a fish among stones. He can believe and he can persuade others that he is telling the truth, when what he says contradicts utterly what he said only yesterday. But in a moment she was not sure even of that.

He put his cup down and rose. 'I must really go, Lotte.'

She walked down the stairs with him. On the way he talked, in a diffident, almost deferential voice, about the decoration of the staircase. She had made her house beautiful he said. He was thinking of building himself a house, and she must give him her advice. In the hall he held her hand in both his for a minute.

When he had gone she stood thinking, trying to enclose the thought struggling in her mind. Perhaps there are times, in the history of a country, when naked forces take charge, needing only the covering of flesh as the hand needs the white glove. They rise from the ground, from the fields left unploughed by the farmer, from the spoiled orchard, from streams poisoned with oil, from dry wells. They fall from the air, as the squadrons veer, wing-tip to wing-tip, over the city. They find their hand and guide it, their brain and charge it with their electricity, their nerve and hold it stretched awaiting their time. The tongue moves but the words are given.

She felt that she had lived in this moment before, and thought these thoughts. She knew before she turned to go upstairs that a servant would be crossing the landing when she reached it, and that this door would be open and that closed. It was as if her mind were living ahead of her body, or as if her body had a foreknowledge it could use, but only clumsily.

CHAPTER IX

When I saw R. B. Tower again, on the nineteenth of June, he was anxious concerning one of his pupils who had been arrested that week for printing or helping to print a communist leaflet.

'I've done what I can,' Tower said. 'But I find that men who would listen to me six months ago now send down a curt message that they are too busy to see me.'

'But what will they do to him?'

'Oh, send him to a camp. They have talked of the death penalty for sedition. It wants a war to put that through. Or I think so.'

'But four or five young men, in a basement, multigraphing[56] their badly-written leaflets – why are they taken seriously? What do they weigh against a million and a half of their kind in uniform?'

I was hoping to find out whether he, Socrates, had anything to do with these shabby men in their basements. He had talked of a skeleton frame, a web. Was this it?

'What was the weight, do you suppose, of a few Christians against the whole Roman empire?' Tower said, smiling. 'These Christians, or communists, have their own ways of carrying on an offensive. It's not my way, but it might have been if I were eighteen, like this poor young chap. As it is, I can only fight in my own way against the common enemy.'

'What is the name of this enemy?'

'Oh. Inertia. The dreary indifference, worse than malevolence. The unliving spirit. One has to struggle not to fall a victim to it.' He chuckled. 'Men like you and me can only ask ourselves every day, in the words of a forgotten genius, *Am I being offensive enough?*'

He shook with inward laughter. Suddenly I found myself telling him about Richard's plans. His heavy eyebrows went up, and his small eyes became alert and very disconcerting to my inner timidity and diffidence.

It was only now that I realised how little there was to tell. I could relate any number of conversations, and good reasons why there should be a plot. But the plot, when I came to it, vanished into air.

Tower nailed this at once.

'It seems to me,' he said, 'that a great deal of hard work will need to be done, by someone, before your plot has any chance. Who is doing it? One man is talking to the Trades Union leaders, another to the army; there is grumbling among the Volunteers. People everywhere expecting a crash of some sort, discussing what is to happen, or what they can pull out of the fire for themselves. Is that a plot? Or have I got it wrong?'

'No. I think you are right,' I said. The poor plot looked like a damp piece of newspaper on the floor.

'And then Denham is not to be trusted,' he said, slowly. 'He is a jackal who serves the *big* lions. As for your brother-in-law.' He stood up and steered past me across the room to one of the windows. There he leaned his arms on a sort of breastwork of books and newspapers, and stared out. He reminded me at once of war pictures I had seen – men clumsy in their khaki and equipment in the angle of a trench, on guard, I suppose. His eyes stared with a quiet, far-watching sight.

'I knew men like your brother-in-law over there,' he said. 'There were two such in my battalion. Officers. Hard, foul-mouthed, violent, yet, do you know, attractive in their way. Physically strong. I've known those two ride forty miles at the end of the day into Amiens, only to have dinner, see a woman, and ride back. I used to wonder what happened to such men in peace time. I didn't realise then either that there would always be some country in eruption, where they could chance their arm. Or that "peace," even in England, would so soon become a state of war. They are the pioneering type gone bad – a more common type in America than here. Your brother-in-law's talk of a second revolution means nothing at all. He is like them an adventurer, fighting for himself. In the conditions of a dictatorship, even a half-willed one, what other sort of adventure, or change, is possible?'

'So you think Sacker can't bring off anything, even for himself?'

'I didn't say that,' Tower retorted. 'But on the face of it, you see that any even loosely constructive idea has come from Smith. It is he who suggested the general strike and the demonstration of Volunteers, and the liaison with the army. Sacker may think he is using Smith, but obviously it is the other way round. I am surprised that Smith, who is a regular soldier, thinks he can use men like Sacker anywhere except in an army in the field. They need the brute force of war to discipline them. Well, well.'

'Suppose someone shot Hillier?' I said.

Tower looked at me as though he could see through to my skull. 'His death now,' he said, 'would bring on only confusion, and the despair of all the middle sort of men who are pinning their hopes on him. He is their last delusion.

Probably, since no other organ is ready, the army would, in effect, take charge.'

'Perhaps Hillier is better than martial law,' I murmured.

'Perhaps,' Tower said, carelessly. 'He can't put the country right, you know. In fact he has already failed – except to lift his little pale figure into the light.'

'Everyone talks of war,' I said. 'Especially here in London. And the depression goes on. Won't that bring the National State down?'

'Why should it? The machine-guns are all on one side. I don't imagine the Council will have worse than riots to face this winter.'

'But the opposition? Liberals, communists?'

'The opposition doesn't exist. Only the *feeling* is growing.'

He left his breast-high wall of books and came over to the disordered table. Poking about there, he picked up a small brown object, like a frail cylinder of wood, as thin as old yellowed paper. It rattled very faintly when he moved it.

'D'you see that? Do you know what it is? It's a child's rattle, about ten thousand years old. Plus ça change! Dictatorships don't change either. Hillier can't right England by the methods of nationalism. He could only do that by reducing the population. Kill three men in four and the rest can live on the country. Provided, of course, that you expose the babies or use other methods of birth control! So he'll fail. A dictator faced with failure can only go to war. So there will be war. As in the past, the last resort of dictators in defence of their prestige, is war. Yes, war.' He was speaking now in a cold, cruel voice.

'And if we were defeated?' I asked. I felt chilled – I think by his voice.

'Neither defeat nor victory matters very seriously,' Tower said quietly. 'It doesn't matter at all now where the heavier stress comes. Another war is another earthquake shock in a world already half ruined. More violence. And so into the dark ages.'

'Plus ça change,' I said, trying to mock my bitterness.

'Not at all,' Tower said airily. An Ariel weighing twelve stone, in a stained shabby suit! 'I don't believe the dark ages are returning. I don't believe it for a moment. I believe in the English. Even if the world comes to a violent end there will still be an Englishman left, and his curiosity and endless patience will set the ball spinning again.'

He held out the toy the child had dropped – where? In Nineveh? His face was alight with a sardonic passion, and a mischief of some sort. 'Why shouldn't we last at least as long as this?'

CHAPTER X

The next day Richard came back unexpectedly to London. He had not visited the two northern commands. The message Lotte had sent caught him up at Northampton, and he came straight back.

He invited Smith, and Body, and Eugene Denham, to dine with him at his house. To my puzzled surprise Denham came. There had been quite a crop of 'incidents' in London during Richard's absence. Eight Volunteer companies had held a meeting of protest against the Council. When some of their officers tried to interfere they were roughly chased out of the place. A dockers' strike lasted one day: when the leaders had been marched off to jail the rest went with sullen quiet back to work. The tamest of all public rabbits, the civil servants, had sent a stout letter to the Council protesting against dismissals, and the new cut in their salaries.

While all this was going on, and worse promised, Hillier announced that he needed a rest, and went off to Scotland for a week. He left orders that he was not to be vexed with business.

This, for Richard, outshone everything else. He pooh-poohed Lotte's fears. He even thought he might have been asked to provide some document or other, and forgotten it.

Flown with self-confidence, after dinner, he sat before the table in his room as though he were in the mess with his chosen companions. 'Tell me that Frank has gone away now for any reason except to leave me a clear field!' he said. 'I told you so. He won't involve himself but he'll thank me afterwards.' He could scarcely contain himself in gravity. He wanted to laugh in their faces.

I watched Denham. No doubt it was my imagination that felt a clear malevolence in him against all the rest of us. He seemed to me to be listening with more than his ears.

'Hasn't it occurred to you,' he said suddenly, 'Hillier may feel himself threatened?'

'Threatened?' said Richard, in a sudden voice. 'What is threatening him? In any case, Frank Hillier is not a coward. If he thought he was in any danger, he'd act!'

'He would act?' echoed George Body. He seemed to feel the word faintly indecent. He blushed slowly. It was the first time he had opened his mouth, except during the meal to put food into it. He even ate with an air of reserve, as though he might be called to account for it.

Richard sent a shrewd guarded glance over their faces. 'Don't forget that no one can take Hillier's place as leader,' he said, with explosive energy.

'Oh, quite,' Smith said in a low voice. He looked down at his long delicate fingers on the edge of the desk. They made me think of a man's fingers on the ledge of rock from which he is dangling in space. I don't know why. He looked secure and suave enough. He was a brave man, too.

'If Hillier were to be killed – or to die – ' he said, slowly, 'no one could take his place. No one man.'

'Who would then?' Denham said with smooth assurance.

'Oh, well, the army, I suppose, would keep order,' Smith drawled, 'until such time as things righted themselves.'

'Do things right themselves?' I asked.

They turned to look at me, all except Richard, as though a piece of the furniture had spoken. George Body's mouth was slightly open. As for Richard, he looked at me in the way that momentarily frightens me. He did not want to hear anything from me then.

'No, they don't,' Denham said smoothly. 'That is surely the reason we are all here. To discover the proper way of righting them.'

'Haven't we got farther than that?' I said recklessly.

'*We?*'

'Well, you, if you prefer it?'

I saw anger drawing the skin of Richard's face. Smith noticed it at the same time, and interfered. His face had its absent ironic smile.

'Denham is quite right,' he said quietly. 'Nothing is to be gained by rushing at events like a bull at a gate. Time is on our side.'

'It's on yours, if you're hoping for the army to be called in,' Richard said. 'It's not on mine. Are you asking me to stand still and let the Council vote my men away from me?'

He must have been angry, or he would not have given himself away like that to the other two. Body did not count. He sat there, his mouth still slack and opened, and made a very curious noise in his throat, like a fish on dry land. He was certainly out of his element. Eugene Denham allowed his eyes to roll away out of sight, and sat sightless.

Smith made one of his civil speeches, about the value of fighting a delaying action in given circumstances. Did he mean anything? It was very hard to tell. I was overwhelmed suddenly with a feeling of the worthlessness of all of them, and their plot. Not one of you, I thought, cares a tinker's curse what happens to England. Major-General Smith is thinking of his ambitions, Denham of saving his place, and Richard of his destructive power and position. Perhaps George Body, that careful hard-working renegade, had actually a touch of feeling for his country and the common men who live in it. It was perhaps only in gratitude for what it had done by nursing him, and lifting him into his comfortable leather-padded chair, and providing a gold ring for his umbrella. But gratitude, even the gratitude of a mouse, as the fable tells, was less squalid than their self-seeking. On an impulse of disgust, and excitement – it is only rarely I feel myself strong enough to make a rough gesture – I rose and walked out of the room.

I went downstairs, to my sister's room. She was sitting there with Ernest. He was on duty. Richard had told him to wait in case he needed him. He and Lotte were playing a game of dominoes at the small table in the window. He had taken his belt off and hung it over the back of his chair. He was sunk in the game, his blue eyes fixed and distant, his hand, the long lean smooth hand of a boy, hovering over the ivory pieces. Lotte was watching him with pursed mouth, half wanting him to win, half mischievous.

I came in and drew my chair near them. Ernest moved his dominoes, one and then another. He looked up at her with a pleased smile, his eyes shining. 'I've won. See?'

'Oh, nonsense,' cried my sister.

'Yes I have.'

He looked at her in triumph, his young face wrinkled with laughter. 'Now you owe me sixpence!' He took the coin she handed silently to him, and slipped it into his pocket. Then he stood up quickly, stretching his long legs. He looked at his watch.

'Poor Steffy,' he said, softly and ruefully. 'I told her to go out and have her supper. I hope she did.'

'You don't cook it for her, I suppose?' Lotte said sharply. She was often critical of Steffy although she liked her.

'No,' the boy said, smiling. He was not to be provoked. A smile like an absurd thought came over his face. 'We go round the corner to a little cafe and eat an egg.'

'Well, it's not enough. You should bring her here. If you two must eat together.'

'I can't do that when I'm on duty, can I?' he said easily. He had picked up a book he had with him – it was a text book of physics – and sprawling on the couch became immersed in it almost at once. His capacity for withdrawing suddenly into his own world was one of the attractive things about him. In less than a minute he ceased to be aware of us.

'What are they doing up there?' Lotte asked me, in a secretive murmur.

'Oh, plotting as usual,' I said.

She glanced sharply at me at the sound of contempt and anger in my voice. 'What's the matter?'

'They're a worthless, useless lot,' I answered bitterly. 'Not one of them cares for any person or idea beyond himself and his muck heap.'

'Why should he?' said my sister. 'If every man minded his own business, and cared only for the one or two people near him, his wife or his woman, or his child, how much happier and better off we should be.'

'But Richard and Smith and the rest are playing with other men's lives. Even Ernest here has been dragged into it.'

'He's quite safe. And he thinks of no one but himself and his Steffy,' Lotte said calmly.

I had raised my voice. It had taken a moment or two for the sound of his own name to reach Ernest in his other world. Now he lifted his long young head, and looked at us with clear eyes. 'What are you saying about me?'

'Lotte is saying that you are as selfish as every other man,' I said maliciously.

He gave a sharp little laugh, and ducked his head again. 'Unselfish people are a nuisance,' he said quickly. 'They think of other people all the time and expect to be paid for it. Yes, they do. I prefer *his* way' – he meant Richard, of course – 'he marches over everyone. At least you know where you are with him.' He hesitated. 'But I'm not like that,' he said, in his quiet young voice. 'I couldn't march over you. Or Steffy. Or, say, Planck or Einstein.⁵⁷ I'm not brutal or hard – I should like everyone to be happy, without any of this fighting and marching. So you see I'm not likely to get very far in the world of to-day.'

He returned into his book, his mind closed against us again. I sat watching him with something like despair in my thoughts. He is right, I thought. What kind of a world have we created for him, and the young men like him? And what can they do to make a better one for themselves? Only fight and struggle and do violence to their spirit.

CHAPTER XI

Hillier was still in Scotland on June twenty-eighth, when Richard went up to Yorkshire. His wife went with him.

They arrived in the evening, when the sun was level with the edge of the moors behind the house, so that they burned a dull bronze, like a ring round the earth to the point where the sea began abruptly. Lotte went into the upper garden to watch it. The feeling of tension and sickness in her body came, she knew, from her certainty that Richard was about to take some decisive step. What step she did not know. She felt him near her, and turned and saw him crossing the grass. He stood with her and looked about him. He was long-sighted and could see the forms of the land where she saw only the dull-gold haze.

'I have been thinking,' she said slowly, 'wouldn't it be a wise thing to let Ernest take a fortnight's leave in Norway? Andy can tell him where to go. He has a week due to him – and you could make it longer. He looks tired. You know a boy that age, and as tall as he is, needs rest sometimes.'

Richard looked at her with narrowed sight. 'You want him out of the way.'

'Well – yes.' It was only now that she felt the weight of her anxiety for the boy. She had been ignoring it, living in a self-hypnotised state, for a long time. Now that she had looked it in the face it seemed impossible to endure it a day longer. Ernest must be got away, must, into safety, or she would lose her mind. He was too young, and vulnerable, to be made to run whatever risks her husband was taking. She pressed her hands on her body.

'I don't think so, Lotte. Ernest isn't a child. You're trying to make him one. He must take his chance with the rest of us.'

'But what are the chances?' she said in a low voice.

'Why, good, I think,' he said. He stuck his hands in his belt, and stood smiling at her.

'In any case,' he went on, 'I was told yesterday, by Denham, that the order to demobilise half the Volunteers has been drawn up and will come before the Council in the middle of next month. So we have less than a month.'

'So much for Frank Hillier's promises,' she said bitterly.

Richard shrugged his shoulders. 'I don't look at it that way. What's gone is gone, and if Frank has had his hand forced by Hebden and Thomas Chamberlayn last week he can have it forced the other way by me. Another week.'

'What are you going to do?'

'I don't like discussing half-made plans,' he said, shortly. 'But I'll tell you the whole thing in a few days. That's a promise.'

Her fear at this moment was so actual that she seemed to lose touch with her senses. Blood darkened her sight, swirling behind her eyes. She saw Richard's lips move, but what he said was inaudible to her. She came to her senses slowly.

'… demonstration in force, in every district.'

'Will there be any fighting?' she murmured.

Her husband's glance became fixed and staring as he looked at her. 'If Fred Hebden had to be carried out of his room I shouldn't be sorry,' he said. He laughed again, and clapped her on the shoulder. 'Cheer up, love. You look as yellow as a lemon. Listen, we'll keep Ernest up here for a week or two. I'll send for him to-night and he can bring his girl with him. How's that?'

'Better,' his wife said.

She roused herself. Richard put his hand up and stroked her cheek, looking at her with a smile. He drew his hand down over her shoulder and breast, caressing her without any thought of her, but an absent kindness. She felt it.

She had the sense that this scene was taking place in the past. It was as though she were looking back on it from some later moment, as though she were already an exile and remembering this place, the garden with its stone wall and wind-bitten lilacs, and the moor beyond. The sun had dropped behind the line of moor and all up there was growing dark and wan. The light still left in the sky seemed not to touch it, a tide ebbing from the earth. The chill wind that gets up at night in these places blew lightly. Lotte felt cold.

'We'll go in, shall we?' he said. He had felt the shiver pass over her. They turned and walked over the grass. It was badly kept, and rough with clover and dandelion roots. The man from the village who looked after it had too much to do. It had been a lawn once.

'One other thing, Lotte. I can't stay here. I'm not going to York and Newcastle. I've arranged for eight of the officers to come to me in a place I've chosen. They'll motor to it at night, to-morrow night in fact, and I'll see them early in the morning. After that, on the thirtieth, I shall probably go back to Winchester. You can stay on here.'

'For how long?' Lotte asked calmly.

'Better stay here until we see what's going to happen.'

'And if it doesn't happen as you expect it?'

'You mean if Frank has me locked up, as a punishment for trying to save him from himself,' her husband laughed. 'In that case I advise you to go with your brother to Norway. I shall feel easier about you if you're out of the country while I'm serving my sentence! I'll come out to you afterwards, and we'll run off somewhere.'

'Why are you laughing?' she asked.

'At the notion of Frank despatching me to jail. Bloody Mary, what a scene!'

'He might have to do it,' she said quietly. 'After all – if you make trouble.'

'Do you know what?' he said. 'I'd go as quiet as a lamb, and wait for him to slip in and smuggle me out. I can see him doing it.'

'Can you?' Lotte said, in a curious voice, with almost a touch of derision. At the same time, her heart lightened a little. She could not remain dejected for very long. She was always sanguine, a little too sanguine, until the worst happened. And then down to the bottom, and then up again, swimming strongly.

In the morning Richard left her. The place he had chosen as a meeting-place was that isolated house in Derbyshire where the desperate young man and his wife were living, or not living. He thought they might already have deserted the place. He had asked Smith to meet him there in the evening. It was not more than four hours from London by road, in Smith's car, and he could go back the same night. Richard had no intention of allowing him to meet the Volunteer officers, or even of telling him that they were coming. He had hardly made up his mind what he wanted to say to Smith, but he had not been able to see him in London after he knew that the decision to disband the Volunteers had been taken. It might be as well to consult him. This might change his views.

He reached the house about seven o'clock. As he came towards it he saw the young woman moving about the fenced yard. She looked up, startled, when the car stopped at the fence. After a moment she recognised him. He saw her lift her hand to her throat.

Leaving the car at the side of the road he came towards her and into the yard. 'Don't be startled,' he said, gently. 'It's all right.' He looked down at her, half deliberately trying to arouse her interest in him as a man, not only as a symbol of authority and very likely of dread. He thought she might have been a spirited creature if she had not been so crushed by her life. She smiled back at him, a wary unwilling smile.

'I want to stay the night here,' he said easily.

'We've only the two rooms,' she answered. 'You saw them.'

'I know. I don't want to take yours. I'll sleep in the other room. Before then I'm expecting a visitor, a man. He won't stay long, but there'll be others first thing in the morning. Nothing to be alarmed about.'

She walked a little ahead of him into the house. He saw that she was nervous. In the small living room there was a sofa on which he could get some kind of sleep, a table, and three or four chairs.

'Where's your husband?'

'He's in the field, we're earthing up the potatoes,' she said rapidly.

'When he comes in I'll speak to him. I don't want anyone to hear about this. Do you understand?' He spoke softly, trying to quiet her.

'Yes,' she said. She hesitated. 'Do you want a meal?'

'No.' She turned away. 'Wait. I'd like glasses and a jug of water.' He set the bottle of whisky he was carrying on the table. She stared at him for a second. She went away and came back with two glasses and a few common white cups on a tray. She lifted the whisky bottle on to the tray. She was thinking of her table.

Smith came at eight o'clock. He looked round the room with his odd half-averted smile, and his fine nose slightly lifted. 'You've a queer enough taste,' he said. 'What book have you been reading?'

Richard looked at him without moving from his chair at the table. 'Will you have a drink?' He had already drunk a third of the whisky.

Smith shook his head. After looking at it carefully he seated himself on the couch. He crossed one leg over the other, and waited, but as Richard said nothing he was forced to speak.

'Well, what have you to say to me?' he asked.

'Did you know that the Order in Council to dismiss half the Volunteers had been prepared?' Richard said. He was ready to be in the devil of a temper if he were provoked.

'I didn't know it,' Smith said. 'But I'm not surprised.'

'Well, what do you think I'm going to do?'

Smith kept his eyes steadily on Richard's face, as though he were trying to control him in that way. 'I can't tell you what you're going to do,' he said quietly. 'I know what I should do in your place.'

'What?'

'I should accept it with as good a face as possible. And immediately set about organising the remainder. They'll hardly touch you again for six months, and that gives us time, me time, to bring round the general staffs to our way of thinking.'

For a perceptible length of time Richard said nothing. He had lowered his head and had the air of considering the advice. But when he looked up again Smith saw that he had made no impression on his mind. He is too drunk, he thought. He felt a little repulsion, and against his will, a slight physical fear. He was not afraid, except of not being able to avert a disagreeable scene.

To his surprise he saw a smile coming on Richard's face.

'You certainly amuse me,' he said. His smile widened. 'You sit there, as quietly as if you were somewhere else, and tell me to cut off my left hand and do with the right. That's splendid, isn't it?'

The other man shook his head slightly, with his polite, friendly smile. His slender body on the couch relaxed. He felt that he could speak directly again. 'Listen, my dear Sacker,' he exclaimed. 'If you think I don't know what it feels like to lose half your command, you might remember that I lost the whole of mine. I'm an unemployed soldier. And do you know anyone with less reason to exist? I'd give both my hands to get back to work. If you'll only have patience I'll do my best for both of us. But the General Staff is not composed of out-of-work soldiers, and they need two things, an adequate incentive and a reasonable prospect of success, before they make up their minds. Do you know that the last time the army in this country made an independent move was in June 1914, in Ireland? I believe the time before that was 1688!'[58]

And you're still of the opinion,' said Richard, 'that their – consent – is necessary before anything can be done?'

Smith moved his hand slightly without answering. This gesture made quite plain his conviction, profound and unalterable, that the whole great Volunteer force was a mob, nothing more, an unwieldy undisciplined mob. Of amateurs. Less than a tenth the number of regular soldiers could disarm and disperse it. And if the air arm were moved – well – . Even trained men were only trained to scatter under an attack from the air. As a soldier, he had no respect for Richard's troops, not the least, although he supposed they might come in useful in an emergency.

'Do you know I can't give you anything to eat?' Richard said amiably. 'These people are poorer than rats. And you won't drink?'

'No, I shall go back.'

He went out, leaving Richard seated at the table, facing the tray with the cups and the half-emptied bottle of whisky. In the yard, the young man and his wife were standing close together against the fence. They looked after him, stolid and in silence, as he passed; he saw the girl's hand close sharply on her husband's arm, and thought, Poor devils.

CHAPTER XII

When my sister and her husband went into Yorkshire I had stayed behind, in the house in Regent's Park. On the morning of June twenty-ninth I had a telephone message from R. B. Tower asking me to see him at once. I was in his room before twelve o'clock. This room never changed. It was always disordered, always books lying everywhere, and in the middle of it the alert shaggy Tower, archangelic mind in the heavy body of a man.

He told me what he had heard – he was not inclined to say how he had heard it. Denham had gone up to Scotland to see Hillier, and it was believed, Tower's friend or informer believed, that something unusually unpleasant was in the wind. For that matter, the belief was common. People, and in the cities especially, were expecting an event. They did not know what they expected. The air was crossed with invisible currents, as before the satisfaction of thunder. People had begun to look over their shoulders before speaking even to a friend. They had begun to avoid strangers. The most common phrase heard, in cafés, at the family table, in the street, was: 'Things can't go on like this.' By 'this,' they meant, according to their circumstance, the new taxes, the price of bread, the unaccountable disappearance of men from their homes, the unrest among the lower classes, the Volunteer riots, the grumbling. People felt that they were not being told the whole truth about many things. Doubt was beginning to be coloured a little with fear. It is easy to magnify this fear and this doubt, and chiefly it was in the cities and large towns. As always, the inert mass of the people was busy only with its private fears and secrets.

'You think that Denham has run off to Hillier to tell what he knows, and make trouble?'

'I think it likely,' said Tower. 'But only from what I know of him, and the fact that his visit is a secret. If you look in *The Times* you'll find he is supposed to be speaking in London to-day, and I'm told that that statement was sent out from his office *after* he had arranged to go to Scotland.'

'What ought I to do?'

'Really, I don't know,' Tower said. 'I'm not at all interested in what happens to Sacker. But I suppose you must feel something for your sister's husband. It's my only interest in telling you the little I have heard.'

I noticed again the inflection of cruelty in his voice. He would never act cruelly, but his contempt for persons whom he held to be worthless or a sham was unforgiving. His mind had no mercy on them.

I thanked him for telling me, and left him. He was on his way to the University on some end-of-term business. I decided that the only thing I could do was to take an aeroplane to Yorkshire, to warn Sacker. I was walking towards a telephone booth, intending to ask them at Croydon to keep a small taxi machine for me or a place in one of the larger aeroplanes which stop to set down beyond York.[59] A car drew up at the curb a short distance in front of me and the chauffeur stepped out. He beckoned to me. I quickened my step a little, he opened the door of the car, and I saw Thomas Chamberlayn leaning forward on the wide seat.

'This is very fortunate,' he exclaimed. 'I want to talk to you. Where are you going?'

'I was on my way home,' I answered. 'I mean, to my brother-in-law's house.'

'I know, I know. In Regent's Park. I'll take you. Please get in.'

Docile, because no other way of taking it occurred to me, I stepped in beside him. He had a rug over his knees although it was a warm, airless day. He fussed with it, placing half of it over me, as though my comfort were a concern with him. Now we were both tucked in under the rug, close together. I felt extraordinarily uncomfortable, as though I had got into the wrong bed. I did not care for the banker as bedfellow.

He was sitting quietly, his gloved hands folded on his knee on the rug. I waited for him to speak, emptying my mind of its uneasiness. I would hear what he had to say.

I expected a rambling speech and to have to probe for the meaning, and I was shocked by his directness.

'I think you are in your brother-in-law's confidence,' he began.

'I doubt that very much,' I said.

He looked at me, turning his head in a way that recalled his coquettish manner at our other meetings, but now he was smileless. He was still extremely polite.

'We needn't discuss it. It will be much better if I tell you what is in my mind, and you can arrange your own course. In short, my dear fellow, we have concluded that there is nothing to be gained by delaying an action we shall be forced to take before long – in view of the financial state – and we are going to disband half or two-thirds of the Volunteers. I know that this will not be to General Sacker's taste, and I am naturally sorry. But I want *you* to understand that we are forced to do this, and that any ideas of opposition, active or passive, can only have the worst effect.' Again, for a moment, he became the elderly and quite virtuous coquette. 'I have no fear of *your* not understanding.'

'But why tell me? Why not talk to General Sacker?'

He looked away from me at once. 'The most exaggerated hopes have been current,' he said softly. 'It was natural. You cannot win an election on cold facts. But the facts are not altered thereby. And the truth is that neither Hillier, nor the National State Party, nor the bankers, nor any person or body of persons, can take less than years to change the condition of the country. The natural *laws* of money have been violated in the past for political reasons. Recovery is possible but a miracle is impossible. A miracle is what has been promised. I am struck dumb when I hear it said that men are more valuable than economics, than finance. My dear fellow, men *are* economics, are the raw stuff of economics, and a nation depends on its finances as a wife depends on her husband's wages. It needs time, and again time, to fulfil a tenth of the promises that the State Party made before it took charge. You do see that, don't you?'

'You mean that Hillier is as conscienceless a fraud as any other demagogue,' I said rudely.

His sly, kind smile peeped out for a second. 'Now I know you're not well,' he said. ' I *thought* it, when I saw you walking towards me. You're looking white and strained. If you were yourself you wouldn't commit the vulgarity of abusing the head of the State. I am sure you, my dear, realise that if the man at the head is not a miracle-worker – and of course he isn't – still less can he step aside for anyone else, who would be just as powerless to work miracles, and perhaps weaker. He is bound, is he not, to defend himself against grumblers and rebels. Otherwise he has simply delivered the country over to despair and chaos. It is precisely as a nation which is threatened must fight or will decay, and it is why wars happen only when there is a doubt which nation is stronger. Don't you see?'

'I see that you really believe it,' I answered.

The car had stopped at the house and I made to get out. He put his hand on me.

'People sometimes speak about me, I know it – they used to write it before the press was disciplined – speak about me as if I were not English, or not human. As if I were an enemy inside my own country. Is that fair?'

He was melancholy about it but not in the least cast down. I pushed at the rug, pushing it off my knees and disentangling my feet clumsily from it. 'They talk and write in that way about strikers,' I said. 'Extremes meet.'

He was folding the rug over himself again when I glanced back, a sinister and curiously righteous figure. If ever a man were certain that he had the way – indeed that he was the way, the truth, and the life – Thomas Chamberlayn, banker, was that man. He would never want to take Hillier's place from him. He had no ambition to be lifted up, was content to be himself. And to know he knew what was best for his fellow-men to do, if they would only do it. It was the one drop of bitterness in his cup – the inexplicable, ineradicable tendency of men to go whoring after their own little tin-pot gods in spite of him. He knew that they must have gods. That, perhaps, was why from the first he had encouraged Hillier. It would be extravagant to say that he welcomed him. He preferred the past, but he would make the present serve. He was in the worst sense a realist.

I reached the house in Yorkshire in the late afternoon. There was no one about, the lower gate was padlocked, and the main door locked. I went round to the back and found Annie in the yard. She looked at me with a bright smile, and asked me cheerfully if she should prepare a meal.

'No,' I said. 'Where is the General?'

She had stooped to gather up some logs, and her face when she stood up holding them against her skirt was very red. 'The master's out,' she said breathlessly. 'He'll be in to-night, I don't doubt.'

'Where is Mrs. Sacker?'

'Mrs. Sacker's out too. She'll be coming in. Yes, she'll be coming in.'

She paddled away from me into the kitchens. I heard her rushing about, it sounded as though she were locking cupboards. I suppose she is mortally afraid I shall take something, I thought. She included me in her distrust of all strangers, always had, for some reason. Perhaps it was my arm. Country people often suspect deformities.

I went out into the lower garden and sat on the wide low wall. This part of England touches my heart. It is beauty without softness, the lines firm and bounding, the colours full. The hard deep moor is veined with streams. They run down into the valleys and make them rich, so that corn grows almost to the heather. Where I sat I could see the church in the village: it is sheltered from the moor and looks down, down, over meadows and pasture to the valley. The sun in its downward wheel had singled out one particular field to shine on it between the clouds with intense brightness, and above this field a lark drew his thread of sound. It was so thin and frail it seemed to be very far away. Many years away. I heard it in my first youth and my boyhood and in my infancy. It saddened me, and gave me courage.

I sat there, tranquil enough, until eight o'clock. I went indoors. There were no preparations for a meal and I began to be anxious again. Annie, when I spoke to her, was evasive or sillier than usual. I began to think she had not understood me when I arrived. I questioned her more closely. She admitted to me at last that Richard had left the house early that morning, but he had not told her when he was coming back. 'I'm sure I thought from what Mrs. Sacker said that he would be home in good time,' she said, looking at me with her sly bright smile. What vexed me most of all was to discover now that Lotte had gone to London by the noon train.

'Did General Sacker know she was going?' I asked.

'I can't say, I'm sure,' said Annie, very brightly.

Even her backward parts as she withdrew them into the kitchen were self-righteous and secretive. I would willingly have whipped her for her peasant suspiciousness. She had not wanted to admit that she was left alone in the house and that she did not know at what hour Richard was coming home. Who knew what ravages I would commit if I thought I had the house to myself!

There was only one thing I could do. I went into the library and telephoned to Lotte in London. I was going to ask her where Richard had gone that morning. After a long delay, nearly half an hour, I was answered that no calls could be put through to General Sacker's house. Why? In London a voice said that the line was under repair. I asked them whether I should be able to use it early in the morning. The voice could not say. 'But repairs don't take long as a rule,' I said. The voice agreed. It was the full resonant voice of a young woman, and without any reason I was reassured by it.

CHAPTER XIII

When Smith had gone, Richard sat at the table in the darkened room until he had drunk two-thirds of the whisky. He had another bottle safely in the car for the men he was expecting between five and six in the morning. He began to think of going to sleep.

First he went out into the yard. He lifted his head and looked all round him and listened. There were no sounds, not even a dog barking. The road beside the house was not the main road to north or south. He heard no car or cart. After a minute his quick ears picked up the noise of an aeroplane flying a long way off to the east. It died away, and the complete darkening silence came back. The house stood almost on the rise of a hill and the ground fell away on two sides, so that there was very little to see. It was as though the earth had contracted and the sky swelled, on an indrawn breath, into desert on desert of darkness.

He went back into the house. The house door opened into the little scullery, in which there were two doors, one into the living-room and the other, he supposed, into a bedroom. He wanted water to drink, but when he turned the tap over the sink it was dry. Not one drop trickled. He knocked on the door of the bedroom.

It opened after a minute, and the young man stood in the opening and looked at him. He held the door with his arm.

'Give me some water. And a lamp or a candle,' Richard said.

The young man took the jug from the table without a word and went into the yard. His wife came from the bedroom with the lamp. 'I'll put this in your room,' she said, unsmiling.

'What's wrong with your tap?'

'The water was cut off. We get it now from a spring.'

He followed her into the room and watched her turn the wick to get a clear flame. Again he thought that if she were not so thin and a better colour she would be pretty. He felt sorry for her, because her life here must be bad for a girl. He would almost have made love to her out of pity if she had been alone, or if she had seemed to want it. It would be easy to send the husband out of the way. But she scarcely looked at him. She did not seem afraid of him at all, but nervous and vexed. He saw her look at the round mark made by his glass on her table.

The young husband came back with the water. 'You needn't be afraid to drink it,' he said, with a little smile. 'We drink it all the time, don't we, Mart?'

She nodded. She went away quickly. Her husband would have followed her, but Richard kept him a few minutes asking him pertinent questions, about the soil, the state of the wells, and his potato crop. He was intensely curious to know how people lived. He would talk to anyone, a rag-and-bone man, about his trade until he had its secrets. The young man was reticent or frightened. He had very little to say. He stood there, stolid and quiet, his dark eyes turning aside when they met the other man's.

After he had gone Richard lay down on the couch. He did not go to sleep at once. He lay on his back, looking at the ceiling. Before he slept he went through a long, a very long conversation with Hillier, convincing him easily that he had been right all the time. Then, easily and convincingly, he killed Hebden in self-defence. When he was young he had spent hours in imaginary exploits. Afterwards he had lost the habit, and it required some unusual occasion, like this waiting, for it to seize him again. His mind was restless with his schemes. He wanted furiously to be about them, to give orders and to feel that things moved. To lie here for another six or seven hours was nearly beyond him. He could not sleep. In time he did sleep. The lamp, which he had not turned out, went out at last for want of oil and stank horribly. The darkness was thick for a short time. Then it changed quickly, as wave after wave of light flowed into it. At last it was all grey sunless light. Then the early morning light. Richard slept on his side on the couch, his knees drawn up.

He did not hear the car which stopped a short distance from the house. It had stopped almost silently, gliding for some yards without the engine. The young wife heard it, because she was awake. She roused her husband, and they stood side by side peering out of the small window of their room. They were the only people who saw Hillier step out of the car and walk directly to their house. They knew him at once. His face was more familiar to them than, say, the King's face. They recognised also one of the men in uniform who followed him.

The girl was the quicker of the two. She had thrust her arms into her long coat and was opening the door when Hillier had his hand lifted to knock. He stepped inside at once. To his two companions he said: 'Wait.' He did not speak to the young woman at all. He looked round, saw one door open into her bedroom and her husband standing there in the middle of the room, gaping, and stepped quickly to the other closed door, and pulled it open. They heard the man inside the room exclaim. Hillier shut the door. The girl looked round her and her eyes dilated with fear. She was afraid for her husband, not for herself.

The two men in the uniform of the Special Guard had stepped into the scullery. Behind them, through the door they had left open, she saw two other cars come up.

Richard had swung his legs over the side of the couch in the act of wakening. In the next instant he realised that it was Hillier who was in the room. He made an attempt to stand up. Hillier put a hand on his shoulder and thrust him down sharply so that he lost his balance and rocked backwards. He recovered himself and sat on the edge of the couch. He looked at Hillier.

'What are you doing here, Frank? Has something happened?'

'Not yet,' Hillier said.

'Aren't you going to sit down?'

Hillier remained standing, and so Richard stood up, too swiftly for the other to stop him. Hillier drew back a step. Richard's belt and revolver were laid on the table beside the tray, and with a sudden jerk of his arm Hillier dropped them both on the floor between the table and the wall.

'What's the matter with you?' said Richard. 'Are you sick?'

Looking at Hillier's face he saw that he was working himself towards the state in which his acts and words became almost automatic. He would be in this state during one of his frenzied speeches: the passions with which he had infected his hearers seemed to pour from himself, leaving him as dazed as a man at the end of a drinking bout. He had not yet reached the state of frenzy – there was still time to avert it. He was still cool.

'Not in the least. I've come here, myself, to ask you why you have been working against me – what in your crazy mind you hoped to gain by it.'

'Bloody Mary, I don't work against you.'

Hillier kept his pale eyes on the other's face. 'I'll tell you now that Smith was arrested at one o'clock this morning when he reached his house.'

'Did he tell you where I was?' Richard smiled.

'No, as it happens he didn't. There were other people who knew you were here.' He watched Richard curiously for a time. 'For instance, your wife knew.'

Richard dismissed that. He knew quite certainly that Lotte had not given him away. There were the Volunteer officers whom he had ordered to come here. Any one of them could have been an informer. Involuntarily he shifted his head a little to glance at the door.

'They were stopped and turned back,' Hillier said.

'Who planned this?'

'Do you mean who discovered what you were doing?'

'Who planned this trap?'

'You planned it yourself,' said Hillier quietly. 'You chose this place. You were not asked to come here.'

Sacker had taken off his boots to sleep. He felt the cold of the stone floor on his feet and legs. 'Do you mind if I put on my boots?' he said, with clumsy irony.

He sat down and pulled them on. Breathing awkwardly from the exertion, he stood up again and faced Hillier. The tension between them had increased. Sacker stood with his head reaching forward a little, and his eyes watchful. He was curiously conscious of Hillier's body, as if it were a new reality, unfamiliar and familiar. It blocked his light. He felt drawn towards it, to put his hand on it.

'What do you think I am?' he whispered.

Hillier did not answer.

'You can't believe I was against you. You.'

Hillier looked at him with the eyes that often seemed to have died, to be only lumps of pale jelly. Yes, he is getting fatter in the body, thought Sacker. It is too much sitting; he drinks too much tea. He thought of the white softening belly under the clothes. Jerking his head, he looked Hillier in the face again. 'You haven't answered me,' he said, in a very low voice.

As Hillier looked at Sacker he felt himself filling with revulsion. He was sickened by Richard's battered good looks, loathing even the deep smiling lines on his face, the bright hazel eyes, forward-set ears and the long prominent lower lip. They seemed to him gross and vulgar, the coarse good looks a servant might have. He would go down well in Hyde Park with nursemaids.

Hillier became rigid in revulsion from the man who had been his intimate friend. He felt his revulsion turning to anger. A curious shudder of anger passed through him. He reminded himself that he wanted to know certain things still.

'How long has this been going on?' he snapped.

'How – what going on?'

'Don't play the fool.'

'Speak civilly,' Richard said. His temper was beginning to be uncertain. His mouth felt sour, he could taste the whisky he had drunk. 'Do you mind letting me get at the table? I want a drink.' Without moving his eyes from, the other man, Hillier reached his arm out behind him and touched the jug of water. He handed it to Sacker, watching him tilt it to his mouth and drink. Then he took it back from him.

'Now, have you something to say?' Richard asked. 'What particularly do you want to hear?'

'I don't want to know why, as commander-in-chief of the Volunteers, you were about to disobey orders. I know that well enough. You imagined you would lose influence when the Volunteers were reduced. You never had any social conscience and I was a fool to think you could acquire one.' Into the last few words he managed to put a trace of what was almost indulgent irony. He almost smiled. 'But I *should* like to know whether you had looked ahead at all to the day after your *second revolution*. Whom you proposed to put in my place – yourself, perhaps?, how you were going to deal with the panic and the collapse of credit? Perhaps you were relying on others to arrange this for you?'

Richard smiled with deliberate contempt and said nothing. He had put his hands on his hips in a jaunty pose. He rocked back on his heels and kept the jeering smile on his face. He thought he had guessed that Hillier was provoking him to lose his temper, so that he would have an excuse for deserting him. He is going to have me tried and jailed, he thought sourly, without lifting a finger to do anything for me. He made up his mind not to make it easy for the other man. But he was not sure of himself. He had a queasy weight of anger in his stomach, and in some part of his mind he was in pain. He would lift his lip over it if he noticed it, in a lewd contempt – but it was there.

'You know better than anyone,' he said, 'that there was no question of replacing you by anyone. You are the head of the party and the State. No one has dreamed of touching you.'

'You were only going to ruin my life's work,' Hillier said acidly.

'I don't understand you.'

'No. There is scarcely anything you understand. You don't understand that after years of economic crisis this country is struggling to recover her national strength and honour. You don't understand that everything in the State, the whole of our policy, is overruled by this historic task. You don't understand, it seems, that without credit, without sound finances, we can't do anything; that whoever interferes in these affairs without authority, and makes a disturbance, and tries to act as though money can be poured out on any kind of useless display – like a million and a half Volunteers – is a blackguard. An enemy of society.'

'So that's what I am now, is it?' Richard said jauntily. 'I'm an enemy of society. I and my Volunteers are enemies of the society that accommodates Hebden and Tom Chamberlayn without having the bellyache. You're right. Vous avvey raisong.'

Hillier set his teeth. The jauntiness and the deliberately mispronounced words set them on edge, as if he were being exposed in some ridiculous position. He could scarcely bear himself as he stood here. With an effort he controlled himself again, but he felt that it was for the last time.

'Any man who tries to act on his own authority against the Government is an enemy,' he said, with difficulty. 'What is the Government for if not to govern? What is it if it does not govern? Am I the man in authority, am I the authority of the State, or am I not? And if I am, *your* job was to obey. You knew that.'

'I knew that without the Volunteers you wouldn't be where you are,' Sacker exclaimed. 'You'd still be a politician on the make. We made the difference. I made the difference.' He smiled.

'You could always boast,' Hillier said.

Steady, now, steady, the other thought. He let his hands fall by his side, the fingers relaxed. The blood was rising behind his eyes. He looked round the room, scheming, trying to make up his mind what to do. He felt his temper getting the better of him as he waited. There was a sudden noise in the scullery as though someone had fallen against the wall, and a male voice blurted a few words.

'Who's out there?' he demanded.

'What?' Hillier drawled.

'I said who's there? Who is the new nurse?'

'You don't imagine I came here alone to arrest you,' said Hillier quietly.

'So I'm to be arrested, am I?'

'Certainly you are.'

'*You* are going to arrest me?'

'But you knew what would happen when you were found out. You're in the same position as any Volunteer would have been who disobeyed your orders when you were behaving properly.'

'What are you going to charge me with?' Sacker asked. He stretched his head forward and stared at Hillier's pale face, at the light eyes and wide pale mouth, as though he were memorising them.

'With treason,' Hillier said, when he had hesitated a moment.

'I'm the last person living you can accuse of treason. If you'd made up your mind to cut your throat and I tried to take the knife from you, is that treason?'

'You're not being asked to excuse yourself.'

'Nor to defend myself, I suppose,' Sacker jeered. 'You come here with your policemen – how many did you bring? – to arrest one man. Why, you ass, I made you. Who would you have been without me? Now I look at you, you look very like a jumped-up errand boy! Why, you're a louse, I ought to have squeezed you when you first began crawling on me'.

'Have you something to say? ' Hillier said. His eyes had their dazed look. He was almost insane with revulsion and the hatred he felt.

'I? No, I was laughing at you. You make me laugh.'

'I've had enough of you,' Hillier said. He worked his mouth, with a speck of foam at the edge of his lips. They showed his pale gums for a moment. He was beside himself now with anger.

'No further orders? Nothing more we can do for you to-day?' Sacker mocked. He spread out his hands, measuring off a yard of cloth and offering it to Hillier with the gesture of a shop-walker.

'You traitor,' Hillier screamed.

Sacker's mockery flew up in rage and bitterness. He, too, had lost control of himself and all sense of where he was. He and the other man might have been alone on the top of a mountain for any awareness he had of other people near them.

'Keep the name for yourself,' he shouted. 'If there is a traitor in this room it is not me. Which of us is betraying the party? You, you. You. I fought for you. I made your success for you, I created the Volunteers. Now you are selling me and them out to the bankers and the Conservatives. What are you getting for it? A title? Lord Hillier of Oxford Street?'

'Take off those things,' Hillier said violently. 'Take them off.'
He reached his hand out to tear the tabs from Sacker's jacket. Richard slapped his face.

'Arrest him, arrest him,' said Hillier, in an exhausted screaming voice.

Sacker stood still as Hebden and another officer of the Special Guard jerked his arms behind him. He felt suddenly emptied, as though he had not eaten for days. Glancing at the door, he saw the scared staring faces of the young man and the girl. He felt a little pity for them. He fixed his eyes on the young woman's and she shrank back. So he looked towards the small window and saw the swifts darting across it in the bright light, small dark bodies with flickering wings. Then he looked sideways at Hebden.

'So it's me and not you,' he said. Hebden did not answer, and he went on, with malicious significance: 'I'm only sorry they couldn't send a whole man for me.'

'I'm whole enough to see you out,' said Hebden. Sacker's arms were tied, and Hebden struck him on the breast, sending him against the table. The tray flew aside, scattering the broken cups and glasses. The girl in the doorway cried out sharply:

'Oh, my cups, Jim, all my good cups.'

Hebden gave an order: two of the Special Guards were placed outside the window and others in the little scullery. Hillier went out. With a glance round the room Hebden went. Sacker was left alone in the room.

CHAPTER XIV

Towards eight o'clock Lieutenant Eckhart came into the room. Richard was leaning over the table. The young man came up behind him and freed his arms, in silence. His face had a boyish candour and gravity, he might have been cutting the knots of a parcel, he went about it with so little interest. Then he laid on the table near Sacker's hand his belt and the revolver. He pushed the revolver a little forward.

'You may need it.'

Sacker pursed his mouth. He gave the young man an intimidating glance, from his half-closed eyes. Eckhart took no notice of it: he was faintly excited by his responsibility and he covered it with an air of indifference. The excitement made him yawn every few minutes; he tried to swallow his yawns, for the sake of dignity, but now and then one escaped him and he put his hand across his stretched rosy cheeks.

'An officer doesn't shoot himself unless he is guilty,' Richard said. 'Don't you want to run away and repeat that?'

Eckhart went out. Sacker's first act was to hold the empty bottle of whisky to the light. There might be a teaspoonful of liquor in it. He poured it into his mouth and drank the rest of the water. Taking the jug in his hand he went to the door and tried it. It was fast. He kicked it until it was opened by a Special Guard, who asked him sharply what he wanted.

'Fill this jug,' he said.

With some hesitation the Guard took the jug and sent another man to fill it in the yard. Sacker had time to see the number and position of his guards before he returned. 'Take this and keep quiet,' the man snapped. He was not altogether easy. Eckhart came into the scullery from outside at that moment and looked at him. 'Don't open that door again,' he said, in his quiet voice.

Richard seated himself on the couch and rested his wrists on his knees. His rage had dropped. He was scarcely conscious of it lying in him like a stone in the pit of his stomach, cold, hard, and unmoving. His mind was clear.

He tried to think out his position, but at first his thoughts wandered curiously. It was as though his mind were seized with the need to yawn, like Eckhart. He found himself thinking of the Ramblas in Barcelona, in the middle of the morning in bright sunlight. Of the flower-women's stalls there, in the centre of that long boulevard, covered with the vivid, tightly-packed bunches, in all the colours of summer, gleaming with freshly sprinkled drops of water. He saw himself like a black shadow in the middle of the chattering, sauntering crowds, who did not know he was there.

He pulled himself up, with a dry feeling of surprise. Again he began to scheme and to feel his way towards an issue from his seeming defeat. He did not accept defeat. He had no fear, or no physical fear. What fear he had was the fear of making a fool of himself in some way. He must be careful to say and do nothing that gave anyone a handle to hold him up to ridicule. When he thought of Hebden triumphing over him in public, sending out his florid messages to the newspapers, his anger began to sicken him once more. His face, his whole body, hardened. The sour rage rose in him to his throat, so that he thought he could vomit it and be rid of it. But he was helpless. He had to swallow it to be able to think again, and to think coherently. The effort made his wrists and hands limp.

Half an hour passed while he sat on the couch, given over to the useless anger. The door opened. Eckhart came in again, looked at him, and looked at the revolver lying on the edge of the table where he had left it. His dark thickly-arched eyebrows rose slightly, without spoiling the youthful calm of his face.

'What, not yet?' he said.

Sacker looked at him without answering, and he went out. After this, he came in every half-hour, during the five hours Sacker was there, and went through the same form. He looked at Sacker and at the weapon on the table, and repeated his 'Not yet?' in the same calm curt voice. Had he thought of it for himself or had Hebden or Hillier given an order?

Sacker stood up and walked to the window. The two guards were facing into the room. When he came close to the window they averted their eyes to a point somewhere in the middle of his body. He stared out between them for a short time.

There was very little to stare at – a strip of garden in which the young wife had planted some hollyhocks which were fading and toppling over for want of water, and beyond them the first potato field. The rows were irregular, the young man had no eye for a straight line and they wavered rather like lines of ribbed sand. They were almost the colour of sand, from the long drought. While Richard was there, a neat grey bird stepped towards him mincingly between two of the rows. The bird was small and elegant, in grey feathers, with a black waistcoat and neat white dog collar – obviously a Church of England clergyman in holiday dress. And how he pecked right and left into the ground, where the young man had been digging it over. His appetite was amazing. Nothing wrong with the

Church, thought Richard. His face relaxed into a sharp smile. He turned away, irritated by the fixed bodies of the two men between him and the light, and went back to the couch.

He did not believe that Hillier would make the charge one of treason. It was a death sentence. And the notion that Hillier intended his death was too remote and unbelievable. He did not believe it. The notion scarcely formed in his mind before he brushed it away. But his mind yawned again and led him on, through a mist, to another interview with Hillier. Now he was faced, for the first time, with the rupture of their intimacy as an event; he had an extraordinary feeling of despair and bodily weakness. At the same time he shook with laughter, almost silently, resting his hands on his knees and relaxing his heavy body. He did not know he had laughed, and afterwards he was able to see himself with the other man as if they were small distinct images on the floor of his brain. The Hillier image begged the other to leave England. And Sacker agreed. He would go to China, where he could find employment of a sufficiently exciting kind, unless he had been absent too long for his name to be remembered. He allowed himself to think that he had been remembered.

Eckhart opened the door softly. He was inside the room before Sacker heard or saw him, and his heart contracted a little with the slight shock. The young man's voice saying 'Not yet?' had a trace of boredom. It released a new spurt of anger in Sacker and he was not able to keep quiet.

'I told you that an officer does not shoot himself unless he is guilty. Send for Hillier. Let him do his own dirty work.'

Eckhart bent his head a little and listened with a vague air, as if actually he were thinking of something else. He paid no attention; he only listened absently, and went out. Richard looked after him with repressed violence. I'd castrate you like your commander, he thought.

The litter of broken glass and china was still on the tray. He felt an impulse to strike out round him, to break what was breakable in the room. But he was sober and he sat still. It was desperately necessary to him to plan his course of action. They would not keep him here much longer. He supposed they would take him to London and once there he would be able to see his wife and to send messages through her, and to prepare his defence. If he were tried by court martial, it would be a just trial and he would be found guilty. But it was not the custom to try Volunteer officers in this way. If they had committed a crime they were handed over to the civil courts, even if the crime only concerned their conduct as officers. In a civil court he would have more time, a cleverer and less scrupulous counsel for the defence, and the chance of popular feeling turning towards him. But it was more likely to turn against him. His mouth stretched into a fixed jeering grin of sarcasm. He knew how it would be moved by stories of his debauches and immorality, a great deal of it true, except that he had made no secret of his tastes, and some of those who were noisiest in disapproval would find an obscene satisfaction in thinking about him and them. I know them, I know, he thought. He covered the whole human race with his filthy contempt for it.

Again he forced himself to turn to his schemes. He started always from the fixed idea that Hillier would not have him hanged, or shot, or whatever was the correct method of punishment for treason. Anything else was possible, and must be considered and prepared against, but that was outside the pale of the credible. He was not simply trusting to his luck in this. It was the ground on which he built up the frame of possible events in which his luck might hold or might fail him. He was nearly certain that Hillier had abandoned him to save his own position. He felt a momentary elation, exhilarating and exciting, with the feeling that he had got the better of Hillier in some way, and yet he wanted to humble him further. And to *know* that he was humbled. But now the question was, How far would he go in treachery? would it be imprisonment or exile? And if it were exile would he be allowed to take his money with him? It was his wife's money, but he thought of it as his.

He invented questions and his answers. He saw himself in court. He saw Hillier look at him with a fixed insensible glare, and outstared him. The men looking in at the window saw him seated forward on the couch, his knees stuck wide apart, and the same vacant unchanging air of jaunty assurance and arrogance.

All this time, from eight o'clock until twelve, when Eckhart came in for the last time, he was aware in his mind of something that evaded him. It could have been the pain he had refused to look at, or the repressed queasy violence. In its restless goings to and fro his mind kept swerving aside, as though it touched a raw place. He felt sparks of anger, and sharp pricks of impatience and bitter resentment. At moments he could scarcely contain himself on the couch in the forced inaction. Eckhart's half-hourly visits were like the flick of a hand over the rawness. He had to control himself to sit quietly through them.

Soon after twelve o'clock he heard a car. Hebden came into the room with four of the Special Guard. Two of these came to him and jerked him to his feet. He struck one of them. At once he received a heavy blow on the temple and a jab in the side which sickened him. The men hustled him into the car and stepped in quickly after him. It moved off, and he saw the frightened girl looking at him from the window of her bedroom. She seemed to be shut up there.

Neither Hebden nor Eckhart came with him.

CHAPTER XV

At half-past twelve that morning I reached the house where Richard had been. There was a lorry and a closed car in the road. As I neared the door of the house Eckhart came out. He did not take the trouble to answer my questions. I followed him into the room on the right of the small kitchen and he shut the door. I found myself in there with him and Colonel Hebden.

I was tired and seated myself on a chair. Eckhart jerked me to my feet and stood behind me. I was facing Hebden. He had an overcoat that came almost to the ground; it was unbuttoned and he stood inside it, his fat heavy body balanced on wide legs. He kept his head lowered, staring into my face, so that I thought of an enraged beast.

'You came here to meet Sacker?' he said.

I answered 'Yes,' to this, after a moment.

'Why? Were you ordered to come?'

'No,' I said.

I was not expecting to be touched in any way, but at the slight movement he made I stepped back. I knocked against the young man Eckhart, who steadied me sharply.

'We know everything about you and your activities,' Hebden said. 'We know that you and Sacker are seditious blackguards, we know what you were doing here. He'll be shot, if he doesn't shoot himself. And you'll be tried and hanged unless you can give us reason to think you were only a tool. Now then, are you going to help us?'

He did not take his cold enraged eyes from my face the whole time he was speaking, and he spoke like a man trying to control his temper. I was at a loss. I was not frightened, in the sense that I did not believe I was in danger of death. As most men in my circumstances would, I believed in the reality of the world I was born into, a world kept in order by a known compromise between force and goodwill. Offenders were punished lawfully. A man was not shot in a room with an oilcloth-covered sofa, a coloured calendar on the wall, and a mahogany table bearing a trayful of broken cups. I was only afraid of making some mistake that would turn things to worse for Richard. Yet I am not a brave man, I am only conventional.

'Are you examining me?' I asked. 'It's very irregular, and I shan't answer any questions here.'

Hebden lost his temper at once. His head filled with blood: his face was darkened by it. When he raised his arm I slipped aside and ran behind the table. I stood between the table and the wall and stared at him. It was ludicrous.

He did not follow me, and he waved Eckhart to go back. He leaned over the table, with his hands supporting him, and shouted: 'You shan't answer any questions, you shan't answer any questions? What are you saying?'

'You have no warrant to examine me,' I said.

'A warrant is not needed,' Eckhart said quietly. 'You ought to know that.'

'He knows he's guilty,' Hebden shouted. 'Lawyer's answers won't help you, when I'm dealing with you, you scoundrel.'

He made an effort to control himself. Against my common sense, which told me that I was safe from an actual danger of being hurt bodily, I was trembling. I leaned my back on the wall.

'If necessary we shall arrest Sacker's wife this evening,' he said in a calmer voice. 'She won't be sent to prison, you know, she'll go to a Training Camp for political offences. That is, if we don't get the information from you.'

'What information do you want?' I said.

'You were involved in this attempt, you were present when it was discussed. If you make a full statement, telling us everything you know, you'll not only be doing your duty, but you'll save yourself and your sister a great deal of trouble.'

There was less than a foot between my face and his when he poked the upper half of his body forward above the table. I noticed the thin red threads on his eyeballs and the swollen veins on his neck and hands. He was an unpleasant sight. He smelled strongly of eau de cologne. My mind noticed these details because it was not capable of dealing with what was going on. I did not know what to do for the best.

'If I make a statement will you guarantee that my sister is left alone?' I asked.

If I had thought this would annoy him I would not have said it. But why should it? It seemed that it infuriated him. He began to speak of Lotte in a brutal way, he told me that a Training Camp was the best and proper place for her, as for me. You could think he had been loathing her all this time. I was astonished. I had watched him paying her flamboyant compliments, rolling his eyes and his heavy body at her, until I was nauseated. And now to hear him – I could make nothing of it.

He began again with his questions about Richard. He had me out from behind the table. He sat down, with his legs apart, so that his trunk was resting on the chair, and made me stand in front of him. I could scarcely stand, I felt my knees

'I've put up with a great deal for the sake of our old friendship. It's not that I mind Sacker's bragging and boasting of his exploits. If he wanted to pose as a hero it did no one any harm but himself. I could even stand the recitals of his love affairs, although a middle-aged Lothario is a pitiable spectacle – '

He said it with an old-maidish spite that in any other place and time would have been cruelly funny. I had nothing to say. He looked at me for a moment, his mouth fixed in its sour smile. His face changed. He began speaking to me as though I were at the other end of the long room. He roared, or sank his voice to a soft whimper. I was exhausted, almost light-headed, and I had to listen to him.

'Yes, I know what you are going to say. You are going to tell me, me, that I made promises to the Volunteers and that I'm breaking them. Understand me when I tell you that malicious talk of that kind is out of date. If I make a speech which is necessary for the safety of the State that is my reason for making it. It is not necessary for me to justify it. It was necessary at the time when I made it and that justifies it. The safety of the State justifies everything.'

He put his fingers under his jacket in the traditional gesture of dictators, Mussolini and what not. It was strange and unpleasant that his features altered from within, as though he had no true face of his own. The next minute it was full of a pained nobility, no longer Caesar but one of his assassins, carrying out an unpleasant job in a disinterested anguish.

'I shirk nothing of my responsibility,' he cried. 'When I say that what I do I do for the State I mean that *I* do it. In the end I am the State. I was chosen by the people. Why? Because they felt the passion in me – because they knew that I had the will to save them from chaos. They put their lives and their souls into my hands on the day when they elected me. Every separate single Volunteer has put his life and soul into my hands. And now that they have done it they no longer have any right to criticise me or anything I do. They have dedicated their wills to me. I on my side dedicate my life to them, to help them. I shall help them, I shall give them new lives. But they must obey me. I must be the master of the lives they have put into my hands.'

He had lifted his arms. He let them fall again on the desk. His voice dropped, too. He began to repeat the very phrases Chamberlayn had used to me, and I fancied he looked a little like Chamberlayn.

'One thing is greater than I am,' he said, 'that is the State. My individual life is nothing – if the only way to save the State were for me to lay down my life I would lay it down gladly. It may come to that yet, to one dying that others may live. But while I live all men must be loyal to me, and to the historic task we have undertaken, to restore England to its greatness, and how can England be great and sound at heart until its heart is sound? And how is that heart sound when the blood shaking it is not sound, and what is that blood if it is not credit, the country's credit? We must cleanse the blood, we must wash the bones and the veins, we must rebuild the credit. The heart of the State is an economic heart. We must be loyal to economics, we must obey the laws of economics ...'

I must have missed something here. I was roused suddenly. He had spoken about Tower.

'What did you say?' I exclaimed.

He looked at me with a sly cruelty. His face was very seldom cruel, and the cruelty was always sly, and as if it were left-handed.

'Some professors and teachers are poisoning the minds of their pupils,' he said quietly. 'We have had our eye on your friend Tower for some time. But I was anxious to be very sure. After all, it does go against the grain to send an educated man to the Training Camps – '

'You're not going to do that to him!' I put my hands on the desk to steady myself. 'Why? Why should you? He has nothing to do with this. Nothing on earth. I assure you.'

'And I assure you,' he said calmly, 'that Denham has given me clear proofs that Tower is not involved only in this, but he has been fomenting an underground disloyalty – sending distorted and malicious letters abroad. It's well time he was shut up.'

I made some gesture. Hillier stood up. He leaned over the desk and shook his arm at me.

'I've had enough of this,' he said, curtly. 'I had you brought here because I wanted you to reassure your sister that nothing will be done to her. She's free to go where she likes. If you take my advice you'll go away now and take her with you – the sooner the better.'

I was afraid, but in a curious numbed way. My senses were numbed by weariness and anxiety.

And Sacker?' I said.

'Sacker has made an ass of himself,' said Hillier, slow, loud, harsh. 'He's done it once too often, and I'm at the everlasting end of my patience. Do you think my life's easy, do you think I have the energy to waste explaining the first and simplest necessities of government to an animal that won't listen? The truth about Sacker is that he's only good for destruction and fighting. When it was a question of destroying and fighting he was in his place. Now that that part's finished he is finished, too. What could I have given him to do! He had only to keep his mouth shut, to find his level and stay on it, and no one would have objected to his swaggering and boasting. If he had stuck to boasts about his part in creating the Volunteers. That *was* his job and very ably he did it.'

I felt myself agreeing with him. It was abominable, to agree with him even for a moment. But in that moment I realised without shock that some of the men who help a leader to power are certain to be the actual men he must murder or get rid of. He needs violent and unscrupulous men when he is struggling. Afterwards they embarrass him. They are a nuisance he can only ignore, and if they will not let him ignore them he has to find ways to silence them. It's the end of Richard, I thought. Hillier was still speaking. He had begun to work himself into a voluptuous excitement. His eyes were glazed and turned upward, and his gestures became looser, like a drunken man. I saw the saviour of his country emerge from him and take full possession. Even in my desperation I was partly fascinated by the sight. He flung his arms up, he roared, moaned, shook his head – and I held myself by the desk and watched him.

'I tell you that death means nothing to me. I shall go on living, I shall escape all sorts of deaths, because my work is not yet done. I can't die and I can't fail. My work is not finished until every man in the country has work, bread, and security. Work, bread, and security for the labourer, security and opportunities for the educated, security and profits for the employer of labour. So I shall not die, Whoever dies, England must not die!'

He held his arms out and said 'England!' very softly, and then with a yell – 'England!'

I felt myself shiver – the effect on my nerves of his loud voice. This, I thought, wearily, is how he did it. People wanted to believe. More than they wanted anything, they wanted belief. Just that – belief. Not reasons or facts. The narcotic of belief. Believe, and ye shall be saved. They had felt insecure for years and he promised them security; he promised the workless to find work for them, and he promised the hopeless a new hope. He promised all of them what they wanted, and in their revulsion from despair and the cynicism of despair they never asked themselves if he were more able than others to give it to them. They believed.

I suppose that when he was speaking and preaching he believed in himself. That was his sublime trick. He caught people into his own ecstasy. For men like Chamberlayn he had another face, but for the common people he had the face of the Messiah. And what a Messiah, I thought. What a rod to their backs. Serve them right for being deceived. Serve them right if they die of him. They chose him and they deserve him.

He was sitting wiping his face. He was very pale, with an air of exhaustion. I looked at the clock over his desk again and saw that it was half-past four. His passion had lasted five minutes, not long enough to exhaust him. He must have been tired before I came.

'Where is Richard? Can I see him?' I asked.

'No – you can't see him.'

'Where is he?'

'I don't know.'

'But it is your business to know,' I exclaimed. ' Or it is someone else's business to tell you. What are you going to do with him? You must know that.'

He looked at me with a queer baffled air. I believe that at this moment he had not made up his mind what to do with Richard. I believe that although he meant to get rid of him, to silence him, he had not made up his mind to murder him. There is no other reason why he had not done it that morning when he arrested him. It would have been very easy to shoot him then, the easiest of all. I believe that he did not want the responsibility. He did not want to give an order. He would have felt relieved if Richard had killed himself or if Hebden had shot him. What else could have been going on in his mind during the hours since he arrested him? Eight or nine hours. He had had time to turn himself inside out and persuade himself of anything. What in pity's name had he thought in those hours?

'I shall act – after consideration – the evil must be cleansed – you can take your sister out of the country, but not the boy. The boy can't leave – '

At the time I did not realise that he was speaking of Ernest Sacker. I was too tired, almost sightless.

'May I go now?' I said.

I did not feel that I was free when I was in the street. I ran up Whitehall in the sunshine until I came on a cab. Each time that we were stopped by the traffic lights I prayed: 'Oh God, make it green.' I was sweating. Even now I could not keep my thoughts on Lotte. My mind was split and spilt over a number of shifting planes of dark and light.

CHAPTER XVI

Sacker was hurried from the car into the place in Tothill Street. He had never set foot inside this building until to-day. The Special Guards were not his business and he had ignored their movements and their headquarters as deliberately as possible. He was taken upstairs to a room on the third floor and left there with two of the men who had driven down with him, a young sergeant and an older man, a private. It was half-past three, with the sun hot in the little room and a blue hot sky beyond the houses. The window of the room looked down into a yard with out-buildings, and across the roof of a lower building to the back walls of taller houses. There were windows in these other houses, and an outside staircase or two; in one window was a large cage filled with green and yellow birds. These windows were near enough for his voice to be heard, if he shouted. He had no impulse to be heard shouting.

He was hungry. He asked for a meal to be sent in and after some minutes he was given a plate of cheese, bread, and a half bottle of thin cheap wine. He turned his back on the two guards while he ate. He felt uncertain, and impotently restless. This being hustled about from place to place, as if he were an unpleasant parcel which no one knew what to do with or where to push out of sight, was on his nerves. He was insulted by it and angered by the insult, and for the time baffled. As he gnawed the rather dry cheese he gnawed on this thought of his helplessness. Since he saw Hebden he had seen no one of higher rank than the sergeant, a youth of twenty odd, who seemed overwhelmed by the responsibility. When Sacker asked, with authority, to telephone to his wife and a lawyer, this young man stammered that he knew nothing and he could not do anything. The prisoner must wait.

The prisoner waited in silence now. His mood changed from anger to a jeering impatience. He expected that Hebden would arrive shortly to 'examine' him and he was prepared with a series of retorts which he turned over in his mind and sharpened with rank humour. He expected to enjoy twitting Hebden – whatever the cost to himself it would be cheap. He was extremely surprised when the door was unlocked to admit Denham's secretary, Sir John Megan.

The old gentleman looked stronger and spryer than he had seemed for years. He was, indeed, lifted out of himself by the excitement. When he had abandoned his party and his friends, and the doctrines he had been preaching for years, he had suffered a curious diminution inwardly and outwardly. Outwardly he had aged and shrunk, and had developed asthma. He would wake at night fighting for breath, with the disagreeable sensation that he was falling into a gulf filled with feathers which were choking him. Inwardly he was as hollow as a penny whistle and the wind blew through him with an extraordinary confusion of sounds from which even his friends could not wring more than a few reluctant drops of sense. He was at his best and most coherent when he was talking about old furniture or swopping anecdotes with old ladies who had dabbled in politics and the arts in their time. But his intellect was not quite extinguished, and on an occasion like this, when it was confronted with a culprit whose guilt was blacker than his own, it leapt almost with its old fire, no smokier than in the past. To be sure, he did not acknowledge that he himself had been guilty; he condemned his old comrades, not himself – and yet he had shrunk and aged, like a rotten filbert in its shell. Nothing revived him but the prospect of being able to condemn another man as Judas. If he saw the Judas tree bearing its fruit he need not, for a time, feel in his secret mind that he ought to be hanging there.

He came forward, holding out his hand, with a subtle forbearing smile. He had always detested Richard Sacker for his looseness and his coarse vigour. Now he hid this even from himself. He had thought a great deal on his way here about common humanity, a phrase which spread a fine glow through his brain and body. He was eager to prolong the sensation.

Sacker looked at him without rising from the table. He tried to guess the meaning of this visit, while his mind ran ahead of him feeling for the simplest way to use it. He felt splendid as soon as he could act.

Megan sat down, and placed his gloves and hat on the table between them. 'I had some trouble in getting permission to see you,' he said gently.

'Who sent you?'

'I sent myself,' Megan answered, with his generous smile. 'I felt it my duty.' A little rosy cloud, bearing the phrase he loved, floated past his eyes. He felt the glow in his slack belly.

'Very kind,' Sacker retorted.' What can I do for you?'

He had seen through the older man as soon as he began speaking in his low and carefully mellowed voice. He has come here to spy, he thought. The jeering humour he had prepared for Hebden awoke and he held it in, to play a little with the old soapy politician.

'Nothing for me,' Megan said. 'But what can I do for *you*, my dear Sacker?'

'Tell me about Smith. Where is he? What has happened to him since he was arrested early this morning?'

Megan's face altered. 'Alas,' he said mildly, 'that unhappy man tried to defend himself from arrest and was shot during the struggle. Shot through the head and breast. He is dead.'

'Shot resisting arrest,' Sacker commented, with a sharp smile. He was startled, and careful not to seem it. This was a heavy score against himself. For the first time he faced a disagreeable thought. He thought that they might shoot him. Involuntarily he looked towards the window. As he sat, he could not see into the yard. 'It has happened like that before.'

'He had no time to consider, or to send a message to his wife – nothing,' Megan said with a sigh. 'He was misguided and I pity him.'

Sacker took this as an unmistakable hint that the other man expected his death. He checked himself sharply. Megan could expect, and be mistaken. 'And Denham?' he said.

'Ah,' Megan said gently, 'surely you know that Denham has acted throughout this – business, yes, business, in the best interests of everyone. If you had taken his advice, my dear Sacker, and discussed your discontents frankly with the Government, and after all, the country and all of us have been indebted to you in the past, I say if you had taken the frankest way out of any doubts you may have felt, and who knows what doubts any of us have had or may have had, and the simple way in this confusion is always the right way, the way of goodwill – '

Sacker could not help laughing. Never had he felt less like it, or laughed more heartily. The sight of the unctuous old man wrapping words round Denham's quite simple act – he has weighed the chances and thrown in his lot with the stronger side, he thought, as we should have known he would do – was too much for him. He shook with noiseless laughter.

'You certainly have a gift,' he said. 'Goodwill is the very word I should have thought of.'

He laughed in Megan's face until the old man, offended, wounded deeply in his vanity, rose to go away. He contrived to throw a world of sorrow into his voice. More in sorrow than in anger, he looked back into the other's derisive face.

'I had hoped to be of use to you, and to your wife, who is a *good* woman. You have, after all, got others into trouble as well as yourself. That unfortunate boy will pay for your misleading him, perverting him, yes, from his duty.'

Sacker looked at him quickly, with narrowed eyes. 'What boy? Are you telling me that they have arrested Ernest Sacker?

'Whether now or later,' Megan said, like a politician, and went out.

Sacker was left facing the possibility of his death. His first feelings were those of pure animal rage. He raged inwardly, seated at the table, with his arm resting on it and his face as nearly stiff as he could keep it. The nearness of the two Special Guards irked him. He could not move without bringing himself closer to them and he sat still. He was confused with anger. Anger passed through him, downwards, like the shock from a blow. He felt cooler, and his mind began its searching and scheming towards an escape. There must be a way out. He could not think for longer than a moment that he was going to die. That he should be at an end was unthinkable: it was not a thought, it was nothing. He turned away from thinking of it, to think of action, some immediate action. What can I do? he asked himself. His mind cleared almost at once. If I could see Hillier again, he thought quickly.

He glanced at the sergeant. The young man was standing between him and the window, his face slightly averted. Sacker could feel that he was very nervous. He had a pale alert face, like a student's – not insensible or overbearing. But when Sacker spoke to him, and asked him to take or send a message he revealed an odd stubbornness. He shook his head. Yet he was not easy; he wanted to do the correct soldierly thing and he did not want to make the mistake of offending a man who might only be under a cloud for a short time. That was how Sacker read his changing looks, and he put forth all his charm to coax and soothe the youth into obeying him.

In the end he gave way. He allowed Sacker to write a short note to Hillier, and gave it to the other guard to take downstairs. He was to send it off at once and to come back. He came back very quickly and said that the letter had gone. The time was now four o'clock.

Soon after this two officers, a captain and a young lieutenant, came into the room. Sacker took offence at once. What did they mean, he asked in an insolent voice, by walking into his room in this way? They took no notice of his question. The senior officer spoke quietly to the young sergeant, and the other stared out of the window.

'If I am on show, will you have the kindness to give me a better room?' Sacker jeered.

The officer half turned to him, frowning, then made a sign with his head to his companion and they left the room again without speaking to the prisoner. He realised that they were not certain of themselves. They are waiting for orders, he thought.

He drew his chair nearer to the window and looked out. For a time his mind went slack, and he wandered in his thoughts. He recalled a trivial scene, the turn of a road where he was walking on some forgotten evening. The scene came alive for him suddenly, he saw the leaves move in the hedge and the colour of the grass at the side. He was on a quay, waiting his turn to come on board a boat, but what boat and what quay or what voyage he was beginning, he could not remember. He came running along a short passage into a room, feeling his revolver in his hand, and lifted it against the man who stood up swiftly as he entered. He had no precise image of the next minutes, but he saw the man he had killed lying across the table. This was the first man he had killed. He was a rat of a creature who had to be put out of the way, and he had felt no doubts and scarcely any excitement. But now his mind dwelt on the affair with an unwilling curiosity. It seemed to him to be important, but he had no idea why. The man was not of importance.

It was now five o'clock, and no answer had come from Hillier. He tried to imagine what Hillier must be thinking, to seize and follow his mind. He is considering – he is weighing effects – effects, causes, effects. He is weighing the effect of my death, he thought. His mind was strangely quiet for a moment. Perhaps in his place I should decide to get rid of me. I have been a nuisance. I have failed – I have – I am, he thought dimly, in a confusion. He was on the edge of conceiving *why* his friend must get rid of him. A sudden fresh rage seized him, rising behind his eyes and blinding him. He no longer understood anything, except that he was being murdered by Hillier. He felt himself losing control, but he controlled himself and sat staring from the window with wide-open bloodshot eyes. He was caught.

His mind was still furiously active. It did not obey him when he attempted to think of Ernest, whom in a way he loved, or of Lotte. They were at a distance from him. He could think only about what he saw, the staircases of the houses opposite, the marks on the wall nearest his chair, his own hands. He stood up, walked a few steps and sat down again. He fell to studying the table, noting the grain of the unpolished wood and the knots in it. He looked again at his hands, struck by the shape of his nails and their pallor on the dark skin.

The young sergeant glanced at him in a furtive way, and after clearing his throat and coughing twice asked him if he would like a drink of water or another meal. Sacker asked him for a cigarette.

'I am sorry, I don't smoke. I have nothing,' the young sergeant answered He sent the other man downstairs again to fetch cigarettes and matches. When he returned two others of the Special Guard came in with him. Sacker looked at his watch. It had stopped and he asked the sergeant what time it was. It was a quarter to six. The men who had come in waited until he had lighted the cigarette; one of them told the sergeant that he was to bring the prisoner downstairs. Is this it, or am I being moved to another place? he thought.

They went down the stairs in a procession, the two guards in front, then Sacker with the sergeant, and the third man in the rear. When they reached the first floor a door opened and an authoritative voice inside the room ordered them to stay where they were. They stood still. This landing was at the front of the house. There was a long window, reaching almost to the floor. From it, Sacker could see a stretch of the street. He moved nearer to the window, the sergeant and another man stepping close beside him. Now he could see one end of the street. He saw that trestles and a plank had been placed across that end, and three Special Guards with rifles stood against the barrier, turning back people who tried to walk along the street. This sight decided him. They are going to shoot me, he thought quietly. His mind seemed to have retreated in some way, so that the thought conveyed no sensation to his body. Next he saw that a few persons, after argument with the guards, were allowed to pass but were hurried roughly along the street by a sergeant. From the glances cast up at the house he realised that the news of his arrest and presence here must have spread abroad in London. Four people passed during the ten minutes he stood at the window: first a young boy with a very red face, which he turned aside after one ashamed glance – he was almost in tears; then a girl who hurried by with averted face; then a known face – Maurice Gardner, who looked up and winced away again at once. Last of all to come past was an elderly woman with a coarse stupid face. She deliberately put her tongue out towards the window, although she certainly could not see him. The old beesom, he thought, amused. He struck the guard next to him with his elbow. 'Did you see that?' he demanded. The man did not answer, and Sacker glanced at him with his quick smile.

'Come, I'm not deaf yet,' he said.

'Be quiet,' the young sergeant bawled suddenly.

At the end of ten minutes, an officer, scarcely known to Sacker, came out of the room and motioned the party to go forward downstairs. He followed them.

They reached the ground floor and stood a minute in the passage leading to the yard. Sacker's attention was caught by words scrawled on the whitewashed wall. 'Forward to victory' was written out largely, and in smaller letters beneath it – 'Hillier our Leader.' He read them without much interest. They were only scribblings on a wall, no more present to him than the door through which he passed next, and the high brick walls and outbuildings of the yard. He felt no anger, almost no curiosity. The sun was in his eyes as he stood, and he blinked and moved his head. His mind was inactive, and he let his glance move about the yard with only the vaguest attention to what it saw. He saw a wall in darker shadow, the branch of a small creeper growing over it, and he saw a man's face rather indistinctly.

He looked between two of the men now facing him at a short distance, with their rifles, and he felt rather than saw the officer move his hand. Then he heard a confused noise inside his own skull and felt a moment's agony and horror. The moment was drawn out. He was lying with his cheek against the rough paving of the yard. He was conscious of it and of the unimaginable weight of the whole space above his head. It pressed on him and broke him, breaking the membrane of his eyes so that he was blinded.

The instant change that follows death was seen in him at once, in the curious pinching of his wide mouth and the turning inward of his sight.

CHAPTER XVII

The house looked as it always did, and the people were lying, sitting and walking in Regent's Park as they had done on fine afternoons ever since it was theirs to walk in. When I entered the house, a red-eyed housemaid told me that Mrs. Sacker was upstairs in her room. And now I knew she was safe, I thought that I should have gone to see Tower first. There was a telephone in the hall and I sat down and called his house. I half expected as I waited that I should hear that the line was not in order or there was no answer. But there was an answer. Tower's voice, slow and impatient, asking me what I wanted.

I had begun to speak. He interrupted me.

'Just a moment,' he said, a little testy, 'some men have come into the room. I must see what they want.'

The noise of the shots followed in the same moment. I heard the shots, my ear was jarred by the instrument falling, and that was all. I knew at once that they had killed him and I trembled in my whole body.

This was the end for me. Other deaths were an echo of this. My first separate thought was that it was the end of the world. There is nothing more to be hoped from a world which, deliberately, with deliberate cold violence, murders the best man living in it at the time. There is no excuse for that world. It is corrupt in every dish. Even the child in its mother's flesh is filthy. None of us is clean anymore, none of us is innocent – none deserves to live.

I went upstairs to Lotte. She was wearing hat and coat, and as I came in she was touching up her lips at a small glass.

'Were you going out?' I asked. 'No. Yes. I don't know. Have you seen Richard?'

I shook my head. I had begun to tell her about Tower, and stopped. It would only alarm her for Richard, and anger me that she cared so little for anything else.

She knew more of what was going on than I did. A number of people had been arrested, rumour said five hundred – journalists, writers, working men, suspected of seditious opinions, that is any opinion not wholly for the Government and Hillier.

'What have we done to deserve this sort of thing to happen in England?' said Lotte.

'We did not prevent it. It is in any case too late to repent.'

'Andy, I don't know what to do.'

'You could take your hat off and sit down,' I said. I put my arm round her, and she stood, stiff and unyielding, within it for a moment. She pushed me away and walked restlessly up and down the room. She told me that the house had been searched in the morning and every letter and paper taken, including her passport. This was a new trouble, and I told her that we must get it back, and begged her to think which of her friends would help her. She seemed to think about it. My sick anxiety got the better of me and I asked:

'Where is Ernest?'

She frowned as though I annoyed her. 'He and Steffy left London yesterday,' she said. 'They were going by train to York, then walking to Quarry House. They'll be on their way there now – I suppose they will arrive to-morrow some time.'

'It would be better for Ernest to go out of the country,' I said.

'We'll discuss it later – to-morrow,' Lotte said irritably.

'To-morrow may be too late. If Richard is going to be kept in prison it won't help him for the boy to be there. Or for you to be in England. He'd be more comfortable if you were safely out of the way.'

'You know quite well,' she said, with a little unforced laugh, 'if Richard is in prison he won't care very much where I am.'

'And if he is released and has to leave the country quickly?'

'Yes, then my passport would be a serious nuisance.'

She stood still in the window, her short jacket strained round her as it might be round a small barrel. Now that she was giving her mind to it she remembered that she had a close friend in the Home Office. We telephoned: he had left, and we caught him at his club. He agreed, I thought with the plainest reluctance, to see Lotte. I took her there, and we were shown into a small dark waiting-room near the door.

Lotte's friend was a man in the middle forties, tall, mild eyed, with a rather distant benevolence of manner. He took her hand very kindly and apologised for not being able to ask her into a pleasanter place.

She smiled into his face, warmly and almost merrily. 'You will forgive me for coming, Edward, but they have taken my passport from me. Please tell me how I can get it back.'

He drew back from her very slightly. Perhaps she did not notice it.

'Who has taken your passport?'

'An officer in Hebden's Special Guards. They searched the house and took every scrap of paper except that in the w.c.'s.'

'But, my dear girl – now, please sit down again,' he said, in a faintly reproachful tone.

'I can't sit down,' my sister said, softly. 'I don't know what is happening to Richard, and I am at my wits' end, Edward.'

I saw that he felt a natural distaste for Richard, and the strongest disapproval. The shadow of this disapproval fell over my sister for having involved herself with a disreputable man, but he made another kindly effort to soothe her. 'Why, you will know what is happening to him long before it happens, Lotte. He will be tried and I suppose dismissed – and really, my dear, I can't do anything about it.'

'I only want you to help me to get my passport back,' she said, in a low voice, smiling at him.

'But – I am sorry – my department has no authority over the Special Guards. It will be returned to you, of course, in time. One can't say when – these things naturally take a little time – but you can feel easy about it. I am sure that you can feel easy.'

There was a fanlight over the door of this windowless room, and the light that came through it was clearer than the feeble light of a small reading-lamp in the corner. It had also, for the glass in it was old and blackened, the curious effect of seeming to surround him in a faint reflection of itself. One could imagine a thin envelope of glass round him, only visible where it took the light. And so he does not hear her, I thought, and he did not hear the shots that finished off Tower. He is wonderfully protected from reality, spotless from the world.

My sister pulled down her jacket, and glanced at me. 'Come, we have kept Edward from his dinner,' she said.

'Not such a severe hardship,' he said, laughing.

'I can't imagine that anything will ever be more distressing to you,' said Lotte.

He gave her arm a gentle and forgiving touch in the hall. We stepped out into the sudden light of Piccadilly. I helped her into the first cab we saw and we went home. Lotte was smiling to herself, I think more surprised than bitter.

In the house she began again her restless walking from room to room. At seven o'clock the telephone bell rang. She took up the receiver herself. She listened, and I watched her. There was no change in her face. She turned to me, her hands putting back the telephone into its place, and said to me very slowly that Richard had been killed.

I spoke to her. 'What shall I do?'

'Do?' she said coldly. 'He said that my husband's body was at my disposal if I wanted it.'

She stood up, and pushed at her hat. It fell on to the ground. She began to run up and down, and when I tried to hinder her she pushed me back. She stood still at last, looked at me, and said: 'I can't do anything about it, can I? It's done. It's finished. I'm finished.' Her hands pulled at her face.

It seemed to me silly to try to comfort her. I said that I would go to the Headquarters in Tothill Street and bring Richard back to the house. I went there. He was laid on a table, unrecognisable at a first glance. His face was not in any way injured, it was just that Richard dead was visibly different from Richard living. Death was palpable, too.

'How am I to get him home?' I asked.

There were four men in the room. They looked at each other, and one, a young sergeant, suggested taking him in a closed lorry, and that actually is what I did.

CHAPTER XVIII

The next morning, that is, the morning of July 1, Harriet English came to see Lotte. It surprised me that Lotte was willing to see her, but I think she was indifferent to what went on round her. She was carelessly dressed and her hair untidy and unwaved. She looked ill and haggard, walked listlessly and spoke as though her mind were empty. Harriet – although she had taken pains to dress as plainly as possible – looked full-cheeked and handsome. And yet Lotte overbore her. The living glowing woman was quenched by the dead-seeming one.

'I came to know whether there is any help I can offer. And to say I am sorry,' Harriet said.

'Thank you. What could you do?' Lotte said carelessly.

'I was very fond of Richard.'

'I know that,' Lotte said, with irony.

'It would give me pleasure and comfort to help you, if you will let me,' said Harriet, defending herself.

'Why should I give you pleasure or comfort? Why you, more than any other of Richard's women?'

'I think I am the only one who has offered,' Harriet said plainly.

She was curiously vulnerable to Lotte's sharp tongue. She could defend herself, but she winced and seemed hurt. And my sister was glad to be able to hurt her. All that was ungenerous and bitter in her was roused by the other woman, and Harriet's own warmth sank, leaving a cold spite. I found the emotion between them unbearable.

'It was courageous of you to come,' I said, 'but there cannot be anything you can do.'

There was a silence, and my sister walked up to the other woman and stood close to her, looking into her face. With a sudden gesture, she held out her arms, the tears running down her cheeks, and kissed her. Harriet held her closely. There was a gleam in her fine eyes that was either triumph or simple happiness. She did not cry. I doubt whether she would ever cry for another's grief. Lotte withdrew herself after a minute and dried her eyes.

'What an absurd scene,' she said ironically. 'I am very tired, and I have never wanted to cry on a woman's shoulder in my life. Perhaps I am becoming childish again.'

'There is nothing you can do,' I said to Harriet again.

'You are going to take her away very soon?'

It occurred to me for the first time that she could in fact be very useful, if she were willing. I told her that I was more than anxious to take both Lotte and Ernest out of England, and that neither of them had a passport. Ernest had never had one and Lotte's had been taken from her. As soon as I had spoken of Ernest, Harriet nodded. She, too, had a suspicion – perhaps she had definite knowledge – that the boy was no longer safe. I thought of him in Winchell and felt the horror of my weakness.

Harriet was very quick with her way out. I began to see in her the qualities that had served her in her career. She was vulnerable but she was strong and sharp, and she had a masculine directness of mind. She told us that a close friend of hers was the owner of a yacht, and the yacht, and her friend with it, was now lying off Filey. She would send a message to him immediately telling him to take his boat round to the harbour three miles from Quarry House, and to wait there until he could take Lotte and Ernest on board. He could, as I thought, land them on any island in South Norway without trouble. He had only to drop anchor off Tjømø, or, avoiding all question, to wait in the outer fjord and row them the three or four miles to the little wharf at Havna and the hotel and stay there for friends of mine to fetch them to Oslo. That was true, Harriet said; she had once stayed in Norway for three months without her passport being required of her until a few minutes before she left, and because she was leaving.

All this time my sister was kneeling in the window, without interest in us. Once she leaned forward on her hands to watch some scene in the Park. Her indifference made her seem very simple, so that the years and their dead tumbled out of sight, and I was reminded of the nursery window and the long field over which it looked: but there were not any bars to this window as there were at the other.

The difficulty, I told Harriet, was to lay my hand on money. All Lotte's money was in the bank in her husband's name, and the supplies I had brought with me from Norway were almost finished. I asked her whether she would lend me fifty pounds, in the certainty of getting it back as soon as I went home. Her face had changed when I began speaking of money, and I told her hurriedly that I did not intend to stay in England an hour after I had settled what could be settled, so that her loan need not be a long one. She said 'Very well,' looked at her watch – it was eleven o'clock – and said she would send the money before three.

'I must go, I am glad I came,' she said to Lotte. 'You know I wanted to come to see you long ago. I wish I had had the courage to come.'

'Then you would not have had the excitement of coming to-day, when no one else is likely to come near us,' said Lotte.

She went back to her window as soon as the door closed on Harriet. I took up *The Times*, which was lying unopened on the table. The bare half column – on the main news page, it is true – given to an account of Richard's court martial, was placed under the heading: Changes in the Administration of the Volunteers. *The Times* is a master in understatement, yet I felt this a thought too negligible. The account was nothing but the curt official announcement: General Sacker had been responsible for a seditious mutiny in the Volunteers; it had been discovered in the last moments, like Guy Fawkes among his barrels, and the mutinous officers arrested: General Sacker had acknowledged his full responsibility, had indeed conceived and instigated the incredible attempt. The court, it went on, had done its melancholy duty in passing the only sentence allowed in the circumstances: and the sentence had been carried out without delay.

There followed another paragraph with an account of Major-General Smith's arrest, how he had shot at and fortunately missed a Special Guard, who had then fired in self-defence and killed the prisoner. No doubt the Guard was the better shot.

On another page a longer paragraph, but in smaller print – the hierarchy of type – announced that Robert Baxter Tower, a professor of London University, had committed suicide when he was arrested on a charge of fostering sedition among his pupils. There was also obituary notices of Smith and Tower on the proper page, but nothing about Richard. Both accounts of their lives had been taken, and I thought hacked off short, from the files of the paper, without mention of their ends. On reflection I did not suppose that the smoothest editing could have brought their notices up to date without a little awkwardness. They went better as they were.

I looked for further comment, and found it being droned out in the second leader, with a coarse and heavy-footed assurance. It was headed: The Democratic National State in Action; and it began:

> If there is any single advantage which a thoroughgoing dictatorship possesses over the wisely qualified democracy which our instinct for political compromise has evolved, it must be the protection that a dictatorship affords against the reckless ambitions of individuals. Yesterday's events have shown that democratic government leaves a number of avenues unguarded against

unscrupulous opponents. It may be doubted whether, but for this licence, it would have been possible for two or three individuals, holding as they did positions of authority, to spread their ambiguous and dangerous ideas through the Auxiliary Forces to the point where armed revolt was in active preparation. General Sacker was, it seems, prepared to risk the happiness and well-being of his country on a gambler's throw. Had his attempt succeeded, the country would have been plunged into untold misery, unpredictable in its consequences ...

Nevertheless, the writer went on to predict them for half a column. He rounded off his inspired musings in the most natural way in the world – with praise and thankfulness for the benefits of good government.

We can congratulate ourselves on the wise boldness in action that characterises our present leaders. MR. HILLIER'S moral courage and energy in facing a situation fraught with peril is not less to be commended than his physical bravery in confronting an armed and irresponsible rebel with the discovery of his plot. We can rest easy in the certainty that every step now taken is a step forward to greater security and tranquillity in our political life. The country is firmly behind MR. HILLIER and the State Council in any further measures they may decide to be necessary for the safety of our lives and traditions.

I did not think I could have rounded the mulberry bush more neatly and prudishly myself.

I thought for a time about Tower. He believed as firmly as *The Times* in the essential decency of England. Perhaps he was right.

Harriet's money had not come at three o'clock. I waited an hour, and rang her up. She was in the bitterest distress. She said she had been mad to promise the money. She could not, it was impossible, spare such a sum. It was utterly impossible. It would drive her mad if I persisted.

I did not persist. 'Have you sent the message to your friend?' I asked. I should not have been surprised to hear that that effort had been too much for her. But I was wrong there. The message had been sent five hours since.

I went back to Lotte. She was still idling in her room. She had changed her dress to a warmer one for the night journey by car, but she had packed nothing. Her face had an absorbed shut-in look that baffled me. I tried to speak to her about Ernest and Steffy. She was anxious, but with a cold mechanical anxiety.

'They will hardly punish Steffy,' she said lightly.

'I suppose not,' I said, 'but the thought of Ernest in a Training Camp, like Winchell, is awful and unbearable.'

'You will never grow out of your habit of trying to bear other people's lives for them.'

'That is not like you, Lotte.'

'What should I be like? Ought I to have been softened by losing Richard? I have nothing to live for any longer. There is no meaning in my life without him. I don't believe that any woman does things for herself alone – she does them to be praised, to make herself finer and more interesting to someone, preferably to one man. I have no reason to exist now. Even if Ernest was my son, he would belong to Steffy. Not to me. I am completely alone.'

'You will find it bearable in time,' I said.

'Yes, when I am old,' cried Lotte. 'Yes, I am to look forward to being old, so that I can't feel, and I forget easily and think that some things are not real and not as terrible as I thought they were when they happened.' She struck the window frame with her hands. 'To think that I could do nothing. That they killed him in spite of me. That I was helpless, useless – like any other woman. As useless as his dear Harriet, who thinks better of herself for coming here to satisfy her curiosity this morning.'

'You're hardly fair to her, my dear.'

'I'll leave that to you,' she retorted. 'You always liked large women, with eyes like oxen – do you remember the governess you fell in love with when you were fifteen? She was just such a fine figure of a woman as Harriet.'

I smiled at her, and in the very middle of my love and pity the thought shot through my mind that women are never so much themselves as when they are, in the common phrase, not themselves. 'Well, forgive me,' I said. 'I'm not defending Harriet English. I don't admire her.'

'Forgive *me*,' Lotte said, in a low coaxing voice, and with an equivocal glance.

'Say anything you like,' I said wearily. 'I don't mind – why should I?'

She jumped up and came close to me. Her hair was falling into her eyes and she looked wild and haggard again. 'Do you know that I have been thinking of Hillier?' she said swiftly. 'He makes me shudder, as if he were something loathsome I had dreamed about. I dreamed once that the yard at Quarry House was filled with eels writhing and twisting together in a long wooden tank and I was almost sick with fright in my dream. I have the same feeling when I think of Frank.'

'Don't think of him,' I exclaimed.

She took hold of my arm and swayed on it. Her eyes were closed. 'There is something I must tell you. Yes, you must know. I simply must tell you. The evening before last, the twenty-ninth, when I had just come back here from the country, Denham came here into this room, and asked me where Richard was. He stood where we are standing, and he told me that Richard would be court-martialled and sentenced to death when they arrested him, which was a matter of time. If I told them where they could find him at once, the sentence would only be imprisonment.' She walked away from me, and spoke as though she were alone. 'I told him. He scarcely thanked me. Yes, that is what is so strange, don't you think? That he forgot to thank me.'

She smoothed her skirt down, and looked at me with a heavy frown.

'Your telling him made no difference,' I said.

'But I can't forget it,' she cried. 'It is the worst thing of all – worse even than the ugly hurried burial this morning. It is the worst thing I have ever done in my life.'

'No, it made no difference,' I insisted. 'All it means is that they would have caught him a day or two later, as soon as he came back to London or to some other town. You had nothing to do with it in effect.'

'I shall think of nothing else until I die,' she said, but she said it indifferently, as though she were thinking of something else already. She looked at herself in the glass. 'You would think I could manage to look dignified on such an occasion!' she cried ironically. She tried to straighten her hair, and laughed at me over her shoulder. Then she came over to me and kissed me lightly. 'My dear good Andy,' she said, in a quick voice, 'you must go and pack, and I must pack, because we must be away as soon as possible. Go and tell them to get the car ready.'

I went downstairs and out through the kitchen to the passage leading to the garage. When I was in the kitchen I told the girl – the others had left the house – to run upstairs and try to help her mistress to pack.

I think I had been in the garage a minute or two when she came in running and trembling to say that Mrs. Sacker had fallen from the window of her room. I ran as quickly as I could move myself to the front of the house. There were already two or three people there, stooping over Lotte, but she was dead. I knew that by the way she was lying, with her head turned round away from her body. A man picked her up for me and carried her into the house to her own room.

When the doctor came I asked him to send someone to the house who would not mind staying. 'Perhaps better two women than one,' I said.

He sent in a middle-aged nurse and an older woman. I told them to make themselves at home and to take charge of the house, because I had urgent business that was taking me out of London for twenty-four hours. They looked surprised and suspicious, but they agreed.

I could not drive the car. I engaged a man from the garage to drive me, and we started at ten o'clock. So near midsummer night it was scarcely dark then. It grew darker as we left London. The houses on both sides of the road had lights in the rooms, with open windows. It was a very warm night, quiet and airless. The sky was still pale, and covered with light clouds and long, barely visible tracts of stars behind them. I had told the man to hurry, and as soon as we could we ran at a great speed. We had the road almost to ourselves, since the bulk of the traffic was coming into the town, and what was going out was chiefly lorries and country vans which we caught up and passed.

The chauffeur was a thin, talkative Londoner, and a bad driver. He swerved round the corners on the brake, jerking and dragging at the car. I could not listen to him or answer him. I was dazed with weariness, and at times I caught myself imagining that Lotte was lying on the back seat of the car, being jolted and bumped by the careless haste. Not able to feel anything more for the time, I found that I was smiling at the thought of her bundled carelessly into the back – it would be just like her to choose that way of coming.

After a time I began to feel impatient. My impatience grew heavier until it was like a burden hung round my shoulders. I was leaning forward on the seat, to get some relief from it. I was afraid that I was too late. Someone had known where Ernest had gone and they had already arrested him, and I should come in time to take a distracted Steffy back to her father. I told the man to hurry, and he retorted amiably that short of fitting wings we could not move quicker than we were now moving. I was angry with myself then for not taking one of the night aeroplanes as far as York. It was only the fear that I should be stopped at the last minute had made me come this way.

When we had been driving for two hours the car stopped. The driver got out and tried to discover what was wrong. I stepped out, too, and stood fuming and agitated beside him. The man was quite ignorant and incompetent, he had no more notion how to put the thing right than he had of driving, which was very little. At the end of a quarter of an hour he scratched his forehead and confessed that he knew nothing at all about cars. He was not a mechanic, he said; he had been doing odd jobs at the garage, and they had sent him because there was no one else at the time to send.

In my fury I struck at him and missed him. He ran away from me round the car, with a face of dismay and surprise. Now beside myself with impatience and anger, I set off on foot, walking and running at the side of the road for half a mile before I realised the stupidity of it. I heard a lorry rattling behind me, and I stepped out into the road and waved to the driver to stop. He poked his head out over the door to ask me where I was going: he said he was on his way north. I climbed in beside him and sat thankfully on the narrow driving seat; he could put me on my way, he told me, as far as Doncaster, and there if I had the money I could catch the train that left ten minutes after he did: he knew all about it, he said laconically, because his brother drove it.

He was a young man, short, with a small handsome bold face, roughened by the weather, and he spoke like a Yorkshireman. His eyes were grey and very bright under their furry brows, with their suggestion of a quick smallish wild animal. Leaning a little forward over his wheel, he had an air of grace and reckless energy that made him very attractive. I felt more comfortable with him than I had felt in the car. After a time I asked him whether he had heard what was going on, the arrests and the death sentence passed on Sacker. He nodded. I tried to draw him out by telling him that these things shocked me. He scrutinised me for a moment, with a flicker of a sardonic grin on his face.

'Let them do what they like,' he said cynically. 'They're nowt to me and I'm nowt to them. I'm fed up with the whole lot of them, whatever they call themselves, and the Labour Party was the worst of the lot, promising and doing nowt. But this lot's as bad. So I'm through with them.'

He was silent after that, and I gave up trying to talk to him. He was a good driver. The darkness was already melting into a watery light, and the fields and hedges had a naked sharpness as though a thin veil had been brushed off them, the veil that descends with the full daylight when the air is shot through with moisture. Nearing Doncaster, there was a stir of life in the villages, but none yet in the town. It was four o'clock. The young driver stopped his lorry near the station for me. 'Any message for your brother?' I asked.

He shook his head, grinning. 'Nay, he knows what I think of him,' he said.

During the train journey I slept without knowing it, waking with a start of fear to find that we were nearly at the end. There was still the long climb from the station, up the steep flinty road to the village and further up still to the house. It seemed to me that I was past any emotion. I trudged quickly, thinking of nothing at all and seeing nothing. When I reached the house and saw Ernest standing in the kitchen doorway, with the girl at his elbow, I had to sit down, without speaking to them, I was so done. My last strength seemed leaving me as I sat there, on the chair on the flagged stones of the kitchen. I looked at the yellow sunlight on the stones and at the scrubbed wooden dresser and thought I was out of the world already. There seemed no bridge between these things and the room in which I had left Lotte; the long desperate drive was not a bridge, it was a breaking-off from one life and my mind had not adjusted itself yet to the other. I had only one desire left: for a warm drink of some sort.

'Can I have coffee?' I asked.

'I'll warm it for you,' Steffy said quickly. 'I made some for our breakfast – hours since.'

She went into the scullery. I looked up at Ernest. 'What time is it?'

'Seven o'clock,' he answered.

'You can't have had your breakfast so very long then,' I said foolishly.

'We had it at four o'clock,' he said. 'We only heard – about him – yesterday evening, when we got here. We've been quarrelling, arguing what we ought to do.'

He looked at me with a hard, blank stare. I could see that he was unable to force himself beyond a certain level of calm. If he went beyond it he would break down, lose control of himself, and above all that horrified him, to feel himself losing control, so that other people knew what he was feeling. Steffy came in carrying a coffee pot and a cup, and set them down on the table. She had heard his last words.

'Tell him it is no use going back to London,' she said to me fiercely. 'They'll arrest him, I know they will arrest him.' She turned on him. 'I shall go off my head if they do anything to you.'

'But I must go to Lotte,' Ernest repeated. He looked at her, as if he were tired of telling her the same thing over and over again.

'Lotte is dead,' I said.

I told them what had happened the evening before. Ernest listened in silence, his head lifted and his gaze fixed on some remote point in his own mind. The girl turned so pale that I thought she was fainting, but he paid no attention to her, and she began to cry, helplessly, with fear. She was afraid of a world in which these things happened, but most of all she was afraid for Ernest. She forced back her tears and went to him, trying to comfort him in her arms. He stood stiffly, not noticing her, and she broke into a thin wail of grief.

Then he heard her. He touched her and said: 'Don't cry, Steffy.'

She started up and threw her arms round him again, holding his head against her thin shoulder. 'My love, my love.' He allowed her to comfort him for a minute, then turned to me with an arm round her and said:

'We must think what to do. What do you advise?'

He was very quiet; he had become older in the last few minutes, as if he had felt for the first time the pressure of male responsibility on him. When Steffy spoke to me about Lotte he winced. I was afraid that the thought of her lying under the window would haunt him.

'She died instantly,' I said. 'She was dead when I reached her, there was no pain in it for her.'

'Of course she didn't fall out,' Ernest said. 'She did it on purpose.'

I nodded. 'Of course. It means that she was thinking only of Richard and herself. It didn't occur to her to wonder what would become of you, or me, or Steffy.'

He frowned, bitterly offended, but I thought that it would sink in later, and help him to forget the image he had had of Lotte falling. As for me, I felt in my own body the sick horror of the fall – and always should. The moment when she felt her last hold go, when she knew what she had done – that moment came in me again and again, whenever I thought of her.

'What shall we do?' Steffy asked.

I told them that I had no doubt Ernest was in danger of being sent to a Training Camp as soon as they had time to bother about him, and to find out where he had gone on leave. They moved closer to each other as I said it, and the blank look came again over Ernest's face. His blue eyes stared at the girl. I went on to tell them that we had arranged a way of sending Ernest to Norway and I explained it all to them.

'We can go down to the port at once,' I said. 'Better go before Annie turns up here.' She slept in the village during the times when Richard and Lotte were not living in the house.

'She won't come,' said Ernest. 'She went off yesterday, pretending that her mother was ill. She's afraid.'

Steffy was standing with her head bent and her face turned from us. Her mouth was closed in a short obstinate line. She glanced up suddenly at Ernest, and said:

'You won't go to Norway without me, will you?'

He looked at her with a queer, half derisive smile. '*Can* you come? You know, you won't be able to come back if you don't like it.'

'I can't live without you,' said Steffy. 'And you want me, don't you? We had better marry very soon. I can promise to love and honour you!'

'Yes, I want you,' he said, serious and diffident now.

'That's all, then – and I'm coming with you now.' She turned to me. 'There is room for me in the yacht, isn't there? I can sleep anywhere, I could sleep on deck.'

'Yes. They were expecting Lotte,' I said. 'There must be room.'

Ernest lifted his face, in the wincing abstracted stare. I thought that for all his calmness and sharp spirit she would not have an easy time with him. He loved her, but he was more interested in other things, in his mathematics for one. And he had been shocked out of his young carelessness.

They had soon made their preparations. Their rucksacks had not been unpacked the evening before. I think they had just slept in the kitchen – there were blankets folded in one corner near the hearth. Steffy had a letter to write to her father, which she gave me to post. She was ready then.

We closed all windows and locked the one door that was open. I did not mean to come back to the house, but to go straight to London as soon as I had seen them on board the yacht. Neither of them said much, they seemed glad to have someone to obey for a few hours. As we were leaving the house Ernest said, with his new quiet insistence: 'You ought not to stay behind. Come with us.'

'I'm not in any danger,' I answered, pleased. 'I must go back to London. I shall go back – and see to her – and come later.'

He said nothing more. We took a narrow path over the edge of the moor that would bring us to the road without passing through the village. It was so narrow that we walked in single file. The morning was very hot now and clear. I saw a lizard sunning himself on the loose stones between the track and the moor. There was no colour in the heather yet, nothing except the harsh vivid green of reeds and the delicate jaunty harebells. At the turn of the path we halted. Now, if ever, was the moment to look back at the house, before we turned downward to the road that went quickly to the coast and the harbour. But Ernest looked straight in front of him, and in the end Steffy was the only one who looked back at the house. She looked, and then turned to follow us. When I glanced at her she was crying quietly. 'Oh, poor Lotte,' she wept.

CHAPTER XIX

At eight o'clock in the morning of July 3 I stood with no other beside me at Lotte's grave. The men were waiting as far from me as they could remove themselves, to fill it in, and I had no wish to prolong the moment. And yet I did not move. I was myself waiting, for her ironic laughter to break out, and it was only after I had waited five minutes longer, and heard the slight noise of a tool of some sort striking the ground behind me, the only sound of impatience these decent embarrassed men allowed themselves, that I moved away. As I was leaving the place I was joined by another man, then by two others. They were the relatives of General Smith, who also had been given permission to bury their dead in this place and time.

Outside, I looked round me for the taxi I had come in. It was gone. The other three had a private car, and they were kind enough to offer to take me in it. We were on the outskirts of north London, in a new raw suburb. The cemetery was a new one; it looked as though it had been snatched only at the last moment from builders' lots, fenced round, and a chapel hastily thrown up.

I looked round me at Smith's relatives, a young man and two men between forty and fifty. They were all three soldiers. That was clear from their manner and way of moving, as well as from their faces, which had all the same blank amiable expression of stiffness and alertness. They were men who knew their job – in a sense, they were dedicated to it, and in the same sense they were carefully or involuntarily insensible to any other life. I had precisely the feeling with them that I should have had as a schoolboy arriving at a new school. Yet they were taking a little trouble to be pleasant to me, giving me leg room, and a rug for my knees.

They exchanged a few words between each other. Then I said diffidently: 'This is a bad business.'

After a slight pause, the young man blurted: 'Damned bad, I think.'

'It may have other effects than the Government are hoping,' I said. I was surprised to find that I had still some curiosity and inquisitive spark in me. I did actually want to know what they were feeling.

'It *will* have other effects,' said the young man. He gripped his hand on the gloves he was carrying, and his nose and mouth became pinched with anger.

One of the older men struck in smoothly. 'There is a time for everything,' he remarked. 'Certainly it is not the time now to have trouble of any sort.'

'You mean that the country is unsettled – mentally and economically?'

'I daresay you are right,' he said, very civil and indifferent.

'The state of the country is bound up with the state of the army,' the third man said calmly. 'The present Government is prepared to spend money on the defence forces. That is a welcome change. It will take a great deal of money and hard work to make up for the neglect of the past.'

'But in time it will be made up,' said the young soldier. He looked out of the window of the car, and a faint smile came on his face round his eyes and nostrils. I wondered whether he were seeing the time when the army would feel that it had been strengthened enough. Enough for what?

I had scarcely been in the house an hour when I was arrested and taken to the Headquarters of the Special Guards. My first thought was that I should be sent to a Training Camp and I prayed that it might be Winchell. I should at least have the satisfaction of putting myself right with Holman and his friends. This sentimental idea encouraged me during the five or six hours I was kept waiting in a downstairs room.

At last I was examined, and questioned only about Lotte's death, and my work in Norway. I had recognised one of the officers who was questioning me as a former head waiter at the cafe I used to visit when I was in England. This so confused me that I thought less about my answers than about the changes in our lives. He had never condescended to me.

When he asked me suddenly where Ernest Sacker was, I answered after a moment that I did not know.

They kept me standing in front of them for an hour, then told me carelessly that I could go. My passport, which had been taken from me at the beginning, was handed back.

'You have to-day and to-morrow to leave the country. But don't come back,' the late head waiter told me.

I was astonished. 'I am free?' I said, slowly and foolishly.

'Yes. Why not?' he said in a contemptuous voice. 'You're not a danger to anyone or anything. Your sister's estate will be held in trust for the time by the Government, but you can take your own personal property from the house.'

I felt humiliated and surprised. When I left the place I thought that the men on guard in the corridor were laughing at me. I caught sight of the young sergeant who had helped me with Richard's body two evenings ago, but when he seemed about to speak to me I turned and hurried out of the place without looking aside.

In the street I bought an evening newspaper and read in it that the Minister of Labour, George Body, had been detained in prison. 'It is believed,' the account went on, 'that he was involved in the attempt to seduce the Auxiliary Forces. A sojourn in a Training Camp will no doubt fit the circumstances of the case. Body was formerly a member of the Labour Party.' I felt a distinct satisfaction in reading this.

The house was full of Special Guards. They were poking into all the cupboards and emptying drawers and shelves on to the floor. One handsome youth had dressed himself in a hat and long coat of my sister's, and was parading up and down her room with her sunshade held over his head. I saw another putting small ornaments from the mantelpiece into his pockets, and another had broken a bottle of scent and was dipping his fingers in it and wiping them on his hair and clothes.

After nine o'clock I left the house and walked about the streets for a time. Some of the shop windows were lighted, and men and women sauntered aimlessly past them, with no idea except to kill time. The only shops into which they looked were the show-rooms of the motor-car firms. When I had walked the length of Regent Street a light shower of rain sent most of them flying into the tube stations and buses. I had no wish to return to the house, and my train did not leave until the morning. Then I remembered that I knew Lewis's address and I set off to visit him.

He lived in a narrow street behind Tottenham Court Road. The street was dark and poverty-stricken as well as narrow. I rang the bell of his house and stood waiting on the empty pavement for a long time. The rain had stopped, but the air was still damp and heavy, and there was the smell of poverty in it in this street. The door opened at last and a woman stood there inside the darkened passage and stared at me. I asked for Lewis, and she shut the door in my face at once. I walked a few steps and stood irresolute. Footsteps were coming towards me from a side-street. I turned round and peered in the darkness at a young man, not more than a boy, who must live in the house, since he stopped at the door and was drawing a key from his coat pocket. I hurried up to him. 'Do you know a man called Lewis who lives, or used to live here?' I asked.

The boy looked at me curiously. 'Are you a friend of his?' he asked softly.

'Yes,' I answered, and to persuade him I went on: 'I have not seen him since the day of Myers's funeral, and he may have moved.'

'No, he is here,' said the boy. 'He is ill – but he is here and you can see him.'

He unlocked the door and allowed me to step in front of him into the house. The woman who had kept me out came into the passage from a room near the door. She drew back when she saw me. 'You promised me not to bring anyone,' she said, reproachfully, to the boy.

'Now, mother, it's all right, don't fuss,' he said, lightly and kindly. 'He is a friend of mine.'

She looked at me with dislike and resentment. 'You can't stay,' she said.

'I have only come to see Lewis,' I began, and the boy himself silenced me, by a gesture. Following him towards the stairs I glanced at his mother and saw in her face that she was only mortally afraid for her son. I would have reassured her but I did not know what to say.

Lewis's room was at the top of the narrow dingy house – it was the attic, and a faint light came into it through the skylight, from the overcast sky. The room itself was quite dark, with only the dispersed smoky greyness directly beneath the skylight. Not even a candle pierced the blackness. After a minute I became sufficiently used to it to make out the bed close to the near wall. And then Lewis spoke.

'Who is there?' he said.

'It is Andrew Hillier,' I said, standing still in the doorway. I felt the boy at my side start a little at the name.

'Come in, then,' Lewis said quietly. 'I am glad you have not been arrested.'

'Shall I go?' the boy asked, in a relieved joyful voice.

'Yes, go. Promise your mother that I shall be able to move out in a day or two. She needn't worry. I'll leave as soon as I can.'

'Then you're not very ill,' I said. 'Why are you lying in the dark like this? And what is wrong with you?'

'I slipped, running down into a basement room, and broke my ankle,' said Lewis. 'But it is almost mended. I am forced to lie here in the dark because this room is supposed to be empty. Fortunately it *was* empty when the police searched the house last week. That was the day I had gone out, and came back with my ankle broken. The boy is a friend of mine – I was coaching him for his examination – he was one of Tower's pupils. And now his mother, poor woman, can't sleep for fear.'

I had found my way to the side of the bed, and I sat down. 'Do you blame her?'

'Not at all,' he said simply, almost merrily. I felt that he was smiling.

'Tell me what you are doing – and what you are going to do.'

'To-morrow at four o'clock I am sailing for Norway. I shall not come back.'

'So you are running away,' Lewis said.

I tried to see, him, but his face was only smudged faintly in the darkness – I could make out his dark eyes and his mouth, but not the expression on them. 'I see no other way out,' I answered. 'It would be useless for me to stay here, in hiding.'

'One becomes used to it very quickly,' smiled Lewis. 'And at least you have seen, or I hope you have, that there is no smooth way out. If there is a war, things will only seem worse. All those who fear change will be drawn together still more closely, and for a time I shall be hard put to it. You will see what will happen. It will turn out as it did before, that in the moment of danger, whatever shape danger takes – even if it is only the danger that so much food will be grown that it will have to be burned to keep it from getting into the hands of people who need it – many whom you thought were enemies of one another are found to have the same wishes at bottom. The industrialist and the labour leader both wish to keep their places and the respect of their fellows, both accept titles for themselves, both bring up their sons to honour what is and to fear what might be. The banker and the grocer at the corner see eye to eye about money and its uses. It is not only the rich who are shocked by the thought of social justice. I have heard a clerk drawing three pounds a week argue that two or three million unemployed were needed in order to put the fear of God into the others, and keep them quiet. I suppose his heart leaps up when he hears that still another young man has hanged himself in despair – '

'Then why are you risking your life to alter the thoughts of these people? Why not let them rot?'

There was a long silence. I fingered the rough covering of the bed, and my foot straying over the boards came on the thin edge of a strip of carpet.

'I can't help myself,' he said at last, in a flat tone.

'But why do you preach violence and civil war?'

'There is no other way,' he said slowly. 'I thought you would have seen that by now.'

'War is never worth it,' I exclaimed. My whole body was in revolt against him at this moment.

'Please do not raise your voice.'

'I am sorry.'

'You are clearly not used to hiding,' he said.

'But I feel that you are welcoming violence,' I whispered. 'You do not want another way out; it gives you pleasure to anticipate it. I hate it and fear it. No war has ever been worth it, no revolution has ever paid for the slaughterings. Besides, I do not believe that it is inevitable in England. The English are different. There is a tough root of belief in them. Compromise, easing of the present, will come in time.'

He moved suddenly, and his hand grasped my wrist. His fingers were roughened at the tips and very bony and dry. 'No, I will tell you what is coming.

The well-off and the powerful are like Saturn, they eat their own children to prevent any change taking place that could threaten them. In the past they have always been defeated by new men and new inventions. Either they will be defeated again or they will relapse, dragging us with them, into barbarism and war. That will be the triumph of Saturn. No revolt against them is quite certain of success. There is always another and worse level on to which they can wriggle. But *we* shall always fight, and one day we shall win. You will see other changes in the meantime. You will see a tussle between Denham and Thomas Chamberlayn for the power of the State, and Denham defeated – changes like that are not important, although you, watching them from your funk-hole, will become excited and think that something is really happening. You won't see what actually is happening. Even when you read one day that I have been shot resisting arrest.'

I did not answer. He sighed, and asked me what my friends in Norway thought of England.

'Oh, they think we are finished,' I said.

'So we should be if all Englishmen were like you,' he answered. His fingers moved on my wrist for a moment. 'Stay, and face it,' he said gently. 'Do you know that I like and trust you?'

'No, I'm not one of you,' I whispered. My hand and arm pressing the bed had become cold. 'I don't believe in your faith, if it is a faith. I believe that England will be saved in her own way, and it won't be yours.'

Lewis did not speak. I felt his fingers slowly leave my wrist. I stood up to go away, only eager now to leave him lying, without a light, in the airless shabby room. When I said: 'Good-bye,' he did not answer. I waited a moment, and heard him breathing, slow quiet breaths. Feeling my way along the wall I found the door. I opened and closed it very gently and crept furtively down the stairs. In the passage I heard the boy's voice murmuring on quietly behind a closed door, and his mother's answers. The street was still empty when I stepped into it. I spent the rest of the night walking about the streets of this part of the city. Not for the world, I thought, can I go back again to sleep in Lotte's house. But when I went there in the morning to fetch my luggage it was empty and some of the rooms had been tidied: there was only one middle-aged Special Guard, a lean bottle-nosed Cockney, in the hall and he was actually trying to restore decency. He looked at me with a half grin. 'Must leave things right,' he muttered.

In the evening at ten o'clock we were out of sight of land. The sea was smooth, moving gently, in dark long furrows, with a gleam of white disappearing rapidly into the darkness. I was tired, but my eyelids strained widely open. I did not realise that I had finished with England, that I should never see or smell or touch it again, and yet it had become shadowy and unreal to me. I thought of the rat courage of Lewis. I thought of Tower. *Was* there an underground movement against the destroyers, and was he part of it? Even so quickly after what had happened I was already uncertain and confused in the welter of motives, greeds, fears, ambitions. I reflected that if all the dead of the past week came to life and met together in one room, still the truth of what each of them had hoped would be hard, no, impossible to tell.

I felt myself empty, except for those who had died. I tried to think of Ernest and Steffy. They, at least, I said, have a future. But the feeling of emptiness in my own spirit returned, and persisted. It seemed that my roots were too firmly and deeply curled round the past, round the old England, the old houses and the old words and thoughts. In between these, the soil was dry and falling away, but my roots only clung the faster to what was left. I was not comfortable any longer in the past. Yet I could neither imagine myself living in a new way, nor wish it. I have lost both worlds, I thought. Even the safety towards which I was going had neither comfort nor attraction for me now.

I stood on deck until I was alone there, then went to my cabin; I closed my eyes, but at first I could only think of what I had lost.

THE END

TJØMØ–OSLO,
July-August, 1935

Notes on the Text

1 (p.7) The reference is to the famous grinning gargoyle of Notre Dâme Cathedral in Paris, much loved of postcard senders.

2 (p.8) Hebden is clearly modelled on Hitler's Reich Commissioner for Air, Hermann Goering (or Göring) (1893-1946), also referred to in his own right in the text. Founder of the Gestapo, Goering set up the concentration camps for political, racial and religious suspects. He had a key hand in the purges of 30 June 1934, the 'Night of the Long Knives', in which he had his former National Socialist comrades murdered, the scenario which provides the model for Jameson's narrative. Goering too, like Hebden here, delighted in a large wardrobe of uniforms.

3 (p.8) As in right-wing circles in the present-day United States, and like the German Nazis and Spanish Falangists, these British rightists lumped socialists and liberals together as a common enemy. In the disastrous 'Third Period' of Comintern policy between 1928 and 1934, until Hitler's accession triggered a rethink, this conviction was shared by the orthodox, Moscow-dominated Communist parties, though non-Communist socialists were usually classified as 'social fascists'. The division between Social Democrats and Communists in the German Reichstag is one of the factors that allowed Hitler to come to power in 1933. The contempt of Communists for well-meaning but ineffectual liberals and socialists is explored sympathetically throughout the novel, through the Communists Myers and Lewis. But Jameson, who admired the dedication of the Communists with whom she worked in PEN International in the 1930s, helping refugees to escape from a fascist-dominated Europe, nevertheless makes clear, through her narrator, her own substantial reservations about their ruthlessness and doctrinaire absolutism.

4 (p.9) While his name appears to recall that of Neville Chamberlain, in 1935-36 Chancellor of the Exchequer in a Conservative 'National' Government, and shortly to become Prime Minister, it is important that Jameson's Chamberlayn is *not* a politician but a supposedly private citizen, immensely influential behind the scenes as a financier and newspaper proprietor. Prototypes for this character include the newspaper barons, Lords Rothermere, who owned the right-wing, Hitler- and Mosley-sympathising *Daily Mail*, and Beaverbrook, owner of the Express newspaper group and apostle of Empire loyalism. Both men were widely attacked by the Left in the 1930s for their personal influence on successive British governments and, through their newspapers, on public opinion. Jameson's friend, W.H. Auden, pilloried them in his exploration of the psychology of military putschists, *The*

Orators: An English Study (1932/1934) as the composite beast 'Beethameer, Beethameer, bully of Britain'. Like Chamberlayn, Beethameer may 'pose in private as a playful kitten', but his newspapers nevertheless 'poison' a 'dumb' public, and 'advertise idiocy, uplift, and fear' which 'succour the State'. Lotte's dry observation, later, that 'he used to be called the Enemy of the People' reminds that, like the National Socialists and Oswald Mosley's British Union of Fascists, Hillier's National Volunteers espoused, before coming to power, a radical anti-capitalist rhetoric akin to that of the Communists. This explains why politically confused young people such as Ernest Sacker can describe themselves as 'socialists' yet be members of the Volunteer militias.

5   (p.10) Governor of the Bank of England from 1920 to 1944, with enormous influence over national and international monetary affairs. In the 1930s he was demonised by the Left as largely responsible for the financial and fiscal policies that destroyed Ramsay MacDonald's Labour Government in 1931.

6   (p.11) Non-Commissioned Officers, i.e., sergeant majors and below.

7   (p.13) 'Fagging': a form of indentured labour in the British public schools, in which younger boys were required to act as unpaid servants of senior pupils, often as sexual objects, a practice which may have led to the slang meaning of 'fag'. In her autobiography, Jameson indicates that the model for the relation between Richard Sacker and Frank Hillier was an encounter charged with homoerotic feeling between two unknown men that she had glimpsed in Spain. See the introduction, p. xviii above, and Storm Jameson, *Journey from the North* (London: Collins and Harvill Press, 1970), vol. I, 334-8.

8   (p.14) the Cape: Capetown, South Africa.

9   (p.22) Stephen Spender (1909-95), poet and critic, most usually in the 1930s associated with W. H. Auden, Cecil Day Lewis and Louis MacNeice as politically committed left-wing writers, frequently referred to as 'the Auden Gang', 'the Pylon Poets' (because of their use of imagery from the modern industrial world), or by the collective name 'MacSpaunday'. In 1936, although essentially a 'liberal', Spender was linked to the Communist Party of Great Britain. In 1937 he went briefly to Spain to participate in the Civil War on the side of the Republican government, and published *Forward from Liberalism* with the Left Book Club, which argues the case for liberal intellectuals to move on into full commitment to Communism as the only way of preserving the European inheritance from fascist barbarism. His arguments are close to those Andy Hillier has to confront from his Communist interlocutors.

10 (p.22) An allusion to the argument of the German-born British philologist and orientalist, Max Müller (1823-1900), that many of the heroes of the ancient world were actually pseudo-historicised versions of mythological

figures, sun gods and other deifications of natural forces.

11 (p.25) Scythia: a term used by the ancient Greeks for the 'barbarian' regions of the Russian steppes and Northern Europe, here applied sarcastically to the social democracies of Scandinavia, and specifically to Andy Hillier's Norway.

12 (p.26) The contrast being made is between the brutal militarist oligarchy of Sparta in ancient Greece, and a supposedly 'democratic' Athens, which was the home of the arts, sciences and philosophy.

13 (p.26) 'Welcome!' in Latvian and Lithuanian, here used apparently to mean 'Cheers!' perhaps because these are Baltic states and therefore included in Sacker's 'Scythia'.

14 (p.26) The hymn 'Silent Night'.

15 (p.29) Penny dreadful: a sensationalised story of crime or horror for popular consumption; the comic book or journal in which it is published.

16 (p.29) Oswald Spengler (1880-1936), German historian whose *Untergang des Abendlandes* (1918, 1922), written in the wake of German collapse in the First World War, and translated into English (1926-29) as *Decline of the West* in time for the Depression years that followed the Wall Street Crash, spoke morbidly of the inevitable decay of western civilisation in an endless cycle of historical rises and falls. His book foresaw an era of soulless, expansionist Caesarism in which the man of action would take precedence over the artist and contemplative. His ideas were much bandied about by the Nazis, though Spengler was not himself a supporter.

17 (p.30) William Ewart Gladstone (1809-98), British Liberal statesman and reforming Prime Minister, returned to office four times between 1868 and 1892. Stanley Baldwin (1867-1947), British Conservative Prime Minister from 1923-29 (briefly interrupted in 1924 by a minority Labour government) and from 1935-37. His political wiliness, disguised by a homely pipe-smoking image, was revealed in his handling of the Miners and the TUC during the General Strike of 1926, and in the skill with which he coaxed the Labour Prime Minister Ramsay MacDonald into a 'National' coalition government in the crisis year 1931. See also n. 30, below. Much despised on the Left, Baldwin returned as Prime Minister while Jameson was writing the novel in 1935.

18 (p.31) Roaming bands of mercenaries in the Middle Ages, often indistinct from vagabonds and bandits.

19 (p.31) The Bodleian: the copyright library of Oxford University; the Henry VII Chapel: in Westminster Abbey.

20 (p.36) *Stravaig[e]* (Scots): To sally forth, wander up and down, ramble aimlessly.

21 (p.40) Probably Harry Pollitt (1890-1960), Secretary of the British Communist Party, 1929-56, and John Strachey (1901-63), Labour M.P. (1929-31) and socialist

intellectual, who fellow-travelled with the Communists throughout the 1930s. Author of many books of political analysis, including *The Menace of Fascism* (1933), and *The Theory and Practice of Socialism* (1936), Strachey rejoined the Labour Party and became Under-Secretary for Air in the 1945 Labour government.

22 (p.42) Sophie Burtt, often referred to but seen only once in the novel, is probably based in part on Jameson's friend, the feminist, socialist writer Vera Brittain (1893-1970), famed at the time for *Testament of Youth* (1933), her pacifist memoir of the Great War, in which she served as a nurse. 'Sophie' derives from the Greek word for wisdom, 'Vera' from the Latin for truth. Besides Brittain, born in Staffordshire, Burtt may incorporate elements of Jameson herself, and of a fellow Yorkshirewoman and mutual friend, the writer Winifred Holtby (1989-1935), who died while Jameson was writing this book, in the same year her own novel, *South Riding*, was published.

23 (p.44) The Ring: the historic city centre of Vienna, and the road which encircles it.

24 (p.52) High society (from the French).

25 (p.52) For Göring, see n. 2, above, and the introduction. The Sforzas: the Dukes, or Signori, of Milan, who held sway over Northern Italy in the later Middle Ages and Renaissance. They were generous patrons of the arts. *Condottieri* were the professional captains of mercenary armies, who sold their military services to princes or states throughout Europe in the same period.

26 (p.53) Short for *mezzo-soprano*, a singer with a voice intermediate between soprano and contralto. This 'middle' position is an appropriate one for Harriet English, given her various mediating roles in the novel.

27 (p.54) Georg Friedrich Handel (1685-1759), German composer who became a British subject in 1726, and spent most of his life in Britain. Henry Purcell (1659-95) is the quintessential English composer. Vincent Wallace (1813-65), in whose musically and dramatically banal opera *Maritana* Harriet English is to perform in a later chapter, was, ironically, Irish, while Michael Balfe (1808-70), an equally lightweight and prolific composer, was born in Dublin. Richard Hillier's patriotic desire for an English national culture is thus exposed in its shallowness by his own inferior musical tastes.

28 (p.56) The foremost London 'gentleman's club', founded in 1824 with a membership restricted to 1,200. On Smith as modelled on the German General Schleicher, see the introduction.

29 (p.56) The Distinguished Service Order.

30 (p.58) The passions, personalities and politics of the Labour movement in the 1920s and 30s, and the betrayals and backslidings of 1926 and 1931, provide the emotional hinterland of this novel. There are many instances of venality

and self-seeking in the troubled history of the Labour Party. Body and
Denham are composite figures representing two recurring stereotypes of
Labour 'turncoat' (the word used of Denham in Part II, ch. VII): the
conservative, social-climbing trade union bureaucrat, and the cold and clinical,
power-hungry upper-class intellectual. Body's prototype is in all probability
the Welsh trade unionist and Labour cabinet minister, J. H. (Jimmy) Thomas
(1874-1949). As general secretary of the National Union of Railwaymen,
Thomas had sought to mediate between the Trades Union Congress, the
government and the mine-owners during the General Strike of 1926. As Lord
Privy Seal in 1931 he joined the Prime Minister, Ramsay MacDonald, and the
Chancellor of the Exchequer, Philip Snowden, in jumping ship to form a
'National' Coalition Government with Conservatives and Liberals, after the
majority of the Labour Cabinet had rejected the Chancellor's plans, faced with
a financial crisis, to cut unemployment benefit and introduce other measures
harmful to the working classes. Thomas continued as Dominion and then
Colonial Secretary in successive 'National' governments until 1936, when he
was forced to resign for divulging budget secrets to his stockbroker son and
a wealthy businessman who had paid him £15,000. It might be thought that
Snowden (1864-1937) is the other 'turncoat' that Jameson has in mind here.
A quondam Christian Socialist and pacifist, who as M.P. during the Great War
had campaigned at some personal cost on behalf of conscientious objectors,
in 1931 Snowden stayed on as Chancellor long enough to implement his
policies, accepted a peerage after the October election, in which he did not
stand, and resigned from the so-called 'National Labour' government in 1932.
But Snowden was a personal acquaintance of Jameson's, and in the section
of her autobiography which spans the genesis of this novel, she registers
mixed feelings when a friend speaks of Snowden as 'The one of the three
rats I don't understand', remembering a meeting with him in which 'the ironic
smile left his pale Yorkshire eyes' (Denham is described in the novel as having
'light eyes without eyebrows'), and adding, 'I knew I could never dislike him,
never condemn him, never not feel for him a sympathy of the nerves and the
northern ice in my veins' (though she also recognises that this response is
'foolishly emotional and irrational') (vol. I, 318). The contempt the novel
evinces for Denham suggests that Snowden is not the prime suspect in this
case. A few pages later *Voyage from the North* speaks of the right-wing Labour
front-bencher and Old Etonian Hugh Dalton (1887-1962), whom Jameson
disliked, in terms the novel uses of Denham. At the 1933 Labour Party
Conference, she wrote, 'Hugh Dalton, large gleaming head tilted back, only
the whites of his eyes visible, smiling, at once cold and hearty, resembled

nothing so much as a Chinese executioner' (322). The novel speaks of Denham being forty-eight (Dalton's age in the year it was written) and of his 'habit of turning his eyes up to the ceiling when he was on view, which gave him the air of a Chinese executioner.' In all fairness to Dalton, it should be recorded that he was never a turncoat, gave sterling service in Churchill's wartime coalition, and as Chancellor of the Exchequer in the 1945 Labour government nationalised the Bank of England, the institution which had contributed to the ruin of Labour and Snowden in 1931. I have suggested in the introduction that one element in the character of R. B. Tower is provided by Jameson's friend Harold J. Laski (1890-1953), the distinguished Professor of Political Science at the London School of Economics and a left-wing member of the Executive of the Labour Party (its chairman, 1945-6). Tower is primarily based, however, on another friend and mentor, the Professor of Economic History at London University, R. H. Tawney (1880-1962), a Christian Socialist. Tawney's books, particularly *The Acquisitive Society* (1926), *Religion and the Rise of Capitalism* (1926) and *Equality* (1931), had a profound influence on the democratic, non-communist Left in the 1930s. As is clear from the novel, Jameson had an unbridled admiration for the intellect and integrity of Tawney. In a letter of November 1940, at a time when the British Communist Party was officially opposing the war because of the Non-Aggression Pact between Hitler and Stalin, she wrote dispiritedly that the people with energy, like the Communists, were dishonest and untrustworthy, brutally illiberal, and opportunistically eager for personal power, while people of the calibre of Tawney, who would willingly accept poverty and loss of privilege for the sake of a new social order, were powerless to do anything.

31 (p.63) Violet Douglas-Pennant, sixth daughter of Lord Penrhyn, a Conservative member of London County Council with liberal views on social reform. During the First World War she helped organise the Scottish Women's Hospital Unit, the Women's Army Auxiliary Corps and the Women's Royal Naval Service. In 1918 she was invited to become commander of the Women's Royal Air Force (WRAF). Believing that the Royal Air Force was not seriously committed to the WRAF, she resigned, but agreed to return on the promise that her complaints would be dealt with. The official report was severely critical of Douglas-Pennant, and this time she was summarily dismissed from her post. Politicians and trades union leaders (one of whom was Jimmy Thomas, see note 30 above) protested at her treatment. An Inquiry was set up into the matter under the auspices of the House of Lords. It found against Douglas-Pennant, who was accused of making false accusations, and subsequently was sued successfully by two libelled witnesses and forced to pay substantial

damages. While Professor Tower here sees this story as an instance of the establishment closing ranks against an innocent whistle-blower, the record suggests this is a somewhat one-sided version, close to the self-justification of Douglas-Pennant's book, *Under the Searchlight* (1922).

32 (p.65) To shark (for): 'to live by shifts and stratagems' (OED).

33 (p.68) Aelbert Cuyp (1620-91), Dutch painter of landscapes, seascapes, animals and still-life, most of whose best works can be found in Britain. Christies, the leading art auction room.

34 (p.72) In 1934, the right-wing Austrian Chancellor Engelbert Dollfuss, who had already suspended the constitution, introduced repressive measures aimed at provoking popular resistance, which he then used as a pretext for armed attacks on the socialist and trade union opposition, including the shelling of working-class housing-blocks in Vienna in which many died. Dollfuss installed a nationalist dictatorship, but was himself murdered later in the year by Austrian Nazis supporting *Anschluss* (unification with Germany). See Stephen Spender's long poem, *Vienna* (London: Faber and Faber, 1934). Rosa Luxembourg (1871-1919) and Karl Liebknecht (1871-1919) (Jameson misspells the name) were socialist intellectuals and charismatic leaders of the left-wing of the German Social Democratic Party. Imprisoned for their opposition to the First World War, they were founders in 1918 of the German Communist Party (KPD), and, in 1919, with the collapse of the German war-machine, led the 'Spartacist League' revolt in Berlin. Taken prisoner, they were murdered by the German army.

35 (p.73) The Cenotaph was erected in Whitehall, London as a memorial for the dead of the First World War. 'On the day' refers to Armistice Day, November 11, commemorating the day in 1918 when the War ended, celebrated each year with a public parade past the Cenotaph and two minutes' silence across the nation.

36 (p.74) Duds: old clothing. The student is recalling Karl Marx, who wrote famously of the revolution working like a mole beneath the surface of capitalist society.

37 (p.76) Whitechapel, in the working-class East End of London, had the largest Jewish population in Britain, comprised mainly of nineteenth and early twentieth century immigrants fleeing persecution in Russia and Eastern Europe. On 4 October 1936, in the 'Battle of Cable Street', local Jews, assisted by socialists and communists, fought a successful battle to repel marauding Blackshirts from Oswald Mosley's British Union of Fascists.

38 (p.76) On *Maritana* and its composer, see n. 27 above.

39 (p.79) George Du Maurier (1834-96), grandfather of the novelist Daphne Du

Maurier, French-born British illustrator, cartoonist and novelist, most widely known for his gentle satires of middle and upper class English life in the pages of *Punch*. His popular novel *Trilby* (1894), about a satanic mesmerist, Svengali, who takes hypnotic possession of a vivacious young woman, has some resonance for Frank Hillier's relation with the British people.

40 (p.79) Park Lane runs alongside Hyde Park and is the site of some of the capital's most expensive hotels, here, together with Devonshire House, Piccadilly, representing, at the heart of Mayfair, the home ground of a privileged and complacent English ruling class.

41 (p.84) In Greek mythology, Athene, goddess of wisdom, sprang fully armed from the head of her father Zeus, chief of the Olympians. See the *Homeric Hymns*, no. 28.

42 (p.88) In the English edition of this novel, at the bottom of page 126, after the words 'carrying away the rest', there is a period mark, followed by a two-em space and three punctuation points (elision mark). Page 127 begins in the middle of a sentence with 'reached it through the field', but without an opening quotation mark to match that with which the half-sentence ends. According to Christopher Storm-Clark, Jameson's executor, the US edition of the novel (New York: Macmillan and Co, 1936) has an open quotation mark before the corresponding dots (elision marks). This would appear to be a printer's attempt to render consistent a flawed text. It does not however address the absence of a capital letter in 'reached'. The text itself speaks of words being carried away by a clanking lorry, and of having 'missed a sentence or two', so the disjunction is clearly in part intentional. However, it is unlikely that anyone inventing the second half of a sentence of which the first half never actually existed would produce something as grammatically confusing as the half sentence here, where the past tense of 'reached' is hard to reconcile with the present tense of 'lie' (even if 'lie' were a present participle following an imputed previous verb taking an auxiliary such as 'could' or 'might'). One is led to conclude that there is perhaps an unintended omission here, complicated by the internal reference to words being lost. In the absence of a manuscript or the original publishers' proofs, consistency can best be supplied by adopting the US emendation.

43 (p.89) *Blutbrüderschaft* (German): blood-brotherhood, a concept beloved of the Nazis, combining a romanticised militaristic tribalism with a sentimental peer-bonding, often with homoerotic overtones. It was particularly prevalent among the generation of German ex-soldiers defeated in the First World War, who formed the backbone of the *Freikorps* and the private militias from which Hitler's Brownshirts were drawn.

44 (p.96) Prince Clemens Lothar Wenzel Metternich (1773-1859), autocratic and reactionary Austrian statesman, a key architect of the Treaty of Vienna (1815), which drew the boundaries of Europe for the rest of the century, and ensured the repression of popular aspirations for civil liberties and constitutional reform, until the revolutions of 1848 toppled half the thrones of Europe and drove Metternich himself into temporary exile. Louis Adolphe Thiers (1797-1877), autocratic French politician, first president of the Third Republic in 1870, responsible in 1871 for the bloody suppression of the Paris Commune, the popular revolt that followed French defeat in the Franco-Prussian War and the German Siege of Paris.

45 (p.97) Montevideo, capital of Uruguay in South America, the location of some of Sacker's arms dealing.

46 (p.99) The text makes plain that Body's conservatism and incompetence in the modern world extend even to such 'new-fangled' devices as fountain pens: he still uses a stylus dipped repeatedly in an inkwell.

47 (p.99) [sic] a bad way.

48 (p.103) E. M. Forster (1879-1970): the novelist was an icon of authentic liberalism to left-wing writers in the 1930s, for his principled opposition to Fascism and defence of civil liberties. A friend of Jameson's, in 'Liberty in England', his address to the International Congress of Writers in Paris in June 1935, he spoke in terms relevant to this narrative and Andy Hillier's own position: 'as for my politics, you will have guessed that I am not a Fascist – Fascism does evil that evil may come. And you may have guessed that I am not a Communist, though perhaps I might be one if I was a younger and a braver man, for in Communism I can see hope. It does many things which I think evil, but I know that it intends good. I am actually what my age and my upbringing have made me – a bourgeois who adheres to the British constitution, adheres to it rather than supports it.... I do care about the preservation and the extension of freedom....' (*Abinger Harvest*, London: Edward Arnold, 1936).

49 (p.105) *Aeropagitica* [sic]: John Milton, *Areopagitica: A Speech for the Liberty of Unlicensed Printing to the Parliament of England* (1644). There are many passages of a radical and patriotic nature in Milton's text that a demagogue might use for his own purposes. Perhaps the one that would best suit Hillier's purpose here, endorsing his claims to having effected a national renewal, and simultaneously flattering his auditors, is the following: 'Methinks I see in my mind a noble and puissant nation rousing herself like a strong man after sleep, and shaking her invincible locks....'

50 (p.117) Broadmoor was established in 1863 as a prison for the criminally insane.

51 (p.121) The country residence of the British Prime Minister, in the Chilterns.

52 (p.121) Originally feudal appointees charged in the middle ages with responsibility for the royal forests. While the novel could here be referring to a military regiment, irony resides in the possibility that this is no more than the 'Royal and Ancient Order of Foresters', a kind of freemasonery cum rotary club, beloved of small-town businessmen and others seeking camaraderie and the mystique of specialness.

53 (p.129) Mesopotamia, 'the land between the rivers' of Tigris and Euphrates, modern-day Iraq.

54 (p.132) In the Old Testament, the wife of Heber the Kenite, who treacherously slew the Canaanite general Sisera by hammering a nail through his head while he slept in her tent (*Judges*, ch. iv).

55 (p.139) 'Better is the enemy of good.' That Body thinks this French aphorism is Latin is not just a cheap jibe at his lack of education, but allows an insight into the complex interplay of legitimate aspiration and social-climbing in the quarter of the Labour movement that Body typifies.

56 (p.151) Multigraph: 'The proprietary name of a small printing machine which uses specially cast type fitted in to grooves on a rotating cylinder … a machine for producing multiple copies of typewritten work' (*Supplement to the Complete OED*, 1987), a normal method of duplication before the invention of the photocopier, capable of producing up to 4000 copies an hour.

57 (p.157) Max Planck (1858-1947), formulator of quantum theory, which Albert Einstein (1879-1955), deployed as the basis for his special and general theories of relativity. Presumably Ernest thinks of these two German-born geniuses of theoretical physics, whose theories replaced the traditional Newtonian system, because he has just been reading about them in his Physics textbook, but they may also be linked by their shared anti-Nazism (Planck's son was executed for his part in the plot against Hitler in 1944) and, possibly, by the implications of their work for the construction of an atom bomb, about which there was much talk in the 1930s.

58 (p.162) A reference to the 'Curragh Mutiny.' Following the passage by the Asquith government of the third Irish Home Rule Bill in May 1914, British officers in the Curragh Barracks, County Kildare, with the connivance of senior members of the Army chiefs of staff, and encouraged by the leader of the opposition Conservative and Unionist Party, Bonar Law, announced that they would refuse to enforce Home Rule or to fire on Ulster Unionists violently opposing it. In the wake of the mutiny, the regional commander General Gough, all his officers, the Army Chief of Staff General French and the War Minister were all required to resign. The outbreak of war in August

1914 led to the suspension of plans for Home Rule. The mutiny, therefore, achieved its aims, and was to prevent the creation of an independent united Ireland for the rest of the century. The events of 1688, celebrated as the 'Glorious Revolution' by Unionists, saw the deposition of James II by the British ruling class, its parliament and army, and the invitation to William of Orange, married to James's daughter Mary, to assume the throne. The year in which Jameson's novel was published witnessed in January the accession to the British throne of the Nazi-sympathising Edward VIII and then, in December, his enforced abdication, allegedly on the grounds of his relationship with an American divorcee.

59 (p.164) Between the wars, Croydon Airport, opened in 1920, was London's official customs airport, the sole point of entry and departure for all international flights and for most internal UK flights. It was replaced by Heathrow in 1946 and closed in 1959.